Crossing the Line

Laura Farr

Skye High Publishing

Copyright © 2022 by Laura Farr

All rights reserved.

No part of this book may be reproduced in any form or by any electronic or mechanical means, including information storage and retrieval systems, without written permission from the author, except for the use of brief quotations in a book review.

Editing: Swish Design & Editing

Cover: SSB Cover & Design

Interior Design: SSB Cover & Design

Chapter One

Hallie

Age Thirteen

Suddenly I'm jolted into the air and cry out, my head coming in contact with the hard floor. My eyelids feel heavy, and as I struggle to lift them, a wave of nausea washes over me. Taking a deep breath, I concentrate on trying not to throw up. It's dark, but not too dark to see. As my eyes adjust, panic threatens to overwhelm me as I realize I'm in the back of a moving van.

I hear voices coming from the enclosed section of the cab, and I force myself to sit up. My body screams out in protest, every part aching from being tossed in the air. I've no idea how long I've been unconscious, but I'm guessing from how my body hurts after lying on the uncomfortable floor, it's been a while.

Dragging myself to the front of the van, I press my ear against the cold metal. Although the voices are louder, they are still muffled, and I sit back unsteadily on my heels, wondering what the hell is happening. The last thing I remember is leaving Jess's house a little after curfew. I was late, so I cut through the park to make up some time. As I exited the park, I felt someone grab me from behind. I tried to scream, but my cries were muffled when something was pressed over my mouth. The next thing I know, I'm waking up on the van's hard floor.

Panic washes over me again as the realization of what's happening hits. I want to bang on the side of the van, make them stop and let me out. I don't, though. I'm terrified at the thought of coming face to face with whoever is driving. Instead, I sit with my back pressed into the corner and my knees drawn up to my chest. My head is pounding, and I squeeze my eyes closed as I will the pain in my head to stop.

It's hard to know how long we've been driving, and I must have fallen asleep because, when the van finally comes to a stop, I jolt awake. My breathing accelerates, and I scramble as far away from the door as possible.

A million thoughts race through my mind. *Why has someone taken me? Are they going to hurt me? Kill me?*

I'm pulled from my erratic thoughts when the cab door opens. Seconds later, it's slammed closed, making me jump. A cry escapes my lips, and I press a hand over my mouth, muffling the sound. A few more seconds pass, and I watch the van's doors with wide eyes as I wait to see who's there.

When they swing open, I'm temporarily blinded by the sunlight that floods the space. I squint against the brightness, raising my hand to shield my eyes. Apprehension bubbles in my stomach as I wait for my eyes to adjust. When they do, I'm surprised to see a woman standing in the doorway. She's beautiful. Her long blonde hair is swept up in a messy bun on top of her head. She has a kind face, a face that erupts into a smile when she sees me. I can't help but feel a little relieved. A woman wouldn't hurt me, right?

"Sweetheart..." She gasps. "You came back." Her hand reaches for me, and I try to push myself back, but there's nowhere to go.

"What do you want?" I croak, tears rolling down my cheeks. "Please don't hurt me."

Her face fills with surprise. "Hurt you? We're not going to hurt you. We've missed you so much." Her voice breaks, and I can't help but feel confused. It's obvious she thinks I'm someone else, and hope erupts in my chest at her words. Surely, once she realizes I'm not who she thinks I am, she'll let me go, and I'll be able to go home.

"We're home, Cora. Your room is waiting for you." I frown, not knowing how to react. *Should I play along or tell her I'm not Cora?* Before I can come to a decision, a man appears beside her. "Oh, Matt, I can't believe she's here."

He puts his arm around her and pulls her into him. "Go inside, Amanda," he coaxes, kissing her head before moving her backward away from the van. "I'll bring Cora inside."

She gives me a small smile before turning around and disappearing out of view. He watches her go before turning to face me. It's the first time I've gotten a good look at him. A thick beard covers his face so it's hard to see his features, but his eyes are dark and cold, and suddenly, I don't want to look at him. A feeling of dread washes over me as I drop my eyes. The back of the van dips as he climbs in and crosses the short distance to reach me. I think he's going to grab me, but instead, he sits down.

"Right, here are the rules. I don't care what your name was back in Savannah, you're a long way from there. Here, you are Cora, and that woman..." he gestures with his head to outside the van, "... she's your mother." He must see the look of confusion on my face and exhales loudly. "Look, I don't want to hurt you, and I won't as long as you don't cause me any trouble. Understand?"

I nod, but I don't understand.

"You'll have your own room, and you'll only be locked in at night. Our house is in the middle of nowhere. There's dense woodland for several miles in every direction. The nearest town is even farther. I promise you, sweetheart, if you try to escape, I *will* find you, and I *will* kill you. Are we clear?" He opens his jacket, and I gasp, seeing a gun in a holster at his side.

I nod frantically, my eyes wide and my stomach churning, but I hold back a sob as a single tear slips down my cheek. I want to go home. I want to see my parents and my annoying older brother. Right now, that seems impossible.

Scrambling out of the van, I'm unsteady on my shaky legs. Taking my time, I look around at my surroundings. Despite what he's told me, my eyes can't help but scour the area for an escape route. He's watching me, but maybe I can get away when he's asleep. It turns out what he said was true. There is a fairly small house set in a large yard, and a thick dense forest fills my eyeline as I whip my head around, taking in every inch of the plot. The only section without trees is a small dirt track beyond the van. My eyes linger there, wondering where the track leads to.

"Cora," a voice yells.

I jump, and it takes me a few seconds to realize he means me. I drag my eyes off the track, turning to where the voice came from.

Matt's standing on the wraparound porch, his face like thunder. "Come inside."

Don't cry, don't cry, don't cry, I chant in my head over and over again as I make my way across the lawn. After slowly climbing the steps, I stop in front of him. Keeping my eyes on the ground, I wait for him to say something. After a minute or so of silence, I gingerly raise my head and look up. He towers above me, a good foot and a half taller. His eyes are still dark and cold, and a scowl covers his face.

"There really is nowhere to run, sweetheart." His hand comes to my face, his thumb caressing my cheek. I turn away from him, recoiling at his touch. His hand drops, and he smirks as he moves to one side, allowing me to pass and enter the house. Desperate to get away from him, I quickly go through the open door, finding myself in a short entryway.

There is a door to the left that's slightly ajar, so I glance inside and see it's a small office. A stairway is directly in front of me, and the kitchen is beyond that. A door to the right leads to what must be the living room.

The walls are covered with picture frames, and I move farther into the entryway to get a better look. Three smiling faces stare back

Crossing the Line

at me from multiple pictures. I recognize the man and woman in the picture as Amanda and Matt. A young girl with shoulder-length blonde hair, similar to mine, is with them. I can't help but notice how alike we look and wonder if she might be Cora. They look happy. The cold, empty eyes that stared at me a few seconds ago are nowhere to be seen in these photographs, and I wonder what happened to change them. I also can't help wondering where Cora is now.

"Cora, sweetheart, you must be hungry? I'm making your favorite." Looking away from the images, Amanda's standing in the kitchen doorway. She's smiling, and I stare blankly back at her. Matt clears his throat behind me, and I glance over my shoulder at him. He nods slightly, his eyes boring into mine. I want to cry and run as far away from here as I can. Remembering the gun under his jacket, I turn back to Amanda, slowly walking toward her.

As I reach the doorway, she pulls me into a hug, and I stand awkwardly, my arms limp by my sides. I pull out of the embrace, but she keeps her arm around my shoulders, guiding me to a small worn table in the corner of the kitchen.

"Your hair is different. Did you cut it?" she asks, frowning as she takes a section of my hair in her hand, letting it slip slowly through her fingers. I have no idea how to answer. I haven't cut my hair, it's the same as it has always been. This woman is clearly insane, truly believing I'm someone else.

"Yes," I whisper, hoping I've chosen the correct response.

"Well, I love it," she exclaims with a smile. I breathe a silent sigh of relief as she pushes gently on my shoulder, coaxing me to sit down. She slides a glass of milk in front of me, and it's only then I realize how thirsty I am. It's been hours since I had a drink, and I snatch up the glass, gulping the milk down noisily.

"Thank you," I mumble as I set the empty glass on the table in front of me. She busies herself at the stove, and I wonder where Matt has gone. As much as Amanda seems crazy, I don't think she'd hurt me, not if she truly believes I'm Cora. It's Matt I have to worry about.

"There you go, your favorite." With a flourish, she places a plate in front of me. Dropping my eyes, I groan inwardly.

Goddammit!

It's an omelet.

I hate omelets.

"Thank you," I tell her quietly, slowly picking up the knife and fork lying on the old wooden table. Despite hating what she's made me, my stomach rumbles, letting me know it's been hours since I last ate. After cutting up the omelet, I fork a piece into my mouth, chewing quickly before swallowing. It's the texture I don't like. Actually, the taste isn't that bad. With how hungry I am, I'd more than likely eat anything right now.

Once I finish eating, I sit silently at the table while Amanda clears up. I have no idea what I'm meant to do now. This all feels surreal. I'm not tied up, but I can't leave. Not yet anyway. Not until I can be sure I can get away. My mind wanders to the office I passed in the entryway. Maybe a phone is in there I can use to call for help? My parents must be frantic. I wish I could let them know I'm okay, even if I have no idea where I am. A tear falls down my cheek, and I quickly wipe it away.

"Where are we?" I ask quietly. "I've forgotten."

Amanda turns from the sink and frowns. "We're at home, silly. In Cedar Falls."

"Cedar Falls?"

"Cedar Falls, Iowa." Her frown increases as she wipes her hands on a towel. "Are you feeling okay?" She moves toward me and places her hand on my forehead.

"I'm just tired, I think. The back of the van wasn't comfy."

"Why don't you go and lie down, sweetheart? It's been a long couple of days. I'll come with you and make sure you have everything you need."

I try not to react to her words as I follow her out of the kitchen. A couple of days? Is that how long I've been missing? And we're in

Iowa? That's miles from Savannah. We must have driven all through the night.

I slowly follow Amanda upstairs. She's talking, but I don't hear a word. My mind is screaming with a thousand questions, none of which I have the answers to. As we reach the top of the stairs, I hear muffled banging. I can't be sure if it's coming from inside the house or outside, but as we make our way down the hallway, the banging becomes louder. We come to a stop outside a closed door.

"Here we go. Your room is just how you left it. There are fresh towels in the bathroom if you want to shower." She opens the door and gestures for me to enter. As I do, I see the source of the banging. Matt is standing in front of the bedroom window, holding a hammer in one hand and what looks like a nail in the other.

"What are you doing?" Amanda asks from behind me.

He turns and looks over his shoulder. "Just making sure Cora's room is secure, baby. I'm nearly done." Turning back to the window, he positions the nail and drives it into the wooden frame, the hammer connecting with the nail until it's barely visible. I wince at the sound, knowing he's making sure I have no chance of escaping. With all the banging I heard on the way up here, I'm guessing he's nailed the window shut.

"Come on, then, if you're done. Cora needs to rest." She holds her hand out to Matt, who moves away from the window and wraps his arm around Amanda. He looks down at her. The cold eyes from earlier have disappeared, and he stares at her as if she is the air he needs to breathe. I'm only thirteen, but even I can see Amanda and Matt are head over heels in love with each other.

His complete shift from psycho to loving husband unnerves me.

I wish I knew what was going on and why I'm here. I'm too afraid to ask though, and I don't want to piss off Matt. I have a horrible feeling he meant every word he said to me earlier in the van, and right now, I don't want to test that theory.

Chapter Two

Haillie

Six months later

As I kneel on the slightly damp grass, I absentmindedly turn the earth over in the garden, the small rake in my hand flicking dirt everywhere. I'm pretending to concentrate on what I'm doing, but instead, I'm watching Matt out of the corner of my eye. It's been a little over six months since I arrived here in the back of his van, terrified and alone.

Surprisingly, the time here has been okay. Far better than I ever thought it would be when I first arrived. Amanda still believes I'm Cora and playing along has kept Matt somewhat happy. I'm locked in my room every night, and the window is still nailed shut, but I'm allowed in the yard during the day. I'm hopeful that one day I'll get to go home. I miss my parents so much it hurts.

Amanda is always nice to me, but I hear her crying at night, and I've found her mumbling to herself on more than one occasion. I think she has some serious issues, ones I dare not ask about. I still don't know why I'm here or where the real Cora is. All I can do is bide my time until I get a chance to escape.

Crossing the Line

The first few weeks I was here, I cried a lot. Matt hated it. I soon learned the less emotion I showed, the less angry he became. I saved all my tears for when I was alone at night in my room, and I cried them silently, not wanting to wake Matt. I still cry sometimes, but I've learned tears get me nowhere.

The sound of Matt cutting the grass brings me back to the present, and as I watch him, I struggle to work him out, even after being here for six months. It's like he's got a split personality or something. One day, he's laughing and joking with Amanda, the next he's moody and sullen. I learned early on to stay out of his way when he was having one of his bad days. All it took was a broken dish when I was clearing away one night, and his true colors emerged as he flew at me, pushing me roughly against the counter. His temper is scary. There's no way I want to be on the end of it again. I don't think he would ever hurt Amanda, but I can't say the same for me.

It's my birthday next week, and I'll be fourteen. Not that Amanda and Matt are aware. Cora's birthday was a few weeks ago, and I was forced to play along, eating pizza and ice cream. I did find out Cora, wherever she is, would have turned fifteen—a year older than me. I wish I knew where she was or what happened to her.

Despite being here under duress, Amanda is kind to me, truly believing I'm Cora. When we're alone, I try and ask questions, pretending I've forgotten the answers I should know if I were Cora. Sometimes she answers me, but other times she gets angry, and I quickly change the subject, not wanting Matt to hear her upset.

Matt's finished cutting the grass, and I realize I've zoned out. I don't sleep much at night, and I'm constantly tired. Snapping from my daze, I turn back to the garden and continue to weed, making it look like I'm not watching him. He walks past without saying a word and climbs the porch steps.

"Cora! Get in here," Matt yells, and even from outside, I can hear the panic in his voice.

Scrambling to my feet, I hesitantly make my way up the steps, unsure of what I'm going to encounter when I get into the house. As I push open the door, I gasp. Amanda is curled up on the floor in the entryway. She's whimpering in pain, her arms wrapped around her waist. Matt kneels next to her, brushing her hair from her face.

"She's burning up. I need to get her to the ER." He stands up and grabs my arm, pulling me toward the stairs. "I need you to go to your room." Before I know what's happening, we're halfway up the stairs. I pull back on his arm, and he stops, looking over his shoulder at me.

"You don't need to lock me in my room. I won't go anywhere."

He lets out a sarcastic laugh and continues to pull me up the stairs. "That's not a risk I'm willing to take. You're going to your room."

"But—"

"No buts," he cuts me off, his grip tightening on my arm.

"You're hurting me," I cry, wriggling to free myself from him.

"Don't piss me off, Hallie," he warns, his voice low.

"You know my name," I whisper, taken aback.

We reach the door to my bedroom, and he swings it open. "Of course, I know your name," he growls. "Stay here. Don't even think about trying to escape. I *will* find you."

His eyes are cold and dark again, and I walk backward into the room, not wanting those eyes directed at me. He closes the door, and I hear the key turn in the lock. Rushing across the room, I press my nose to the window. A minute or so later, Matt walks across the lawn with Amanda in his arms. He somehow manages to open the door to the van, setting her on the passenger side. I watch as he climbs into the driver's seat and starts the engine. My heart is pounding, and I jump as the tires squeal on the loose gravel of the dirt track, spraying dust behind them. A few seconds later, the van is out of sight, and silence descends. I have no idea how far away the hospital is, but if the house is as isolated as Matt told me it is, they'll be gone for at least a few hours.

This is my chance to escape.

The first chance I've had since I arrived, and I'm not going to let it pass me by.

Crossing the Line

Throwing on a sweater and some sneakers, I look around the room for something I can use to break the glass in the window. Deciding on the desk chair, I pick it up. Adrenaline is surging through my body, and I'm easily able to hold it at shoulder height. Taking a deep breath, I throw it as hard as I can against the window. The noise is deafening, and I close my eyes, wincing as the sound of shattering glass pierces the silence. When I open my eyes, I'm relieved to see most of the glass is gone from the frame. There are a few jagged pieces jutting upward, impeding my escape, and I rush into the bathroom, snatching up a towel from the laundry basket. Wrapping it around my hand, I knock out as much glass as I can before laying the towel over the frame. Peering out of the now-smashed window, the desk chair and broken glass litter the bushes bordering the house. I will need to be careful to avoid landing on any of it when I jump down. The last thing I need is to break my ankle.

Deciding to use the comforter to soften my fall, I toss it out the window, watching as it falls over the top of the bushes. It won't provide much of a cushion, but I guess it's better than nothing. Taking one last look around the room I've been trapped in for the past six months, I suddenly can't wait to get out of here.

Excitement bubbles in my stomach at the thought of going home and seeing my parents again. I can only imagine the hell they've been through these past months, not knowing what happened to me.

Moving toward the window, I slowly climb onto the frame. Suddenly, my foot slips on the towel, and in a panic, I move my hand to steady myself. Pain tears through my palm as a shard of glass pierces my skin. I stifle a scream as blood trickles down my arm. Closing my eyes, I take deep breaths as I wait for the pain to subside. When it does, I take my chance and jump, not wanting to lose my footing again. The comforter does a good job of breaking my fall, and by some miracle, I miss any glass.

"Shit," I whisper to myself as I sit on the ground, leaning back against the bushes surrounding me. I can barely believe I've jumped from a second-floor window. My heart thunders in my chest. My hand is bleeding heavily, and I need to wrap something around it to stem the bleeding. I take my sweater off and wrap it around my hand, hugging my bandaged arm against my chest.

I stand and walk quickly across the yard. My eyes dart everywhere as I make for the dirt track leading to the road. Logically, I know Amanda and Matt have gone, but part of me still expects to see them barreling toward me. I stay close to the edge of the track, ready to hide in the surrounding woodland should I hear a car or truck approaching. Of course, this doesn't happen. No one has visited in the six months I've been here, not even a mailman.

I've been walking for about ten minutes, and I'm still on the track. I always wondered if Matt had exaggerated about how isolated the house was to keep me from trying to run away. It seems he hadn't lied about it, and I can't help but shiver, thinking if he hadn't lied about the location of the house, he probably hadn't lied about causing me harm if I chose to run. I try not to think about it as I continue to walk quickly. My hand is throbbing with each step, but I think I've managed to stop the bleeding. I don't want to unravel my sweater to check, but there doesn't seem to be any new blood soaking into the material.

My senses come alive when a car horn blares in the distance. I dart into the trees at the side of the track and wait for a few seconds. My stomach churns with nerves, and I wait in the shadows of the trees, listening for any approaching vehicle. When nothing comes, I eventually venture back onto the track and run as best I can with an injured arm.

Slowly, I hear more traffic noise, and tears fall down my cheeks as I realize how close I am to safety.

Suddenly, the track becomes wider, and cars, trucks, and motorcycles race along a busy interstate. Coming to a stop, I drop to my knees at the edge of where the dirt track meets the road. The tears are still falling, and I can only imagine what I look like, bloodied and crying on the side of the road. A minivan passes me, slowing to a stop a hundred yards or so up the interstate. Scrambling to my feet, I frantically look around, slowly walking backward away from the car. I suddenly realize I haven't thought this through. Who's to say someone stopping to help me isn't as bad as Matt? How do I know who I can trust? I don't have time to think about it when a woman walks toward me.

"Are you okay?" she calls, her eyes dropping from my tear-stained face to my bandaged hand. She looks kind and genuine, but so did Amanda. As she comes to stand in front of me, she frowns. "Can I call someone for you?"

My heart leaps at her words, and I nod frantically. The thought of speaking to my mom after being away for so long is a little more than I can bear, and I choke back a sob.

"Oh, sweetie. What's your name?" She moves to put her arm around me, and I flinch. "I won't hurt you, I promise." She glances back to her car and beckons to it with her head. "My daughter's in the car along with my phone. Why don't you come with me, and you can make that call?"

"Okay," I mutter, knowing I need to make a decision. I silently pray I'm making the right choice. "My name's Hallie," I say quietly as I follow her to the car.

"Hi, Hallie. I'm Taylor." She smiles over her shoulder, and as we get to the car, I can see a toddler strapped into a car seat in the back. She opens the driver's door and leans inside, reaching for her phone.

"Do you know the number?" she asks kindly. I nod before telling her the number to the landline at home. I hope to God someone is there. She dials the number before passing the phone to me, smiling encouragingly. As desperate as I am to speak to my parents, I can't help but feel nervous, and I gingerly take the phone from her and place it to my ear. It rings and rings, and when I think no one will answer, I hear a voice on the other end of the line.

"Hello." The voice is breathless, and I can tell my mom has rushed to answer the call.

"Mom," I whisper on a sob, dropping to my knees at the side of the road.

Taylor is by my side in a second, her arm around my waist.

"Hallie, is that you?" Her voice is as quiet and unbelieving as mine, and more tears track down my cheeks. I'm silent, unable to speak. "Hallie," she cries, louder this time.

"It's me," I tell her, holding back a sob, somehow managing to pull myself together enough to speak.

"Oh, thank God! Where are you? Are you okay? Brett! Brett!" she shouts, calling for my dad. "It's Hallie."

"I want to come home, Mom." I sob. "I want to come home." Taylor takes the phone from me as I collapse at the side of the road. She's talking to my mom, but the noise rushing through my ears makes it impossible for me to hear what's being said. A few minutes later, Taylor is helping me off the ground and into the passenger seat of her car. She must see the panic on my face as I realize what's happening, and she forces me to look at her.

"Hallie, you are safe. I'm taking you to the ER. The sheriff will meet us there. I'm going to call your mom back when we've got you sorted."

"No!" I cry, shaking my head wildly. "He's there. I can't go to the ER. Please. I can't see him," I beg, hysteria taking over.

"Who is there, Hallie?" she asks, her voice soothing as she holds my hand.

"Matt. Matt is there, and he'll kill me if he knows I've escaped. Please don't take me there."

"Okay, okay. We'll go straight to the sheriff's office. Your hand can be looked at there. You're safe now, I promise."

I sigh with relief as I let her help me into the car.

As we pull into the traffic, I turn my head, taking one last look at the dirt track I've emerged from. I'm grateful I'll never have to see that place again.

Chapter Three

Hallie

Ten years later

"Mom, it's time. I'm twenty-four!" I admonish as I pack the last of my boxes into the trunk of my car. She wipes her eyes before blowing her nose loudly. My dad slips his arm around her shoulder, pulling her into his chest.

"She's only moving a few blocks away, sweetheart, and she's right, it's time. We can't keep her with us forever."

"I worry..."

"I know," he soothes, kissing her hair. "Come on. She's going to need some help with all those boxes."

I smile gratefully at him as he ushers her toward his car.

Nervous excitement swirls in my stomach as I climb into my Jeep, placing my beloved camera on the passenger seat. It's the only thing I couldn't bring myself to pack. My parents gave it to me a few years after I'd returned from Cedar Falls, hoping to encourage me to get out of the house more. It had taken a while, but it had worked, and now I rarely go anywhere without it. My bedroom walls were full of images I'd captured, and I hope to transfer some of them onto the walls of my new apartment.

Glancing over my shoulder, I take in all the boxes piled into the back. There are so many I can barely see out of the rear window. My whole life is in these boxes, and although I'm anxious about living alone, I also can't wait to start this new chapter in my life. It seems like it's taken a lifetime to get to this point. A point where I'm not constantly looking behind me, scared to leave the house.

It was almost ten years to the day Taylor found me on the side of the road, bloodied and scared. After meeting with the sheriff, Matt and Amanda were picked up at the ER and arrested on kidnapping charges. Only that's not where the hell ended. A search of the house and land where I'd been held uncovered horrors that made me question how I'd ever gotten out of there alive. The remains of five young girls were found buried in shallow graves behind the house. One turned out to be Cora, their daughter. The others were girls like me, girls Matt had taken from the streets and kept locked in the room I'd slept in. Matt would never say what happened to Cora, but the police believed either he or Amanda had accidentally killed her. The girls, me included, were somehow a replacement for Cora.

I'd felt desperately sorry for those girls and their families, and it had taken a long time to overcome the guilt I'd felt at surviving when they hadn't. Even though both Matt and Amanda are locked up back in Iowa, it's only now, ten years later, after hours of counseling, I'm able to move forward with my life, finally putting what happened behind me. I've worked hard with my therapist over the past twelve months, building up to moving out and living independently. While I'll be nervous, I'm ready to do this and move on with my life.

I shake thoughts of Matt and Amanda from my head as I pull up outside my new apartment block. I don't want to think about them, especially today. As I climb out of the Jeep, I sling the strap attached to my camera over my arm and watch as my parents climb out of their car. My mom has her tears under control and smiles as she links her arm with mine.

Crossing the Line

"My baby is all grown up," she mumbles as she looks at the block in front of her.

"Max moved out last year, and you didn't cry this much then," I tell her with a chuckle.

"Oh, she did, believe me," my dad says as he comes to stand behind us. "She simply did it when she thought no one was looking." My mom turns and swats him on the stomach, making him laugh.

"Anyway, Max moving out was different. He's six foot two and a Marine. He can look after himself," she says, shooting a look at my dad.

"I can look after myself. I'll be fine, Mom," I promise as I pull her toward the entrance. She doesn't answer, and I know she worries about me. After what she and Dad went through when I was taken, I understand why. For years afterward, I needed them to go everywhere with me, but things are different now. I refuse to let what happened to me define my life.

"Let's get a picture," I tell them. "The start of a new chapter." The three of us stand with our backs to the entrance, and I hold the camera out in front of me, guessing when all of us will be in the shot. "Smile," I cry as I press down on the button. Turning the camera around, by some miracle, we're all in the frame, and I beam.

"That's one to go up on the wall," my mom says, kissing my cheek.

I key in the security code, then push open the heavy door. We'd chosen this apartment complex because of the heightened security it offered. There's an intercom on the main door and security cameras in the shared lobby. The added security makes me feel better, and it's something my parents insisted on. My apartment is on the fifth floor, and I press the button for the elevator, squeezing my mom's arm that's linked with mine. Dad appears behind us as the doors to the elevator open. I smile at him as I see he's carrying two boxes. He must have gone back to the car after I'd taken the photograph.

"No point going up empty-handed," he says with a wink as I step aside to allow him into the elevator first. I've had the key to the apartment for a couple of days. Most of my furniture has already been brought up by a moving company. I'm moving in for real though, and tonight will be my first night on my own. My stomach flips at the thought, but I don't have time to overthink it as the elevator doors open, and we walk out into the corridor. Taking a left, we walk down the short hallway, stopping outside apartment fifty-five. I open the door with a flourish and walk in, my parents following closely behind me.

The apartment is relatively small, consisting of a living room with an open-plan kitchen, two bedrooms, and a bathroom. It's perfect for me though, and I fell in love as soon as I viewed it. Even though I was here a couple of days ago to show the moving company where to put the furniture, I excitedly go from room to room, planning in my head where all the stuff in my Jeep will go.

"Where do you want these boxes, Hal?" my dad calls out from the living room.

"Put them in the spare room for now. I'll sort them all out in a bit," I shout as I flop down onto my bed.

"What time is Jess coming over, sweetheart?" my mom asks, poking her head around my bedroom door.

"Not until after work."

"Let's get as much unpacked as we can, then, before she arrives." She disappears back toward the living room, and I sit up, excited to show my apartment off. Jess is my only friend these days. I had a lot of friends before, but when I came back, people were different. I didn't go out much, and I missed a load of school. Jess was pretty much the only person who bothered. I'm so grateful she never gave up on me.

A few hours later, I'm sitting in the spare room surrounded by boxes. My parents left about an hour ago, my mom making me promise to call her after Jess leaves. She won't get any sleep tonight worrying about me. I wish I could convince her I'm going to be fine.

Standing, I grab one of the boxes marked 'books' and head over to the other side of the room where my bookshelves sit. I've got at least five boxes full of books. I've always loved to read, but after I got back from Cedar Falls, I found myself reading more and more, losing myself in story after story. Those stories stopped me from falling into the abyss, one I knew if I allowed myself to fall, I couldn't be sure of ever getting out.

I pull out book after book from the box, lovingly flicking through the pages, sometimes stopping to read a paragraph or two before transferring them to the shelves. As ridiculous as it sounds, the characters on these pages felt like friends. I could pretend I was part of their lives and not stuck in the hell that was mine.

After unpacking all five boxes, I stand back and smile, appreciating my handiwork. The rest of the apartment might be in total chaos, but the bookshelves are full, and I love them. As I wander out of the bedroom, there's a knock on the apartment door. That can't be Jess already, unless I've spent longer sorting my books than I thought. I glance at the clock on the wall in the kitchen, seeing it's not even six yet. The intercom hasn't rung either, so it must be someone already inside the building. Walking to the entryway, I pause before gingerly opening the apartment door. Standing in the hallway is a woman around my age holding a bottle of wine.

"Hey there. I'm Kitty. I live across the hall." She smiles, holding out the bottle for me to take. "Welcome to the building."

"Thank you. I'm Hallie." I return the smile, shocked at her kindness before taking the bottle from her outstretched arm.

"Nice to meet you, Hallie. I thought I'd say hi. If there's anything you need, feel free to knock." She waves as she turns and heads to her apartment. I bite my lip as I look down at the bottle in my hand. I don't trust people easily, and with good reason, but today feels different. Today I want to try.

"Kitty," I call as I step out into the hallway. I wait for her to turn around. "Do you want to come in for a drink?" I hold the bottle up and wait for her reply.

A smile breaks out on her face. "Sure, that would be great." She follows me into the apartment, closing the door behind her.

"Please excuse the mess, I'm nowhere near unpacked."

"Pshhh, this is nothing. My apartment looks worse than this most days, and I've been here for six months."

I walk into the kitchen, searching through a box on the floor for the corkscrew. "Take a seat. My corkscrew is in here somewhere. Ahh, here it is." With a flourish, I hold the corkscrew up triumphantly. "Now to find the wine glasses."

Kitty laughs from the living room. "Should I grab some from my apartment?"

"No, no. They're here somewhere. I bought some new ones last week." I continue to hunt through boxes and bags.

"So," I call from the kitchen, breathing a sigh of relief as I finally find the glasses. "What do you do for a living?" I quickly open the wine and pour us each a glass. Sitting next to her on the couch, I pass one over to her.

"I'm a nurse at County. How about you?"

"I work at the library in town." She nods and takes a swig of her drink. Her phone vibrates in her pocket, and she slides it out with her free hand. Staring at the screen, she groans before putting it back in her pocket. "Everything okay?" I ask, not wanting to pry.

"Yeah, just my dickhead ex saying he's left his jacket at my place. He can wait." She takes another drink. "Enough about me and my sad excuse for a love life. What about you? Please tell me your love life is better than mine, that you have an amazing man in your life, and not all men are douches?"

"Afraid not. The only men in my life are my dad and brother." I shake my head and take a mouthful of wine. "I think I win the crappy love life contest."

"So, you have a brother... is he hot?"

"Eww... he's my brother. He used to pick his nose and eat it. I'm not sure that qualifies as being hot."

She bursts out laughing and leans back on the sofa. "Yeah, you've kind of put me off him."

"Seriously, he's a great guy. A couple of years older than me, but he's away a lot. He's a Marine and deployed at the moment." Her eyes widen, and I roll mine. "What is it with women and men in uniform?"

"You're kidding, right? Men in uniform are hot!"

"I guess." I shrug my shoulders, not wanting her to think I'm weird. I've never had a boyfriend. Well, not one who wasn't in middle school. After I came back from Cedar Falls, I rarely went out. Guys were the last thing on my mind.

"This is a great apartment." She stands from the sofa and walks to the large window overlooking midtown, the Savannah River in the distance. "You have a great view. My apartment is on the other side of the block. I can't see the river. You'll have to come over for takeout and a movie sometime?"

"That sounds great. I'd love to." Our conversation is interrupted when the intercom sounds. "I bet that's Jess," I tell her, standing and crossing the room to buzz her in.

"I'll get going if you have company." She finishes her wine and walks toward the kitchen, placing her glass on the counter.

"We'll get a date arranged for that movie night. Thanks for the drink." I walk her the short distance to the apartment door and hold it open.

"Great to meet you, Kitty, and thanks for the wine."

"Sorry, I drank half of it!"

"Hey, here's Jess," I say as the elevator doors open, and Jess walks toward us, a bottle of wine in her hand. "Why don't I introduce you? Maybe the three of us could go out sometime?"

"Sure. Sounds good."

"Hey, Jess." I step into the hallway and pull her into a hug. "This is Kitty. She lives across the hall. She brought a bottle of wine over to welcome me to the building."

"Hey," Jess says with a smile.

"Good to meet you. You too, Hallie. I'll leave you to it. Have a good night." She offers her hand up in a wave and walks the short distance to her apartment.

I wave back, tugging Jess inside and closing the door.

"She seems nice," Jess says, placing the bottle of wine she's brought on the breakfast bar and slipping off her jacket.

"Yeah, she is. Come on, I'll show you around."

After a quick tour of the apartment, we're back in the kitchen, deciding which pizza to order.

"I can't believe you've finally moved out. How are you feeling?" Jess asks, sipping on the glass of wine I've poured her.

"Honestly? I'm good. A little apprehensive, but it's time. I'm ready to get on with my life."

"I'm happy for you, Hal."

I smile and pull her into a hug.

A few hours later, after far too many glasses of wine, I close the apartment door after saying goodbye to Jess. I've had the best day. Moving out of my parents' house was both the easiest and hardest decision I've ever made. Part of me wanted to stay in their protective bubble forever, but a bigger part of me wants to be normal. I want my space and the satisfaction of knowing I *can* be on my own. I feel at home immediately here, and more importantly, I feel safe, something I'd struggled to feel for years. I knew from the brief meeting with Kitty earlier that we'll be friends, which only cements the fact I'd made the right decision.

This is the beginning of the rest of my life.

Chapter Four

Hallie

The next few weeks pass quickly, and my apartment is finally box-free. My nights are no longer spent unpacking, and I've become something of a DIY superstar. Okay, so maybe not a superstar, but I've managed to get all my framed photographs on the walls throughout the apartment without the help of my dad. Although, I was a little nervous the first time I picked up the hammer, worried I might bring the wall down. The apartment is finally beginning to feel like home, and I love it.

Tonight is girls' night. Jess and Kitty have been to my apartment a couple of times for takeout and a movie, but tonight we were going to a bar. I'm a little apprehensive, and as I stand in front of the long mirror in my bedroom, I frown at my choice of outfit. I don't get out much and rarely feel comfortable on a night out. I don't want people to notice me. I'm happy to fade into the background.

When I got back to Savannah ten years ago, the press hounded us. They spent weeks camped outside my parents' house, desperate to get a glimpse of the girl who'd survived when so many others hadn't been so lucky. I was terrified to go outside anyway, but the press made it even harder. I slowly changed how I looked, coloring my shoulder-length blonde hair a dark brown and growing it out. I introduced bangs a couple of years ago, and when I look in the mirror now, I struggle to see the Hallie from back then.

I frown again as I look at my reflection to see the black skinny jeans and electric-blue top I've chosen. I'm debating getting changed when I hear a knock on the door. Kicking off my heeled pumps, I make my way through the apartment, swinging the door open.

"Wow, you look great," Kitty says as she stands in the hallway outside the apartment holding a bottle of wine.

"Really? I was thinking about getting changed." I gesture for her to come in.

"Don't, I like it." She heads for the kitchen, getting down three wine glasses. "When is Jess coming?"

"She should be on her way." I've barely gotten my reply out when the intercom sounds. "That'll be her," I declare with a chuckle as I reach for the intercom phone. After buzzing her up, I open the door in readiness. Kitty has poured three glasses of wine, and I take one from her and sip the bubbly drink.

"Looks like I'm just in time," Jess says as she sweeps into the apartment, pulling me and then Kitty into a hug. She plucks a glass of wine off the breakfast bar, then flops down on the sofa. As usual, she looks stunning. She's wearing a tight black dress and heels so high, I don't know how she can walk without falling over. Her long blonde hair hangs over her shoulders in waves, her makeup flawless. She looks incredible.

"You look beautiful, Jess," I tell her.

"So do you. I love that color." She gestures to my top, and I smile at her before smoothing my hands down the soft material, feeling better that both Jess and Kitty approve of my outfit.

"I'll grab my shoes and purse, and we can get going." I take another mouthful of wine, then set what's left down on the breakfast bar before heading back into my bedroom. I slip my heels on, then apply a coat of lip gloss in the mirror, checking my reflection once more. Snatching up my purse, I head back into the living room. Kitty and Jess are sitting on the sofa, chatting. It's great we've all clicked so quickly.

"Ready, guys?"

They both stand, following me into the entryway.

"Don't forget your wine," Kitty says, scooping up my glass and holding it out in front of me. Laughing, I take it from her and drink what's left, leaving the empty glass on the small table by the door.

It's a short walk to the bar Kitty suggested. Despite working shifts as a nurse, she has a pretty busy social life. Walking through the door, it seems as if she knows everyone here. I swear it takes ten minutes to get to the bar with everyone stopping her to say hi.

"First drink's on me," she shouts when we finally reach the front of the line. "What does everyone want?" Jess and Kitty stick to wine, but after the hangover from hell a few weeks ago, I know not to drink more than one glass. I choose vodka and lemonade instead, and we head to a free table once we have our drinks.

"So, I have news," Jess says excitedly as we slide into the booth. Turning to face her, she has a huge smile on her face.

"Well, tell us, then," I beg when she doesn't elaborate.

She laughs before taking a sip of her wine. "Grayson finally asked me out," she cries, her eyes sparkling with excitement.

"Oh my God! When?" I ask, scooting closer toward her.

"Today, at recess."

"Who's Grayson?" Kitty asks from across the table.

"Grayson is the hot PE teacher who works at the school where Jess teaches," I interject before Jess can answer. "She's been crushing on him since he started back in the fall."

"I have not been crushing on him," Jess exclaims before taking a mouthful of her wine.

"So, you don't run past his apartment block three times a week hoping you'll bump into him?"

She looks sideways at me. "You make me sound like some crazed stalker," she states, and I laugh, slinging my arm around her shoulder.

"I'm pleased for you, Jess. I know how much you like him."

"God, he's so hot. I can't wait."

"Where's he taking you?" Kitty asks. "And more importantly, does he have any friends?"

"I thought you were sworn off men after your ex?" I ask with a chuckle.

She waves her hand and shakes her head. "I'm so over him. I'm ready to play the field again. What about you, Hallie? Any guys you like the look of?" She gestures with her head to the packed bar, and I glance out at the sea of people.

"Nah, I don't have time to date." I brush off her question, hoping she isn't going to force the issue.

"Girl, you have to make time," she pushes.

"I know, I know." I wave off her comment before taking a sip of my drink, attempting to hide my face.

"Shall we dance?" Jess asks, knowing I'm uncomfortable.

"Great idea," I affirm, swallowing down the last of my drink before standing up. I whisper a thank you to Jess, and all three of us make our way to the dance area, our previous conversation forgotten for now. After about thirty minutes of dancing, Kitty stops and leans in close to Jess and me.

"That guy over there..." she gestures with her eyes to the corner of the room, "... blue shirt, blond hair?" Jess and I turn to look at who she's talking about.

"What about him?" I ask.

"Do you know him? He keeps looking over here."

I steal a glance again, only to see him staring at me. "I've never seen him before, but he's cute. Do you know him, Jess?"

She shakes her head.

"Well, I'm going to say hi." Kitty wriggles her eyebrows at us, and I smile as she makes her way toward him, his eyes now fixed firmly on her. She flirts with him, placing her arm on his chest before throwing her head back and laughing at something he's said.

"She's not shy, is she?" Jess says with a laugh. "Come on. Let's get a drink. It looks like she's going to be busy for a while."

Crossing the Line

I turn back to where they both are. Kitty's arms are already around the guy's neck, and she's kissing him. I can't help but feel a little envious of her. I'd never have the confidence to walk up to a guy in a bar like that, let alone kiss him within a few minutes of meeting.

"You okay?" Jess asks me, her hand slipping into mine and squeezing it gently. Pulled from my thoughts, I drag my eyes off Kitty and turn to face her.

"Yeah, fine. Shall we get that drink?"

When I follow her to the bar, we get served quickly. Finding a table where we can see Kitty, I flop down on the chair, the balls of my feet burning from my heeled pumps.

"Looks like it's going well," Jess says, gesturing to where Kitty and the guy are slow dancing on the edge of the dance floor.

"I think we've lost her for the night. Can't say I blame her." My voice sounds melancholy even to my ears, and I can see by Jess's face she's picked up on my tone.

"Grayson's got a brother, you know." She grins and winks at me, and I burst out laughing. "I'm serious, though. If it goes well with us, I'll set you up."

"What is it with people offering up with their brothers?" I say, laughing. "Dana from work tried to set me up a few weeks ago."

"Well, you haven't said no. I'm taking that as a win." I shake my head at her and smile.

She means well, and I love her for it. The thing is, I have no idea how to date. Sure, I had the odd date in middle school but nothing serious. While all my friends were experimenting with boys and dating, I was having nightmares and weekly counseling sessions, terrified to leave the house.

Matt and Amanda stole six months of my life when they kept me a prisoner in Cedar Falls.

In reality, I lost so much more.

I lost my teenage years and every experience that comes with that. I never went to parties or college. Hell, I barely finished high school. I never experienced spring break or girly vacations. I didn't even get my driver's license until I was twenty-two. I might be twenty-four now, but I sometimes wonder how I made it to where I am today, seemingly skipping the last ten years of my life.

After another couple of hours of dancing, along with too many drinks to count, I'm ready to call it a night. Kitty's still wrapped around her date, if that's the right word for him, and we slowly fight our way across the dance floor toward them. Coming up behind Kitty, I tap her on the shoulder.

"Hey, you two," she shouts over the music as she turns and sees us. "This is Nick." She winds her arm around the guy next to her, a huge smile on her face. "Nick, these are my friends, Hallie and Jess."

"Good to meet you," he shouts. He's tall, about six foot two, and up close, even better looking than he seemed when Kitty first spotted him across the bar. He has messy blond hair and bright blue eyes that match the color of the shirt pulled tight across his chest.

"Hi," Jess and I say in unison, and he chuckles as he pulls Kitty closer to him.

"So, we're heading home, Kitty. Are you about ready to go?" She glances at Nick and nods before going up on her tiptoes to kiss him. I'm thankful she hasn't insisted on staying. I wouldn't have been comfortable leaving her here with a man she's just met.

"I'll call you tomorrow, babe," Nick says as he steps back. "Great to meet you, ladies."

I smile and link arms with Jess as Kitty waves over her shoulder to him.

When we're outside, Kitty stops and squeals. "Oh my God, isn't Nick amazing? I'm sorry I ditched you. I never intended to stay with him all night."

"He is hot, Kitty. We don't blame you," Jess assures her as she flags down a passing cab. We climb into the back and head to Jess's place first. Kitty is talking nonstop about Nick, and despite watching them kiss all night, it does seem they talked quite a bit in between sucking face.

"He's an investment banker at Bank of America," she gushes,

turning to look at me and then Jess. "An investment banker," she repeats, her eyes wide. "Can you imagine how hot he'll look in a suit?" She pauses and then grins. "Can you imagine how hot he'll look out of his suit?"

The cab driver clears his throat, and the three of us laugh.

"I think we'd better save this conversation for another time," I say with a giggle as we pull up outside Jess's apartment. We say a quick goodbye, with Kitty promising to keep Jess informed on how things progress with Nick. We watch her until she's in her building, then wave as the cab pulls off.

It's only a five-minute drive from Jess's place to mine, and despite Kitty's initial flurry of conversation, she's quiet as her fingers fly over the screen of her phone. There's a huge smile on her face, and I'm guessing it's Nick messaging her already. As we pull up outside the apartment entrance, I pay the driver and guide Kitty out of the cab, her eyes still fixed on her phone.

"He wants to take me out tomorrow," she tells me excitedly as I punch in the code for the main door.

"That's great, Kitty."

She follows me into the elevator and slips her phone into her purse. "I really like him, Hallie. I hope I don't mess it up." I turn to look at her in surprise. This is the first time I've seen a vulnerable side of her. She's always been so confident with everything. It never occurred to me it might all be a front.

"Why on earth would you mess anything up?"

"Well, I'm twenty-seven, and I've managed to mess up every relationship I've ever been in, so…" she trails off and shrugs.

"Doesn't mean it'll happen this time. Take your time, see where it goes." She gives me a small smile as the elevator doors open on our floor. I link her arm, and we walk slowly down the hallway, coming to Kitty's apartment first.

"Thanks, Hallie. And I'm sorry for being a crappy friend. Next girls' night out, I promise to not disappear on you."

"It's fine. There'll be plenty more nights out. Let me know how tomorrow goes?" She nods as I pull her into a hug. Throwing a wave over my shoulder, I head across the landing to my apartment. My feet are killing me, and I'm glad to kick off my shoes as I close the door behind me. The clock on the wall reads almost two o'clock, and I yawn, suddenly exhausted. I lock the door, then head to the bedroom, knowing I'll be asleep before my head hits the pillow.

Chapter Five

Hallie

"Ughhh!" I groan as my phone's shrill ringtone blasts out from the nightstand, waking me far earlier than I'd planned. Reaching my hand out from under the comforter, I blindly feel around, refusing to open my eyes. As my hand lands on it, the ringtone cuts off. Rolling over, I ignore whoever was calling, knowing they can leave a message if they need to. Seconds later, the ringtone starts again, and I sigh, forcing my eyes open. Reaching for my phone, Jess's name illuminates the screen. I hit the answer button and bring it to my ear.

"Hey, Jess—"

"Turn on *CNN*, Hallie," she interrupts, her voice strained.

"What?"

"*CNN*," she repeats. "Turn it on."

"Okay, hang on..." I swing my legs to the side of the bed, and with the phone still on my ear, I walk into the living room. I look around for the remote, then snatch it up, pointing it at the screen. I scroll through the channels and stop as I land on *CNN*. As the screen fills with the newscaster, I hear Jess again.

"Have you got it on?"

"Yes, but what am I looking—" I stop mid-sentence, gasping as I see why she wanted me to turn on the television.

"Hallie, are you okay?" Jess asks, the worry evident in her voice. "Hallie," she repeats a few seconds later when I don't answer.

"She's dead," I whisper as I sit down heavily on the sofa, my legs giving way. A wave of nausea washes over me, and a cold sweat breaks out on the back of my neck. I recoil as images of Amanda fill the screen in front of me. Words are scrolling across the bottom, and I read them aloud, even though Jess is watching on the other end of the phone.

"The body of Amanda Bryant was found today in her cell at Iowa Correctional Facility. She was serving a life sentence for her involvement in the murders of five young girls and the abduction of thirteen-year-old Hallie Anderson just over ten years ago. Bryant and her husband were arrested after Hallie, who was kidnapped from Savannah in 2009, escaped. Following the arrest, a search of their property in Cedar Falls, Iowa, uncovered the bodies of five more girls buried in shallow graves in the woodlands surrounding the house. It's not yet known if her husband, Matthew Bryant, will be granted leave from Anamosa State Penitentiary, where he's serving five life sentences, to attend her funeral."

"You don't think they'll actually let him out, do you?" I stand then pace the small space in my living room. "They can't," I whisper before Jess has a chance to reply.

"Hallie, listen to me... he's not getting out. Even if they let him attend the funeral, he'll be restrained. You're safe." I can hear what she's saying, but somehow, the words don't penetrate the fog that's descended in my mind.

"They've told everyone my name," I mumble as I absentmindedly walk around the living room.

"It'll be okay, Hal." The intercom buzzes, but I barely hear it, my eyes fixed on the television. It sounds again a few seconds later, and I'm pulled from my haze. Realizing Jess is still on the line, I pull the phone back and check the call hasn't dropped.

"I've got to go. Someone's at the door," I mutter as I tear my eyes off the television and head for the intercom phone.

"I'll call you later."

I nod, even though she can't see me, and end the call.

"Hello," I say shakily as I pick up the intercom phone.

"Hallie, it's Mom." I can hear the concern in her voice, and I know she's seen the news.

"Come on up," I whisper, pushing the button to release the door.

Slipping into my bedroom, I throw on some yoga pants and a tank before tying my hair up. I'm in the kitchen getting a bottle of water from the refrigerator when a knock sounds on my apartment door. Even though I've buzzed my mom up, I use the peephole to see who's outside the door. Breathing a sigh of relief, I swing the door open, my mom immediately pulling me into her arms.

"Hallie," she whispers, holding me tightly. Looking over her shoulder, my dad gives me a small smile. Standing behind him are two men in suits.

Frowning, I pull out of the embrace. "Mom?" I ask, looking past my dad to the strangers in the hallway.

She sighs as she turns around. "Hallie, this is Detective Wilmot and Lieutenant Phillips. They're here to talk to you."

"Good morning, ma'am," Detective Wilmot says. He's a little older than my dad, with a kind face and salt-and-pepper hair. The officer with him is younger, maybe early thirties. The fact they're here can't be good, and I wonder what they need to talk to me about.

Pulling myself together, I step aside. "Come in," I tell them, gesturing to the open door with my hand. I wait until they're inside my apartment before taking a deep breath and following them. My stomach churns with nerves as I cross the room and sit next to my mom on the sofa.

I thought this was all behind me.

That Matt and Amanda no longer had control over my life.

It seems I was wrong.

"Miss Anderson—" Detective Wilmot begins.

"Call me Hallie, please," I interrupt.

He smiles kindly and sits on the footstool across from the sofa. "Hallie, I know by now you will have seen the news." His eyes flick to the television still on the *CNN* news channel, the story of Amanda's death playing on a loop. Picking up the remote next to me, I turn it off. "We put a ban on the stations broadcasting the news, but it was leaked. We wanted you to hear it from us."

I shrug, my fingers playing with the hem of my top. "What difference does it make? It doesn't change anything." My eyes stay on my fingers as I fight back tears. She's dead. I only wish Matt was dead too.

"No, but we wanted to talk to you about what happens now."

I lift my head sharply and frown. "What do you mean? What happens now?" My mom reaches for my hand, squeezing it tightly. I flick my head around, and she bites down on her bottom lip, her eyebrows drawn together. "What aren't you telling me?"

"Amanda was found dead in her cell over a week ago. Her funeral is the day after tomorrow. We wanted it to be all over before you found out."

"Why?" I ask in confusion.

"Matthew Bryant has requested to attend."

"Okay," I say slowly. "Is he... is he allowed to attend?"

"I'm afraid so. He'll be under guard and shackled the entire time..." he trails off and swallows heavily. An uneasy feeling washes over me, and I know he's holding something back.

"There's more, isn't there?" I say, my voice barely a whisper.

"The funeral will be held here in Savannah." My chest feels tight as my breathing accelerates. My fingers tingle, and black spots appear in my vision. I can hear my mom telling me to calm down, but her voice seems far away and muffled.

I'm having a panic attack.

I've had enough over the years to know.

Regardless of that, I'm powerless to stop it.

Suddenly, someone is kneeling in front of me, a paper bag in their hand. They're encouraging me to breathe into it, and I somehow manage to follow their instructions. After a minute or so of breathing into the bag, I can feel my fingers again, and the black spots have disappeared.

Looking up, my dad's kneeling in front of me.

"Sweetheart, are you okay?" I hear my mom's worried voice clearly now, so I know the worst has passed.

I nod slowly, and my dad passes me an open bottle of water. Putting it to my lips, I take a small mouthful. I had panic attacks regularly after I came home from Cedar Falls, and the therapist I saw helped me control them. It has been years since I last had one, but it came on so quickly, I was unable to put the strategies I'd been taught to use.

"I'm so sorry, Miss... Hallie. I can only imagine how upsetting this is for you," Detective Wilmot says, his voice full of genuine remorse.

"Why is the funeral being held here?" I croak out, taking another mouthful of water.

"Amanda's only remaining relative is an aunt who lives in Savannah. We tried to talk to her, but she was very insistent she is buried here."

"I can't believe *he's* going to be here in Savannah the day after tomorrow." My voice breaks, and my mom pulls me close.

"Why don't you come home for a few days until all of this is over," my mom suggests.

"I am home, Mom. I live here. I've put my life on hold long enough. I'm not being chased out of my own home."

She sighs. "Okay, sweetheart. I'm just worried about you."

"I know." I turn and pull her into a hug. "I'm done letting them rule my life. I lost ten years. I don't want to lose anymore."

"If you're sure you are okay, we'll get going," Detective Wilmot says kindly. "The funeral arrangements haven't been made public, but I can't guarantee no press will contact you, not now that the story's been leaked. We can't stop you from speaking to them, but we believe it's in your best interest not to." I stand up to see them out. "You're safe though, Hallie. You have my word." He holds his hand out, and I take it, shaking it briefly. Lieutenant Phillips nods in my direction before heading for the apartment door.

"Which cemetery is it at?" I ask quietly, not wanting my parents to hear. Detective Wilmot's hand pauses on the door handle, and he sighs as he slowly turns around. His eyes flick behind me to my parents before landing back on me.

"Colonial Park. I don't advise you to go, Hallie," he warns, his voice low. I don't say anything, reaching past him to open the apartment door. He stares at me before sighing again and walking through the open door, followed by Lieutenant Phillips.

Closing the door, I pause, briefly composing myself before heading back to my parents. They're talking in hushed tones, falling silent when I walk back into the living room.

"What's going on?" I ask.

"Are you sure you don't want to come and stay with us for a couple of nights? It'll be fun. We can have a girly night with a movie and popcorn?" I can hear the pleading tone in my mom's voice, and as much as I'd love to run back to the safety of my parents' house, I can't.

"Mom, I'm fine. My apartment is closer to work, and I have friends here. I'm not running away." Although I can see she isn't happy, she seems to accept my decision.

"How about breakfast on me?" my dad asks with a smile.

"That sounds good," I tell him, grateful he's diverted the conversation away from me moving back home. "I'll quickly hop in the shower." Kissing his cheek as I pass him, I'm about to head into the bathroom when I hear another knock on the door. "I'll get it," I call out as I head into the entryway. Using the peephole, Kitty is standing in the hallway. As I swing the door open, she throws her arms around me.

"Oh, Hallie. I've just seen *CNN*. Why didn't you tell me?" I shrug as I step out of her embrace and think about lying for a fraction of a second. I want to be the Hallie who lives across the hallway and gets drunk on half a bottle of wine. I don't want to be the Hallie from ten years ago, the poor girl from Savannah who was abducted by a serial killer. But most of all, I don't want to see the look that's currently on Kitty's face. The look I've seen hundreds of times before on everyone from the mailman to my schoolteacher. That look changes how people see and treat you. I'm still me. I don't want people's pity.

"It was a lifetime ago," I mumble, my eyes not finding hers. "Can I catch up with you later? My parents are here and taking me out for breakfast." Finally meeting her eyes, they flash with hurt before she forces a smile.

"Of course." She pulls me in for another hug, giving me a small wave as she makes her way back to her apartment.

"Hope your date with Nick goes well," I call after her.

I like Kitty and don't want to lose her as a friend. I know I'm pushing her away right now, but I'm not ready to talk about what happened.

She turns around and gives me a proper smile that reaches her eyes. "I'll fill you in later." She winks. I smile and close the door before heading for the shower.

As I stand under the hot spray, I replay the last hour in my mind. Amanda is dead, and the day after tomorrow, the man who abducted me ten years ago will be in Savannah, just two and a half miles from where I work. I thought I'd put Matt and Amanda behind me ten years ago. It seems life has other plans for me.

Chapter Six

Hallie

It's the day of Amanda's funeral, and it is like I've been hit by a freight train. I haven't slept properly since I saw the news of her death on *CNN*. My nights are filled with dreams of ten years ago, and the thoughts that race through my mind aren't rational.

Despite knowing Matt is under guard, I need to see for myself. I need to see that he can't get to me, and that I'm safe.

It didn't take me long to find out the time of the funeral. A few Google searches and the information is there for anyone to see.

Jess has been around to my apartment a couple of times to check on me since I found out about Amanda's death. As close as I am to her, I haven't told her of my worries, putting on a brave face whenever she's there. I'm sure she can see right through me, and that's the reason for her multiple visits, but even so, she hasn't called me out on it yet.

I've called in sick to work, and I'm sure my colleague, Dana, is worried. She's seen the news like everyone else but thankfully, hasn't pressed me to tell her anything. I couldn't be more grateful to her for that. She's offered to listen if I need to talk, but that's the most she's said to me about it and I am grateful.

Crossing the Line

Leaving the apartment, I head down in the elevator to the parking garage. It's only a ten-minute drive to the cemetery, and I want to get there before the service starts. I need to see Matt, but I don't plan on letting him see me. Nerves swirl in my stomach as I make the short drive across town. The cemetery is quiet, and I wonder if they've not scheduled any other funerals today. Armed guards and a high-profile prisoner aren't exactly what people expect to see when they are laying a loved one to rest.

Parking my Jeep in the small lot, an area a little way from where I'm standing is set up for a service. A handful of chairs are positioned around an open grave, and I pull out my phone to check the time—fifteen minutes until the service is due to start. Slipping my phone back into my pocket, I walk in the opposite direction, needing to put some space between me and where Matt will shortly be standing. My phone rings, and I jump, my heart racing. Sliding it from my pocket, Jess is calling.

"Hey," I say, my voice sounding more confident than I feel.

"Hey. So, I stopped by the library. Dana said you were sick. I swung by your apartment, but you weren't there. Everything okay?" I bite down on my bottom lip as I contemplate lying. I'm a terrible liar though, and she can usually see straight through me.

"Umm, yeah, I'm okay."

"So, you're not sick?" I can hear the confusion in her voice, and I close my eyes, knowing she's going to think I'm crazy when I tell her where I am.

"No, I'm not sick, but you might think I am when I tell you what I'm doing."

"Why? What's going on, Hallie? Where are you?" I'm silent for longer than I should be. "Hallie, talk to me."

"I'm at the cemetery," I mumble, closing my eyes as I wait for her reaction.

"The cemetery... oh, Hallie, no! Come home. You don't want to see him."

39

"I need to do this, Jess. I need to see him vulnerable and locked up."

She sighs down the phone. "Okay, I'm coming. Which cemetery are you at?"

Before I can answer, a large gray van pulls up the driveway. As it gets closer, I can see the words 'Prisoner Transport - Stay Away' splashed on the side in white writing. My breathing accelerates, and I think I'm going to throw up.

"Hallie. Hallie, are you still there?" Jess shouts down the phone.

"He's here," I whisper, my eyes wide and glued to the van.

"Shit. Which cemetery, Hallie?"

"Colonial Park," I mumble.

"I'm on my way. Stay out of sight."

I end the call, switching the phone to vibrate. The last thing I need is for my phone to ring and give away my hiding position. There's a large tree to my left, and I scoot behind it, using it to shield myself from view. The funeral cars haven't arrived yet, and as I peer around the side of the tree, two guards step out of the van, their eyes constantly surveying the area.

"What the hell am I doing here?" I mutter to myself, dropping my head against the hard bark of the tree. I should go home. I simply can't force myself to move. I'm still standing in the same position when I hear another vehicle approaching. Looking around the tree, nerves swirl in my stomach as the funeral car carrying Amanda's body pulls up outside the chapel. My eyes are fixed on the casket, and I watch its removal from the car and placed on a trolley. Another car pulls up, and an elderly lady slides out. I'm guessing this is the aunt Detective Wilmot told me about. There are no other mourners, and after what she was a part of, I can't say I'm surprised.

As the casket is wheeled over to where the service will take place, my eyes flick to the prison van. The two guards are opening the back doors, and my breath catches in my throat as a man dressed in an orange jumpsuit steps out. His hands are cuffed, and his ankles are shackled. There is a small length of thick chain linking the shackles on his ankles, allowing him to shuffle along slowly. His head is bowed, and despite not seeing his face, I know it's him. His hair is the same as it was except for a few streaks of gray, and he looks as built as he was ten years ago. A shudder runs through me as he lifts his head, and I see for the first time in ten years the hard, cold eyes that terrified me—eyes that haunted my dreams for years. Eyes I never thought I'd see again.

My phone vibrates in my hand, and I look down, seeing Jess is calling me.

"Hello," I whisper as I put the phone to my ear, my eyes still firmly fixed on Matt.

"Where are you?"

"I'm hiding behind a tree across from the parking lot."

"Okay. I see you. I'm coming over."

"You can see me?" I whisper scream down the phone, frantically looking around. *If Jess can see me, can anyone else?* Fear erupts inside me, and I pray I don't have a panic attack. This was a bad idea. I should leave now with Jess and come back later for my car.

"Calm down. I parked on Burlington and came in the back way. I'm coming up behind you." I close my eyes and drag in a mouthful of air trying to calm myself down. When my breathing evens out, I turn around, seeing her walking across the cemetery, her phone to her ear. Giving a small wave, I end the call, pushing the phone into my pocket. A few seconds later, she's behind me.

"Hey, you okay?" she asks quietly as she pulls me in for a hug. "I can't believe you're here, Hal."

"Me either. I had to come. I can't explain it... I just had to." She squeezes me a little tighter before releasing me and peeking around the tree.

"Why aren't you at work?" I suddenly ask, realizing it's mid-afternoon on a school day.

"School's closed. The drains are backing up, and there's sewage everywhere." She looks at me and pulls a face before looking back around the tree. "Where is the bastard then? Oh, I see him, shackled like an animal. I can't think of anyone more deserving." Her voice is thick with disdain, and I can't help but get a little emotional knowing my best friend has my back.

"Thank you," I say quietly. "For coming and humoring me. I know you think I'm crazy, but I'm glad you're here with me."

She turns and smiles. "I don't think you're crazy." Tilting her head, she screws up her nose. "A little weird maybe, but never crazy."

"Hey," I exclaim, feigning hurt.

"I'm joking," she says with a laugh. "Seriously though, Hal, I will always be here for you whenever you need me. Granted, this is probably the weirdest thing we've ever done, stalking a serial killer, but there's no way I'd want you to be here on your own." I pull her into another hug before we go back to peering around the tree.

As the service is about to begin, a black sedan pulls up, and Jess nudges me in the side. "Who's that?" I shrug as the car door opens, and Detective Wilmot climbs out along with Lieutenant Phillips.

"They're the officers who came to my apartment," I tell her in a hushed tone. "I wonder what they're doing here."

"Probably extra support for the guards. I did think there would be more police for someone as high profile as him." I nod and turn my attention back to the officers. They haven't approached the graveside. They lean up against their car, watching from a distance.

A few minutes later, and aside from Matt, the prison guards, and the elderly aunt, no one else has turned up. I watch Matt intently through the service, and no emotion passes his face. He really is a heartless bastard if he can't shed a tear at his wife's funeral. I shouldn't be surprised, I guess. A man who can kill his daughter along with four other young girls, can't possibly be emotionally stable. The graveside service is surprisingly long considering there are hardly any mourners.

"Do you want to go, Hal? It's almost over," Jess asks as they lower the casket into the ground.

I shake my head. "I need to see him get back into the van." She takes my hand, squeezing it gently before giving me a small smile. As

Matt throws dirt onto the casket, a black van squeals into the cemetery, stopping right next to where the service is being held. Three masked men jump out with guns in their hands. Before I know what's happening, gunshots ring out in the peaceful cemetery, and the two prison guards fall to the ground.

Jess tugs on my arm, and we fall to the grass, lying as low as possible. Her hand clasps mine, and we lie pressed together in the dirt below the tree.

"Fuck, Hallie! What's happening?" Her voice is shaking, exposing she is terrified. I am too. My heart pounds in my chest as more gunshots are fired, this time from farther away, and I wonder if Detective Wilmot and Lieutenant Phillips are returning fire.

Slowly lifting my head, I look across to where the service was being held. Both prison guards are lying motionless, blood pooling on the ground beneath them. The pastor is cowering behind a chair, his arm wrapped protectively around the shaking elderly aunt. Matt has taken cover behind a tombstone, his face once again emotionless. He doesn't look surprised at what's happening. I'd bet my life he knew these men would come.

I gasp and drop my head as another round of gunshots rings out.

"Shit, Hallie, if they find us, they'll kill us!" Jess whispers, the terror in her voice is evident.

"If we stay quiet, they won't know we're here," I promise her, guilt washing over me that I've put us in this position with my stupid need to be here. Lifting my head again, I look at the black sedan where Detective Wilmot and Lieutenant Phillips are taking cover behind their car doors. Two of the three men are still firing at them, and both front tires deflate, bullets piercing the rubber. The third shooter has moved toward Matt, his gun replaced with bolt cutters.

I look on in horror as Matt's shackles are cut, and he stands up, running toward the black van. As he climbs into the back, another hail of bullets rings out, and I drop my head again, my eyes squeezed tightly shut.

The sound of squealing tires forces me to open my eyes, and I watch in disbelief as the black van holding the man who once threatened to kill me races out of the cemetery.

"Are they gone?" Jess asks, her face still pressed against the dirt.

"I... I think so," I stutter, not wanting to move in case they return. "They cut his shackles, Jess. He's free." I let out a cry I can't contain before clamping my hand over my mouth. "God, he's free," I mumble again from behind my hand. "He's going to come for me. He said he'd find me if I escaped." Tears track down my face, and Jess sits up, pulling me up with her.

"Shh, it's going to be okay, Hallie. It's going to be okay." She wraps her arms around me as my body trembles.

"It won't ever be okay. Why couldn't it have been his funeral today?" There is no answer to my question, and we hold each other as we both sob, the realization of what's happened hitting us hard. The sound of police sirens echoes in the distance, and soon there are five or six police cars along with two ambulances filling the small parking lot.

"We need to let the officers know we're here," Jess says, standing up. Her voice sounds calm, but her shaking body tells me she's anything but. Wiping her eyes, she holds a hand out to me, then pulls me to my feet. I follow her out from our hiding place, my vision blurred from all the tears.

Detective Wilmot spots us and runs over. "Hallie, what are you doing here? Did you witness all of that?" His eyes pass from me to Jess before returning to me. "Are either of you hurt?" I shake my head, my eyes dropping to the ground. He sighs as he guides us past the open grave toward his car. Glancing over, the EMTs are taking care of the pastor and the elderly aunt. They don't seem hurt, just shaken up. I know how they feel. I can tell from how much blood has pooled on the grass, that both prison guards are dead, and I avert my eyes as we walk past. I don't want the image of them in my mind.

"Do either of you need to see an EMT?" Detective Wilmot asks. We both shake our heads. "Office Dennison, I've a job for you," he shouts to one of the officers taping off the crime scene. He quickly finishes up with the cordon and makes his way over to us.

"Yes, sir?"

"Can you take Miss Anderson and her friend to the precinct, please? I'll be along shortly." The officer nods and gestures with his arm to his police car. "Oh, and Dennison, can you send a car over to her parents' house and pick them up? I'll catch a lift back with one of the other patrol cars when we're done here." The officer nods again and walks over to his car, opening the door for us.

"Thank you," I mumble as we walk past the detective and climb into the back of the police car. Exhausted, I drop my head back on the seat. My mind is working overtime as I process the fact that Matt has escaped. Despite Jess trying to convince me everything will be okay, I know it won't be. How can it? The words Matt said to me when I arrived in Cedar Falls all those years ago play in a loop over and over in my mind.

"I promise you, sweetheart, if you try to escape, I will *find you, and I will* kill you."

It might have been a promise he made ten years ago, but I have a feeling it's a promise he has every intention of keeping.

Chapter Seven

Sawyer

As I'm stepping out of the shower, I hear my phone ringing from the nightstand in my bedroom. Wrapping a towel around my waist, I jog into the bedroom, grabbing my phone before the call cuts off.

"Hello?" I say, not having looked at who's calling.

"Sawyer, it's Logan. I know you're on leave, but something's come up, and they're asking for the best we have. That's you. Can you come in?"

I close my eyes and sigh. "Sure, give me an hour." I end the call and dry off, throwing the wet towel in the laundry basket in the corner of the room. Tugging on a pair of jeans and a T-shirt, I head into the kitchen, picking up the sandwich I fixed before showering. I take a soda from the refrigerator and move into the living room to eat. I've only taken a mouthful of my sandwich when a news bulletin interrupts the program that's on in the background.

A serial killer has escaped in Savannah.

Putting two and two together, I can only assume the job I'm being called in for has something to do with that. The prisoner's name flashes up on the screen, along with a mugshot. It's not a name I'm familiar with, but he looks like a sick bastard. They always do.

I finish my sandwich, pull on my boots, and head out of the apartment. The elevator takes me to the parking garage, where I jump on my motorcycle and pull my helmet on.

As I'm about to start the engine, my phone vibrates in my pocket. Sliding it out, there's a message from Logan.

Logan: *Change of plan. Can you meet me at the precinct instead of the office?*

Me: *Sure thing. On my way.*

I'm in Tybee Island, about a thirty-minute drive from the center of Savannah. On a good day, I can make it in twenty, and as I open the throttle on the motorcycle, the world rushes past me. I've driven a motorcycle since I was old enough for a license, and it never gets old.

As I get closer to Savannah, I hit some traffic, and it looks like roadblocks have been set up on routes in and out of town. Officers are stopping vehicles going in both directions, and it takes a while to get through. When I've finally navigated the traffic, I hit more as I near the precinct. There are at least twenty or so reporters, some with television crews camped outside. It seems an escaped prisoner in town is big news. I find somewhere to park the bike and fight my way through the crowd surrounding the entrance. Inside, Logan is waiting by the front desk for me.

"Sawyer," he calls across the room. I acknowledge him, shaking his outstretched hand when I reach him. "Thanks for coming in on such short notice."

"No problem. I'm guessing it's something to do with all that out there?" I gesture with my head to the entrance, and he nods.

"Come on. I'll fill you in as we head upstairs." Following him, we head to the elevator. "Around ten years ago, a thirteen-year-old girl was abducted from a park in Savannah. She disappeared for six months, turning up again on the side of the road in Cedar Falls, Iowa.

Matthew Bryant and his wife, Amanda, were arrested on abduction charges. When their house was searched, the bodies of five young girls were found in shallow graves in the woodlands behind their property, one of which was their daughter."

"Bastards," I mutter as the elevator doors open, and we step inside. Logan pushes the button for the third floor, and the doors close behind us.

"Amanda Bryant died in prison a week ago. She'd been unwell for some time but refused treatment. Today was the funeral. By some cruel twist of fate, the service was held here in Savannah."

"What the hell? Why would they do that?"

"Apparently, her only living relative lives here." He raises his eyebrows, and I nod in silent agreement.

"I doubt very much it was a coincidence."

"I thought the same."

"So, how did he get away?"

"Three guys with semi-automatics and a pair of bolt cutters. It took less than a minute. Two dead and four shook-up witnesses."

"What do you need me for?" The elevator chimes and the doors open onto an open-plan office space. Desks fill the area, and the hum of voices carries through the air.

"One of the witnesses was the girl Bryant abducted, Hallie Anderson. She's twenty-four now. Wilmot thinks he's going to come back for her."

"Does she know Wilmot's asked for protection?" He shakes his head, and I sigh. I've worked for Safe Haven Security as a close protection officer for the past five years. For the last two, the company has had a contract with the Savannah Police Department, providing protection when needed. I've worked with the police a handful of times but trying to protect someone who doesn't want protection or thinks they don't need it, is a pain in the ass.

We come to a stop outside an office door. "We're meeting with Wilmot first, then the girl. Her parents have arrived, and she's here with her friend. Both of them witnessed what happened at the cemetery today." Logan knocks on the door, and I follow him inside.

"Logan, Sawyer, good to see you both. Take a seat," Detective Wilmot says, gesturing to the spare seats. In the room with him are three other senior officers sitting around a large conference table. Papers and images are scattered across the table, and as I take a seat, my eyes drop to the image directly in front of me. A young girl stares up at me. Her face is smeared with dirt, and her eyes are red and puffy from crying. There's blood on her clothes, and her hair is messy and tangled. I'm guessing this is Hallie Anderson after she managed to escape the Bryant house. I can't help feeling angry as I look at her picture. She must have been terrified at what that bastard did. I'm glad she got away but I can see from the images on the table others weren't so lucky.

"Any sightings?" Logan asks as he sits in the seat next to mine.

Wilmot shakes his head. "No. We've set up roadblocks, but they've changed vehicles. We found the black van from the cemetery abandoned by Forsyth Park. They either had another car waiting or they stole one." He sighs and runs his hand through his salt-and-pepper hair. "He could be anywhere by now."

"Any prints found in the van?" I ask.

"CSI has managed to lift a print. We've run it through the database, but there's been no match," Wilmot says.

"It wasn't Bryant's print then?" Logan asks, and Wilmot shakes his head.

"You think he's here for the girl?" I ask.

"I think there's a good chance. Hallie's parents have approached me. They're keen for her to move out of Savannah with protection while we catch him. They've warned me they don't think she'll be keen on the idea, though."

"She doesn't think Bryant's a threat?" I raise my eyebrows in question, and he shakes his head.

"She was terrified at the cemetery. From what her parents tell me, she already feels like she's lost ten years of her life at the hands of this man. They don't think she'll want to put her life on hold again." He shrugs and shakes his head. "We need to convince her she needs you. As much as she won't want to admit it, she's vulnerable."

"What are we looking at? Round-the-clock close protection?" Logan asks from next to me. He's asked the question, but we already know the answer. With a threat this great, there's no other option.

Wilmot nods. "We can put you both in a safe house out of town. She's going to take some convincing, though." He stands up. "I'll get the Bryant file emailed to you so you can have all the information on this bastard."

"I'd appreciate that. I need to know what I'm up against."

He gestures to the door. "She's down the corridor with her parents. I'll take you to her."

Standing, we follow him out of the room, coming to a stop three offices down. "She's still pretty shook up. That might work in our favor in convincing her she needs protection," Wilmot says, his hand on the doorknob.

He opens the door, and we follow him in. "Hallie, I'd like you to meet someone I think can help you," he says. The room is set up like the one we've just left but on a much smaller scale. Four people sit around a small conference table and glancing round, I can pick out Hallie's parents, but I'm unsure which of the girls is Hallie—the blonde or the brunette. Both look shaken up, and despite seeing a picture of Hallie after she was rescued, neither looks like the photograph.

"Have you found him yet, Detective Wilson?" Hallie's dad asks.

"I'm afraid not, Mr. Anderson. We have every available officer looking and setting roadblocks up on the outskirts of town. His picture is on every news channel. He can't hide forever."

Hallie's dad sighs as he reaches for his wife's hand.

"Hallie, this is Sawyer Mitchell. He's a close protection officer working with the Savannah Police Department," Wilmot explains as he pulls out a chair, motioning for Logan and me to take a seat.

"Sawyer, this is Hallie Anderson." He gestures across the table to the brunette.

"Nice to meet you, Hallie. I wish it were under better circumstances. How are you doing?" I ask. Her frightened eyes meet mine, and despite the worry etched on her face, I can't help but notice how beautiful she is.

"A close protection officer?" She frowns. "As in a bodyguard?"

"Well, yes, but we don't use the term bodyguard anymore."

"I don't need a bodyguard."

"Hallie, we're concerned for your safety now that Matthew Bryant has escaped," Wilmot explains. "We all think having someone look out for you would be a good idea. Just until he's caught."

Hallie turns to her parents. "Do you think this is a good idea?" Her voice is quiet, but I can hear the emotion in her tone.

"Yes, sweetheart. We lost you once, and we can't bear to have anything happen to you again. That man is dangerous. We need to know you're safe," Hallie's mom says, reaching over and taking her daughter's hand.

She sighs and drops her head on the table. "I want this all to be over."

"We're doing everything we can to catch him, Hallie," Wilmot promises.

Lifting her head, she stares across at me. She looks lost and scared. I understand her dilemma. I've seen it in people countless times. She's hanging on by a thread. If she lets me in, she's got to admit she *is* in trouble and needs my help. I don't think she's quite there yet.

"How would this work then?" She's still looking at me, confusion filling her eyes. "Do you just follow me around?"

"The best option is to move you out of Savannah to a safe house—"

"No, no way." She shakes her head determinedly. "Surely, there's another option."

I sigh and close my eyes. There is another option and my jaw tics as I contemplate it. It's not an option Logan will like. It's not an option I'm too keen on either. I glance across at Logan, and he subtly shakes his head, knowing what I'm thinking.

"I move into your place." Her eyes widen, and she swings her head to look at her parents.

"What? That's worse than the safe house! You can't be serious?"

"Sweetheart, it's close protection," her dad says sympathetically. In order to protect you, he needs to be close. It won't be forever."

"I can't believe you think this is okay. I have no idea who this... this man is." She waves her hand across the table at me, her frustration evident.

"Sawyer is the best we have, Miss Anderson. You'll be safe with him," Logan interjects. "Although, I think the safe house is the better option." His eyes flick to mine, and I look away.

"Like when Detective Wilmot said I'd be safe? Excuse me if I don't believe you."

"Hallie!" her mom chastises. "These people want to help you." She sighs and runs her hand through her hair.

"I'm sorry. I don't want to waste another minute on him. I've lost so much already. Now I have a life, a job, friends." She throws her hands up in the air. "I don't want my every move to be watched, and I definitely don't want to leave Savannah."

"I think you should accept their help, Hal," her friend says quietly. Hallie swings her head around to look at her. "I want you to be safe."

She groans before picking up the glass of water in front of her. She swallows a mouthful, then bangs the glass down on the table, droplets of water splashing on the polished wood. I can't help but feel for her. It sounds like she's got some sort of normality in her life, and now she's going to have to let a stranger into her home and life. It's going to be tough.

"You could move home, Hallie. Have Sawyer come there," her mom suggests.

"No way. If Matt finds me there, that puts you and Dad in danger too. If it has to be like this, it must be at my apartment." She sighs, and tears fill her eyes.

"Look, you won't know I'm there, Hallie. I've done this before. I'll stay out of your way," I say, trying to reassure her. I'm not lying. I've done close protection at a client's home before. It's not easy, but it's doable.

"What do I tell my friends, my neighbors, my work colleagues? Am I meant to stay inside? Put my life on hold until they catch him?" The tears that were threatening to fall track down her face, and before I know what I'm doing, I reach across the table and take her hand. Her eyes shoot up to mine, and I give her a small smile.

"No, Hallie. No one's asking you to put your life on hold. You can still do all the things you normally do. I'll just be with you when you do them." She pulls her hand from mine, and I slowly pull back my arm, wondering why I felt the need to touch her.

"I work in a library. What are you going to do all day?"

"I like to read. It'll be fine."

"I work in the children's section."

"That's okay. I like children's books too." I shrug, and she shakes her head, a small smile playing on her lips.

"Maybe I should take some time off. I'm due some leave."

"Does that mean you'll let Sawyer help, sweetheart?" her mom asks.

Hallie looks at everyone around the table before sighing loudly. "Okay," she whispers. Her mom pulls her into a hug, the relief evident on her face. "So, what now?"

"You come with me," I tell her, standing up.

"Right now?" She looks unsure, and I nod.

"I need to swing by my place and pack a bag, then I'll take you home."

"Can't I wait here while you do that?"

"Afraid not. You're under my protection now. Where you go, I go, and right now, I need some clothes."

She rolls her eyes, and despite the fear and innocence I've seen, I think I might have my work cut out protecting her. "Fine," she grumbles.

"We'll call you later, Hallie," her mom says as she stands and pulls her into a hug. "We'll take Jess home."

"Thank you. All of you, for everything."

After a round of hugs, I hold the door open, and she follows me through the open-plan office to the elevator. As we ride the elevator down to the front desk, she shifts nervously from foot to foot, her hands twisting together in front of her.

"We need to go out the back of the building. The press was circling when I arrived." She closes her eyes and sighs before dropping her head. Once we exit the elevator, I lead her through the back doors and onto the sidewalk. My bike is parked around the front, but with the press focused on the entrance, I'm confident we can get away without being noticed.

Rounding the building, Hallie gasps when she sees the number of press gathered on the precinct's front steps. There are even more now than when I arrived an hour ago. "My bike's here," I tell her. "We'll be out of here soon."

"Hell no," she exclaims. "I'm not getting on that." The worry and nerves of a few minutes ago disappear as she crosses her arms defiantly across her body.

"I've got a helmet for you. I'm a good rider. You'll be safe."

"No way."

I sigh and drag my fingers through my hair. "Come on—"

"Hey," one of the reporters yells. "Hallie, Hallie Anderson."

"Shit. Hallie, we gotta go." I push the helmet over her head and climb onto the bike. "Get on."

She glances back at the approaching reporter, then looks back to me, knowing she has no other option. Swinging her leg over the back of the bike, she climbs on behind me, her arms snaking around my waist. I can feel from her grip, and her racing heart as she presses her front to my back, she's terrified. Covering her hand with mine, I ride as fast as possible to get her as far away from her nightmare.

Chapter Eight

Hallie

As my hands grip tighter onto the material of Sawyer's T-shirt, I press my body closer to his, convinced that with every turn of the bike I'm going to fall off. One of his hands is covering mine in what I think is a gesture of reassurance. It's not working. I'm terrified. I've never been on the back of a motorcycle, and if that reporter hadn't noticed me, I'd still have my feet planted firmly on the ground.

We've been riding for about five minutes, although it feels like five hours when Sawyer pats my hand and looks over his shoulder. "You okay?" he shouts over the noise of the air rushing past us.

"Don't turn around! Look where you're going," I yell into his ear, feeling the bike slightly turn as he moves. His stomach ripples under my fingers as he laughs, and I smack his stomach, my hands letting go briefly on the death grip I have on his T-shirt.

"I'm going to pull over," he shouts, laughter still evident in his voice. I drop my helmet-covered head onto his back, opening my eyes as the bike slows down, eventually stopping on the side of the road. Releasing my grip on him, I climb off, my legs shaking as I stand. I pull at the helmet to get it off, but it's stuck, so I panic, pulling harder on the strap under my chin.

"Hey, calm down. Let me..." Sawyer reaches over, his hand gently pushing mine away. Within seconds, he's released the clasp on the helmet and is gently lifting it off my head. I drop my hands to my knees and draw in mouthfuls of air as I calm down. I'm overreacting, but I am powerless to stop it.

"Are you okay?" Sawyer asks, his voice full of concern.

Taking in a few more breaths, I stand up, my cheeks flushed with embarrassment. He thinks I'm freaking out about being on the bike. He's right, but it's not only that. I've never been this alone with a guy before. I've never allowed myself to be in a position where any guy can get close. But I can't tell Sawyer that. I'm sure he already thinks I'm crazy. Instead, I tell him what he already knows.

"I'm sorry. I've just... never been on a bike before and after everything today..." I pause, "... it's too much."

Taking my hand, he pulls me gently away from the road, sitting with me on the curb next to where he's parked the bike.

"Take as long as you need. There's no rush to be anywhere."

"But I have to get back on there, don't I?" I gesture to the bike before meeting his eye.

He flashes me a small smile. "I'll go slow. I promise." He stares at me with sympathy and confusion, trying to figure me out. One minute, I'm yelling at him, and the next, I'm crying. Hell, at this point, even I can't figure myself out. He doesn't stand a chance.

"How far away is your place?"

"Tybee Island."

"Shit! That's far."

"Not that far." We sit in silence for a few minutes, the traffic rushing past. Knowing I have to get back on the bike, I eventually stand and take the helmet from Sawyer's hands.

"Come on, let's get this over with." I pull the helmet on, and now that my hands have stopped shaking, I'm able to do up the clasp.

"I bet you end up loving this bike," Sawyer says with a grin as he pushes away the kickstand and throws his leg over, settling into the seat.

"Don't count on it." I climb on the back, my hands immediately going around his waist again.

"Try keeping your eyes open this time and less of the death grip. I promise you won't fall off."

"How did you know I had my eyes closed?"

"Lucky guess." He chuckles.

I roll my eyes and increase my grip around his stomach. He laughs again and starts the engine, waiting for a gap in the traffic so we can join the interstate. Spotting one, he opens up the throttle, and if at all possible, I hold on even tighter as he pulls away, my body moving backward slightly. I start to close my eyes but remember what he said and keep them open. I never got the chance to do anything reckless as a teenager. While riding a motorcycle at twenty-four isn't up there with the craziest of things, it's the craziest thing I've ever done.

My parents, understandable after what happened, were reluctant to let me out of their sight when I returned from Cedar Falls. I can't help but smile now as I think about how much my mom would freak if she knew my close protection officer had me on the back of a motorcycle. I don't think she'd have been so quick to push me into agreeing to protection if she'd known.

Despite not wanting to admit Sawyer was right, the longer I spend on the back of his bike, the more I enjoy it. The wind whips my long hair around my helmet, and dropping my head back, it almost feels like I'm flying. I'm still holding on tightly to Sawyer, but maybe not as tight as I was. I feel so free like nothing and no one can touch me. Sawyer squeezes my hand—he must be able to tell I've relaxed a little.

"Not far now," he shouts. "Just a few minutes." Even though he can't see me, I nod and take in my surroundings. We're on a suburban street, and he slows the bike down as kids play on the sidewalk. I've been to the beach on Tybee Island hundreds of times, but I've never been where Sawyer's taking me. The street is lined with trees, and the houses are nice. I wonder if he lives in one of them and how much a close protection officer earns if he can afford to live on a street like this. We don't stop at any of the houses, though. Instead, we come up alongside an apartment block not dissimilar to mine. He slows the bike down a little more as we go into an underground parking lot.

"This is me," he says once we've parked. I climb off the bike, slipping my helmet off.

"Shall I wait here?" I ask, unsure what I should do.

He chuckles. "You're not getting this close protection thing, are you? You're with me, Hallie." He gestures toward an elevator across the parking lot, and I follow him. Entering the elevator, we stand in silence as the car travels up to the third floor.

"How long have you lived here?" I ask, needing to break the awkwardness.

"About three years. I'm not here a lot, though. The job takes me all over." As the doors open, I follow him along the hallway. Stopping outside apartment fourteen, he turns to me and grimaces. "I... umm wasn't expecting visitors, so my apartment might be a little messy."

"It's fine, Sawyer."

He opens the door, and I follow him in. It's a nice apartment, twice as big as mine with a large open-plan kitchen and living space. A hallway leads off to the left, which I'm guessing goes to the bathroom and bedrooms.

"Make yourself at home. I'll pack some stuff." He disappears along the hallway, and I walk farther into the apartment. For a guy, it's tastefully decorated. Modern art fills the walls, and despite minimal furniture—a sofa, a few side tables, and a huge television on the wall—it still has a homey feel to it. Spotting a set of double doors leading out to a balcony, I cross the room and pull them open. It's warm for early May, and the heat from the Savannah sun hits my skin. It's late afternoon, but the sun still has some heat, and I gasp as I look out over the balcony at the most perfect view of South Beach. There are colored parasols dotted along the entire stretch of the beach, and I can hear squeals of delight from both adults and children splashing in the warm waters of the Atlantic.

"Wow, Sawyer..." I shout from the balcony. "This view is amazing."

"It's pretty special, isn't it?" I spin around to see him standing on a balcony a little way up from the one I'm standing on. I hadn't noticed it before, too taken in by the views.

"Your bedroom has a balcony? That's so cool."

He shrugs. "I guess. Help yourself to a drink. There are some sodas in the refrigerator." He walks back into his bedroom, and I take one last look at the ocean, vowing to make it down here soon with the girls. It's been too long since we had a beach day.

I'm suddenly dragged back to reality when I realize a beach day is nearly impossible with everything going on with Matt. Sure, Sawyer said I could carry on my life as normal, but I'm not stupid. I know that won't happen until that asshole is caught. I can't have a girls' day at the beach with a close protection officer watching my every move.

Sighing, I close the balcony door and make my way to the kitchen. Sawyer was right when he said the apartment was a mess. Dishes litter the living room, along with empty soda cans and magazines. I hope he doesn't think he can live like this in my apartment.

"Hey, do you want me to clean up a bit?" I call out. "If you're going to be away for a while, all these dishes will go bad."

"Nah, leave it. I have a house cleaner come in once a week. I'll pay her extra this week for all the mess."

"I bet she loves you," I mutter while gathering all the dishes and stacking them in the sink. I take a soda from the refrigerator, then walk back through the living room, taking a seat on the balcony. I watch the people on the beach enjoying the last of the day's sun, wishing I was down there with them, carefree and happy. Instead, I'm sitting on Sawyer's balcony, my mind full of Matt and what happened this morning. I shudder as the images of those two men lying dead on the ground fill my mind. Despite not being cold, I pull my knees up to my chest and wrap my arms around them. I can't believe I'm here running scared from a man I thought I'd escaped ten years ago.

Half an hour later, and I'm still waiting on Sawyer. My soda's finished, and the last of the beachgoers are leaving, their arms full of towels, umbrellas, and beach toys. I stand and wander back into the living room. It's quiet, and I slowly walk down the hallway to where I think Sawyer is packing. A door to the right is open, and I peek inside as I walk past. Seeing it's the bathroom, I carry on down the hallway. There's a door slightly ajar a little farther down, and I come to a stop outside it when I hear movement.

"Sawyer?" I call out, pushing lightly on the door. I gasp when the door opens, and he's holding a gun. He lowers it as soon as he sees me, holstering it on his waistband before covering it with his T-shirt.

"Hey, Hallie. Come in. I'm almost done." He turns back to the bed, where a mountain of clothes lies on his crumpled comforter. My eyes are drawn back to the waistband of his jeans as I slowly walk in.

"Do you really need that?" I mutter, my eyes still fixed on where the gun is stored.

"Need what?" he asks, his back to me. When I don't answer, he turns around.

"The gun. Do you really need the gun?"

His hand drops to where it's holstered. "I'll probably never need to use it, but I always carry it whenever I'm working." My eyes widen when I think of him bringing it to my apartment. He rakes his hand through his dark hair. "It's just in case, okay? What you saw today has left you shaken. I can't say I'm surprised. Guns aren't good in the wrong hands. But I'm careful with mine. The safety is always on. Okay?"

"Okay," I mumble. He throws a handful of clothes from the bed into a carryall. I frown. "How are we going to get that on the bike?"

"We'll take my car back to Savannah."

"Oh, okay." Even I can hear the disappointment in my voice, and I know for sure by the look on his face he's heard it too.

He smirks, and I roll my eyes. "You wanted to go on the bike, didn't you?" he teases. "I knew you'd end up liking it."

I smile. "I'll wait for you in the living room." My attempt at sounding flippant doesn't work. He's right. Despite hating the motorcycle at first, I loved it once I'd put my fear to the side. I still don't one hundred percent feel comfortable with Sawyer. It will take more than a couple of hours with him before I let my guard down, but I'm freaking out anymore. It's also helping to take my mind off what happened today. If I stop and spend too much time dwelling on it, I might burst into tears. I don't want to do that in front of Sawyer. I'm sure he already thinks I'm unstable. I'll leave my tears until I'm alone in my room tonight.

Ten minutes later, Sawyer emerges with a couple of bags and his pillow under his arm. "Ready to go?" I nod as he locks the balcony doors before heading for the door.

"I do have bedding, you know," I tell him, gesturing to the pillow under his arm.

"I'm sure you do. I sleep better with my own."

I shrug and follow him out of the apartment, waiting while he makes sure the door is locked.

The drive back to Savannah is quiet, apart from the radio. The music is a welcome distraction from the awkward silence that's descended. I pretend not to notice as I stare out the window, my eyes darting from faces on the sidewalk to drivers in passing cars. My mind works overtime, and every face I see is Matt's, his dark, cold eyes penetrating my soul.

Knowing I'm going to drive myself crazy, I drop my head back against the seat and close my eyes, hoping against hope those eyes don't follow me into my dreams.

Chapter Nine

Sawyer

The first night is always the worst. No matter what kind of person you are, sharing your home with a stranger has got to be tough. I'm rarely at home these days, and aside from preferring my pillow, I can sleep pretty much anywhere. Hallie, however, seems to be struggling.

Since arriving at her apartment an hour ago, I've barely seen her. She showed me around, which didn't take long, and then disappeared into her bedroom. After unpacking the small amount of stuff I'd brought with me, I make my way into the living room. The apartment is much smaller than mine, but it feels more like a home. My place is a base, and because I'm never there, it doesn't feel much like a home.

Walking around the small room, I stop to look at the multiple photographs adorning the walls. Some I recognize as Hallie's parents, and there are a couple of shots of a guy in uniform. I don't know if he's a brother or a boyfriend. I haven't heard her mention either, but I'd like to think if she had a boyfriend, he'd be here after everything she'd been through. There are other images too, including sunsets over the ocean, wildflowers, and scenic shots. They're good. Really good. I wonder if it's Hallie behind the camera.

Crossing the Line

I feel a little uneasy making myself at home, so I perch on the arm of the sofa and take out my phone. Seeing I have an email from the Savannah Police Department, I click on the first of the two attachments. It's a background file on Bryant, including his rap sheet. My eyes flick through the report—he's been in and out of the foster care system since the age of six. In trouble with the cops from the age of ten. Small things to start with—theft and social disturbances—then things escalated to assault and aggravated assault in his early twenties, when he spent nine months in jail. He seemed to go quiet after that as if he'd turned his life around. If only that had been the case.

Opening the other attachment, it's the file on the Anderson/Bryant case Detective Wilmot promised to send over. It doesn't make for easy reading, and my stomach churns as the detailed accounts of the injuries sustained to the bodies of the girls found at the Bryant property are listed. All but one had been sexually assaulted and tortured before their deaths. The killings had occurred over three years, and it seemed none of the girls were with them for longer than a year, some merely weeks. Hallie had been lucky Amanda had fallen ill. If she hadn't, I'm not sure there would have been a way out for her.

I've read enough to know I'm dealing with a sick bastard, and I close down the email app, slipping my phone into my pocket. There's still no sign of Hallie, and I need to get her out of her room. This is her place. She shouldn't have to be locked away feeling uncomfortable.

I reach her bedroom door and knock lightly on it. "Hallie, are you awake?" I speak quietly, knowing after what she's been through today, she could be asleep. I can hear movement and take a small step back as I wait for her to open the door.

"Everything okay?" she asks as she swings the door open. The outfit she wore earlier has been replaced with sleep shorts and a tank, her face free of makeup. Her long brown hair has been piled on top of her head and secured by a hair tie. My eyes track over her body, and I can't help but think she looks even more beautiful this way. I close my eyes and shake away my irrational thoughts. I'm her close protection officer. I've never been attracted to a client before, and I'm not about to start now. When my eyes meet hers, she's looking at me strangely, probably wondering why I'm staring at her.

"Hey, do you umm... want to get pizza? I can order in?" My voice sounds strained even to my ears, and I smile, hoping she hasn't noticed.

"Sure. The menus are in the top drawer in the kitchen." I smile and turn away from her. Going to the kitchen drawer, I grab the takeout menu.

"Hey, Sawyer, would you mind getting me a soda?" she asks as she sits on the edge of the sofa.

"Sure." I reach into the refrigerator and pick up two cans. "Do you mind if I have one?"

"Help yourself."

"I'll get some groceries in tomorrow. I don't want to eat all your stuff," I assure her as I walk into the living room, handing her one of the soda cans. She takes it from me and repositions herself on the sofa, tucking her legs underneath her.

"Maybe we can pool some money and buy together? Seems stupid to buy separate food." She flicks her eyes to mine, and I see the uncertainty there.

"Works for me." I hand her the takeout menu. Attempting to get her talking, I gesture to the photographs on the wall. "Did you take all of these?" She nods, and I walk toward one of her parents. "I recognize your mom and dad. Who's this?" I ask, pointing to one of the photographs of the guy in uniform.

"That's Max, my brother. He's a Marine. He's deployed at the moment." A strange feeling of relief washes over me when I hear it's her brother and not her boyfriend.

"They're good, Hallie. I love this one." I point to the image of the sun setting over the ocean, and she smiles.

"That was on vacation when I was seventeen. It was taken off the end of the pier at Myrtle Beach. I love it there."

Crossing the Line

"Why aren't you in any of the pictures?"

"I prefer to be behind the camera rather than in front of it. I have some with me in them, but I prefer not to put them on display." She shrugs, and her stomach rumbles. Her eyes meet mine, and we both laugh.

"Maybe we should get you fed. What do you want?"

"Barbecue chicken," she replies, not even looking at the menu.

"Do you want to think about it?" I joke, a smile tugging on my lips.

"It's my favorite. What are you getting?"

"Hawaiian," I reply without hesitation.

"Eww, that's gross! Pineapple on a pizza shouldn't be allowed."

"What? Pineapple on a pizza is the best."

"It's fruit on a pizza. It's wrong on every level." She opens her soda and brings it to her lips, swallowing a mouthful.

"You can try a slice of mine. I bet you change your mind."

"Not gonna happen."

I let out a laugh as I dial the number on the front of the menu. Ordering the two pizzas for delivery, I give over the address before ending the call.

There is only one sofa and a footstool in the small living room, and I have no choice but to sit next to Hallie. She turns on the television, flicking quickly through the list of channels. Inwardly, I groan as she stops on a channel showing a cheesy reality show where women compete for a guy's attention. The women are bitchy, and within five minutes, they're arguing over who kissed Brandon in the hot tub. I glance sideways at Hallie, seeing she's transfixed by what's happening on the screen.

"You like this?" I ask, unable to hide the disdain in my voice.

"I love this!" she says, her eyes never leaving the screen. "You'd better get used to it if you're going to be living here for a while. It's the start of a new series, and it's on every night for a month." I groan loudly and drop my head back against the sofa. Hallie laughs, her eyes still on the screen. "I bet you're hooked by the end of the week."

"I seriously doubt it!"

"Trust me, it's addictive."

"I'll take your word for it." I let out a sigh and drag my hand through my hair. "I think the stack of romance books in my room is favorable to watching this."

She turns to look at me, her eyes wide. "Those books aren't for reading." She looks a little crazy, and I hold my hands up.

"Okaaay... what are they for then? Surely *you've* read them?"

"I've read them on my Kindle. I haven't read the paperback copies."

"So, you paid to read them on your Kindle?" She nods. "Then you paid again for the paperback copy, but you never *read* the paperback copy?" She nods again. "Okay, I'm confused. Why would anyone do that?"

She laughs, and I turn slightly in my seat next to her. "Oh, God! You make me sound insane!" She drops her head in her hands and laughs.

I laugh too. "I'm just saying it as I see it. So, why don't you ever read the paperbacks?"

She lifts her head from her hands and shrugs. It's a strange conversation to be having, but I'm glad I've finally got her talking. "Most of them are signed by the authors. I don't like to read them once they're signed. I don't want to crease the spines." She looks at me out of the corner of her eye and grins. "I know that makes me strange. I like to see them on the shelves. I flick through them from time to time, though." I smile, thinking how cute she sounds trying to justify her massive collection of unread books. "I'm shutting up now. It's clear you think I'm nuts."

"No, no. Not at all," I rush out, not wanting her to feel uncomfortable. "I sort of get it. I used to collect comics when I was a kid."

"Unread comics?" she asks, a smile pulling on her lips.

"Well, no... I'm not that weird." I bump shoulders with her and wink when she looks at me. "Okay, enough teasing."

"Thank you."

"One more question, though?" She rolls her eyes and looks at me skeptically. "How did you get them all signed?"

She turns in her seat to face me. "I've met a couple of the authors at signings at Barnes & Noble. Others I've ordered from the author's website, and some I've gotten through book box subscriptions." Her whole face lights up as she talks about her book collection. I suddenly feel bad for teasing her.

"What are book box subscriptions?" I ask, loving seeing the excitement on her face.

"Each month I get a box in the mail with a couple of signed paperbacks inside, along with some author swag. It's always a surprise to see which authors are included, and I've found some great new-to-me authors in those boxes."

"So, you read the books that come in the mail?"

"Umm... no. If I like the book's cover or the blurb sounds good, then I get it on my Kindle."

"And what exactly is author swag?"

"Pens, keyrings, lip balms, bookmarks, postcards... anything that promotes an author's work. I have tons of swag. I never quite know what to do with it all, but I love collecting it."

Despite her crazy obsession with all things books, I'm in awe of how passionate she is about what she loves, and it's the most I've heard her say all day. Books are definitely a conversation starter, I'll have to remember that. Before I can respond, the intercom sounds.

"That'll be the pizza," she says as she unfolds her legs from underneath her and stands. "I'll buzz them in."

I follow her and watch as she pushes the button to release the door downstairs.

"Dinner's on me. I'll grab some cash." I head for the small hallway that leads to the bedrooms, pausing in the entryway. "Hallie, don't open the door. Wait for me." Her eyes meet mine, and she nods. I grab some cash off the nightstand, and I'm back in the entryway before the delivery guy even has a chance to knock on the door.

"It's just the pizza delivery," Hallie whispers, her wide eyes fixed on the waistband of my jeans. My eyes follow hers, and I drop the hand unconsciously resting on my gun.

"Shit." I sigh and shake my head, knowing I've freaked her out. "I know—" She jumps as a knock sounds on the apartment door, cutting off what I was going to say. "I'll get it." I walk toward the door, looking through the peephole. Waiting in the hallway is a young guy holding two large pizza boxes. Turning to check on Hallie, she's watching me from the archway that leads into the kitchen. "Just the pizza," I confirm. Swinging the door open, I take the pizzas from the young guy and tip him before closing the door.

Hallie takes the boxes from me, and I follow her into the living room. We sit in silence for a few minutes as we eat our pizza. The annoying television show fills the silence as another argument breaks out on the screen. Despite hating the show, I'm grateful for the noise.

"You okay?" I ask once we've finished eating, and the silence has become awkward. She nods and turns to face me.

"I'm sorry." She sighs and pulls her knees up to her chin, her arms going around her legs. "I guess it's going to take a while for me to get used to seeing you carrying a gun around my apartment."

"Hallie, that isn't something you should ever have to get used to."

"This is all so surreal. This time last week, I was normal, happy. Now... now it's ten years ago all over again, and I'm a prisoner. Locked up by *him*." She spits the word 'him,' and I shake my head.

"No. That's not what's happening. You aren't a prisoner here. This is your home. Sure, we have to be careful, but you don't have to put your life on hold for that asshole again. We can go out and have fun, be normal. I *will* keep you safe." She gives me a small smile, but it's sad, and I know she doesn't believe me. Not yet anyway.

"Do you... do you know what he did? Matt?" She straightens her legs out, setting her feet down on the floor. She doesn't look at me as she waits for my reply, her fingers twisting in her lap.

"Yeah. I've seen the file," I say quietly. "I'm sorry for what happened to you, Hallie."

"I was lucky. I got away." I doubt she knows the true extent of

Crossing the Line

how evil Matthew Bryant is. What he did to those girls, she doesn't need to know. She is more than lucky. It's a miracle she escaped his clutches.

"Do you think he'll try to find me?" Her terror-filled eyes meet mine before dropping to her lap.

"I don't know, but I won't let him get to you. I promise." I move across the sofa so I'm next to her. Her hands are still twisting in her lap, and I reach for one, enveloping it in mine. "Look at me." I wait until she lifts her head, her eyes slowly finding mine. "I promise," I repeat.

She gives me a sad smile, and I hope to God I can keep that promise.

Chapter Ten

Hallie

When the sun finally begins to streak through the drapes, I throw off the comforter and sit up. Despite being exhausted last night, I hadn't been able to sleep. The events of the day had swirled around in my head, and every time I closed my eyes, all I could see was *him*. Unlike most mornings, today I was happy for the sunlight to break through the drapes and chase the darkness of yesterday away.

I climb out of bed and quietly open my bedroom door. Padding across the small hallway, I knock lightly on the bathroom door, not wanting to walk in on Sawyer. Thinking of him staying in my spare room makes me nervous.

When silence greets my knock, I enter, locking it behind me. I can't wait to stand under the hot spray of the shower and let the water wash away my restless night. I strip off my sleep shorts and tank and lean across the tub, flicking on the shower. I brush my teeth as I wait for the water to heat up. When steam begins to fill the small room, I step into the tub. Standing under the hot spray, I close my eyes and drop my head back. I probably spend far too long under the spray, and my skin is pink from the hot water as I turn the shower off and wrap a towel around my body. I dry off a little before opening the bathroom door, steam escaping into the hallway.

"Morning," Sawyer calls from the direction of the kitchen. "Sleep well?" My eyes widen as I poke my head around the door. Catching sight of him standing in front of the coffee machine wearing nothing but a pair of shorts, my mouth goes dry. He's facing away from me, and I take full advantage of his inability to see me. My eyes track up and over his tanned, muscled back. His hair is messy from sleep, and as I stare at him, a wave of heat travels up my neck and over my face. Thankful I'm hidden from view as I drag my eyes off him and force myself to speak.

"Morning," I croak. "I'll... be right back."

I hear him chuckle softly as I rush across the hallway, darting into my bedroom. Closing the door behind me, I press my back to the wood, my heart pounding. I'd been so caught up with everything that happened yesterday, I hadn't taken a minute to notice how hot Sawyer really is.

"Fuck," I mutter to myself as I drop the towel. "Why couldn't my close protection officer be overweight and bald?" I snatch up some underwear from my dresser drawer and slip them on. "Now I have to spend God knows how long sharing my apartment with someone who looks like he should be starring in a Hollywood movie instead of babysitting me." Tugging on a pair of yoga pants, I hop around my bedroom as the material gets stuck on my still wet leg. Losing my balance, I fall onto my ass, groaning as I hit the floor.

"Everything okay in there?" Sawyer shouts through the door seconds later.

"Yes! Fine," I cry, scrambling to stand up. "I'll just be a minute."

"Okay." I stare at the door as I hear him return to the kitchen. Dropping my head into my hands, I groan.

"Way to go, Hallie," I mumble as I finally get my yoga pants on. After I finish getting dressed, I brush my wet hair, braiding it in a plait down my back. Taking a deep breath, I make my way toward the kitchen. Sawyer is sitting at the small breakfast bar with a plate of scrambled eggs and bacon in front of him. Still shirtless. I try not to stare as I get nearer.

"Hey, Hallie," he says as he looks up, his eyes tracking the length of my body. I clear my throat, and he drops his eyes and gestures to the stove. "I kept some eggs and bacon warm for you."

I look over at the stove in surprise. "Thanks. You didn't have to do that." He shrugs.

"I like to cook. Plus, if I'm eating your food, I thought I'd better make you some too." He looks at me sheepishly. "I hope it was okay to help myself."

I laugh and reach for the plate he's left on the side. "Anytime you want to cook, I'm good with that," I assure him, filling my plate with eggs and bacon. "So, what now? What do we do all day?" I ask as I stand in the kitchen and eat.

"I need to check the building. The security in the lobby looks good. Does the building have a parking garage?"

I nod. "What are you looking for?"

"I need to know the layout of the building, that's all." In other words, he needs to know how to get me out if Matt discovers where I live and shows up at my apartment. At that thought, I swallow down the lump that formed in my throat and take a deep breath.

"I need to go to work. I'm going to take some time off, but I have to speak to my boss in person."

"We can do that. What time do you want to leave?" I glance at the clock on the wall and see it's seven-fifteen.

"About eight-thirty?"

"I'll be ready." I watch as he finishes his eggs and bacon. "You said you worked in a library?"

"Yeah. I work in the children's section at Bull Street Library."

"You enjoy it?"

"I love it. As you know, books are important to me, and watching the kids fall in love with reading is my favorite part of my job."

Crossing the Line

"I take it your colleagues know what's going on?"

"They saw the news like the rest of Savannah," I say with a sigh. "There's me and Dana in the children's section. I hadn't told her about my past, so it came as a surprise to her, but she's been great. She hasn't pushed me to talk to her, but I know she's there if I need her. She's a good friend."

"She sounds it," he says with a smile. "I'm looking forward to meeting her."

"Would you mind if we told people you were a friend of my brother's or something?" I bite my lip as he frowns at me. "I don't want people knowing I need a close protection officer. I wish people didn't know anything about my past. Now that it's been splashed all over CNN, everyone knows. All I want is to be normal, you know?"

"We can tell people whatever you want, Hallie."

"Thanks."

"I know you live alone, but umm... any boyfriend going to be stopping by?" His eyes meet mine, and heat floods my face.

"No. No boyfriend." He stands to bring his plate to the sink.

"I'll clean up. You cooked," I tell him, taking the plate from his hands and setting it down in the sink. Turning on the water, I wait for it to heat. When he sits back at the breakfast bar, I turn to face him. "So, how long have you been a close protection officer?" Turning back to the sink, I start washing up.

"About five years."

"And you like it?"

"Yeah. No two jobs are the same, and I get to travel around a lot."

"Ever worked with anyone famous?" I ask, looking over my shoulder.

He laughs and shakes his head. "Not so far. Before I started working with the Savannah Police Department, it was usually businessmen and their families."

"And what about before you were a close protection officer?" He doesn't answer right away, and I turn from the sink, drying my hands on a cloth. "I'm sorry. I don't mean to pry. You don't have to tell me."

"No... it's okay. I was a cop." He doesn't elaborate, and I don't push him to tell me. We're virtual strangers. He doesn't owe me any kind of explanation. "Tell me about your brother. Is he older or younger than you?" Clearly, he wants to change the subject, and that's fine.

"He's three years older than me. He joined the Marines straight out of school. He's in Afghanistan right now."

"I hope I get to meet him one day, especially if I'm meant to be a friend of his." He smiles and winks before standing. "I'll shower, then we can do that perimeter check before we head over to see your boss."

"I'll get changed too. Thanks for breakfast." My eyes follow him as he heads for the bathroom. Despite not pressing him about what led him to leave the police force, the nosy side of me is desperate to know, and as I head for my bedroom, I hope I'll get to find out.

Thirty minutes later, we're heading down to the parking garage in the elevator. Sawyer has thoroughly checked the building, asking to see every entrance and exit. It makes me nervous knowing he's mentally plotting escape routes in case he ever needs to use them. Despite feeling uneasy, I know it needs to be done. It's not like that asshole will just buzz my apartment if he does come looking for me. Sawyer seems impressed with the security at the building's main entrance and the cameras in the lobby, which makes me feel better.

As we ride down in the elevator, I explain my apartment comes with one allocated parking space. As the elevator stops and the doors open, I walk Sawyer to where my car is parked. He's looking around as we cross the garage and still looking as we reach my car.

"There doesn't seem to be any cameras down here."

"Is that bad?" I ask, unlocking my car and placing my purse on the back seat. He walks around to the driver's side, reaches inside, and scoops up my purse.

"We'll take my car. And it's not bad, just a little surprising considering how good the security is in the lobby."

"I'm happy to drive."

"I'd feel better if we took mine."

"Okay."

"Is the way into the garage secure?" he asks, his eyes still flicking around the well-lit space.

"No. You just drive in. You need a key fob to access the elevator from down here, though." I lift my keys and show him the small gray fob that dangles from my 'I've lived a thousand lives' book-shaped keyring. He glances at the fob.

"That's good," he mumbles. "Right," he says a little louder. "You ready to show me where you work?"

"Sure." I lead him out outside, emerging on the sidewalk. His car is parked across the street and a little way up from the building. Spaces were limited when we arrived home last night, and we had to park where we could. "Maybe later we could take your car back and get your bike. That way, you can park it at the back of my space inside instead of having to leave your car out here."

He stops on the sidewalk and grins at me. My stomach flips as I notice how gorgeous he is when his smile reaches his eyes.

"Sounds like you've given that quite some thought?"

I can't help but laugh. "Okay! You were right. I like your bike."

"I knew it!" I roll my eyes as a smug expression fills his face. "Maybe that means I'm right about Hawaiian pizza being the best too."

"No way! I will never agree with you on that one."

He chuckles as we reach his car. Unlocking the passenger side door, he holds it open for me. I'm about to climb in when my name is called. Turning around, Kitty's running across the road toward us.

"Shit," I mutter, and Sawyer's entire body changes from relaxed to alert. I put my hand on his arm. "It's my neighbor." Before I can remove my hand, Kitty is standing in front of me.

"Hallie! I saw on the news that guy had escaped. Are you okay?" Her eyes go from me to Sawyer and then drop to where my hand is still resting on his arm. I can see she's thinking this is some guy I've picked up, and that makes me a little sad as I realize how little I've opened up to her. If she knew me at all, she'd know I'd never have the confidence or the experience to pick up a guy. Sawyer is here because he needs to be, not because he wants to be. Dropping my hand from Sawyer's arm, I take a step away from him.

"Hey, Kitty. I've been meaning to catch up with you." She messaged me yesterday when the story of Matt escaping hit the news. With everything that happened, I'd never gotten around to replying. "Things have been a little crazy. I'm okay, though."

"I can see that." She winks at me before looking over again at Sawyer.

"Kitty, this is Sawyer. Sawyer, my neighbor, Kitty." I gesture between the two as I introduce them. "Sawyer is a friend of my brother's. He's staying with me for a few weeks."

"It's good to meet you, Kitty," Sawyer says, holding his hand out for her to shake.

Grinning, she takes it. "Good to meet you too. Are you a Marine as well?" she asks as she drops his hand.

"Umm..." He looks over at me with wide eyes. Despite agreeing earlier to tell people he was a friend of my brother's, we hadn't actually discussed the details.

"Yeah, Sawyer's a Marine," I reply quickly. "He's stationed with Max in Jacksonville." The lie rolls easily off my tongue, and before I can stop myself, I'm elaborating. "He's recovering from an injury and taking some time off." Out of the corner of my eye, I see Sawyer trying not to smile, and I concentrate on not looking at him.

"Well, I'm a nurse, Sawyer, so if you need any help with your... injury..." She trails off suggestively.

Sawyer coughs uncomfortably and looks at me.

"How's Nick, Kitty?" I bite out, a little annoyed at her flirting. Even though I've introduced Sawyer as my brother's friend, she doesn't know he didn't just get out of my bed.

"Oh, he's great," she gushes. "We're going out tonight." She suddenly claps her hands together and bounces up and down. "I have the best idea. Why don't you two come with us?"

"Oh, no," I reply quickly. "You and Nick have only just started dating. We wouldn't want to intrude."

"Not at all," she insists. "I want you to meet Nick properly, anyway. It'll be like a double date." I look across to Sawyer for some help, but he just shrugs.

We can't go on a date. He's my close protection officer. Not that I can use that as an excuse now, not when I've lied to Kitty about who he is.

"Oh, we're not dating, Kitty. He's my brother's friend."

She raises her eyebrows in question and then leans in closer to me, whispering in my ear, "Girl, are you blind? That man is hot! You need to get on that."

My cheeks flush with heat, and I realize, despite Kitty whispering, there is no way Sawyer didn't hear her. She smiles at me and wiggles her eyebrows. "Anyway, gotta run, or I'm going to be late for my shift." She takes a step away from me. "Sawyer, it was great to meet you. Hallie, I'll message you later with the details for tonight. Have a good day." Before I can respond and tell her we won't be there, she's gone.

"Well, she was... interesting," Sawyer says, a smile pulling on his lips.

"I'm sorry. We definitely don't have to go out with them. I'll message her."

"No. I think we should go."

I look at him in surprise. "You want to go?"

"Sure. Don't get me wrong, your friend is a little scary, but we're allowed to go out. It beats watching your crazy reality TV show."

I laugh. "So, that's the reason you want to get out of the apartment? Don't worry, you won't miss it. I've got it set to record."

"Oh great," he mumbles, and I bump his shoulder.

"If you're sure you don't mind going out with my friends."

"It'll be entertaining if nothing else."

"I hope you can lie a lot about the Marines…"

"I'm sure I'll manage. Come on." He opens the car door for me, and I climb in, watching as he jogs around the front and climbs into the driver's seat. I give him directions to the library, and we drive the short distance in comfortable silence.

Chapter Eleven

Hallie

Looking down at my phone, I'm messaging my mom as we pull up at the library.

"We're here, Hallie," Sawyer says as he turns off the engine.

Pushing my phone into my pocket, I take a deep breath as I climb out of the car. I glance up at the impressive building in front of me. Despite working here for the past five years, I'm still in awe at how beautiful this building is. Bull Street Library is the largest of three libraries in Savannah. It's a grand old building with large stone steps leading to imposing pillars outside the main entrance. Inside, ornate staircases take you through four floors of books, conference rooms, and computer suites. Although I love working here, my boss can be difficult, and I have no idea how he will react to me wanting time off with no notice.

"Ready?" Sawyer asks from next to me.

"As ready as I'll ever be." He follows me across the parking lot, and we silently climb the stairs to the entrance. Once inside, there are more steps to the children's section on the second floor. When we reach the top, I turn to Sawyer. "I'll go and see Dana first, then I'll find Mr. West."

"Mr. West?"

"My boss."

Pushing open the double doors, I walk through the low stacks of books and past the brightly colored carpet, Sawyer following behind me. I reach the check-out desk and smile seeing Dana sitting behind her computer. She jumps up when she sees me, quickly making her way around the desk.

"Hallie, sweetie, how are you?" She pulls me into a hug, and I hug her back tightly.

"I'm okay." She pulls out of the embrace, her eyes searching mine.

"Really?" I shrug, and she gives me a small smile. "It's okay not to be okay." Her gaze flicks behind me, and I pull out of her embrace, turning to Sawyer.

"This is Sawyer. He's deployed with Max and staying with me for a few weeks while he gets over an injury. Sawyer, this is Dana."

"Hi, Dana. Good to meet you." He holds his hand out, and Dana takes it.

"Good to meet you too, Sawyer." She looks between us, a strange expression on her face, and I wonder if she's figured out Sawyer isn't who I've said he is. Despite being close to her, I'm not ready to admit I have a close protection officer.

"I'm going to be off for a while until this blows over. I hope that's okay?" I hear the uncertainty in my voice, and I'm sure Dana hears it too.

"Hallie, of course, it is. Don't even think about work. Take as long as you need."

I smile gratefully, noticing from the corner of my eye that Sawyer is moving toward the window overlooking the front of the building.

"I need to see Mr. West. I wanted to stop by—"

"Hallie, we need to get out of here," Sawyer calls from the window, interrupting me. I walk toward him when he jogs over to me and grabs my hand. "Is there a back entrance to the library?" I don't answer as fear creeps up my spine. "Dana, is there another way out?"

She nods. "There's the back stairs through the staff room. I'll show you."

Sawyer squeezes my hand as he tugs me along with him. We pass through the staff room until we come to the stairs.

"Who's out there, Sawyer?" I ask, my voice trembling.

"The press. I don't want you to have to deal with them." He turns to Dana. "Where do the stairs come out?"

"At the back of the building. You'll have to walk back past the entrance if you're parked out front, though."

"That's okay. I'll think of something."

"Take care, Hallie. If there's anything you need…" Dana trails off, pulling me in for another hug. My hand drops from Sawyer's as I hug her back.

"Tell Mr. West I'll call him," I mumble.

"I will. Don't worry about him." She gives me a sad smile as I pull out of her embrace.

Sawyer takes my hand again, and we jog down the flight of stairs. When we reach the ground floor, he pushes on the emergency exit door, and suddenly, we're outside. He moves me to his right side, his arm going around my shoulder as he shields my body with his. We walk around the side of the building, and I look up, seeing reporters and television crews setting up by the entrance.

"They're going to see me," I mutter, panic overwhelming me as my breathing speeds up.

"No, they're not. Keep your head down and stay close." I drop my eyes to the sidewalk and focus on my breathing as I let Sawyer lead me back to the car. As we get closer to the entrance, I hold my breath. Before I know it, I'm climbing into Sawyer's car.

As he gets in the car, I finally allow myself to look up. The large stone steps leading up to the library's entrance are full of reporters, television crews, and cameramen. "Shit."

Sawyer throws the car into reverse and speeds out of the small parking lot.

"How did they find out I worked here?" I ask.

"Those reporters can find anything out, Hallie."

"Even where I live?" He looks across at me and gives me a sad smile. "That's a yes, isn't it?" He nods before focusing back on the road.

"They won't be able to get into your apartment block. I promise you're safe in your apartment." I stare out the window, the streets of Savannah rushing past the window.

Am I? Surely a man who can abduct five girls off the street in broad daylight can gain access to an apartment block. I want to believe Sawyer. I really do.

"This will blow over. All those reporters back there, they'll latch on to somebody else when another story hits." He's right. Today's news is tomorrow's trash. But today, right now, I'm the one they're chasing, and I really wish they weren't.

Chapter Twelve

Sawyer

Hallie speaks to her boss on the phone while I keep driving, and due to his incessant shouting, I can hear every word he's saying. Instantly, I dislike the guy. He's pissed the reporters are camped outside the library. Like it's Hallie's fault. When she starts to apologize, I've heard enough. Reaching over, I take the phone from her ear and end the call.

"Sawyer!" she cries, snatching the phone back. "What did you do that for? That was my boss."

"Your boss is an asshole," I growl.

"My boss is pissed no one can access the library because of all the fucking reporters who have turned up."

"And that's your fault?"

"Right now, yes!"

"No, Hallie. Not ever. He's got no right to speak to you like that."

"And you've got no right to end my calls." She crosses her arm and turns her head away from me.

I sigh and pull the car over to the side of the road. "You're right. I'm sorry. I saw red. Do you want to call him back?"

She turns from looking out of the window and sighs. "Nah, he is an asshole." She gives me a small smile, and I sigh in relief she isn't annoyed with me. "I will give Dana a call, though. She'll be worried about me." She gets out of the car and paces up and down as she talks to her friend. After a few minutes, she ends the call and climbs into the car.

"Everything okay?" I ask as she buckles her seat belt. She sighs, and despite it still being early, she looks exhausted.

"Dana is holding down the fort, and I've asked her to speak to my boss, tell him I'll be off until this is over... whenever that might be. I feel so guilty leaving Dana to deal with all of this. She's got enough going on without all of my shit as well."

"What do you mean?"

"Her husband walked out on her last year, and she's trying to raise twin boys on her own. She struggles. She's shattered most of the time as the boys don't sleep well. The last thing she needs is to be covering my job as well."

I reach across the car and take her hand, squeezing gently. "She's your friend, Hallie. I'm sure she's more worried about you than her at the moment. Don't beat yourself up." She sighs again and drops her head back on the seat, closing her eyes.

I was going to suggest picking up my bike and going for a ride away from all the shit in Savannah. Looking at her though, I think she needs to sleep.

"Okay, I've got an idea." Turning the car around, I head back toward the center of Savannah.

Her head snaps up, and she looks at me. "What idea?"

"I was going to suggest we pick up the bike and go somewhere, but you look like you could fall asleep at any moment. So... I was thinking of a movie day on the sofa. We can get my bike another day." As silence fills the car, I wonder if I've said something wrong. "If you don't want to—"

"No!" she states, cutting me off. "I didn't sleep great last night, so movies on the sofa sound perfect. Thank you."

I smile across the car at her, and she smiles back. "Target for snacks it is then. I'm guessing your movie collection is full-on romance if your bookshelves are anything to go by?"

"Hey," she exclaims, swatting my arm. "I have every *Mission Impossible* movie, actually. I love those."

I raise my eyebrows in surprise. "I'm impressed."

"*The Hunger Games* too, and the *Divergent* movies."

"So, no chick flicks at all?"

"Well, I didn't say that." She looks across at me and wrinkles her nose. "A girl's still got to have her favorite chick flicks to fall back on, especially with endless re-runs of football games on TV."

"Not a football fan then?"

"Nope. Although I've never been to a game."

"What? Not even in school?" I can't hide my surprise. I thought everyone went to football games in high school.

"I didn't socialize much at school. Football games were always big events, and I was never comfortable being part of them. School was hard enough with everyone talking and whispering behind my back. As soon as classes ended, I was the first one out of there."

I groan inwardly, silently cursing myself at how insensitive my question was. "Hallie, I'm sorry. That was a stupid question."

"It's fine." She waves her hand. "You like football then? Did you play in school?"

"I do, and I did. I was the quarterback."

She laughs. "I can totally see that."

I pull into a parking space at Target. "You can?" I ask as I turn off the engine, wondering what she means.

"Sure. Hottest guy in school. Star quarterback. It all makes sense." She shrugs and opens her car door, climbing out.

I stare at where she was sitting, a little taken aback at her comment. I climb out and walk around the car to where she's waiting for me.

"How do you know I was the hottest guy in school?"

A flush of pink makes its way up her neck and over her cheeks as she realizes what she said. "I... I..." She's flustered, and I try not to laugh. "I only mean that all high school quarterbacks are usually the hottest guys in school. It comes with the job."

I nod, a smile pulling on my lips. "Let's get what we need and head home." I don't tease her anymore. I can see she's mortified.

Thirty minutes later, we're back in the car, surrounded by bags full of snacks. We have far too much, but Hallie is the most indecisive person I've ever met, and she couldn't make up her mind about what she wanted. In the end, we got everything. I'm a little apprehensive as I drive back to Hallie's apartment. After seeing the reporters camped outside the library this morning, I know it's only a matter of time before they find out where she lives. I hope for her sake it isn't today. I'm not sure she could handle it.

I sigh in relief when I pull up outside her building, and it's clear.

"I thought we'd get here, and there would be reporters," Hallie says quietly from the passenger seat. I park right outside the entrance and turn off the engine.

"Me too," I admit. "I'm not going to lie, Hallie, I think it'll happen."

"Let's hope the bastard gets caught before they figure out where I live then." She climbs out of the car before I can reply, and I follow her.

A little while later, we're sitting on the sofa, trying to decide what to watch. Hallie has changed into her 'comfy pants' as she calls them, and the snacks we bought from Target are set up on the table in front of the sofa. Despite Hallie having a handful of action movies, there are a load more romance movies than she confessed to in the car. I think I may have set myself up for a day of chick flicks.

"How about I choose first?" Hallie suggests. "You can choose after. I've got movies on the TV too."

"Sure. I'm pretty confident you'll be asleep in half an hour. I can put on what I want then," I tell her nonchalantly.

From the corner of my eye, I see her reach for one of the sofa cushions. Before I can react, it hits the side of my head as she throws it at me.

"Hmph," I let out as she chuckles.

"For that comment, I'm putting on my favorite movie." She unfolds her legs from underneath her and moves toward the television. Reaching into one of the drawers in the unit, she takes a DVD case out, then slides the disc into the player.

"Should I ask what it is?"

"*Pride and Prejudice.* The version with Keira Knightly." I groan inwardly as she picks up the bowl of popcorn. She flops on the sofa next to me, holding the bowl out. "Want some?"

"How many times have you watched this?" I ask, taking a handful of popcorn as the screen comes to life.

"God, I've lost count. I'm guessing you haven't seen it?"

"Nope."

"You're in for a treat!"

"Can't wait," I joke, tossing some popcorn in my mouth.

My prediction Hallie would be asleep in half an hour was pretty accurate, but my comment that I could put whatever movie on I wanted once she was asleep wasn't quite panning out. What I hadn't counted on was her falling asleep on me. The sofa we're sharing is pretty small, and not long after she'd fallen asleep, her head had found my shoulder. I've been pinned to the spot ever since. Truth is, I'm enjoying *Pride and Prejudice* more than I like to admit. I don't need to let Hallie know that, though.

As the credits roll on the movie, I glance down at her. She'll be mortified when she realizes she's fallen asleep on me. I can tell she's nervous around me. I'm guessing it's down to that asshole and what he did to her. Not wanting her to feel uncomfortable, I gently lift her head from my shoulder and move off the sofa, laying her down. She stirs briefly but stays asleep. I grab the blanket draped over the back of the sofa and cover her with it. Letting out a sigh, I take the opportunity to watch her sleep. She's beautiful, and despite only just meeting her, I find myself wanting to know everything about her.

She sleeps for a massive four hours, finally waking around two o'clock.

"Morning, sleepyhead," I tease as she sits up and raises her arms above her head in a stretch. Her hair is messy from how she's been lying, and her face has the imprint of the cushion on it.

"How long have I been asleep?" Her voice still sounds sleepy, and I pass her a bottle of water from the side table.

"About four hours."

"Shit. Sorry. I didn't mean to sleep for that long."

"It's fine. I got to watch exactly what I wanted." I wiggle my eyebrows at her, and she laughs.

"No *Pride and Prejudice* then?"

"Nah, I turned that off. Watched *The Matrix* instead," I tell her, not wanting to admit I couldn't turn it off, or that I actually liked it.

She rolls her eyes and stands. "I'm starving. Did you eat lunch?"

I nod. "I made a sandwich. I made you one too. It's in the fridge." I get off the footstool I've been sitting on and walk into the kitchen, taking the covered sandwich from the refrigerator.

"You didn't have to do that. Thank you." She takes the plate from me, and I shrug.

"I was making mine. It was no trouble."

Hallie's phone chimes from the living room, and I follow her out of the kitchen and back to the sofa. She groans as she looks at her phone.

"It's Kitty. She's booked a table at The Fitzroy."

"I've heard it's good there."

"Are you sure you don't mind hanging out with her?" She bites down on her bottom lip as she looks uncertainly at me. "I can guarantee she will think we should be dating. She can't get her head around me not wanting to meet guys."

"I'm more than happy to go out with her. I think it will be good to get out. Be normal for a while."

"If you're sure?"

"I'm sure."

Her fingers fly over her phone screen as she types a reply to Kitty.

Crossing the Line

I wait until she's finished, her words from a few minutes ago swirling in my mind.

"So, you don't date at all?" I ask. She must have guys who are interested in her. She's beautiful.

"No." She doesn't elaborate, and I don't push the issue. As much as I'd like her to open up, it's nothing to do with me.

"What about you? Do you have a girlfriend?" She takes a bite of her sandwich, and I shake my head.

"No. This job doesn't lend itself to relationships. I don't get much downtime."

"What about your family? Do they live in Tybee Island?"

"My parents do. My sister is here in Savannah."

"You have a sister? What's her name? Is she older or younger than you?"

I chuckle at her succession of questions.

"She's younger. Twenty-six. Her name is Brooke."

"I always wanted a sister. Older brothers are pretty mean. At least Max was while we were growing up."

"Little sisters are annoying! I'm siding with Max on this one. You'll probably get to meet Brooke. My parents too."

"Will I?"

"Brooke's getting married in a few weeks. If I'm still here..." I trail off. She's not

going to want to think I might still be here in a few weeks.

"You don't want me at your sister's wedding. Surely, you can get the day off?"

I shake my head. "We're a small security company. There's only me, Logan, and two

other guys. Both are on cases. I'm afraid you're stuck with me."

She frowns and turns to face me on the sofa. "So, you're telling me that no matter how long this goes on, you can't have a single day off? That's ridiculous. I'll be fine here for one day. You said yourself the building is secure. I'll stay in my apartment."

"No. Not happening. Yes, your building has good security. It's

89

not impenetrable, though. Hell, Bryant could walk right in behind someone." Her eyes widen, and I sigh. "Look, I'm not saying this to scare you, but there's no way I'm leaving you here alone while I go to my sister's wedding. It's my job to protect you. Plus, I'd have a shit time if I was worried about you all night. If I'm still here, we go together, okay?"

She lets out an inpatient huff. "Fine, but I'm not happy about it." She pouts, and I have to hide a smile. "I hope Matt is caught by then," she whispers, a sadness crossing her face.

"I hope that happens too. Come on. We have time to watch one more movie before getting ready to go out. I'll even let you choose." I reach for the popcorn, tossing a handful across the sofa at her. The sadness clears from her face, and she bursts out laughing before picking up a piece of popcorn and putting it in her mouth.

"I know just the movie." She grins at me, and despite having to sit through another chick flick, I'm glad to see she's smiling again.

Chapter Thirteen

Hallie

Standing in front of my open closet, I try to choose an outfit to wear tonight. I have a couple of dresses, and knowing Kitty will look stunning, I want to feel nice too. After the last few days, I could do with a confidence boost. I reach for my favorite black bodycon dress and stand in front of the mirror, holding the dress against me and turning from side to side. Slipping it on, I do the zipper at the back, twisting awkwardly as I slide it up. Smoothing the dress down with my hands, I look in the mirror again. The soft material falls mid-thigh and clings to my body. It's short but not uncomfortably short, and I find as I look at my reflection, I like what I see. My long hair is curled in waves down my back, and I've pinned small sections up so it's out of my face. My makeup is minimal, which is how I always wear it, and I choose some black patent heels, adding a couple of inches to my five-foot-three frame.

"Hey, Hallie, you almost ready?" Sawyer calls through the door. "We gotta go if we're going to make the reservation."

"Be right out," I say, quickly reapplying my lip gloss. Taking one last look in the mirror, I push my feet into my heels, grab my purse, and make my way to the living room where Sawyer is waiting for me.

Seeing him steals my breath. He's standing next to the sofa, his head bowed as he looks at something on his phone. Thankfully, he hasn't noticed me yet, and I can appreciate how incredible he looks. He's wearing dark denim jeans and a white shirt. The sleeves are rolled up, his tanned forearms on display. On his feet are lace-up boots, and his jeans are tucked into them. It's a pretty simple outfit, but on him, it's stunning. Dark stubble covers his face, and his hair is styled like he's spent hours running his fingers through it. He finally looks up from his phone. His eyes meet mine before quickly tracking over the length of my body.

"Wow, Hallie. You look beautiful." Heat travels up my neck and over my cheeks at his compliment. Avoiding eye contact, I grip tightly onto my purse, my fingers fiddling with the clasp.

"Thank you. You look good too," I tell him quietly.

"You ready to go?"

I nod before heading for the apartment door. We're meeting everyone at the restaurant, and as we leave the apartment, Sawyer leads me to his car.

"We can get a cab," I tell him. "You don't have to drive."

"I'm still working. I won't be drinking."

"Oh, of course. Sorry." I frown and look down at his shirt. "Have you brought the gun?" A wave of panic rushes through me, and I stop walking. "You can't take it to the restaurant. What if we go somewhere afterward? You won't get through security. They'll stop you. Everyone will know—" My breathing comes out in gasps, and he turns to face me, his hands coming to rest on the tops of my arms.

"Hallie, breathe." His thumbs circle the skin on my arms, and I try to even out my breathing. After a minute or so, I've calmed down.

"I'm sorry." I cringe inwardly at Sawyer witnessing my mini-breakdown.

"You don't need to apologize. I've got a license for the gun. No one will even know it's there."

"Maybe we should stay home?" I bite my bottom lip and sigh

loudly. Sawyer drops his hands from my arms and reaches for my free hand, squeezing gently.

"No way. Your friends are waiting for you, and you look stunning. You can't waste that." He tugs on my hand, pulling me along the sidewalk. "Come on. It'll be fun." I let him pull me to where his car is parked. He holds the door open for me, and I climb into the passenger seat.

As we drive toward the restaurant, Sawyer glances over at me. "You okay?"

I nod, my fingers twisting nervously on my lap. "I'm sorry I lost it back there." I stare out of the window. "*He* had a gun... Matt. He never used it, but he threatened me with it." My voice is almost a whisper, but I know Sawyer hears me when he reaches his free hand across and laces his fingers with mine.

"I'm sorry, Hallie. I'm sorry he did that to you." He squeezes my hand before letting go. "My gun won't ever put you in danger."

We're both quiet for the rest of the short drive to the restaurant, and when we pull up, I realize we haven't talked about our cover story.

"So, Kitty's never met my brother. I'm pretty sure she won't question you on anything. I'm sorry we have to make up some stupid story."

"I'm quite looking forward to some role play. I can put my acting skills to use." He wriggles his eyebrows, and I burst out laughing.

"What acting skills?"

"Well, okay, I don't actually have any..." he trails off and shrugs his shoulders.

"I'll try to keep a straight face while you're in character then." We climb out of the car and head into the restaurant. I give our name to the waitress, and she shows us to the table where Kitty and Nick are already seated. The restaurant is packed, and it's a wonder Kitty was able to get a table at short notice.

Thanking the waitress, I sit down, taking the menu from her. "Hey, sorry if we're late," I say, reaching for the water pitcher on the table. I pour a glass and drink the cool water, my mouth suddenly dry.

"You're right on time," Kitty says, her eyes flicking to Sawyer. "Sawyer, this is Nick. Nick, Sawyer."

"Good to meet you, man," Nick says, reaching his hand across the table.

"Likewise," Sawyer replies, shaking Nick's hand.

"Kitty tells me you're a Marine?" I swallow nervously as I wait for Sawyer to answer.

"Yeah, on leave right now, and Hallie has kindly lent me her spare room for a few weeks." He turns and smiles at me before turning back to Nick. "What about you? What do you do?"

"Investment banker. Not quite as exciting as a Marine." Sawyer and Nick's conversation fades into the background as my eyes track around the restaurant. I can't help but wonder if Matt is out there somewhere, watching me, laughing at how his escape has transported me back to the scared thirteen-year-old girl I was when he last saw me. Despite it being warm, I shiver.

"You okay, Hallie?" Kitty asks from across the table.

Sawyer's head flicks around to me, his eyes filled with concern. "Hallie?" he asks.

I force a smile. "I'm good. Shall we order?" He holds my gaze, knowing I'm full of shit. My eyes plead with him to drop it, and eventually, he does, his eyes going from me to his menu.

Kitty is watching us both, a smile pulling on her lips. It's obvious she thinks his concern is something more than it is. I force myself not to roll my eyes at her, instead concentrating on what I want to eat. My stomach churns, and I'm not sure how much of anything I'll be able to eat right now. I knew coming out tonight was a bad idea.

Ten minutes later, the food is ordered, and I have a vodka lemonade in my hand. Kitty has been grilling Sawyer ever since the waitress left with our order. Despite my initial apprehension about our cover story, Sawyer is answering all her questions. Even I'm beginning to believe he's a Marine.

When she's finally satisfied with all of his answers, she turns to me. "How are you doing, Hallie? I'm guessing it's been a pretty shitty week?" I reach for my drink, swallowing a mouthful.

"I'm okay," I say quietly. "How's work?"

"Busy as ever." She smiles across the table.

Kitty continues to talk about her job, and I'm thankful the attention isn't on me.

The restaurant is busy, and despite our food taking a while to arrive, the conversation is finally flowing. I've relaxed a little, and by the time the waitress places my salmon in front of me, I find I'm enjoying myself. Watching Kitty and Nick, it's easy to see how besotted Nick is with Kitty. He constantly finds a reason to touch her and whisper things in her ear. It's sweet, and I'm happy for her.

"Are you guys up for a drink and some dancing after here?" Nick asks as the waitress clears our plates. His arm slips around Kitty's shoulders, and he leans in to kiss her cheek. "There's a great bar not far from here with live music." I look across at Sawyer, and he smiles.

"Sure, why not?" I say. "Sounds like fun."

After settling the check, we head across the sidewalk to the bar. Sawyer places his hand on the bottom of my back as we follow Kitty and Nick. A cold sweat breaks out on the back of my neck, and nerves swirl in my stomach as we join the line for the security check. Sawyer is standing close behind me, and as if reading my mind, his hand moves from my back to my waist, where he squeezes gently.

"Breathe, Hallie. It'll be fine," he whispers, his breath hot on my neck. Closing my eyes, I try to enjoy the feeling of his hands on my waist. When I open them again, Kitty's purse is being checked, and she and Nick disappear through an archway that leads into the bar. I shuffle forward toward the burly security guard. Handing my purse over, I drop my eyes to the floor as he searches it. When he's done, he hands it back, his eyes going to Sawyer, who stands behind me.

Sawyer pulls something from his pocket and passes it to the security guard, who looks it over before glancing at him again. A few seconds pass, and I literally hold my breath, only exhaling as he finally nods, passing the piece of paper back to him. I stand rooted to the spot until Sawyer takes my hand and tugs me through the entrance.

Stopping, I turn to face him. Going up on my tiptoes, I shout in his ear, "Is that it? He just let you in with a gun?"

He laughs. "Yeah, he did. You might not want to shout too loud about me having a gun, though." I clasp my hand over my mouth, my eyes wide. He laughs again and removes my hand from my mouth. "I'm joking. It's that loud in here I barely heard you." He looks around. "It is busy though, Hallie, so I want you to stay close. If you need the bathroom, I'm coming with you."

"What? You can't come with me. It's the girls' bathroom," I state incredulously. "Kitty will think we're up to God knows what."

He leans in close, his lips half an inch from my ear. "I don't care what Kitty thinks. I'm here to protect you, and I plan on doing exactly that." His voice is low, and his hot breath on my skin makes me shiver. "Let's get you a drink." His hand is still in mine, and I let him guide me across the packed room toward the bar where Nick and Kitty are waiting.

Ten minutes later, we find a table on the edge of the dance floor. Across from where Sawyer and I are sitting, Kitty is making out with Nick. It's a little awkward, and I glance at Sawyer. "Do you think we should go and leave them to it? I feel like we're intruding." I pull a face, and he laughs.

"I think they're coming up for air." He gestures with his head across the table, and I follow his gaze.

"Do you want to dance, Hal?" Kitty asks when she's finally stopped kissing Nick.

"Umm…" I discreetly slide my eyes to Sawyer, thinking back to his comment about staying close. When he slightly nods, I smile at Kitty. "Sure." Jumping down off the barstool, I place my purse on the table.

"Stay close, ladies. It's busy tonight," Sawyer says.

"Sure thing, Mr. Marine," Kitty replies, taking my hand and

pulling me the short distance to the dance floor. Laughing, I look over my shoulder to see both Sawyer and Nick watching us.

"Those two look smitten," Kitty yells in my ear as she begins to move her body to the music.

"What? Nick for sure. Sawyer definitely not. We're just friends."

"Keep telling yourself that, Hal." I shake my head, and she giggles. "He hasn't taken his eyes off you since you turned up at the restaurant. I saw your little moment on the way into the bar too. Looked like he was getting pretty close."

"Whatever." I wave off her comments. Little does she know he's paid to stay close to me and watch my every move. "We're just friends."

"Yeah, you said that already." I ignore her and lose myself in the music, my arms above my head as I close my eyes and imagine my life hasn't gone to shit the past few days. We dance to a couple more songs before Nick slides in next to Kitty, his arms circling her waist.

"I'll leave you two to dance," I shout to them. Kitty looks past me and raises her eyebrows.

"I think someone is coming over to dance with you." She's smirking, and I turn my head. Sawyer is walking toward me.

"I was heading back," I yell as he reaches me.

"How about one dance? I brought your purse." I take it from his outstretched hand and nod. The band is playing Shawn Mendes' "There's Nothing Holdin' Me Back," and I move closer so I'm dancing next to him. It feels weird but in a good way. I've never danced with a guy before. Even though we're not dancing like Nick and Kitty—bodies pressed together and arms looped around one another—it still feels good. I frown to myself. It's not like I want to dance with Sawyer like that. Do I? I mean, he's hot. Really hot. What's not to like? He can't see *me* that way though—I'm a client—a fucked-up client he needs to protect. Despite knowing this, it doesn't stop my stomach from tightening as I think how hot he is.

"You okay?" Sawyer shouts as he moves toward me. Before I can answer, the song ends, and the band goes straight into Ed Sheeran's

"Perfect." I stand there like an idiot as the first few words of the song are being belted out. Couples all around us begin to slow dance, and I move uncomfortably from foot to foot. I'm about to make my way back to the table when Sawyer slips his arms around my waist and gently pulls me against him. Although I'm caught off guard, my arms automatically wind around his neck, and I rest my head on his chest. He smells incredible, and with my ear pressed against him, I can feel the pounding of his heart through his shirt. We sway gently to the music, and I can't help but think my first slow dance couldn't have been better.

As the song comes to an end, I go to drop my arms from around his neck when he squeezes my waist. "One more song?" he whispers in my ear. Surprised, I lift my head and nod when my eyes meet his. He smiles and pulls me even closer. My heart's racing, and I know if I'm this close to him, there's no doubt he can feel the effect he's having on me. I've no idea what song we're dancing to because I'm too caught up in how it feels to be in his arms.

All too soon, the song's over, and I drop my arms from around his neck. He slowly removes his hands from my waist and takes a step back. Neither of us has said a word, and not wanting to make things awkward, I gesture to the bar. "Drink?"

He nods and follows me off the dance floor toward the crowded bar. It's about four people deep, and it takes a while before we reach the front. With drinks finally in our hands, we make our way back to the dance floor. The table we had been sitting at is now occupied, so we stand to the side, away from the crush of the dance floor. Leaning back against the wall, I yawn, covering my mouth with my hand.

"Tired?" Sawyer shouts over the chatter of the people around us. Despite sleeping this afternoon, my crappy sleep last night is catching up with me.

"Yeah. Do you mind if we head back after this?" I hold my drink up to him, and he nods. It's hard to chat with the noise from the crowds, so we stand in comfortable silence as we finish our drinks. I notice Sawyer's eyes flicking around the room, and I look out into the crowd surrounding us.

"What's wrong?" I ask, putting my hand on his arm to get his attention. Nerves bubble in my stomach as I wait for him to look at me.

"Everything's fine." Taking the empty glass from my hand, he places it on a nearby table, along with his own. "Let's find Kitty and Nick. Tell them we're calling it a night." I follow him into the crowd of people, his hand tightly encased around mine.

After saying goodnight, we head out onto the sidewalk. I've only had a few drinks, but with the cool night air hitting my skin, I suddenly feel tipsy. Sawyer drops my hand as we leave the crowded bar behind us. Despite no longer holding my hand, he stays close on the short walk back.

"Thank you for tonight," I say quietly as we stop by the car. "I had fun."

"Told you we would." He grins as he holds the car door open for me.

"My head is spinning," I say as I climb in and drop my head back on the seat. Sawyer walks around, and I hear his door close. "I think that last drink was my downfall."

"It'll be the fresh air," he says with a chuckle. "Not a big drinker then?"

"Nah. I'm a lightweight. Lack of practice," I tell him with a grin.

"Let's get you home. I don't want you throwing up in my car."

"Not a chance." My eyes close as he starts the engine.

Chapter Fourteen

Sawyer

The next week is rough. Hallie is the most withdrawn I've seen her since I took on the assignment, and as much as I try to help her, I'm not sure I am.

As I'd thought, it didn't take long for the vultures to descend. The morning after going out with Kitty and Nick, the apartment block was surrounded by reporters and television crews. I'd managed to intercept the first intercom call before Hallie woke, saving her the upset of having to speak to anyone. That wasn't the end of it, though. Despite Detective Wilmot sending officers down to the sidewalk, all they were able to do was keep them out of the entryway. Five days later, they're still there.

Despite visits from Jess and Hallie's parents, neither could get her out of the apartment. Hallie's dad moved my car around the back of the building the last time he was here. If I ever manage to get her to leave, I don't want her to face all the reporters.

Kitty and Nick have also visited a couple of times. The first time she was asleep, and they didn't stay long. The second time, I managed to convince her to come out of her room for half an hour. Something has to give.

I'm in the living room when I hear her talking. She must be on the phone. The bedroom door opens, and she walks into the kitchen, her phone pressed to her ear. Her hair is messy, and she's still in her sleep shorts and tank. Pretty much how she's been for the past week.

"Are they still at the library?" she asks. She drops her head as she hears the reply. "Shit. Yeah, they're here too. God, Dana, what a mess." She takes a bottle of water out of the refrigerator before returning to her room. Her eyes meet mine briefly before she disappears down the hallway. I sigh and drop my head back on the sofa. I need to do something to get her out of here. I'm beginning to climb the walls myself.

Feeling my phone vibrate, I slide it out of my jeans pocket to view the message.

Logan: *There's been a development. Where are you?*

Hitting the call button, I put the phone to my ear and wait for him to answer.

"Sawyer," Logan says as he answers the call. "Where's Hallie?"

"She's on the phone with a work colleague."

"You have eyes on her?"

"Of course, I do." I silently move across the apartment toward Hallie's room, pressing my ear to her door. Hearing she's still talking on the phone, I move back to the living room, pacing the small space. "What's happened?"

He sighs, and an uneasy feeling settles in the pit of my stomach. "A young girl has gone missing."

"When?"

"Last night."

"Do they think it's Bryant?"

"Not at first. Not until an eyewitness came forward this morning. The witness thought he saw someone forcing a young girl into a van... at Morrel Park."

"The same park Hallie was taken from," I mutter. "Why didn't he report it last night?"

"He'd had a few to drink, apparently. Wasn't sure what he'd seen.

When he woke this morning, he thought he'd better report it. Turns out a young girl had been reported missing by her parents an hour after the witness saw the incident with the van."

"Fuck! It's a hell of a coincidence the week Bryant escapes, a girl goes missing from the same park Hallie was taken from."

"Too much of a coincidence."

"I agree. What about CCTV?"

"It's being checked..." He pauses, and I know he has more to say. "Sawyer, this is going to hit the news, and soon. We can't keep a lid on it. As much as I hate the press, we need them in a missing child case. We want the missing girl's face everywhere in the hope someone spots her."

I sigh, knowing he's right. I wonder how hard this will hit Hallie. It won't take the press long to put the two cases together and assume they're linked. There is no way this story is blowing over anytime soon.

"How old is the missing girl?" I ask, somehow already knowing what Logan's going to say.

"Thirteen." I close my eyes and drop my head—the same age Hallie was when she was abducted.

"He's up to something, Logan, and whatever it is, it's got something to do with Hallie."

"Keep her safe, Sawyer. That's all you can do."

Just then, Hallie appears from her bedroom, and I stop pacing.

"I gotta go," I tell him, her eyes holding mine. Ending the call, I flip the phone over in my hand. "You okay?" I ask as she sits on the sofa in front of me. She nods halfheartedly, her eyes bloodshot and dark from lack of sleep. She's not sleeping well, I can hear her crying through the apartment's thin walls.

She glances down at my phone. "I, umm... saw you on the phone. Everything okay?"

I hesitate, not wanting to lie. "It was Logan. He was checking in." It's not exactly lying, I'm just not telling her the whole truth. I'll have to tell her soon, but right now, I want to get her to agree to come out with me for the day. Leave all this behind her for a bit. Sitting on the sofa, I turn to face her. "Let's take my bike out today. We can ride up the coast and stop off at the beach."

She screws her face up and shakes her head. "Not today, Sawyer." She turns on the television with the remote control and settles back on the sofa. I take the remote control from her hand and turn it off.

"What are you doing?" she asks, reaching across me to try and take it back.

"We are not spending another day sitting in this apartment, Hallie." I hold the remote control out of her reach, and her face floods with anger as she scrambles to reach it. "We're going out."

"You *go!*" she yells at me. "No one is asking *you* to stay." She sits back on the sofa, tears welling in her eyes.

I ignore her words, knowing she's projecting her anger at the situation onto me. "We've been inside for almost a week." I soften my voice and take her hand. "I'm worried about you." Her hand fits perfectly in mine, and I'm acutely aware of how much I touch her. It's like I can't stop myself. I've never allowed myself to get this close to a client before. I've never wanted to. With Hallie, I find myself wanting to comfort her whenever I can. Hearing her cry at night kills me, and I constantly battle with myself not to go to her. It's something I need to get under control and fast.

"I'm okay," she whispers, a single tear tracking down her cheek.

My stomach twists. "You're not, but that's okay," I tell her softly. "You don't have to pretend with me." I've watched her put on a brave face when her parents visit, and I've seen the relief of being able to drop the act when they leave. "Do you trust me?" She wipes her face as more tears fall before slowly nodding her head. "Then you know I'll keep you safe."

She sighs loudly. "What about all those reporters?"

"My car is around the back. They won't even know we've gone." She bites down on her bottom lip, and I think I've convinced her.

"I need to shower."

"Yeah, you do. It's like living with a homeless person." My voice is deadpan, and her eyes widen in surprise before a smile pulls on her lips. Picking up a cushion, she throws it at my head. "That's the second time you've attacked me with a cushion. I think I'll be the one needing protection soon."

She laughs before falling silent. "Thank you," she says quietly.

"For calling you a homeless person?"

"No. For making me get my head out of my ass. For making me laugh. I'm sorry I was such a bitch."

"Hallie, you weren't a bitch. I get how hard this is for you. I don't want that asshole to win. You deserve better than that."

Smiling, she stands. "I'll go get ready."

"I'll be waiting."

I watch as she heads to her room, noticing she's left her phone on the sofa. Grateful she hasn't got it with her, I pick it up and drop it on the small table in the entryway. I'm hoping she'll forget it when we go out, but I know it's unlikely. I want to keep her in our bubble, safe and unaware of the horror happening outside.

I'm heading back to the sofa when a knock sounds on the door. Frowning, I cross the room. We're not expecting anyone, and there was no intercom call, so it must be someone from inside the building. Using the peephole, I sigh in relief when it's Nick standing in the hallway.

"Hey, Nick," I say as I swing the apartment door open.

"Hey, Sawyer. Sorry to bother you. Kitty's sick. Does Hallie have any Tylenol?"

"I'm sure she does. Come in." Standing to the side, I hold the door open as Nick enters the apartment. "I'll check the bathroom. I don't think Hallie's in there yet." Leaving him in the entryway, I head down the short hallway to the bathroom. Not hearing the shower, I knock lightly on the door. When I'm met with silence, I go on in. The bathroom is empty, and I open the vanity above the sink. I find the Tylenol and make my way back to Nick, who's still waiting in the entryway.

"Here you go. I hope Kitty's feeling better soon."

"Thanks, man. I'm sure she will once she's had these." He holds up the Tylenol. "Catch you soon."

Thirty minutes later, Hallie's ready. We've snuck out the service entrance at the back of the building. There are no reporters back here, and Hallie's dad has hidden my car out of sight behind a dumpster. I can see she's nervous as she slides into the passenger seat, her eyes darting all around as she scans the area. I smile reassuringly at her as I close the door and jog around to the driver's side. Pulling away from the apartment block, we leave the reporters and the stress of the last week behind us. Hallie visibly relaxes the farther we get away from Savannah, her whole body almost sagging with relief.

Traffic to Tybee Island is light, and we drive in comfortable silence. Hallie has fallen asleep, and I go over and over in my head how I'm going to tell her what Logan told me. I want her to find out from me and not *CNN* like she found out about Amanda. The suggestion of a bike ride was partially a selfish one as it buys me more time. She can't have her phone in her hand when she's on the bike. There's no danger of her reading about the abduction as a bulletin on her phone, and she, of course, grabbed it before we left.

As I pull into the parking garage of my apartment, Hallie is fast asleep. Maybe a bike ride isn't a great idea if she's this tired. Parking the car, I climb out and go around to the passenger side. I open the door, kneel, and gently shake her shoulder.

"Hallie, we're here," I say quietly. I wait a few seconds, but she doesn't stir. "Hallie," I try again, this time a little louder. Still no response. Knowing she can't be comfortable in the car, I reach over her and release the seat belt. Scooping her up, I lift her out of the car and hold her close to my chest. Her head drops on my shoulder, and I wonder if moving her might wake her up. Glancing down at her face, she's still asleep. Having her in my arms makes me think back to holding her while we danced the other night.

Like then, it feels good.

Too good.

I sigh, knowing I must get this attraction to her under control. Getting too close is dangerous. It's always harder to protect someone you care about. I kick the car door closed and make for the elevator, hitting the button for my floor when I get there.

Managing to open my apartment door with her still in my arms, I'm pleased to see Josie, my house cleaner has been, and the apartment looks a lot better than the last time I was here. I walk through the apartment with Hallie in my arms and stop by the sofa, gently placing her on it. She still hasn't stirred, and I make my way into my spare bedroom, grabbing a blanket from the bed. Coming back to the sofa, I sit beside Hallie and cover her with the blanket. A piece of her long dark hair is over her face, and I brush it off her cheek, tucking it behind her ear. Her skin is soft, and I gently stroke her face with the back of my hand. She's beautiful, and I wish this weren't happening to her.

No one deserves this.

The problem is my gut tells me this may only be the beginning.

I'm sitting on the balcony while Hallie sleeps. I can't bring myself to wake her knowing how little sleep she's had this week. Logan has messaged to ask how she took the news. I told him I hadn't managed to speak to her yet. It turns out the area where the girl was taken from isn't covered by CCTV. Right now, the police have nothing to go on. Logan also tells me the story is scheduled to hit the midday news bulletins, which gives me under two hours to talk to Hallie.

Soft whimpering sounds break into my thoughts, and I stand, making my way into the living room. Hallie is still asleep but agitated. Her hands grip the blanket that's covering her, and a single tear falls from her eye.

"Hallie," I whisper, sitting next to her on the sofa. "Hallie, you're safe." I uncurl her fingers from the death grip she has on the blanket, holding her hand in mine. My thumb slowly traces circles on the back of her hand as I attempt to comfort her. The whimpering increases, and she grips my hand tightly.

"No!" she cries. "No!" Her eyes are still closed, and her head thrashes from side to side.

"Hallie, *wake up*," I say loudly, my free hand gently squeezing her shoulder. Her eyes fly open, and I can see the terror in them as she looks around, unsure of where she is. "Hey, it was a bad dream. You're safe," I reassure her.

Her eyes find mine, and she sits up, throwing herself against me. My arms instinctively wrap around her, and she clings to me, her whole body shaking as she sobs against my chest. I reach up and stroke her hair. "I won't let anyone hurt you," I soothe, holding her close. I hold her for a few minutes until her sobs subside.

"I'm sorry," she whispers, her head still buried in my chest. I try to pull back so I can see her face, but she stops me. "Don't. I'm embarrassed."

I tighten my arms around her. "There's no need to be embarrassed. It's only me. Do you want to talk about it?" I ask gently. She's silent for a few minutes before sighing loudly and pulling out of my embrace. Her head is down, and she won't look me in the eye. "Hallie, look at me." When she doesn't, I put my finger under her chin and gently lift her head. Her face is red and puffy from crying, and her makeup is streaked down her cheeks. Her eyes finally meet mine, and I give her a small smile of encouragement.

"I was back in Cedar Falls. He was chasing me through the woods." Her voice catches, and she closes her eyes tightly as if shaking the memory away.

"It's over. You're not going back there."

"If he comes for me..." she trails off, her voice catching.

"If he comes for you, he has to get through me." She doesn't look convinced, but I mean it. Assholes like Matthew Bryant who pick on innocent little girls don't intimidate me.

"I'm sorry I fell asleep. I haven't been sleeping well," she says a few seconds later before taking a deep breath and wiping her tear-stained face with the back of her hand. She frowns and looks around. "Hang on. How did I get on your sofa?"

"I tried to wake you, but you were wiped out. I carried you up from the car."

She groans and drops her head into her hands. "God, I'm sorry. My mom always said I sleep like the dead."

"Will you stop apologizing? It's fine, and you should have come and found me when you couldn't sleep." I didn't want to make her feel worse and tell her I was awake most nights, listening to her sob through the wall.

"What good would that have done? If you're going to save my ass, I need you well-rested." Her voice is deadpan, but there's a sad smile on her lips. She shakes her head. "God, I hate this. I hate this control he has over me and how pathetic it makes me."

"It doesn't make you pathetic, Hallie, and he has no control over you."

She lets out a sarcastic laugh. "Sawyer, I can't sleep, I can't go to work. Hell, I can't even *live* alone. I think that counts as him being in control."

"He's not in control right now. Let's take the bike and head out for the day. Anywhere you want to go." The conversation with Logan swirls in my head, but I push it down for now, selfishly not wanting to see the look on her face when I have to tell her. She sighs and drops her head in her hands.

"Okay. Why not? Let's go escape for a while." She looks up at me, her eyes filled with sadness. I'm desperate to see her smile again despite the news I have to tell her later.

"It'll be fun. Come on." I hold my hand out to her, and she takes it. I pull her to her feet. "The beach or somewhere else?" I ask.

"Definitely the beach. There's something calming about the ocean, and I could do with that today."

"The beach it is then."

Once in the parking garage, I fire up the bike and climb on. I hand Hallie her helmet and watch as she puts it on, then climbs on behind me. Her hands snake around my waist, and she scoots closer.

As much as I shouldn't like the feel of her pressed against me, I do, and suddenly, my love for the bike takes on a whole new meaning when she's riding with me.

I'm in trouble.

Big trouble.

Chapter Fifteen

Hallie

We've been on the bike for about thirty minutes, and my heart races as I cling to Sawyer. It's only the second time I've been on the back, and although I'm still nervous, I love it. When I'm riding with him, all my worries seem to disappear. It's like no one and nothing can touch me. After being trapped in the apartment for the past week, being on the back of Sawyer's bike is exactly what I need. Everything will still be the same when I get home later, but for now, I can forget everything for a few hours.

Turning my head, a sign for Hilton Head Island appears, and I figure that's where we're headed. Tightening my grip on Sawyer, I drop my head back, feeling invincible. My palms rest on his stomach, and one of his hands moves over mine. Electricity tingles up my arm as our fingers entwine, and I'm a little taken aback. He held my hand the last time I was on the bike, but he knew how nervous I was. This feels different somehow. More intimate.

I've tried not to read too much into how tactile he is with me. I've put it down to him trying to comfort me. There is no way a guy like Sawyer will be interested in me—he's just doing his job. He could have anyone he wants. With all the shit going on, he's more than likely feeling sorry for me rather than anything else. Still, his hand in mine feels good, and nervous excitement bubbles in my stomach as I can't stop my mind from working overtime.

This past week is the longest I've ever spent with a guy. Despite my initial apprehension when we first met, Sawyer's never once made me feel uncomfortable. In fact, I can't believe how comfortable I feel when I'm around him. It's like I've known him forever.

Feeling the bike beginning to slow, I look around, seeing Sawyer is pulling off the coastal road and parking. He turns off the engine, and we sit in silence for a couple of minutes, his hand still entwined with mine. I drop my head on his back and feeling him sigh, I untangle my hand from his, climbing off the back.

"Wow. This is beautiful," I say, ignoring the moment I think we might have just had. We've parked in a graveled area next to a small marina. The water is full of elegant bobbing yachts and beautiful sailboats, and a red and white striped lighthouse is on the water's edge. It looks like something from a picture postcard. "I wish I had my camera. This would make a great picture."

"My phone takes a pretty mean picture." He holds up his phone. "Let's get a shot with the harbor and the lighthouse behind us."

"Okay." Moving to stand next to him, I leave a small gap and wait while he puts the camera in selfie mode.

"Come here." He slips his arm around my waist and pulls me against him, closing the gap I'd left. "Smile." I'm a little blindsided when his hand latches onto my hip but smile as he takes the picture. With his arm around me, I'm reminded of when we danced at the bar last week and how good it felt to be close to him. His arm stays wrapped around my waist as he pulls up the picture he's taken.

"Looks good," I mumble.

He smiles at me and slowly drops his arm. "What shall we do?" he asks as he slips his phone into his pocket.

"Beach?"

"Sure."

He checks the bike is secure before we head away from the marina in search of the beach. Shops, bars, and restaurants fill the sidewalk, and although it's the middle of the week, the town is full of people. We pass a handful of hotels before the sidewalk opens out, and a golden sandy beach appears ahead of us.

I slip off my sneakers and hold them in my hand as I walk onto the beach, my feet sinking into the hot sand. Sawyer has walked on ahead as I stand and savor the feeling of my feet disappearing beneath the surface. I watch him as he walks backward toward the shore. His eyes are fixed on mine, and he smiles, my stomach flipping. He is so attractive. He's wearing cut-off jean shorts and a tight white T-shirt. Earlier, his arms around me felt good, and I can't help but imagine what it would be like to kiss him. A real kiss, like the ones I've read about. A kiss I know would be better than the one I got from my middle school boyfriend when I was twelve.

"Hey, Hallie," he shouts from the shoreline, pulling me from my thoughts. "Come and dip your toes in."

I give him a wave, slowly pulling my feet from the sand. I need a minute to get myself together before heading over to him. When I get to the shoreline, the water laps gently over my feet, and I take a sharp intake of breath as the frigid water hits my skin.

"It's cold." I laugh, hopping from foot to foot.

"Wimp," he teases, and I bend down, scooping some water into my hand. "Hallie, don't you dare."

I grin as he eyes my hands while slowly backing away.

"Who's the wimp now!" I cry, tossing the handful of water at him. It hits his white T-shirt, making parts of it see-through. He inhales sharply as it soaks him, and I hold my breath, waiting for his reaction. He stares at me for a few seconds before laughing and throwing his shoes onto the sand.

"Oh, it's on," he shouts, running the short distance toward me and scooping up handfuls of water on his way.

"No, no, no," I squeal, throwing my sneakers alongside his and running away from him through the swell. He's quicker than me, though. A splash of water hits my back before his arms reach around my waist, and I'm lifted into the air. I scream as he spins around with me in his arms, my legs kicking up the water as he does. I'm laughing so hard I can barely breathe. When his fingers begin to tickle me, I try to push his hands away, my breathing becoming even more difficult.

"Sawyer... no... put me down," I gasp out between fits of laughter.

His fingers still, and he gently lowers me onto the wet sand. His hands remain around my waist, and he turns me so I'm facing him. My breathing is labored from all the laughing, and I cling to him while I catch my breath. His fingers dig into my sides, and embarrassed, I drop my head into the crook of his neck. He smells good, and I breathe in deeply, inhaling his scent.

"You okay?" he asks softly, and I nod, my face still buried in his neck. After a few seconds, I stand up and step out of his embrace, his hands falling from my waist.

"Shall we get something to eat?" I ask, looking anywhere but at him. He doesn't answer straightaway, and I look up, meeting his eyes. Something crosses his face, but it's gone before I can figure out what it was.

"Sure. There was a burger place that looked good as we were walking up," he replies eventually.

I gesture up the beach to where we left our shoes. "Better grab our shoes before the tide takes them out."

"I'll get them." He jogs the little way up the beach and scoops up both pairs before coming back. "Let's go. I'm starving," he says before handing me my sneakers. Walking side by side in silence, we head off the beach. I try not to think too much about what just happened. It's not as though my life has suddenly become one of the romance books I read. Real life isn't like that.

The burger place we passed earlier looks busy. Sawyer asks for a table, and luckily, they have one. We're seated in a booth at the back of the restaurant, and I thank the waiter as he hands me a menu. Everything looks good, and I glance around to see what the people at the neighboring tables have ordered.

"Everything okay?" Sawyer asks, his eyes flicking to where I'm looking.

"Yeah, I'm being nosy. Checking out what everyone has ordered. What are you getting?"

He glances back down at his menu. "It's a tough one... I'm thinking the ranch burger. You?"

"Good choice. I'm going to go with the Monterrey Jack burger."

He calls the waiter over and gives him our choices, adding fries and a Coke each to the order. Once the waiter has left, I take a look around the restaurant. It's a cross between a diner and a sports bar. The restaurant has booth-style seating like the one we're sitting in, but there's also a pool table across the other side of the bar. There are a few large-screen televisions hanging on the walls, each one showing a different sport. The one closest to us is showing a baseball game.

Sawyer's phone chimes with an incoming message, and he pulls it from his pocket. I watch as he reads the message and frowns. His fingers fly over the screen as he replies. My attention is drawn back to the television when the screen turns red, and the words 'BREAKING NEWS' flash up. An uneasy feeling washes over me as I wait to see what's happened. An image of a young girl fills the screen along with the words 'AMBER ALERT.'

"Sawyer," I whisper, my eyes fixed on the screen. The television is muted so I can't hear what's being said, but I know what an Amber Alert is. It's a missing child. Words roll across the bottom of the screen, but as we're a little away from the television, I can't read them all. I can make out one word though, and the word is Savannah.

"Sawyer," I say again, this time a little louder. Tearing my eyes from the screen, I look across at him. He's still focused on his phone, a scowl firmly on his face. The uneasy feeling I have intensifies, and I reach across, my hand touching his. His head shoots up, and his eyes find mine. "Look," I whisper, gesturing to the television. He glances to where I'm pointing, and the expression on his face changes.

"Shit," he mumbles as he closes his eyes and drops his head. His hand laces with mine, and he squeezes gently. "I'm sorry, Hallie. I wanted to tell you myself. I wanted you to forget the stress of last week before I gave you more to worry about."

I pull my hand from his and frown. "Tell me what?" My eyes widen as realization hits me like a smack in the face. "~~Matt!~~ He has her, doesn't he?" A sob escapes my lips, and I clamp my hand over my mouth, hot tears tracking down my cheeks.

"Hey, we don't know yet..." he trails off, and I know he's not telling me everything.

"But?" I prompt, swiping away my tears with the back of my hand. He looks across the table at me, a pained expression on his face. "Sawyer, *tell me*!"

He takes a deep breath. "She was taken from Morrel Park."

"No," I mutter, dropping my head into my hands as more tears fall down my cheeks. "Oh, God. That poor girl. When did he take her? How old is she?"

"It was last night. She's thirteen." I lift my head.

"It has to be him, Sawyer."

"We don't know anything yet. There was a witness, but he couldn't tell us much."

Picking up my napkin, I wipe my face and blow my nose. "How long have you known?"

"Logan called me while you were on the phone this morning."

"You should have told me."

"I didn't want to worry you."

I'm about to say something when Sawyer's phone rings. With his eyes fixed on me, he picks it up, answering on the first ring. "Logan, what have you got?" he asks. I can't hear what Logan is saying, but I can guess from Sawyer's expression it isn't good.

"What? Where and when?" His eyes leave mine, and he looks all around the restaurant. He's making me nervous, and I can't help but follow where he's looking.

"Hilton Head Island. I gotta go... I'll let you know... I will." He ends the call and stands. Reaching for his wallet, he tosses some bills on the table and slips his phone into his pocket. "We need to go." He takes my hand and pulls me up. "Keep hold of my hand. Stay close and do what I say."

"Sawyer, you're scaring me. What's going on?" He's already making for the exit, tugging me behind him. Fear swirls in my stomach, and I feel like I'm going to throw up. My eyes dart desperately around the restaurant, expecting to see Matt in front of me at any second.

"I'll explain everything, but right now, we've got to leave."

As we near the door, I pull on his arm, forcing him to stop. "Sawyer," I whisper, my voice trembling.

He turns to face me, his fingers slipping from mine. He cups my cheeks with his hands and brings his face to mine. "I've got you, Hallie," he says softly. He closes his eyes and rests his forehead on mine. "I've got you," he repeats, his voice a whisper. He pulls his head back and brushes his lips against my forehead before taking my hand in his again.

Once we're on the sidewalk, we walk quickly back to his bike. He keeps me pressed against his side, his eyes scouting all around us as we walk. He's quiet, and I don't ask any questions. I don't want to distract him. My heart thunders in my chest, and I can almost hear it beating with each step I take. My hands feel clammy, and I wipe the one that isn't enveloped in Sawyer's on my jean shorts.

Despite not having been far from where we parked the bike, it feels like it takes an eternity to reach it. I can't help but feel relieved when it's still parked where we left it. Sawyer wastes no time pushing the helmet over my head, then putting on his own before jumping on the bike. He holds his hand out, I take it and climb on behind him. I've barely got my hands around his waist before he's speeding off, leaving dust and gravel spitting up behind us.

Chapter Sixteen

Sawyer

Adrenaline is pumping wildly through my system while leaving Hilton Head Island faster than I should. I'm aware Hallie is scared, but I can't stop to explain. Not yet. Once we're a safe distance away, and I'm certain no one is following us, I'll pull over.

Logan's message after we arrived at the restaurant told me we had a potential problem—a reported sighting of Bryant. At first, it wasn't too much to be concerned about. The cops have received hundreds of sightings of him since the news of his escape broke. So far, none have come to anything. This sighting was by a cop though, so a little more credible. He'd tried to stop a man who resembled Bryant. When the car sped off, the cop reported it. Logan then called a few minutes later, telling me a traffic camera had picked up an image of the driver of that car running a light. They were pretty sure it was Bryant, and it was on Hilton Head Island. As soon as I'd heard that, I knew we had to leave. As much as I hated scaring Hallie, I needed to get her out of there.

Pulling off on the smaller roads that lead away from the island, I join the interstate and feel Hallie hold on even tighter than she normally does. Her front is pressed to my back, and I swear I can feel her crying. Reaching my hand to her leg, I squeeze her thigh before taking her hand in mine. My gesture seems halfhearted. I want to stop the bike and hold her, but I can't. Not yet. I know exactly where I'm headed, and instead of riding toward Savannah, I ride in the opposite direction.

I silently question myself as we ride away from the island. Did I miss someone tailing us as we left my apartment earlier? Did Bryant follow us here? It's surely too much of a coincidence for him not to have followed us. Was I too caught up with having Hallie on the back of the bike that I took my eye off the ball? Are my feelings for her affecting my ability to protect her? These questions and more swirl in my mind, and despite not knowing the answers, I push them down. I have to concentrate on getting Hallie someplace safe.

I've been watching the road for the past thirty minutes, and I'm confident no one is following us. Seeing a rest stop ahead, I steer the bike off the interstate and park away from other vehicles. I turn off the engine, and we sit in silence for a few minutes. Hallie slides her hand from mine and dismounts the bike. Kicking out the stand, I remove my helmet, watching as she pulls hers off. My heart drops when I see her face is streaked with tears, her eyes red from crying.

"What's going on, Sawyer?" she asks quietly. Taking her helmet from her, I place it on the ground next to mine. "Why did we have to run out of the restaurant? And where are we?" She finally looks up and glances around the rest stop.

"I'm sorry I scared you. I didn't have time to explain, I needed to get you out of there."

"But why?" She looks confused, and I don't blame her. I don't want to tell her what I know. It's going to tip her over the edge.

I sigh as I lead her to a grassed area. "There's been a sighting of Bryant." Her eyes widen, and I can see the terror in them. "It's not been confirmed yet," I rush out, seeing she's about to lose it.

"But... but..." Her eyes flick around every inch of the rest stop, and I take her hand.

"He's not here, Hallie." I sit and tug gently on her arm until she sits next to me.

"Where, then? The Island?" she asks, putting two and two together. I nod. "Did he follow us?"

"I don't know yet. I'm waiting for Logan to get back to me once they've checked the CCTV."

"What if he followed us here?"

"We weren't followed, I made sure."

"If he followed us from Savannah…" she trails off and bursts into tears. "He's going to find me," she says through her sobs. Before I can think about what I'm doing, I pull her onto my lap and wrap my arms around her. Her legs straddle mine, and I hold her against me while she cries. Despite my head screaming that I'm crossing a line, my need to comfort her is stronger, and I have to hold her.

"He's not going to find you. I won't let that happen," I whisper in her ear, my fingers stroking her hair. My stomach twists as I hold her trembling body. I hate seeing her cry. Goddammit! I've seen her cry too often.

After a few minutes, her sobs subside, and she slowly lifts her head from my shoulder. Her face is flushed, and her eyes are red and puffy. She's still the most beautiful woman I've ever seen. I drop my hand from her hair and gently swipe my thumb under her eye, wiping the last of her tears away.

"Are you okay?" I question gently when her eyes meet mine. She nods and bites down on her bottom lip. My eyes gravitate to her mouth. "Don't," I whisper, easing her lip free of her teeth with my thumb. Her breathing accelerates when I brush my thumb across her bottom lip.

Whatever this is between us, I think she feels it too.

I'm not about to take advantage though, especially when she's so vulnerable. I shouldn't even be touching her. The more time I spend with her, the harder I'm finding it to remain professional.

"We should go," I say. As much as I like her in my arms, I need to get her somewhere she'll be safe. We can't go back to Savannah, and we can't risk going back to my place, either. Instead, we're heading somewhere not even Logan knows about.

"Home?" Hallie asks, and I shake my head.

"We've got to assume for now the sighting was Bryant, and that possibly he followed us from your apartment. We can't go back there."

"But we went to your apartment as well this morning."

"We can't risk going there either."

"What?" she whispers, her face falling as the realization of what this means hits her.

My hands rest on her waist, and I squeeze gently. "Hey, this is going to be okay. I have a place we can go. My parents own a cabin a couple of hours from here. It's remote. No one will know we're there."

"A couple of hours? On the back of the bike?" She shakes her head. "No. I can't do that." Her face is filled with panic as she pushes against my chest and stands.

Jumping up, I reach for her. "Hallie." I take her arm, but she brushes me off. She's beginning to panic, and I need to calm her down before we get back on my bike. My parents' cabin is our only option right now. I just need to convince her.

"This isn't forever. Maybe a night or two until we know what's happening. It's our best option..." I pause. "Hallie, it's our *only* option." She's pacing up and down in front of me, her hands wringing together. Standing in front of her, I force her to stop. "This is going to be okay," I repeat, hoping I'm right.

She takes a deep breath and finally looks up at me. "There's no way we can go home?"

"Not right now."

"What about clothes and all the other stuff we need? This is all I have." She gestures to the jean shorts and tank she's wearing.

"The cabin is well-stocked, and I think my sister may have left some clothes there. If not, I'll have something you can wear." I reach down and take her hand. "We'll make it work. Okay?" She still looks uncertain, but I'm relieved when she nods her head.

"Can we stop halfway? I don't think I can sit on the bike for that long."

"Sure. Let's get going." I pick up her helmet and hand it to her.

"Maybe if he is following us, he wasn't the one to take that girl in Savannah? If he did take her, he would have to leave her somewhere alone while he followed us," she says as she tugs her helmet on.

"Maybe," I agree as I reach under her chin and fasten the clasp on her helmet. I don't say anything else. She's desperate to hear the abduction is a coincidence, and Bryant isn't about to ruin another young girl's life. I wish I could give her that assurance. Right now, I can't. I'm not a big believer in coincidences, but I don't tell Hallie that.

Once we're both back on the bike, I rejoin the interstate and open the throttle. It's a long ride to the cabin, and I want to get as much of the journey done as possible before it becomes too cold to be on the bike. Although it's mid-afternoon and the May sun is still warm, we probably only have an hour or so before Hallie will be freezing.

I ride as quickly as I dare, my eyes constantly checking my mirrors for any vehicle that might be following us. I weave in and out of traffic, but I'm sure no one is tailing us.

Just over an hour into the journey, I can feel Hallie shivering. I need to find a motel where we can stay until morning. Seeing a rest stop coming up in a few miles, I squeeze her hand before pointing to the road sign. Hallie squeezes my hand in acknowledgment, and I move to the inside lane as I prepare to take the exit. I've no idea if there's a motel, but there should be one nearby if not. As we pull in, I breathe a sigh of relief as Sunbeam Motel flashes into view. Deciding to park the bike out of sight, I ride behind the motel and stop between two dumpsters.

"We'll stop here for the night. It's too cold on the bike to go any farther, and we have at least another hour to go," I tell Hallie as I pull off my helmet. She climbs off and removes hers. Handing it to me, she wraps her arms around her body to keep warm. I can see the goosebumps on her bare skin and exhaustion on her face. "Let's get inside."

Taking her hand, I lead her around the front of the motel and into the reception area. Despite the motel being at a rest stop, it's fairly decent. We make our way to the counter, and a middle-aged woman greets us.

"Hey there. Do you have a reservation?" she asks.

I shake my head. "We're looking for a twin room if you have one?" I tell her, hoping they aren't fully booked. She checks the computer screen in front of her. Hallie hasn't said a word since we arrived, and I'm worried about her. She's had over an hour on the back of the bike, overthinking everything that's happened today. I need her to open up and talk to me.

"We only have doubles available." She looks up at me expectantly.

"A double is fine," Hallie says before I can respond.

I turn to her and raise my eyes in question. "Are you sure?"

"What choice do we have? As much as I like being on your bike, I've had enough for today." She sounds dejected, and I hate seeing her like this.

"We'll take the double," I tell the woman behind the counter. She nods and processes our booking. After handing over some cash, I pick up the key and follow the directions she's given us to our room. I push open the door, and Hallie passes me, flopping facedown onto the double bed sitting in the middle of the room.

"How are you feeling?" I ask, sitting next to her.

She rolls over, propping herself up on her arm. "Like I could sleep for a week."

"How about we eat first, and then you can sleep? We never did get lunch."

"What are we going to eat? I doubt they do room service." She glances around the room and frowns. I follow her gaze. It's not the best room I've ever stayed in, but it's clean. There's a large double bed on one wall with a nightstand on each side. On the opposite wall is a small vanity unit with a mirror above it. A hairdryer and a small television, along with a mini-fridge sit on the countertop. In the corner is a lounge chair, and down from it is a doorway leading into what I'm assuming is the bathroom. It's basic but fine for the night.

"There's a Wendy's across at the rest stop. Let's order to go, and we can come back here to eat." She lets out a long exhale before sitting up and sliding off the bed. Pulling her phone from her pocket, she sighs.

"My phone was going crazy on the way here. My battery's dead now. How will I let everyone know I'm okay?"

"Shit. I need to call Logan back." I drag my hand through my hair while I decide what to tell her. I don't want everyone to know where we're going. The fewer people who know, the better, but her parents will be worried. "I'll call Logan when we've eaten and ask him to let your parents know you're safe. I don't want you contacting anyone."

"I have no way of charging it anyway." She tosses it onto the bed.

"Food first, then I'll call Logan."

A little while later, we're back with armfuls of food. Neither of us has eaten since breakfast, and it's only once we're waiting to order we both realize how hungry we are. It's safe to say ordering food when you're starving is never a great idea. We've come back with far more than we can eat.

When we've both eaten more than we should, Hallie kicks off her sneakers and flops back on the bed. "I'm stuffed," she mumbles, her arm covering her face. Her tank has ridden up, exposing her tanned, flat stomach, and I can't keep my eyes off her as she lies there with her eyes closed. Knowing I'm staring, I force myself to look away, clearing up what's left of the meal.

"Here, I'll help," she says, sitting up and taking the trash from my hand. Climbing off the bed, she spots a trash can under the vanity unit and throws everything inside. She walks into the bathroom and then pokes her head back out. "I'm going to have a shower. I'll have to put the same clothes back on, but I'm achy from being on the bike. I can't wait to stand under the hot spray."

I wait a few minutes until I can hear she's under the water before reaching for my phone to call Logan.

"Hey, man. It's me. Any news?" I ask as I sit on the edge of the bed.

"Sawyer, it's been hours. Where are you? Are you both okay?" Logan asks, the worry evident in his tone.

"We're good. Sorry I didn't call sooner. I needed to get Hallie as far away from Hilton Head Island as I could..." I pause and run my hand through my hair. "Was it him? Did the CCTV show anything?"

Logan sighs, and I already know the answer. "Yeah, Sawyer. Multiple cameras in the town picked him up. It was definitely him." I close my eyes and drop my head. I was hoping the sighting was a false alarm, our need to leave so quickly unnecessary. It seems I'd made the right call.

"Did the cameras show which way he came in and out of the town?"

"We saw him come in off the coastal road, but the interstate cameras are out."

"Shit. So, we lost him?"

"He's either still on the Island, or he left via the interstate." He exhales. "But yeah, we've no idea where he is."

"What about the girl? Any news?"

"Nothing. It's a clusterfuck. Where are you? Do you need me to organize a safe house?"

"No. We're good. We're about an hour or so from Hilton Head Island. I'm taking Hallie to my parents' place outside of Summerville."

"Do you think that's a good idea? Wouldn't a safe house be better?"

"It's my call, and I'm taking her there. It's secluded, and no one knows about it. Can you let her parents know she's safe? Her phone is dead, and we don't have a charger."

"I trust you, Sawyer. I'll let her parents know."

"Thanks. Keep me in the loop."

"Will do. Stay safe." I end the call and lie back on the bed. Noticing I can no longer hear the shower, I roll to my side as the bathroom door opens and Hallie walks out. Her long hair hangs wet down her back, and her face is pink from the hot water. She still has her shorts and tank on, but as my eyes sweep over her body, I see she's not wearing a bra. My eyes widen as her nipples pebble against the material of her top, and my cock hardens. Thankfully, she hasn't noticed me staring at her. I quickly adjust myself and avert my gaze before she sees how much I want her.

"God, that feels better." She stands in front of the mirror and braids her long hair in a plait down her back. "Did I hear you on the phone?" She finds my eyes in the mirror and raises her eyebrows in question.

Sitting up, I hold her gaze. "Yeah. I checked in with Logan. I've asked him to contact your parents."

"Thank you. I can't imagine how worried they are." She walks to the side of the bed and pulls the comforter back. I stand, and she climbs into the bed, wrapping the comforter around her.

"When we get to the cabin, you can call them from my phone. I'm sure speaking to you will put their minds at ease. For now, they know you're safe." She smiles before letting out a yawn. "Go to sleep," I say with a chuckle. "I'm going to take a shower. I'll sleep in the chair tonight." I gesture to the lounge chair in the corner of the room.

"You won't get any sleep in that. The bed is big enough for both of us."

"Hallie—" I start, but she cuts me off.

"Sawyer, it's fine. I trust you." She rolls away from me, indicating the conversation is over, and I walk to the bathroom.

Her words play over and over in my mind.

She might trust me, but I'm not sure I trust myself.

It's going to be a long night.

Chapter Seventeen

Hallie

Lying under the comforter while I wait for Sawyer to finish in the shower, my mind swirls with everything that's happened today. Although no one knew for sure Matt had taken the young girl on the Amber Alert, I knew it was him. There were too many coincidences for it not to be. It broke my heart knowing how terrified and alone she would be feeling. I almost wish I could take her place, save her the heartache I know only too well she will face.

When Sawyer took the call from Logan, I could tell something was wrong by his face. Knowing Matt had followed and had no doubt watched us while we had been on the beach made my skin crawl. I'd been that close to him without having any idea, and that scared the hell out of me.

It finally hit me.

I wasn't safe anywhere.

If he'd found us in Hilton Head Island, what was stopping him from finding us here or at Sawyer's parents' cabin?

Hearing the shower end, I tug the comforter around my chest, a million butterflies taking flight in my stomach. As well as having to deal with all the shit Matt was throwing my way, I would now have to share a bed with Sawyer. Despite telling him I trusted him, which wasn't a lie, I'd never slept in the same room as a guy before, let alone in the same bed. There was no denying I was attracted to Sawyer. My whole body seemed to come alive when he touched me. As much as I tried to control my feelings for him, it was hard with how attentive he was. I was acutely aware that under the comforter I was only wearing my tank and panties. My jean shorts were uncomfortable to sleep in, and I'd taken them off once he'd gone to shower.

"Hey," Sawyer says as he emerges from the bathroom.

I sit up slightly, holding the comforter around me. He's wearing his boxers, and I can't help but stare at the impressive bulge. Dragging my eyes upward, I take in his broad, tanned chest and wide shoulders. As my eyes land on his face, I'm mortified he's watching me gawk at him, a small smile playing on his lips. Heat floods my face, and I drop my head back on the pillow, my fingers fiddling with a loose piece of cotton on the comforter.

"I thought you'd be asleep." He finishes toweling off his hair before tossing the towel into the corner of the room. There's a small light above the bed, which he flicks on before turning off the main light. Despite it still being early, the room is plunged into darkness except for a slight glow the light right above the bed is giving off.

"I couldn't switch my mind off enough to fall asleep," I admit as he pulls the comforter back before sliding into the bed.

He turns to face me, a sad smile on his lips. "Do you want to talk about it?" he asks gently while holding my gaze, but I shake my head.

"What's there to say? It's a mess." I shrug halfheartedly and continue to fiddle with the edge of the comforter. "How about we talk about something to take my mind off it all?"

"Sure. What do you want to talk about?"

"Tell me about you. You know pretty much everything about me and my fucked-up life. You said Brooke was your younger sister? So, how old are you?"

"Your life is not fucked up."

I raise my eyebrows at him. "It's pretty fucked up, Sawyer. Stop avoiding the question. How old are you?" He rolls his eyes and props himself up on his elbow.

"I'm thirty-one. What else do you want to know?"

"Are you close to your parents?"

"Fairly. I don't get to see them as much as I'd like, especially when I'm working."

"What about Brooke? Do you like her fiancé?"

"What sort of question is that?" he asks with a chuckle. "Of course, I like him. Liam's a great guy."

"You're not one of those older brothers who think no one is good enough for their baby sister then?" I prop myself up on my elbow, mirroring him while I await his reply. The small light above the bed is positioned directly above us, and it's only being this close I realize how beautiful his eyes are. They're green, but not like any green I've seen before. They remind me of the ocean with flecks of blue edging the green. They're perfect, and I find myself staring into them. It's only then I notice Sawyer staring back. Our eyes remain locked for a few seconds, and my stomach flips before I finally look away, breaking the connection.

"I think you've read too many romance novels." He smiles, his whole face lighting up.

"Probably."

"Even though I protect people for a living, I'm not overly protective of Brooke. I'd be the first there if she needed me, but Liam adores her."

"That must be nice," I say wistfully.

He frowns. "What must be nice? That Liam adores her?" I nod. "You could have that, Hallie. You're beautiful." I close my eyes, embarrassed by his compliment. "You really don't date?"

I'm taken aback by his question but shake my head.

"Why not?"

Dropping back onto my pillow, I stare at the ceiling. "Matt and Amanda took away my confidence. I found it hard to trust people when I came back, guys especially. I never went to parties or proms. I couldn't bring myself to go." I let out a sarcastic laugh. "I was never even asked. Once I came back, I faded into the background. I didn't want to be noticed. Instead, I got lost in books and photography, and that was enough."

"And now?" he asks gently.

I shrug. "I wouldn't even know *how* to approach a guy, let alone what to say to him."

"But you talk to me."

"That's different."

"Why?"

"I dunno. It just is." We're silent for a minute or so, my eyes still on the ceiling. "When we danced the other night, it was the first time I'd ever danced with a guy." My voice is quiet, and although I'm embarrassed to admit it, I'm glad it's dark, and he can't fully see my face. "I'm experiencing more than one 'first' with you."

"Look at me, Hallie." I turn my head toward him, and he smiles. "What have been your other firsts with me?" he asks, his eyes holding mine.

"First time on a bike. First time I've had a guy in my apartment... a guy who wasn't my dad anyway." I chuckle and move back onto my side. "First time I've shared a bed with a guy." My voice is quiet as I admit to the last 'first,' and I roll onto my back and cover my eyes with my hand.

"I wonder if we can tick off any more 'firsts?'" His fingers tangle with mine as he moves my hand from my face.

When my eyes open, he's moved closer to me. My heart races as his eyes drop to my lips. Unconsciously, my lips part as my breathing accelerates, and nervous excitement bubbles in my stomach. His hand cups my face, and his fingers stroke my cheek. He lowers his head and gently brushes his lips across mine. I gasp before reaching my hand up and tangling my fingers in his damp hair. He moves back slightly, but I cover the small distance and capture his lips again, pulling his head to mine. This time he kisses me with more urgency, and his tongue swipes across my bottom lip, seeking entrance. Opening my mouth, his tongue duels with mine, and I pull gently on his hair as he consumes me.

My whole world implodes with his kiss, and I never want it to end. It's everything I imagined it would be and more. His hips push against my leg, and I can feel his hard erection pressing against me. I'm taken aback that I am having this effect on him.

Pulling back, he rests his forehead on mine, his breathing labored. I continue to run my fingers through his hair as his breathing evens out. Kissing me once more on the lips, he opens his eyes and moves back.

"I shouldn't have done that." His voice is pained, and disappointment floods my body. Tears sting my eyes, and I quickly blink them away, not wanting him to see how much his words hurt me. "Shit," he mutters. "That came out wrong." His hand still cups my neck, and his fingers continue to stroke my cheek. "I shouldn't have done it, but I've never wanted anything more in my life."

"What?" I whisper, confused by what he's saying.

"You, Hallie. I've never wanted anyone like I want you." He drops his hand from my neck and lowers his head. "But I'm crossing a line. I should be protecting you." He looks tortured, and I reach my hand under his chin, forcing him to look at me.

"You *are* protecting me, Sawyer. I've never felt safer."

"I took my eye off the ball. If I hadn't been so caught up with how it felt to have you wrapped around me on the back of the bike, I might have noticed Bryant tailing us from Savannah."

"You can't know that. He could have followed us without you knowing." He shakes his head and sits up, my hand falling from his chin.

"It's my job to know. What if he'd—"

"No what-ifs," I say, cutting him off. "Nothing happened. We're safe."

"But—"

"No buts either." I sit up next to him and put my hand on his arm. It's going to break me to say what I have to say next, but I need to. "I'm not going to sit here and pretend that wasn't the best kiss I've ever had. But if that's the one and only kiss I get, then so be it. I can't see that tortured look in your eyes again. A look I put there."

He swings his body around to face me. "You didn't put it there, Hallie. I did. Don't ever think you did anything wrong." He sighs and drags his hand through his hair. "If anything happened to you because I let my feelings get in the way, I'd never forgive myself."

"It's okay, Sawyer."

"It's not. It sucks." His fingers brush my cheek, and he smiles sadly at me.

"Yeah, it sucks."

"Let's get some sleep. It's an early start in the morning." I hold his gaze before lying down. He turns the light off, and the room plunges into darkness. I lie on my side with my back to his, my body as close to the edge of the bed as I can be without falling out. He's doing the same, and the gap between us seems bigger than it's ever been.

Needing to know one thing, I roll over onto my back. "Sawyer?" I whisper.

"Yeah?"

"If things were different..." I trail off, turning my head to the side. It's dark, but I can make out his shape in the shadows.

He sighs, his shoulders sagging. "If things were different, Hallie, I'd still follow you around and not because I had to."

Tears prickle my eyes at his words, and I brush my fingers across my still-tingling lips. I can't help thinking my first proper kiss, one I know I'll compare all other kisses to, may have just messed up something that could have been amazing.

Chapter Eighteen

Sawyer

The next morning, I wake up with my body tangled around Hallie's. My arms are wrapped around her, and her head rests on my bare chest. I've no idea how we managed to gravitate toward each other when we fell asleep with what felt like an ocean between us. I'm not ashamed to say when I kissed her last night, I saw fireworks. I realize that sounds like a cliché, but it's the truth. For a few minutes while I lost myself in her, everything was perfect. Until it wasn't, and reality hit me like a smack in the face. Hallie isn't someone I should be kissing, despite how much I want to. She's a client. Someone I must protect and not someone to take advantage of.

She stirs in my arms, and I still, not wanting to wake her. My head might be up to speed with the fact I shouldn't be holding her, but my heart hasn't quite caught up. I stay with her lying in my arms for a few more minutes before forcing myself to move. Gently sliding my arms from under her, I guide her head to the pillow, covering her with the comforter. I swing my legs over the side of the bed and sit on the edge, dropping my head. I wish things could be different. They can't, though.

"Is everything okay?" Hallie asks from behind me, her voice sleepy.

Looking over my shoulder, I force a smile. "Yep, all good." I try not to notice her beautiful face, still soft with sleep. Strands of her long hair have escaped from her braid, and I lace my fingers together in an attempt not to reach out and brush them off her face.

"What time is it?" She sits up, and the comforter falls away from her. Her tank has ridden up, exposing her stomach, and my eyes fall to her tanned skin. She tugs the material down, and I snap out of my daze.

Shaking my head slightly, I pick up my phone from the nightstand. "It's early," I say quietly as I check the time. "We should get moving though, before the traffic gets heavy." She stretches and pushes the comforter off her legs. She still hasn't looked me in the eye, and I watch as she pads across the room and into the bathroom, closing the door behind her.

I hate myself for making things awkward.

If only I'd been strong enough not to kiss her.

I couldn't deny the attraction between us.

It was always going to happen.

It had only been a matter of time but I knew it couldn't happen again. I only hoped I could keep that promise to myself.

A few minutes later, Hallie comes out of the bathroom fully clothed, her hair braided down her back. Her tank is crumpled from sleeping, and I hope Brooke has some clothes stored away at the cabin for her to change into. I'm no expert when it comes to women's dress sizes, but I'm pretty sure Hallie and Brooke are a similar size.

After using the bathroom, I dress quickly. When I come out, Hallie is sitting on the edge of the bed waiting for me. She holds out the bike key, and I take it, her eyes finally finding mine.

"Are you okay?" I ask as I reach for our helmets and hand Hallie hers.

She shrugs as she takes it from me. "I want this all to be over and for things to be how they used to be. I want my life back." I want to take her in my arms, hold her, and tell her everything will be okay. I can't do either, so I offer her a sad smile before gesturing to the door.

"Let's go. Things will look better once we get to the cabin." It's bullshit, even to my ears, but the cabin is beautiful, and you can't help but love it there. It's the best I can do right now, and I think Hallie knows that. She offers me a small smile as I hold the motel room door open for her.

"How far do you think we are from the cabin?" she asks as we round the back of the motel, stopping in front of the bike.

"I think maybe an hour. Weather's good, so it might be a little quicker, depending on the traffic." She slides her helmet on, and I start the engine, waiting for her to climb on behind me. She sits farther back than normal, her hands resting on either side of my waist rather than looping around me like they usually do. I reach back, taking her hands in mine then pull her gently. She slides closer to me, and I wrap her hands around my stomach. She's not holding onto me like she usually does because of what happened last night, and I hate it.

As soon as I'm on the interstate, my hand goes to Hallie's, and our fingers entwine. I'm giving her mixed signals, but this is how we've always ridden, and it always will be. She doesn't move her hand, so I keep mine where it is, occasionally squeezing it to check she's okay.

The traffic is light, and less than an hour later, I'm pulling off the interstate. I've never taken my bike to the cabin before. It's fairly remote, and the roads near it aren't the best. I'll have to take the rest of the journey slowly. The last thing we need is to hit some gravel and fall off the bike. I release Hallie's hand when the bike's back wheel slips. I hear her muffled scream through her helmet, and she grips tightly onto my T-shirt. Righting the bike, I pull over because I can feel her shaking behind me, and I remove my helmet.

"We're okay," I assure her as I turn around. "I should have told you the roads aren't good."

She climbs off the bike, pulling off her helmet. "Fuck! I thought we were going to fall off. Is it much further? Maybe I could walk from here?"

I chuckle and kick out the stand. "You can't walk. It's about another ten minutes, that's all," I tell her as I remove my helmet.

"I could totally walk that."

"No walking. I'm not equipped to fight off bears."

"Bears?" Her eyes widen, and she looks around.

"Occasionally, we see bears. It's up to you. Bike or bears?" I'm trying not to laugh as I wait for her reply. There are bears in this area, but I've only ever seen one since my parents have owned the cabin. Even then, it was when my dad and I were out fishing one time, an hour or so from the cabin.

"I think I'll stick to the bike." She pulls her helmet back over her head and climbs on behind me. This time her arms immediately wrap around me, her grip a little tighter than normal. Pulling away, I hold the bike steady, wanting to make sure we get there in one piece.

Fifteen minutes later, I breathe a sigh of relief as we pull off the road, the dense trees we've been riding past open, and the cabin comes into view. I stop the bike and hear Hallie gasp. I downplayed the cabin when I told her about it, so I know what she's looking at now isn't at all what she was expecting.

"Sawyer," she exclaims as she pulls off her helmet. "This isn't a cabin... it's huge." I follow her gaze. Admittedly, I made it sound like my parents had a small vacation home in the mountains. The reality is a two-story 2500-square-foot building with a wraparound porch and hot tub.

"Well, it's still a cabin... just a big one. My parents always planned to retire here. When they had it built, they had visions of grandbabies and family get-togethers."

"Did that not happen? The family get-togethers, I mean?"

"Sure. We spent summers here and quite a few Christmases as kids. Not so much now. It's been a few years since we were all here together." We've climbed off the bike, and I can see she's itching to get inside. "Do you want to look round?"

"Yes!" she cries, and I go to take her hand but stop myself, instead gesturing for her to climb the steps leading to the porch.

I key in the code to the key safe, then reach inside and take out the spare key. Unlocking the huge wooden door, I push it open and follow Hallie inside. The cabin is something special and probably something I've taken for granted over the years. The entryway opens into a massive living room centered around an open fireplace. There is a large rug in front of the fireplace with leather sofas and a checkered loveseat surrounding it. To the right are floor-to-ceiling windows leading to a huge patio. Hallie walks to the picture window and peers outside. The patio area is completely secluded, overlooking the forest surrounding the cabin.

"Is that a hot tub?" she whispers, gesturing to the covered wooden tub sitting off to one corner. She turns to look at me, and I nod. She grins before frowning. "I don't have a bathing suit." She pouts, and I can't help but laugh.

"I know for sure Brooke has bathing suits here. She's got a load of them."

"I can't wear your sister's bathing suits. I've never even met her."

"She won't care," I tell her, brushing off her concern. "She won't even know. We can launder them before we leave. It'll be fine." She looks unsure, but she needn't worry because I know Brooke won't care.

Hallie wanders through the living room, running her fingers along the loveseat's woolen material. "This is beautiful, Sawyer. Are you sure your parents won't mind us being here?"

"Not at all," I assure her, making a mental note to drop them a message to let them know we're here. With everything that's happened, I haven't gotten around to contacting them.

"Is this the kitchen through here?" she asks, gesturing to a doorway off to the left.

"No, that's the den." I push the door open, and she peers around the doorframe.

"That's bigger than my whole apartment." She chuckles. "And look at the size of the television. It's like a movie theater screen."

I laugh. It is a large television, although not quite as big as a movie theater screen. "My dad is a lover of watching sports. My mom, not so much. She banishes him to the den whenever he wants to watch anything. He upsized the television a couple of years ago. She can barely get him out of here now."

Hallie laughs, her whole face lighting up.

God, I want to kiss her again.

She sees me staring, and a flush spreads over her cheeks.

"Your parents sound great. A lot like mine, I think."

I show her around the rest of the downstairs, and she falls in love with the kitchen as I knew she would. It's a massive space with marble counters and a huge island in the middle. Pots and pans hang from a rack suspended from the ceiling, and a big bay window looks out over the forest. Opening a few of the cupboards, I sigh in relief to see the kitchen is well stocked. We'll need some fresh supplies, but we will be able to take the Jeep my parents keep here for that purpose.

"I'll show you upstairs. You can take one of the guest bedrooms. You'll have your own bathroom then too." I lead her up the staircase and along the hallway.

"Which one is your bedroom?" she asks shyly.

"This one." I come to a stop outside a closed door. "The guest bedroom is across the hallway." I open my bedroom door, and she peeks inside.

"Every room in this house is stunning. The views are incredible."

"Wait until you see the view from your room." Unable to stop myself, I take her hand and tug her across the hallway, opening the door to where she'll be sleeping. The guest bedroom has a queen-size bed, a walk-in closet, and double doors leading to a private balcony. Pulling her across the room, I open the doors and lead her outside. I watch her face as she takes in the view of the small lake that sits almost in the cabin's backyard.

"Why is this the guest room? Why isn't it your room or your parents' room? This view is amazing."

"I was fifteen when my parents had this place built. I didn't care about the view then. My room is bigger, and that won out. My parents have the same view, though. Their room is next door."

"I love this place."

"Let's find you some clothes from Brooke's room." I turn to head back inside but stop when she doesn't follow me. "Hallie?"

"I'll be okay with what I'm wearing. I don't want to wear your sister's clothes without her even knowing." She looks uncomfortable, and I can tell I'm not going to be able to change her mind.

"What about if I lend you some of my T-shirts? They'll be big on you, but we can launder everything you're wearing then."

"Okay," she agrees. I leave her in the guest room while I get her some things.

I sort out a handful of T-shirts, along with a couple of pairs of shorts. They'll all be big on her, but at least she'll have something clean to wear. While making my way across the hallway, my phone vibrates in my pocket. Glancing down at the screen, I notice Logan is calling. After placing the clothes on her bed, I hold the phone in the air.

"I'll leave you to get changed. I've got to get this." I can see the apprehension on her face, her eyes flicking to my phone. I smile reassuringly before closing the door and heading back to my room. I hate to leave her feeling unsure, but I need to speak to Logan.

"Hey," I answer as I close my door. "Any news?"

"Yeah, and you aren't going to like it," Logan replies cautiously.

"Go on..."

"Can Hallie hear me?"

"No. She's in another room."

"Her apartment's been ransacked. I'm sorry, man." I close my eyes. "You still there?" Logan asks when I don't respond.

"Yeah, I'm here. God! When are we going to get a break? Did they check the cameras in her building?"

"Yeah. There's nothing on them."

"What? How did he get in, then? There are cameras in the lobby."

"The service entrance at the back of the building was forced. Cameras don't cover there. Once inside, he would have had a clear run to her apartment. No cameras to pick him up."

"Fuck!" I slam my hand against the wall in frustration. "I should have picked that up when I surveyed the building."

"Sawyer, this isn't your fault. You're the reason she's safe. You followed your gut and got her away from Savannah. You could have been there." He's right, but fuck, it feels like I didn't do enough.

"Who called it in?" I ask.

"One of her neighbors. They saw the door open and went to check."

"Kitty?" I ask. "I don't know her surname."

"Umm..." I can hear papers being moved around, and he's obviously checking the file. "No, it was a man. The guy in the apartment next to hers. Jake. Jake Owens. You met him?"

"No. I've only met her friend across the hallway." I drop down on the edge of the bed. "I guess we won't know if he took anything until Hallie can come back and check."

"We've got her parents going around this afternoon once CSI has finished dusting for prints."

"Okay. Keep me updated."

"You'll be the first to know. Are you at your parents' place now?"

"Yeah. We got here not long ago."

"Stay safe, Sawyer. I'll be in touch."

I end the call and flop backward on the comforter. My stomach twists at the thought of having to tell Hallie what's happened. She's still reeling from everything that occurred yesterday. I'm not sure how much more she can take before she breaks.

Chapter Nineteen

Hallie

After Sawyer leaves me to get changed, I strip out of my clothes, quickly pulling on one of his T-shirts. It falls mid-thigh, and although it's big on me, I don't feel comfortable wearing nothing under it, so I slip on a pair of his shorts too. They're huge, and I roll the waistband over three times so the material sits at my knee. I look hideous, but with no other clean clothes, these will have to do for now.

It's the first time I've been alone since Sawyer kissed me yesterday, and I can't help but replay it over and over in my mind. Other than the occasional kiss on the cheek from my middle school boyfriend when I was twelve, I'd waited twenty-four years for the perfect first kiss. Sawyer certainly hadn't disappointed. The look in his eyes though, as he told me how he felt but that we couldn't be together, broke me. He appeared tortured, somehow thinking he'd crossed a line only he'd put there. Either way, I care too much about him to ever want to see that look on his face again. Maybe there's a chance for us when all this is over, if this is ever over. I hope so.

Opening the bedroom door, I can't help but wonder what Sawyer's talking about on the phone. I could see it was Logan calling him, and from previous experience, Logan only seems to call with bad news. I edge out of the bedroom and onto the landing. I can hear Sawyer talking through his bedroom door, but I can't make out what he's saying. Despite wanting to know what's going on, I don't want to get caught eavesdropping. Instead, I make my way downstairs and into the kitchen. Neither of us has eaten this morning, and my stomach reminds me of that as it rumbles loudly.

There's no fresh food in the house, and although it's only ten-thirty in the morning, I pull a pizza from the freezer. It takes me a few minutes to figure out the oven, but I finally turn it on, sliding the pizza onto one of the racks. I'm just about to get a can of soda from the refrigerator when I hear Sawyer shouting, "Hallie, where are you?" His voice sounds strained, and immediately I'm on high alert.

"I'm in the kitchen," I yell, making my way to the foot of the stairs. "What's wrong?"

He's rushing down the stairs, and he breathes a sigh of relief when he sees me. "Shit, nothing. I didn't mean to scare you. I thought you'd be in your room. When you weren't..." he trails off as his eyes drop to what I'm wearing. "God, Hallie, are you sure you don't want to borrow some of Brooke's clothes?"

"Why, what's wrong with this?" I grin and spin in a circle, showing off my outfit. Unfortunately, my spinning is too much for the huge shorts I'm wearing, and the waistband I'd rolled over unravels. Before I can stop them from falling, they're around my ankles. Thankfully, the T-shirt I'm wearing is long enough to cover everything, but I'm still mortified. I kick off the shorts and vow to only wear my jean shorts again. Sawyer, however, is almost hyperventilating he's laughing so much.

"Glad you think it's funny," I tell him, my voice deadpan.

When he's finally stopped laughing, he takes my hand and tugs me upstairs. "This is stupid. Come on. I'm getting you some of Brooke's clothes and don't argue. Okay?"

"Okay," I concede. He's right, I look ridiculous, but I hate to admit I quite like wearing his T-shirt. "Can I... can I keep this one to sleep in?" I ask, gesturing to his shirt. We've come to a stop outside a room I'm guessing is Brooke's, and he turns to face me. His eyes track up and down my body, and he swallows heavily.

"Of course, you can," he says quietly. His eyes hold mine, and I find myself wishing he'd kiss me again. As much as I tried not to cling to him on the bike like I usually did, he pulled me against him and gave me no choice. It felt a little like I was walking on eggshells with him, not knowing how to act, and I hated it. I'd always felt so comfortable with him. And now I want things to go back to how they were.

Sawyer leads me into Brooke's bedroom, and I gasp. It's even more beautiful than the guest bedroom I'm using. There is a huge bed on one wall and a large dressing table on the other. A door leads to what I'm guessing is a bathroom, and there's a dressing room through an archway on the other side of the room. The walls are pale gray, and the comforter and drapes are pastel pink with small flowers all over them. It's stunning.

"Help yourself to whatever you need. The closet's through there." He gestures to the archway across the room before flopping on the bed. "I'll wait here while you change."

I feel uncomfortable walking into Brooke's closet. Would I like it if someone I'd never met wore my clothes? I'm not sure. I'd like to think I'd want to help someone if they needed it. Maybe Brooke is a better person than me and really won't mind. I've no idea.

There aren't a lot of clothes in the closet, but then, if she doesn't come here often, I guess she wouldn't leave loads of clothes here. Opening a couple of drawers, I find some yoga pants and tanks along with a black two-piece bathing suit. I have no idea if it will fit, but I'll give it a try later. Taking Sawyer's T-shirt off, I slip on a pair of yoga pants. They're a perfect fit.

"Hey, Sawyer," I call as I pull on one of the tanks. "Was everything okay when you spoke to Logan?" He doesn't answer, and I frown. Gathering up another outfit for tomorrow, along with the bathing suit and Sawyer's shirt, I make my way back into the bedroom. As he hasn't answered, I'm assuming he's left the room, but as I come out of the closet, he's lying on the bed. He's not asleep, so I wonder if he didn't hear me. "Sawyer," I say again. "Was everything okay with Logan?"

He sits up and pats the space next to him. "Not really. Come and sit down."

"What now? Don't tell me something else has happened." As anxious as I am to hear what he has to say, I figure it can't be any worse than what we've already faced over the past week.

"It's your apartment." He sighs before taking my hand in his. My eyes drop to where his fingers entwine with mine, and I suddenly feel sick.

"What about my apartment? What's going on, Sawyer?"

"Someone broke in, Hallie."

"What?" I whisper, my voice trembling. "Matt?"

"We don't know yet. CSI is there checking for prints." Hot tears sting my eyes, and as they begin to fall, I pull my hand from Sawyer's, covering my mouth as I cry. Before I know what's happening, Sawyer's reaching for me, and I'm in his arms.

"Shh, sweetheart. Please don't cry," he soothes, his hand stroking my back.

"What does he want from my apartment?" I ask between sobs. Tears track down my cheeks, and I angrily swipe them away. "How dare he go through my stuff. I hate him, Sawyer. I hate him." My voice has dropped to almost a whisper as my emotions swing between upset and anger. "I'm so sick of crying."

"I hate that he's doing this to you. It kills me to see you cry." His face is etched with worry as he stares at me, and I find myself cupping his face with my hand. His eyes close as he turns his face into my palm. Reaching up, he covers my hand with his before turning his head slightly, his lips pressing against my palm. I want to feel his lips on mine again. It's selfish, but I need him.

"Sawyer," I whisper as I pull my hand away.

He opens his eyes, dropping his gaze to my lips. "Why is it so hard to stay away?" he mumbles seconds before his lips crash to mine.

I instinctively reach my arms around his neck, and we fall back on the comforter. Sawyer's body moves over mine, his weight pushing me down into the mattress. My hands tangle in his hair as his tongue pushes into my mouth. His fingers dig into my waist before his hand slides up my body, brushing the side of my breast. I gasp and arch into him, my whole body screaming for more.

More of what? I don't know.

I just know I want more.

His leg rests between mine, and I find myself shamelessly rocking against him in an attempt to dull the ache that's building. As Sawyer's lips brush around my jaw and down my neck, I moan, his teeth nipping against my skin. My entire body feels like it's on fire, and I've never experienced anything like it. Even when I've given myself an orgasm, it's never felt half this good.

"Oh God, Sawyer," I mumble, my hands reaching underneath his T-shirt. My fingers stroke his skin when he suddenly stops and sits up. Opening my eyes, my heart sinks as I wait for him to tell me it was a mistake again.

"Do you smell burning?" he asks, breathless from our kissing. I frown, wondering what he's talking about when I remember the pizza.

"Shit! I put a pizza in the oven while you were talking to Logan."

He jumps off the bed and runs out of the room. Scrambling after him, I race downstairs. As I enter the kitchen, he's opening the oven door. Smoke billows out, and he steps back, waving his hand to clear the smoke. Using a cloth, he pulls the blackened pizza from the oven, dropping it on the counter. I quickly move to the window, opening it wide to clear the burning smell from the area.

"Remind me never to let you cook." He looks at me and bursts out laughing.

"I'm so sorry," I say, relieved he's not pissed at me for nearly burning down his parents' place. "In my defense, I was a little... *preoccupied*." My cheeks heat as I acknowledge what we were doing.

He doesn't respond but takes another pizza from the freezer. After removing the packaging, he places it in the oven.

"Sawyer, what are we doing?" My voice wobbles, and I say a silent prayer I don't burst into tears. He's got his back to me, and he sighs, his shoulders dropping. He runs a hand through his hair before turning to face me. I drop my eyes to my clasped hands, not wanting to see the same tortured look on his face from yesterday.

"I'm a selfish bastard." His voice is low, and I'm taken aback by his reply. My eyes shoot up to meet his. Seeing the confusion on my face, he takes a step toward me. "You were upset. I took advantage."

"Yes, I was upset. You'd told me my apartment, the place where I felt safe, had been broken into. You didn't take advantage, Sawyer. I'm a grown woman. If I didn't want you to kiss me, I'd have said no."

He shakes his head. "I've crossed the line again. My job is to protect you."

"What line? This line you keep talking about is something only you can see. Why can't you kiss me and protect me?" I try not to sound pissed, but I'm not sure I succeed. I am pissed. It's obvious there's something between us. I'll be damned if I'm going to beg him to want it. "I'm going to lie down. I've got a headache."

I don't wait for him to reply as I turn on my heel, almost running from the room. I can't deal with all this shit. With everything that's happened over the past twenty-four hours, it's a wonder I haven't gone crazy. I can't go home because of that asshole, Matt, and even if I could, he's managed to turn one of the only places I felt safe into somewhere I'm scared to return.

I hate everything to do with that asshole.

And I detest him with every fiber of my being.

Chapter Twenty

Sawyer

While standing in the kitchen, I watch her walk out. I want to go after her, but I'm paralyzed. She sounds hurt and upset, and I can't say I blame her. After kissing her at the motel yesterday, I knew what I'd felt developing between us was something real. I also knew a relationship seemed impossible. I can't pretend I am able to keep it professional anymore, though. I hate seeing her cry, and the need to hold her won over.

Kissing her again felt right.

And as much as I argue with myself, I want her.

I can't deny it any longer.

Maybe she is right, and the line I thought I'd crossed isn't an issue. Maybe we can give whatever this is between us a chance.

I need to talk to her.

Once the pizza's cooked, I fix us both a drink and head upstairs, balancing everything on a tray. I'm apprehensive. I hurt her yesterday, and I don't want to hurt her again. As I walk along the hallway, I can see the door to the guest room is slightly ajar. I frown when I hear Hallie talking to someone. Pushing open the door with my foot, she's standing at the side of the bed, her phone at her ear. When she hears me, she spins around.

"I've got to go, Mom... no, really, I'm okay." Her eyes fix on mine, and I can see she's been crying again.

Dammit! I feel like the biggest jerk knowing I most likely added to those tears.

"I love you too. I'll call you soon. Bye." She whispers the word 'bye' before ending the call and putting the phone on the nightstand.

Placing the tray on the dresser, I push down the desire to pull her into my arms. "You need to turn your phone off, Hallie. I don't imagine Bryant has the knowledge or ability to track your phone, but I'd rather not risk it."

"Track my phone? Is that why you didn't want me contacting anyone?" I nod, and she reaches over, powering down the phone. "I found a charger in the nightstand drawer... I wanted to speak to my mom."

"You can speak to your mom anytime you want. But you must use my phone." She sighs. "You okay?" I can see she's upset, but something is different. She's put up a barrier.

"They've been to the apartment... my p-parents..." Her voice breaks, and she reaches a hand up to her mouth, stifling a sob. I move toward her, but she holds out her hand, taking a step away from me. "Don't," she whispers. "I can't."

Knowing she doesn't want me to comfort her hurts more than I'd like to admit. As hard as it is not to pull her to me, I respect her wishes and stay where I am.

"Do they think anything was taken?"

She shakes her head. "They've no idea. It's such a mess they can't tell. Every drawer's been emptied and thrown around the apartment. All my clothes... my underwear..." she trails off and sits down heavily on the bed. "How can I ever be there again knowing *he's* been there? Knowing that man has touched all my stuff? I feel like this nightmare is never going to end."

"Hallie, it's going to be okay, I promise." My words feel empty, and I wish I could say or do something to make this better for her. "He's getting careless, though. He was seen on CCTV numerous times yesterday, and now he's broken into your apartment. It's only a matter of time." I sit next to her, leaving a small gap between us.

She's silent for a few minutes before turning to me. "Thank you," she says quietly.

"What for?"

She shrugs. "Listening to me. Making me feel like I'm not going mad."

She's incredible. I can't believe after everything, she's thanking me.

"Look, what happened before—"

"It's fine, Sawyer. It's for the best anyway," she says, cutting me off.

"What's for the best?"

"That we don't get involved. It's too complicated." She sighs. "My head's all over the place. It wouldn't be good for either of us." Her words hit me hard like someone punched me in the stomach. "I need to concentrate on getting through this. Anything else is too much to deal with."

I say nothing, not trusting myself to speak. If I do, I might beg her to change her mind, and from what she's said, her mind is made up.

We're silent for a few minutes, neither of us knowing what to say. When the silence becomes too much, I stand, bringing the tray containing the pizza to the bed.

"I cooked another pizza. I think this one is a little more edible."

She turns to me and laughs before scooping up a piece. "Yeah, it looks a little better than my attempt." We both eat a couple of slices, the silence more comfortable now. When we're done, I gather everything back onto the tray.

"Movie in the den?" I ask as I stand up with the tray in my hand.

"Do you mind if I have a nap? I really do have a headache, and I think I'll feel better if I sleep it off."

"Of course not," I tell her, concerned she's not feeling well. "I'll see if I can find you some Tylenol. I'm sure Brooke will have some in her bathroom."

I put the tray down and jog across the hallway to Brooke's bedroom, where I find a box of Tylenol in the vanity unit and take it back to Hallie. I pass them to her, and she swallows two down with a swig of soda.

"I'll let you get some rest." I pause, not wanting to leave her alone but knowing I have no choice. "I'll be in my room if you need anything."

"Go and watch a movie. You don't have to sit in your room because I want a nap."

"I'll be in my room, Hallie."

She sighs, lying down on the bed. Taking that as my cue to leave, I pick up the tray and head into the hallway, shutting her door gently behind me.

Closing my eyes, I drop my head back on the door. That didn't go at all how I'd planned. She's right, though. She is going through hell and doesn't need me and my fucked-up feelings adding to her turmoil. Maybe if I hadn't pushed her away at the motel, things would be different. I did push her away though, and now I have to live with Hallie's decision.

I take the tray to the kitchen, leaving it on the countertop. I'll clean up later when Hallie wakes. I want to be near her, just in case. With everything that's happened this week, I need to be ready for anything. As secure as the cabin is, the closer I am to her, the happier I'll be. After closing the window Hallie opened when the pizza burned, I quickly check the rest of the windows and doors are locked before heading back upstairs. Pausing outside Hallie's room, I press my ear to the door. It's quiet, and I force myself to walk away and into my bedroom.

About an hour after Hallie went to lie down, I fell asleep too.

Despite sleeping okay at Hallie's apartment, I'm a light sleeper and easily woken. I hear a scream, and my eyes fly open. I jump off the bed, and my hand reaches for the gun holstered at my waist.

"Hallie," I mutter as I raise my gun and slowly open my bedroom door. My eyes track up and down the hallway as adrenaline pumps through my body. Seeing the hallway is clear, I silently cross the space, stopping outside her door. She screams again, and I push the door open, hearing it smash against the wall. My eyes flick to Hallie, who's sleeping, albeit agitated, on the bed. Quickly looking around the empty room, I check she's alone—obviously having a nightmare. Holstering my gun, I climb onto the bed beside her and take her hand. My thumb strokes her skin, and the frown on her face intensifies. Her hand is sweaty, and she thrashes her head from side to side.

"Hallie, wake up," I tell her, my hand reaching up to cup her face. "Wake up. It's a dream. You're safe." Her eyes fly open, wide in terror. She looks at me and then sits up, her eyes tracking around the room. Relief floods her face when she realizes where she is, and she flops back down on the bed. Her breathing is coming out in small gasps, and she puts her arm over her eyes before bursting into tears.

"Hey," I soothe. "It's okay. Don't cry."

She shakes her head, her arm still covering her face. "It's not okay," she says through her tears. "It'll never be okay. He's always going to be in here." She lifts her arm and jabs her finger against her temple. Her face is wet with tears, and my heart breaks. "Every time I close my eyes, he's there. He *will* find me. He's not going to give up." A sob catches in her throat, and she rolls onto her side, her back to me. Her whole body wracks with sobs, and I can't sit and watch anymore. I remove my gun and place it on the nightstand before reaching for her. Rolling her toward me, I wrap my arms around her body, holding her against my chest. She stiffens, but I keep my hold strong.

"Sawyer, what are you doing?"

"Please. I need to hold you." A few seconds later, her body sags against mine. Her sobs eventually subside, and I bring my lips to her head. I shouldn't after what she said earlier, but I can't bear to see her fall apart. I care about her too much. We lie like that for a few more minutes before I pull away slightly, my eyes finding hers.

"Do you want to talk about it?"

She moves away from me a little and props herself up on her elbow. My hand rests on her hip, and I'm aware I could move it now that she's calmed down, but I don't.

"I was at the cemetery for Amanda's funeral. I saw those two guards die again. There was *so... much... blood...*" Her eyes close, and I squeeze her hip gently. "On the day of the funeral, Jess and I hid behind a tree. We lay on the ground, holding each other as bullets flew through the air. I was terrified. We both were. I felt so guilty for putting Jess in that position."

"You didn't know what was going to happen. No one could have predicted that outcome."

"I should never have gone. It was stupid. I needed to see he couldn't hurt me." She lets out a sarcastic laugh. "Didn't work out like that, did it?" Her question is rhetorical, but I answer anyway.

"I will never let him hurt you, Hallie."

She stares at me, and I can see the indecision in her eyes. After a few seconds, her hand reaches up, her fingers cupping my cheek.

"I know," she whispers. "I trust you." Her eyes drop to my lips, and I know what she wants. I want it too. As hard as it is, I let her close the distance, needing the decision to be hers. Just as her lips are less than an inch from mine, a loud noise sounds from downstairs.

"What the fuck was that?"

The fear is back on Hallie's face as I jump up and grab my gun off the nightstand. She sits up, her eyes wide.

"Sawyer," she says, reaching for my arm. "Don't go out there. Please."

"I have to. I need to check what that was." I move my hand to her face. "It will be okay." I'm torn between telling Hallie to hide in the bedroom and bringing her with me. When another loud bang comes from downstairs, the scared look on her face makes my decision for me. I can't leave her alone. She's already terrified.

"We're going to go down the stairs slowly. I want you to stay right behind me, okay?" She nods then she slowly climbs off the bed. Her body is shaking, and my heart races as I make for the bedroom door.

"Wait," Hallie whispers, and I turn to face her. Going up on her tiptoes, she brushes her lips across mine. "I didn't mean what I said. I don't want you to go down there not knowing that."

I brush my fingers gently over her cheek before turning back to the door.

Hallie stays close behind me, her hand gripping the bottom of my T-shirt. Looking over my shoulder, I put my finger to my lips, indicating for her to stay quiet, and she nods in understanding. Opening the bedroom door, I raise my gun as I look up and down the space. Hallie steps closer to me then drops her head onto my back. I know she hates the gun, but right now, I need it. I can hear more noise coming from downstairs as we edge into the hallway. When we reach the top of the stairs, Hallie releases my T-shirt, her fingers going straight back to the material as we hit the bottom step. The stairs open out into the hallway, and we walk silently toward the kitchen. Edging the door open, I twist sharply to the left as the back door swings open. My gun is out in front of me, and Hallie lets out a scream.

"What the fuck, Sawyer! Don't point that thing at me!" I lower the gun, holstering it at my waist as my sister stands in the doorway.

"Shit, I'm sorry. I thought..." I trail off and spin around to face Hallie. Silent tears are streaming down her cheeks, and I cup her face.

"It's okay. It's Brooke." I drop my forehead to hers as she closes her eyes. "It's Brooke," I whisper. Moving my hands from her face, I wrap my arms around her and pull her in close. She clings to me, her hands still pulling on my T-shirt.

"Sawyer, what's going on?" Brooke asks from behind me.

Concentrating on Hallie, I step back and lift her chin so she's looking at me. "You okay?" She nods, despite trembling in my arms. "Seems like my sister's come to visit."

"Sawyer, what are you doing here?" another voice says. Looking over my shoulder, my mom's standing in the doorway, my dad behind her. I groan inwardly. Hallie stiffens, and I look back at her, panic and embarrassment etched on her face. The last thing she needs right now is to meet my family.

"Do you need a minute before you meet everyone?" I whisper. She shakes her head, her hands still clinging to my T-shirt. I turn to face my parents and sister patiently waiting for me to answer them.

"Sorry about that, Brooke," I say sheepishly. "I thought you were... someone else." She waves her hand and comes into the kitchen, dropping a paper bag on the counter.

"Well, it looks like my idiot brother isn't going to introduce us," she says, grinning at me. "So, I'll do it myself. Hi, I'm Brooke."

"Sorry. Brooke, this is Hallie. Hallie, my sister, Brooke, and these are my parents, Sophia and Owen."

"Hi," Hallie says quietly, raising her hand in a small wave. My mom's eyes find mine, and I know she's figured out who Hallie is. It wouldn't be hard. Her name and picture are all over *CNN*. A smile comes over her face, and she moves toward us, kissing me on the cheek.

"Hello, Hallie. Lovely to meet you." Taking Hallie from my side, she wraps her up in a hug. I can see Hallie is a little surprised, but my mom hugs everyone. I would have warned her had I known we'd be seeing them.

"Are those my yoga pants?" Brooke asks, tilting her head to one side as she looks at what Hallie is wearing. As Hallie pulls out of my mom's embrace, she looks down at her pants.

"I'm so sorry. Yes, they are," Hallie says quickly, her face flushing pink. She turns to me, her eyes wide. Taking her hand, I squeeze it reassuringly.

"We didn't realize we'd be coming to the cabin. We never got a chance to pick up any clothes. I told her you wouldn't mind if she borrowed some of your stuff," I tell Brooke.

"I don't mind at all. Borrow anything you like."

Hallie sags with relief next to me, and I squeeze her hand again.

"I'll make sure everything is clean before we go," Hallie says quietly. Brooke smiles at her and goes about emptying the grocery bag she brought in with her.

"Have you been here long? I didn't see your car out front," my dad asks as he comes in and shakes my hand.

"We got here this morning. I was going to let you know, but it's been a little crazy. My bike's around the back out of sight."

"You brought that poor girl here on the back of your bike?" my mom cries. "It's a wonder you didn't fall off."

"We nearly did," Hallie interjects.

"We did not," I say with a chuckle. "You were perfectly safe."

"I'm going to unpack, then I'm going in the hot tub," Brooke exclaims. "Do you want to come in, Hallie?"

Hallie glances at me, and I smile.

"I'd love to. Can you give me a minute?" she says shyly.

"Of course. Take your time. I'm going to get changed." Brooke picks up her overnight bag and heads out of the kitchen toward the stairs.

"I'll head up to my room and let you catch up with your parents."

"Are you okay?" I step in front of Hallie, shielding her from my parents' view. I need to see she's okay and not pretending because they're here. Lifting her chin, I raise my eyebrows in question when she looks at me.

"I'm good. I promise."

I hold her stare for a few seconds before taking a step away from her. "I'll be here if you need me."

She smiles and makes her way out of the kitchen. Stopping in the doorway, she turns around. "Nice to meet you. Sorry to have shown up unannounced."

"Nice to meet you too, honey, and this cabin is as much Sawyer's as it is ours. He's welcome to bring his friends here anytime he likes." My mom smiles at Hallie, her eyes flicking to mine on the word *friends*. I know exactly what she's thinking, and I am confident I'm in for a grilling once Hallie goes upstairs. I might be thirty-one, but that doesn't stop my mom from asking a million questions.

When Hallie leaves the room, I turn around to see my parents staring at me. "What?" I ask as my mom raises her eyebrows.

"There's something going on with that girl, isn't there?" she asks.

"Yeah, Mom, there is. The bastard who abducted her ten years ago escaped. Now we think he's after her again. I'm her CPO."

"I recognize her from the news. That's not what I meant, though."

"And what is it you meant?" I know exactly what she means, but I'm not volunteering any information.

"I saw the way you looked at her. The way you were holding her hand. What's going on?"

"Sophia, leave him alone. He's a grown man."

I smile gratefully at my dad, despite knowing my mom will take no notice of him.

"I'm his mother. If I don't question him, who will?"

"No one needs to question him. What he does is up to him," my dad argues.

"Look," I say, interrupting them. "Hallie's been through hell. We came here because I couldn't trust anywhere else to be safe."

"But you like her?" my mom pushes.

Groaning, I drag my hand through my hair. "Yes, Mom. I like her. I shouldn't, but I do. It's a shitty situation."

"Do you think you're a little too involved now to be protecting her, son? Could you ask Logan for someone else to take over?" my dad asks.

"No. I don't trust anyone else. She's with me. There's no one else available anyway."

"There's always someone else."

"Not happening."

My dad holds his hands up in defense. "Your call, Sawyer."

My mom is strangely quiet, and she's smiling when I look at her. "You really like her, don't you?"

"Geez, Mom. I said I do. What are you all doing here anyway?" I ask, attempting to steer the conversation away from Hallie and me if only for a few minutes.

"Last family weekend away before the wedding. Liam is heading up later. We did invite you, but you never responded," my mom says, and I feel like an asshole. I've been so caught up with work, even before meeting Hallie. I haven't spent as much time with everyone as I should.

"God, I'm sorry. It's been so crazy lately."

"We understand, Sawyer, and you're here now," she says with a smile.

"I'm not sure how long we're staying, but yeah, I'm here for now. I'm gonna go check on Hallie. I'll leave you to your unpacking." A huge grin has reappeared on her face as I mention Hallie, and I roll my eyes as I leave the kitchen, groaning inwardly.

I think my mom's definitely going to enjoy having us at the cabin.

Chapter Twenty-One

Hallie

As I reach the guest bedroom, Brooke is waiting for me, her arms full of bathing suits.

"I figured you'd need something for the hot tub. I grabbed a few suits from my closet for you to try," she says, holding them out to me.

"Thank you." I take them from her, heat rushing to my cheeks. "Actually, I already borrowed a black two-piece from your closet. I hope that's okay?"

"Hallie, it's fine. I think these might look better, though." She gestures to the suits in my hand. "The black one's a little boring." She screws up her nose, and I smile.

"I can't believe how nice you're being. I'm not sure I'd be as understanding if someone rummaged through my closet without me knowing."

She shrugs. "My stuff here is things I only wear at the cabin. It saves me packing loads when I come. I don't mind."

I smile gratefully and drop the suits onto my bed. "How long are you here for?"

"Just the weekend. A bit of family time before the wedding. I don't know if Sawyer mentioned I'm getting married in a couple of weeks."

"Yeah, he did. Congratulations."

She smiles, excitement dancing in her eyes. "Liam is coming later..." She pauses. "I know you're here because you have to be, and Sawyer's your close protection officer..." she gives me a sad smile, "...but I think we can still have a fun weekend. Starting with bubbly in the hot tub! Get one of those suits on and meet me downstairs." She winks and turns around, heading for the door.

"Brooke," I call, and she spins back. "Thank you. This is exactly what I need."

She smiles before walking out and closing the door behind her.

Sitting on the bed, I sort through the bathing suits she's given me. My eyes are drawn to a beautiful flowered pink two-piece, and now that I've met Brooke, I can see we're a similar size. Holding the soft fabric in my hands, I shake my head as it hits me how different things could have gone if it hadn't been Sawyer's family downstairs. As I clung to Sawyer's T-shirt when he led me down the stairs, gun out and ready to fire, I'd been terrified. I was sure we'd come face to face with Matt. The relief I felt when I knew it was Brooke and her parents was indescribable, and I fought back tears as I met them all in the kitchen.

Standing, I head into the bathroom, pulling off my tank and yoga pants. As I slip the swimsuit on, I go up on my tiptoes to try and see myself in the vanity mirror. I can't see much though, as the mirror is too small. There's a full-length one in the bedroom, and walking out, I let out a little squeal as the bedroom door opens and Sawyer walks in.

"Holy shit," Sawyer gasps as he closes the door behind him. Heat pools in my stomach as his eyes rake over me. Self-conscious, I wrap my arms around my body.

"Brooke lent me a swimsuit," I whisper. "Is it too much? I've got a black one if it is." He crosses the room and stands in front of me. Removing my arms from around my body, he waits for me to look at him. "Hallie, you look..." He shakes his head as he trails off. Butterflies swarm in my stomach as I wait for him to finish his sentence. "You look incredible."

"Thank you," I mutter, my eyes dropping from his.

"So, it looks like we have some company while we're here. I'm sorry you were scared earlier. Are you okay?"

"I'm good. Your parents seem great, Brooke too. She brought me all those swimsuits to try." I gesture to the pile still on the bed.

"Told you she wouldn't mind you borrowing her stuff. Despite her being my annoying little sister, I know how great she is."

"Are you sure they don't mind me being here? I don't want to intrude on a family weekend."

"Not at all. My mom's excited to have you here. Brooke too. She has a hot tub buddy now."

"Am I putting everyone at risk? What if Matt finds me?"

He reaches a hand to my face, his fingers gently stroking my cheek. "No one knows we're here, Hallie. Bryant has no idea about this place. We're good." I let out a breath I didn't know I was holding, involuntarily leaning my face into his touch. "You kissed me earlier," he mumbles, his free hand slipping around my waist. He pulls me against him, and I gasp as our bodies meet, my arms looping around his neck.

"That was when I thought we might die," I tell him, my voice breathless.

A smile tugs on his lips, and I can't help but smile too. "So, you don't want to kiss me now?"

"No..." I close my eyes as his fingers slide from my face into my hair.

"You sure about that?" His mouth has dropped to my ear, and he whispers the words, his breath hot on my skin. His hand is warm on my bare back and his touch has me feeling like I'm burning from the inside out.

"Hmm," I mumble as he brushes soft kisses against my neck. He chuckles against my skin before peppering kisses along my jaw.

His kisses stop, and he asks, "Is that a yes? You want to kiss me, or—"

"It's a yes," I exclaim, cutting him off. Winding my fingers into his hair, I pull his face to mine. My lips find his, and it's like I can't breathe unless I'm kissing him. One of his hands stays in my hair while the other strokes up and down my back, his touch setting me on fire. Our tongues collide, and I tug on his hair, moaning into his mouth. A knock sounds on the bedroom door, and Sawyer groans before pulling out of the kiss, his forehead resting on mine. His breathing is labored as he takes a minute to catch his breath.

"You in there, Hallie?" Brooke calls out from the other side of the door.

"She'll be down in a minute," Sawyer says as he lifts his head, his eyes fixed on mine. "I'm not ready to share you yet," he whispers, and I smile.

"Okay," Brooke replies.

"You've had me to yourself for almost two weeks," I tease, my arms still around his neck.

"Yeah, but not like this." He kisses me again, and I'm soon lost in him. Doubt begins to creep into the edges of my mind though, and after a few minutes, I pull back. My heart is racing, and as much as I love being in his arms, I need to know what's happening. Biting down on my lip, I look up into his worried eyes.

"You okay?" His fingers squeeze gently into the skin on my waist as he awaits my reply.

"Are you sure this is what you want?" I hear the uncertainty in my voice, but I need to know he's okay with this.

"Am I sure I want you?" His gaze lingers on me, his eyes soft. "Yeah, Hallie. I'm sure." He closes his eyes and sighs. "I was a jerk before. I was fighting with myself. But it was never because I didn't want you. Never think that."

"You're not fighting now?" I whisper.

"The need to kiss you." He plants a soft kiss on my cheek. "To touch you." His lips move down my neck, his teeth nibbling on my

Crossing the Line

skin. "To hold you." His mouth finds mine, and I moan against his lips. "All that won out. Now that I've done all those things, I know they will *always* win out."

My heart flips at his words, and a smile crosses my lips. "Wow," I mutter as I stare at him.

"What?" he asks with a smile. I shake my head, too embarrassed to say. "Tell me."

"It's like... like something out of one of my books." I smile, and his thumb strokes my cheek.

"And that's good?"

"Very good," I tell him as I go on my tiptoes and brush my lips against his.

"Let's get you in the hot tub, baby. We'll continue this later." He winks at me, and butterflies explode in my stomach. I kiss him once more before he drops his arms from around me.

"Are you coming in?" I ask as I dash into the bathroom and grab a towel.

"Not this time. I'm going to catch up with my dad if that's okay with you?"

I walk out of the bathroom with the towel in my hand. "Of course, it's okay."

"I'm definitely going in the hot tub with you before we leave," he growls, his eyes heated as they track over my body. He pulls me to him again, and I drop the towel on the floor. "I can't stop kissing you now that I've started," he mumbles, his lips brushing against mine.

My hands rest on his chest, and I can feel his heart pounding under my fingers. I never believed someone like Sawyer would be interested in me. I'm damaged goods with enough baggage to drown anyone in close proximity. But feeling his heart racing under my fingertips... *can he really be as affected by me as I am by him?* I'm beginning to think he might be.

"Stay in my room tonight?" he whispers, his lips almost touching mine. My eyes go wide, and I still in his arms. He must feel my awkwardness, and he steps back.

"Hey, look at me." I raise my eyes to his, and I'm sure I look terrified. As much as I like him, and I *really* like him, I'm not ready to sleep with him.

"I'm not asking you to do anything you're not ready to do. I simply want to hold you, okay?"

Relief washes over me. "I'd like that." I smile at him, nervous butterflies fluttering in my stomach.

He smiles back and kisses me. "I need to stop kissing you, or we'll never get out of this room." Reaching for the towel I dropped on the floor, he wraps it around me before taking my hand and leading me out of the bedroom and into the hallway.

Grinning like an idiot, I follow him, knowing I'd follow him pretty much anywhere.

Chapter Twenty-Two

Sawyer

"You not going in the hot tub too, son?" my dad asks as he sits next to me on the leather sofa in the living room. Glancing through the large picture windows that look out onto the patio, I smile as I watch Hallie laughing.

"Nah. Hallie's been stuck with me for almost two weeks. She needs some girl time." He holds a bottle of beer out to me, and I hesitate. "I shouldn't... I'm working."

"We're in the middle of nowhere, Sawyer. No one knows you're here. One won't hurt." He gestures with his head to the bottle, and I grimace as I take it from his hand. I never drink when I'm working. I need to be fully focused. But hell, it's been a rough few days, and he's right, we're safe here.

"Just the one then," I say as I clink my bottle with his. We sit in comfortable silence for a few minutes, and I find myself staring out of the window at Hallie. It's the first time I've seen her properly relax the entire time I've been with her. I've tried to take her mind off everything as much as I can, but it looks like Brooke has the magic touch. I wonder what they're talking about.

"She's not going anywhere, Sawyer," my dad says with a chuckle.

"Huh?" I mutter, tearing my eyes off Hallie.

"Your girl." He gestures with his head to the hot tub. "She's not going anywhere."

"Force of habit. She's not been this far away from me in two weeks."

"Seems you've got it bad."

"I guess I have. I've never felt like this. I wish…" I trail off and stare out of the window again. "I wish I'd met her under different circumstances."

"Sawyer, you're so focused on your job, how would you ever have met her?"

"That's true. I can't remember the last time I even went on a date."

"Have you thought about what happens when this assignment is over, and you move on to the next one?"

"Not really." I sigh and take a pull of my beer. I'm not an idiot. This job doesn't lend itself to relationships. It was never something I wanted to do forever. I always saw myself meeting someone and having a couple of kids. I just never thought I'd fall so quickly and for someone off-limits.

"What's the latest with Hallie? I've seen the news, but are they any closer to catching the guy?" Taking another pull of my beer, I look out onto the patio again. Hallie must sense I'm watching her, and she turns to look at me, a smile erupting on her face. I wink at her, and she gives me a small wave.

"Her apartment was trashed last night. No CCTV footage or prints. It had to be him, though. He's getting careless."

"You think he took the girl from Morrel Park?"

"Seems too much of a coincidence for it not to be him," I say with a frown. "I hope to God she's still alive. It's been radio silence since she went missing." I stand. "I'm going to check Hallie's okay." My dad laughs, and I shake my head. "I *am* her CPO." I leave him chuckling as I head out onto the patio.

Crossing the Line

"Having fun?" I ask, sitting on the edge of the tub close to Hallie. Her shoulders are out of the water, and without thinking, my hand goes to her bare skin. My fingers gently stroke her shoulder, and she turns, smiling at me.

"Hey," she says, her eyes fixed on mine. "You coming in?"

"Maybe later." There's no way I'd be able to keep my hands to myself if I were in there with her. She looks beautiful. Her hair is piled on top of her head, and her cheeks are flushed pink from the heat of the water, or maybe it's the prosecco she's drinking. Whatever it is, she looks the happiest I've seen her in days. I can't take my eyes off her.

"You two are so cute. I think my brother's finally in love," Brooke exclaims from the other side of the tub. Hallie's eyes widen, and I drop my head, brushing her lips with mine. Squeezing her shoulder, I turn to Brooke. "Stop freaking her out, Brooke."

"Exactly how close does a close protection officer get?" She's smiling, but I can feel Hallie tense beside me.

"Brooke," I warn.

"I'm kidding. I think it's great. You'll bring her to the wedding, won't you?" she asks me before scooting across the hot tub to sit next to Hallie. "You'll come, won't you, Hallie?" Hallie glances up at me, her cheeks even pinker than before. I'm guessing this time it isn't the warm water or the prosecco making her flush.

"We'll be there," I tell her.

"Great. I'm going to get showered before Liam arrives. I think Mom's making lasagna tonight."

"What time's he coming?" I ask, passing over her towel as she climbs out of the hot tub.

"About five. He needed to go to the office this morning." She wraps the towel around her and picks up her glass. "I'll see you both later. Thanks for keeping me company in the hot tub, Hallie."

Hallie gives her a smile and a small wave. "I really like her, Sawyer," she whispers in my ear as she walks past me and into the cabin.

Going back to Hallie, I take the empty glass from her hand and place it on the ground. "You okay? You're quiet." She's chewing on her bottom lip, and her face is full of uncertainty.

"Do you feel sorry for me?"

"What?" I ask, sitting next to her on the edge of the tub.

"Do you feel sorry for me?"

"Where's this coming from? Is this because of what Brooke said?" I could kill my sister. She rarely engages her brain before she speaks.

"You haven't answered me," she says quietly.

"I know what you're thinking..." I pause as I wait for her to look at me. When she does, I slip my hand around her neck, my thumb stroking her face. "You're thinking I kissed you because I felt sorry for you?" She shrugs. "No, Hallie. I kissed you because I had to since every fiber of my being is drawn to you. I couldn't stop myself." I drop my head to hers and capture her lips with mine. She tastes of prosecco, and as her tongue pushes into my mouth, I moan. Her hands grab my T-shirt as our kiss intensifies, and I wish I was in the hot tub with her. A few seconds later, she pulls back, and I rest my forehead on hers.

"I'm sorry," she mutters. "I just..." she trails off. "I have no idea what I'm doing."

"You don't have to have all the answers. God, I know I don't."

"Everything's such a mess. I shouldn't even be thinking about how happy I am when I'm with you. Not with that lunatic still out there somewhere with that poor girl."

"Hey. You deserve to be happy. Yes, it's a mess, but even more reason to grasp every second. You, more than most, know how fragile life can be."

"It feels wrong."

I frown as I sit up. "It does?" I can't help but feel hurt by her words. For me, being with her has never felt more right.

"That came out wrong. I'm sorry." She covers my hand with hers, and I turn my palm upward, lacing my fingers with hers. "I don't mean *this* feels wrong." She holds up our joined hands. "I wish things were different. I wish we could be together and not have all this shit hanging over us."

"I want that too, Hallie. We won't be hiding away forever, I promise." She gives me a sad smile, and my heart aches. I want to take all her pain and uncertainty away. Knowing I can't, I lower my head and capture her lips with mine. It's a gentle kiss. One I hope shows how much I care for her.

"I come with so much baggage, Sawyer. It's suffocating. You could have someone who has it all together," she says, shaking her head.

"Hallie, I don't want anyone else. I want you. You are the strongest, most amazing woman I've ever met. There aren't many people who've been through what you have and come out the other side." I cup her face with my hand, softly stroking her cheek. "No more self-doubt, sweetheart. Okay? I'm exactly where I want to be." I pause and frown. "Well, not exactly where I'd like to be. I'd like to be in that hot tub with you."

She giggles and flicks water at me, wetting my top. "Why don't you get in then?" she asks, running her wet hand up my arm.

"I may as well, now that you've soaked me." I lower my head and kiss her. "Trust me, when everyone has gone home, you won't be able to stop me from getting in there," I whisper against her lips. She shivers, and I don't know if it's my words or whether she's getting cold. I'd like to think it's the effect I'm having on her.

"Hey, you two," a voice shouts from inside. Looking up, Brooke's standing by the doors that lead onto the patio. "Do you want to watch a movie?"

"Do you want to?" I ask Hallie.

"Sure. I'll have a quick shower while you choose something if that's okay."

"Of course, it is." I hand her the towel and try not to stare as she stands. Droplets of water run over her breasts and down her flat, toned stomach, and my cock strains against my jeans. As she steps out, I wrap the towel around her and pull her close. "Don't be long," I whisper as I lead her into the cabin. She smiles up at me before disappearing upstairs. I stare after her as Brooke clears her throat behind me.

"I've never seen you like this," Brooke says as she comes to stand next to me.

"Like what?" I ask as I turn to face her.

"In love."

"What? I'm not in love," I lie, knowing full well I am. "I've had other girlfriends. It's not like you've never seen me in a relationship before."

"You've never looked at any of your previous girlfriends the way you look at Hallie. She's different, isn't she? She's the one."

I sigh heavily and run my fingers through my hair. "I've never felt like this before, Brooke..." I trail off.

"But?"

"What if, when this is all over, she feels differently? I'm her CPO. What if her attraction is because I'm protecting her?"

"Do you honestly believe that?"

I shrug, not knowing what to believe. "I don't want to believe it."

"Sawyer, she looks at you the same way you look at her. Whatever's happening between you two, the feelings are mutual."

"I shouldn't be getting close to her when she's so vulnerable, but I can't stay away. I'm drawn to her and not just because I'm protecting her. She's amazing."

"I'm willing to bet she feels the same way about you. Is this all going to be over soon for her? Are they any closer to catching the bastard?"

I shake my head. "We've no idea where he is. I hope to God they catch him soon. I'm not sure how much more she can handle."

She squeezes my arm before giving me a sad smile. "Let's pick a movie and escape for a couple of hours."

Smiling gratefully, I follow her into the den, flopping down onto

Crossing the Line

one of the large sofas while I wait for Hallie to join us. I hope Brooke is right, and Hallie's feelings for me mirror my own. She's clearly having doubts about our relationship if our conversation at the hot tub is anything to go by. It physically hurts to think about losing her, so I'll do anything to show her what she means to me.

Chapter Twenty-Three

Hallie

After climbing out of the shower, I dry off before slipping on some yoga pants and a tank. I quickly dry my hair, arranging it into a messy bun. Staring into the mirror, my mind wanders back to the conversation with Sawyer in the hot tub. I didn't mean to sound so insecure. I just struggle to see why he would want to be with me. He's the hottest guy I've ever seen. He could easily have his pick of any woman. The last thing I want is for him to be with me out of pity or a misplaced sense of duty.

The past two weeks have been intense, and we've pretty much lived in each other's pockets. We're bound to have grown close. How do I know that closeness hasn't been misinterpreted for more intense feelings? For me, it hasn't. I've never felt like I do when I'm with him. What I'm feeling is real, and I hope Sawyer feels the same.

Standing up from the vanity unit, I glance across the room at my phone, where it's sitting switched off on the nightstand. I wish I could speak to Jess. I could use her advice right now. Maybe I could send her a quick message? I could turn it straight off again and check for a reply in a bit. Biting my bottom lip, I cross the room and pick up the phone. There's no way Matt could have put a tracker on it. Sawyer himself said it was unlikely.

"Shit, Hallie, do you want to risk it?" I mutter to myself as I turn the phone over and over in my hand. "It was unlikely he'd ever escape, but he did. I can't turn it on and put everyone here in danger." Placing the phone back on the nightstand, I sigh before heading out of the bedroom and onto the landing.

Once downstairs, I can hear voices coming from the den. Pushing open the door, I find Sawyer and Brooke on the large leather sofa that faces the television.

"Hey, we're deciding which movie to put on. Come in," Sawyer says as he stands from the sofa and makes his way toward me. "You okay?" He lowers his head and brushes his lips against mine. I don't think I'll ever tire of his kisses. Brooke watches us as she moves from the sofa to the loveseat with a smile on her face.

"I'm good. What movie did you choose?"

"I'm trying to convince him we need to watch something romantic, but he says he's had his fill of romance movies," Brooke says, rolling her eyes.

"I think that might be my fault," I say with a laugh. "We had a movie day last week, and I subjected him to *Pride and Prejudice*. I think I may have scarred him for life."

"It was very painful," Sawyer says, trying not to laugh.

"I'd have loved to have seen him sit through that."

"What about the latest *Mission Impossible* movie? A bit of action for Sawyer and Tom Cruise for us?" I suggest.

"Sounds perfect," Brooke agrees. "You happy with that, Sawyer?"

"More than happy." He slips his arm around me and pulls me against him. "Do you want a drink?"

"Sure. Do you have any soda?"

"Yeah, I think so. I'll go check. Brooke, you want anything?"

"Wine, please. Hallie, you sure you want a soda? There's plenty of wine."

"I'm good with a soda, thanks."

"Wine and soda coming up," Sawyer says as he climbs off the sofa and heads out of the den. Despite chatting to Brooke earlier, I can't help but feel a little nervous and unsure of what to say now that we're alone. She's sitting on the loveseat next to the sofa, searching the cable channels for the movie.

"So, how are the wedding plans coming along?" I ask, not wanting to sit in silence.

"Wonderfully," she gushes, her whole face lighting up at the mention of the wedding. "I have my final dress fitting the week after next. Do you want to see a picture of the dress?"

"Oh, sure. I'd love to." I'm pleased but taken aback she wants to show me. I haven't been to many weddings, but I always thought the bride's dress was kept a secret from guests. She pulls her phone from her jeans pocket, her fingers flying across the screen.

"Here it is." She moves from the loveseat to sit next to me on the sofa. I gasp as an image of her wearing the most beautiful dress I've ever seen flashes on the screen. It's a strapless gown with a sweetheart neckline. Delicate lace covers every inch of the dress which hugs her body's curves. Brooke has an amazing figure, but this dress makes her look even more incredible. Halfway down her legs, the dress tapers out into a fishtail.

"Oh my God, Brooke, you look beautiful. Your dress is stunning. Has Sawyer seen you in it?"

"Has Sawyer seen what?" he asks as the door to the den pushes open, and he enters carrying drinks. Brooke quickly locks the screen on her phone, pushing it back into her pocket.

"No, he hasn't, and he won't until the day." She puts her fingers to her lips as she moves from the sofa back to the loveseat.

"Don't worry, your secret's safe with me," I promise as I take the can of soda Sawyer is holding out to me.

"What are you two talking about? Keeping secrets from me already, Hallie?" Sawyer teases as he passes Brooke her glass of wine.

"It's my secret she's keeping. Girly wedding talk. Nothing to concern you," Brooke tells him. "Let's get the movie on."

Crossing the Line

He chuckles and holds his hands up in surrender. "Wouldn't dream of getting involved in your girly wedding talk. I'll get the lights."

The room plunges into darkness, the only light coming from the giant television screen on the wall.

As the movie begins, Sawyer sits next to me. I curl my legs underneath me, cuddling up against his chest. His arm envelops me, and I can feel the rhythmic pounding of his heart under my ear. Nothing has ever felt more right, and I find myself wishing I could stay like this with him forever, tucked away in the cabin, the worries of real life forgotten.

Halfway through the movie, Brooke's phone rings. Standing, she holds it out, a huge smile on her face. "It's Liam, he must be on his way." The excitement is evident in her tone, and I smile as she makes for the door. "Hi, babe. You nearly here?"

The den door closes behind her, leaving Sawyer and me alone. During the course of the movie, we somehow ended up lying on the sofa. My legs are tangled with Sawyer's, and his arms are wrapped around me.

"Alone at last," Sawyer mutters. Before I know what's happening, he's flipped me onto my back, his body hovering over mine. My breathing accelerates as his eyes gaze into mine. "I've been wanting to kiss you since the opening scene." Before I can respond, his lips crash against mine, and butterflies erupt in my stomach. His kisses seem to ignite something deep inside. Something I've never felt before. Something I can't put into words. Reaching up, I wind my fingers into his hair, holding his mouth to mine. As the kiss intensifies, Sawyer moans, and I find myself tugging at the hair on the base of his neck. My body feels like it's burning from the inside out, and I've no idea how to extinguish it. Right now, I'm not sure I ever want to. Sawyer's kisses drop from my lips, his hot mouth finding the hollow of my neck. Pulses of electricity race through my body, and in my lust-filled haze, I struggle to decide if I prefer Sawyer's mouth on my lips or my neck. Both are equally addictive.

"God, I should stop," he says against my skin. His breathing is labored as he lifts his mouth, resting his forehead on mine. "If I kiss you one more time, I don't know if I'll be able to stop." My stomach flips, and I bite down nervously on my bottom lip. I'm not sure I want him to stop. His words make me flustered but excited at the same time. I feel so comfortable with him. I can't imagine being in this position with anyone else.

The door to the den suddenly opens, and my cheeks heat. I hadn't even thought about Brooke coming back when I'd been making out with Sawyer. If she had come in a few minutes earlier, I'm not even sure I'd have noticed if she were dancing around the room. Pushing on Sawyer's chest, he chuckles as he moves off me.

"Everything okay?" I ask as I sit up. Realizing my tank has ridden up, I hurry to pull it down, covering my exposed stomach.

"Liam's almost here. He needed some last-minute directions," Brooke replies excitedly as she sits back down on the loveseat. Thankfully, she seems swept up in Liam's call and doesn't notice she walked in on us making out.

"Fuck! I hope *you* didn't give him directions. He'll never get here," Sawyer says, his voice deadpan.

"Hey! I'll have you know I'm great at directions," Brooke exclaims. Sawyer raises his eyebrows, and she laughs. "Okay, okay," she concedes. "I gave the phone to Dad, and he gave Liam directions."

"I knew it!"

"Doesn't he have GPS?" I ask.

"The GPS sends you about five miles down the road for some reason. Always has," Brooke says with a shrug. "He's about twenty minutes away. Just in time for dinner."

"Does your mom need any help?"

She shakes her head. "I've offered. She likes the kitchen to herself."

Sawyer pulls me gently back against him.

"Might as well finish watching the movie while we wait for

Liam." His arm snakes around me, and I sink into his side. "You okay?" he whispers into my ear. I nod, not wanting to tell him of my embarrassment. I'm not exactly experienced when it comes to guys. I don't want him to think I'm being childish.

"I don't care who sees me kissing you, Hallie," he whispers. "You'd better get used to it. I don't plan on stopping anytime soon." I look at him in surprise. It's as though he read my mind. He's wearing a contented smile on his face, and I can't help but smile myself before settling back against him.

* * *

An hour or so later and the six of us have finished dinner. Liam arrived shortly after Brooke spoke to him, and it's easy to see how happy they are together. He hasn't stopped touching her since he arrived, and the glances between them show how much they love each other. He seems like a great guy, and Brooke clearly adores him. The conversation over dinner is relaxed, and no one mentions my situation or why Sawyer and I are here, which I'm grateful for.

Once we've cleared away the dinner dishes, it's beginning to get dark outside, and I can't keep my eyes open. Sawyer notices and comes to stand by my side.

"You okay?"

"Just tired. The last few days have caught up with me." I smile reassuringly at him. "I think I'll go up to bed. I'll say goodnight to everyone."

"I'll come with you."

"No, stay. It's still early."

He shakes his head. "I want to be with you."

I reach up and cup his face with my hand. "Spend some time with your family. You don't see them as much as you'd like." I can read the indecision on his face, and my fingers stroke over the stubble on his cheek. "I'm fine, Sawyer. I promise."

He sighs. "I'll come up with you, make sure everything's okay, then I'll come back down... just for a little while, though."

I smile and go up on my tiptoes, gently kissing his lips. "Thank you," I whisper against his mouth.

He takes my hand and leads me into the living room, where everyone has gathered after dinner. Brooke and Liam are sitting cuddled up on the sofa while Sawyer's parents are sitting opposite them in separate armchairs.

"Hallie's calling it a night. It's been a long couple of days," Sawyer says from beside me, his hand still nestled in mine.

"Thank you so much for dinner, Mrs. Mitchell. It was delicious."

"You're more than welcome." She rises from her chair and crosses the small space between us. "And please, call me Sophia." She pulls me in for a hug, and I drop Sawyer's hand to embrace her. "If there's anything you need, let me know."

"Thank you." I wave goodnight to Sawyer's dad, who waves back.

"Night, Hallie. See you tomorrow," Brooke calls from the sofa, and I offer her and Liam a wave before Sawyer takes my hand and guides me upstairs.

"Are you still staying in my room tonight?" he asks as we stop outside my bedroom door. My heart pounding in my chest seems so loud, I swear he can hear it.

"Yes," I mumble. "I'll get my sleep shirt." He watches me from the doorway as I grab a few things. When I've got everything, I make my way back to him. Following him across the landing, nerves swirl in my stomach. I shared a bed with him at the motel the night before, but somehow, this feels different. It *is* different. We weren't together then.

"I'll let you get some sleep. If you need me, I'm only downstairs, okay?"

"I'll be fine. Spend some time with your family. I can see how much they miss you." He still looks unsure. "I'm just going to sleep. Go. I'll be fine," I tell him again.

Eventually, he backs away toward the door. "Night," he says, his eyes fixed on mine.

"Night." When I think he's about to leave, he closes the space between us and pulls me against him. His mouth finds mine, and he kisses me until I'm breathless. When he pulls away, my eyes are still closed, and it's like I'm floating on air.

"Sleep tight," he mutters as he leaves the room and closes the door behind him.

Falling onto the bed, I sigh and brush my fingers against my lips. How he thinks I'll be able to sleep after kissing me like that, I'll never know. Despite that, I'm exhausted and know I need to try and sleep. I change into his T-shirt, climb under the comforter, and close my eyes, hoping I can fall asleep quickly and my dreams won't be full of Matt.

Chapter Twenty-Four

Sawyer

It's irrational not wanting to leave Hallie alone, but I feel better when she's with me, and I know she's safe. Making my way downstairs, I stop off in the kitchen, sliding my phone from my pocket. I need to check in with Logan. The police are working nonstop to try and find Bryant, and I need to know if anything new has come up.

"Logan," I say as he answers my call. "Any update?"

"Hey, Sawyer. I was going to call you. I think we may have something. Wilmot thinks the net is closing in on him."

"Really? How come?" I pace the kitchen, my senses on high alert as I wait for him to explain.

"The car he was driving when he was spotted on CCTV in Hilton Head Island was found abandoned. His prints were all over it."

"Anything in there to suggest where he might be?"

"No, but Wilmot's made a trip to Anamosa State Penitentiary. Turns out Bryant was an asshole in prison, and the guy he shared a cell with was more than happy to talk. Seems Bryant was quite vocal about what he would do if he ever managed to escape. He talked about Hallie a lot and held a massive grudge against her. For him, she's the reason he was behind bars, and he couldn't let that go."

"And Wilmot believes this guy?"

"It's the best we've got to go on at the moment. Apparently, Bryant spent a summer in Savannah after dropping out of college. It was during that time he met Amanda. They slept in an abandoned warehouse until they moved on. Wilmot spoke to Amanda's aunt for what good it did. She was so confused she didn't seem to know what day it was. Thankfully, her memory from back then seemed clearer. He did manage to get out of her that Amanda's parents didn't like Bryant and didn't approve of the relationship. When he'd finished in Savannah, she went with him. Wilmot has a team checking out some abandoned warehouses in and around Savannah in case he's gone back to where he stayed as a kid."

"They think he's somewhere in Savannah?"

"It's a possibility. It'll take some time to get around to all the sites. I'll keep you updated, but Sawyer..."

"What aren't you telling me?"

"The abandoned car. It was found outside your apartment." I can feel the hairs on the back of my neck stand up at his words, and it's as if my blood has run cold.

"What?" I ask in disbelief. "He followed us," I mutter to myself, knowing for sure now that I'd been too wrapped up in Hallie to do my job properly.

"It seems that way. I'm guessing he's been watching Hallie all along."

"He must have thought we were heading back to my place. Thank God we lost him when we left the island." Dragging my fingers through my hair, I pace up and down. "Does anyone else know where Hallie and I are?"

"Just me and Wilmot. You're safe, man."

"I'd better go and check on Hallie. Call me if you hear anything."

"I will. Stay safe, Sawyer." I end the call and silently climb the stairs back up to the second floor. Pushing gently on my bedroom door, I watch a sleeping Hallie from the doorway. Despite only leaving her ten minutes ago, she's fast asleep. Crossing the room, I sit on the edge of the bed, my hand resting on her sleeping form. I pull my phone from my pocket and send a quick message to Brooke, telling her I'm staying with Hallie and won't be back downstairs tonight. She replies with a sarcastic comment which I ignore, placing my phone on the nightstand.

After taking a quick shower, I pull on some sleep shorts and slide into bed next to Hallie. She's still fast asleep, her breathing even. When I turn off the lamp on the nightstand, the room is plunged into darkness. The only light is from a small sliver of the moon that finds its way through the drapes. As I lie staring at the ceiling, the earlier conversation with Logan replays in my mind. Bryant must have followed us from Hallie's apartment to mine, and then from there to Hilton Head Island. I can't believe I didn't notice someone tailing us on either journey. I'd fucked up and put Hallie in danger. Something I swore I'd never do.

Rolling onto my side, I find my eyes have adjusted to the dark room, and I can make out Hallie's face on the pillow next to mine. Her long dark lashes rest on the skin under her eyes, and her flawless face looks so peaceful as she sleeps. I should never have crossed the line with her and jeopardized her safety. I should have waited until all of this was over. But I didn't, and now there's no going back. She means everything to me, and I can't give her up. I'm in too deep. I'm damn good at my job, and I don't trust anyone else to protect her. I must stay focused.

"Sawyer, is that you?" Hallie asks, her voice thick with sleep.

"Yeah, baby. It's me. Go back to sleep." She sighs contentedly and pushes her body against mine. Wrapping my arms around her, I pull her close, her head resting on my bare chest.

"How long have I been asleep?" she asks.

"Not long. I didn't mean to wake you." I brush my lips against her head, and she pushes herself up on my chest, her face level with mine.

Crossing the Line

"You didn't go down and spend time with your parents, did you?"

"No." She drops her forehead on my chest, and I tangle my hand in her hair. "I wanted to be with you."

"Your family must think I'm so needy."

"I'm pretty sure they know it's me wanting to be with you and nothing to do with you being needy, sweetheart," I tell her with a chuckle. "Plus, I know you're safe if you're with me."

She tenses in my arms and lifts her head. "Has something else happened?" Her voice comes out as a whisper, and I tighten my hold on her.

"No, Hallie. I'm sorry. I didn't mean to scare you." I'm not being totally honest with her, but she doesn't need to know we found Bryant's car and especially not where it was. If what Logan said was right, then Wilmot is close to catching the bastard, and I'll soon be able to tell her this is all over. She finally relaxes, and her fingers trace circles across my chest as she lies at my side. My cock twitches as her fingers continue to brush over my skin, and I drag my hand up and down her arm, itching to touch her more. When I can't take it any longer, I flip her onto her back. A squeal escapes her lips as my body slides over hers.

"Your touch is driving me crazy," I whisper in her ear, my lips finding the hollow of her neck. A shiver passes over her body as my mouth brushes over her skin, eventually finding her lips. My hand slips under her T-shirt, and her skin feels like silk under my fingers. She gasps as my finger brushes her nipple.

"Sawyer," she whispers against my lips. I roll her nipple between my fingers, feeling it pebble under my touch. Needing to see her, I pull my hand away and lift her T-shirt up and over her head, tossing it on the floor. Despite the room being dark, I can see her cheeks flush as her arms come across her body, hiding herself from me.

I frown. "Don't hide from me, baby. You're beautiful."

"I've never... I've never done this before," she whispers, her eyes fixed on my chest.

Leaning down, I capture her lips with mine. "We don't have to do anything you aren't ready for. You're in control, baby," I whisper, resting my forehead on hers. I pull back when she stays silent and wait for her eyes to meet mine. She's biting down on her bottom lip, and I know she wants to say something.

"Talk to me."

"I want you to touch me." She hesitates. "It felt good."

Smiling at her, I push a stray piece of her hair off her face. I want nothing more than to make her feel good, but I can tell she's nervous and I want her to be comfortable with me.

"We'll go slow, sweetheart."

She reaches her arms around my neck, pulling my face to hers. She kisses me, and the noise that escapes her lips as I push my tongue into her mouth makes my cock jump. The thin material of my sleep shorts does nothing to hide my erection, and I try not to push against her, not wanting to freak her out. As my lips move down her neck and my mouth finds her nipple, she lifts her hips, gasping as she grinds herself against my hard cock.

"Oh, God," she mumbles, her hands tugging on my hair.

Releasing her nipple my hand slides down to the edge of her panties. "Is this okay?" I ask as I run my finger under the elastic of her panties.

"Yes. Don't stop," she begs, her voice breathless. Chuckling, I kiss her before gently tugging off her panties and tossing them on the floor next to her T-shirt. It's fairly dark in the room, but my eyes roam her body, and my mouth goes dry.

"God, you're beautiful, Hallie. So beautiful." I slip my fingers between her folds, and her back arches off the bed as I touch her. "You're so wet, baby," I whisper against her mouth as my thumb circles her clit. Slipping a finger inside her, my cock twitches when I feel how tight she is. She gasps into my mouth as I push another finger inside, her nails scratching against my back.

"Sawyer," she moans as I move my lips from her mouth to her chest, my tongue circling her nipple. "Oh, God!" she cries out as her walls flutter around my fingers, telling me she's close. Releasing her nipple from my mouth, I whisper in her ear, "Come for me, baby. Let go." I increase the pressure on her clit and pinch her nipple with my other hand. She calls out my name as she comes on my fingers, her whole body shaking. Gently removing my fingers, I hold her as she comes down from her orgasm.

"God, that was... wow," she whispers. She bites down on her lip again, her hands reaching for my chest. She pushes me gently off her, and I roll to the side.

I frown, wondering if I've moved too fast for her. "Hallie," I start.

"I want to touch you, Sawyer," she says quietly, her eyes dropping to my still erect cock my thin shorts barely concealing anything. Her hand reaches inside my shorts' waistband before I can respond.

I grab her wrist, and she stills.

"You don't have to do this, baby," I tell her. "I can wait until you're ready."

"I am ready. I want to, Sawyer. Please." After releasing her wrist, I lean over to kiss her, gasping into her mouth when her hand slides inside my shorts. I inhale sharply as she grips my cock. Her hand slowly moves up and down my shaft, and I drop back onto the bed, my hand gripping the sheets.

"Fuck, Hallie," I mutter as I watch her.

Her eyes find mine, and she gives me a shy smile. "Is this okay?" she asks, her voice betraying how nervous she is.

"It's more than okay." I lean over and capture her mouth with mine. Her hand squeezes me tighter as she strokes up and down my length. It won't take long for me to come with her touching me the way she is.

Needing to feel her, my hand cups her breast, my fingers rolling and pinching her nipple.

"God, Sawyer," she whispers, her hand gripping my cock like a vise.

That familiar ache in the pit of my stomach increases, and I know I will come soon. My hips lift off the bed, and I thrust into her hand.

"I'm going to come, Hallie," I warn before ropes of hot cum

explode from my cock all over her hand. My breathing is labored as I come down from my orgasm, and I kiss her again, pouring everything I feel for her into that kiss.

After several long seconds, I pull back, and I can tell she feels embarrassed.

She has no need to be.

"That was incredible. You've never done that before, right?"

She shakes her head.

"It was perfect," I whisper. "Let's get you cleaned up."

Hallie's quiet during our shower, and I worry that things are moving too fast for her. Climbing into bed, I sigh in relief when she scoots over to me, pressing her body against mine.

Wrapping my arms around her, I kiss her hair softly, her head resting on my chest. "Tell me what you're thinking, Hallie. Talk to me."

My fingers brush up and down her arm as I wait for her to respond.

Mercifully, it doesn't take her long. She sighs loudly before she lifts her head to look at me. "Do you think the girl who was taken is still alive?" Her voice cracks with barely concealed emotions.

"Yeah, baby. I do." I have no idea if she is or not, but I hope she is.

"Do you know her name?"

I jerk up my chin. "Poppy. Poppy Wells."

"I hope she's okay," she murmurs, her words barely a whisper.

"Me too, Hal." She drops her head back onto my chest, and I tighten my hold on her. I love having her in my arms, and this is fast becoming my favorite way to fall asleep. It isn't long before her breathing has evened out, and she's sleeping.

Despite not knowing her for long, I'm falling hard for her, and I want nothing more than to make this whole nightmare disappear.

I only hope we get some good news and soon.

Chapter Twenty-Five

Hallie

Opening my eyes, I find myself tangled up with Sawyer, my head on his chest. I can tell from his even breathing he's still asleep, and I gently tilt my head to see him better. A fine layer of stubble covers his face, and I trace my fingers over his cheek, not quite believing he might actually be mine. My mind goes back to the night before, and I can't help but smile as I remember where Sawyer had touched me and how he'd made me feel. Remembering his touch makes heat pool in my stomach, an ache quickly forming between my legs.

Glancing down his body, I can see his erection tenting his shorts. I might have never been with a man, but I'd read enough romance books to know guys wake up with morning wood. I'd also read enough erotic romance to know how to wake a guy up in the best possible way.

The heroines in the books I read are rarely twenty-four and never been kissed. Biting on my lip, I glance back up to his face seeing he's still fast asleep.

"Fuck it," I mumble. "I want him."

Reaching my hand under the waistband of his shorts, I grip his hard erection, slowly moving my hand up and down. He lets out a moan in his sleep, his hips lifting slightly off the bed as he pushes himself into my hand.

"Hallie," he mutters. His hand cups my face, his mouth finding mine. "What a way to wake up," he whispers against my lips. "Come here." His hands go around my waist as he moves me so I'm straddling him. "Morning, baby," he mutters, his fingers digging into my skin.

"Morning." I smile and lean down to kiss him. His hands come to my hips, and he moves me over his hardness. I gasp against his mouth as his erection hits me right where I need him, and I rock myself shamelessly against him, the ache between my legs building with every move.

"Sit up, Hallie," he says, his voice strained. I do as he says, my eyes never leaving his. His hands stay on my hips as I continue to rock against him. Moaning, I drop my head back as the same feelings from last night begin to build. Suddenly, his hands are off my hips and my T-shirt is up and over my head. He quickly cups my breasts, and I can barely breathe as his fingers roll and pull on my nipples.

"Don't stop," I beg as I reach behind me, my hands holding on to his legs as I push my chest into his hands. My hips move against his length, and I can only hope this feels as good for him as it does for me.

"You look so beautiful like that, Hallie."

"Does this feel good for you?" I ask, my voice breathless.

"Yeah, baby. So good."

"I'm going to come," I mumble, lost in a haze of lust.

"Me too," Sawyer says, his fingers still working my nipples. I feel like my whole body is about to explode. As I fall apart, his name falls from my lips. My orgasm must trigger his own as he thrusts up against me, calling out my name as he comes. His body shudders underneath me, and I continue moving my hips, chasing the last of my orgasm. His hands still me, and I collapse on his chest, both breathing like we've run a marathon.

"Oh my God," I mumble into his chest. His arms wrap around me as he chuckles against my skin.

"That good, hey, baby?" he asks, his voice cocky.

"Well, I've nothing to compare it to other than BOB, but yeah. Wow."

"Who the hell is Bob?" he asks, rolling me so he's on top, his weight pressing me against the mattress. I can't help but smile when he frowns at me.

"Jess introduced me to BOB around six months ago. It was her gift to me last Christmas." His frown turns to a look of confusion, and I giggle. "BOB," I repeat. "My battery-operated boyfriend." Heat rushes to my cheeks as I admit to owning a vibrator.

"Your what?"

"My battery-operated boyfriend." I raise my eyebrows, but he still doesn't get it. "My vibrator, Sawyer."

His eyes widen as a smile forms on his lips. "You have a vibrator?"

"Is that such a big surprise?"

"Yes. No. I mean..." he trails off and licks his lips. "And you use it?"

Laughing, I nod. "Yeah, I use it. I think Jess brought it as a bit of a joke when I kept refusing to date. Believe me, the joke was on her!" I wiggle my eyebrows at him, and his mouth falls open in shock.

"That I need to see," he mutters before kissing me like I'm the air he needs to breathe. Nervous excitement swirls in my stomach as I think of using my vibrator in front of him. I'm not sure I'd be able to, and as good as it feels when I use it, it's nothing compared to how he makes me feel when he touches me. Pulling out of the kiss, I can feel him hard against me again.

"Already?" I ask in surprise, my eyes widening.

He laughs and rolls off me, tucking a stray piece of hair off my face. "It's you. I can't keep my hands off you, and all that talk of BOB got me worked up." He climbs off the bed and adjusts himself before walking over to the window. He opens the drapes, and light floods the room.

I know without a shadow of a doubt he would do anything to keep me safe, and I'm beginning to think it isn't because he's paid to. I can feel how much he cares about me every time he kisses me, and I hope he knows I feel the same. I'm falling in love with him, and as much as that scares me, I pray to God he feels the same, and when all this is over, we can be together. I'm not sure I'd survive him walking away.

Thirty minutes later, we're both showered and ready to head downstairs. My stomach chooses that moment to rumble, and Sawyer laughs. "Hungry, babe?" I nod, and he reaches for my hand. "Let's get you fed." I'm nervous as we make our way downstairs. Everyone was so nice to me yesterday. I have no reason to be nervous, but I can't help how I feel.

"Do you think I'd be able to call Jess later?" I ask as we walk hand in hand down the stairs.

"Of course. You can use my phone." He stops, and I turn to face him. "You can't tell her where we are though, Hallie. The fewer people who know, the safer you are. Okay?" I nod, knowing he's right but also knowing Jess would never give away where we were. As if reading my mind, he squeezes my hand. "I know you trust her, but it's safer this way."

"Okay," I whisper. He leans down and brushes his lips across mine.

"It sucks, I know."

"Who does know we're here?" I ask, wondering if *anyone* knows where we are.

"Just Logan and Detective Wilmot."

"And you trust them?"

"With my life, baby." He gives me a sad smile before tugging on my hand, encouraging me down the stairs. "Enough shop talk. Let's go eat and see what my sister has planned for us today."

"Your sister has plans for us?" I ask in surprise. "How can she have plans for us? She didn't know we'd be here."

"Brooke always has plans. It likely involves the lake."

"Can we go?" I ask, excitement bubbling in my stomach. "Is it safe?"

"Yeah, we can go. We'll stay on this side of the lake and close to the cabin. It'll be fine. Plus, I get to see you in a bikini again." He wriggles his eyebrows, and I hit him gently on his arm.

"Pervert," I tell him, laughing.

"Who's a pervert?" a voice asks from behind, and my eyes widen as I realize Sawyer's dad has followed us down the stairs.

"Me, Dad. I'm the pervert. According to Hallie anyway." He laughs, and I want the ground to literally open up and swallow me.

"Sawyer!" I mutter, glaring at him.

"I don't think I want to know," Sawyer's dad says with a smile on his lips. "Come on. Your mom's made pancakes." My stomach growls again, and they both laugh. "I think your girl needs feeding," he says, slapping Sawyer on the shoulder.

Sawyer had been right about Brooke's plans for a day at the lake. We'd barely sat at the kitchen table before she's excitedly talking about swimming and sunbathing. Her excitement is infectious, and despite what had forced us to come to the cabin, I have to admit, I am looking forward to a day relaxing in the sun.

After eating far too many blueberry pancakes, Sawyer and I make our way back upstairs to change into something suitable for a day at the lake. I put on one of the bikinis Brooke brought to my room yesterday, and she also loaned me one of her cover-ups to wear.

When Sawyer comes to my room, he looks hot in his black swimming shorts, and I already can't wait to be alone with him later.

Making our way outside, we head toward a path that winds through a small wooded area. It suddenly opens up, and a small sandy beach comes into view. A wooden jetty juts out, and a small rowboat is tied up and bobbing in the water next to it. It looks like something from a picture postcard. It's that beautiful. It's only now that I realize how isolated the cabin is. There's only one other cabin edging the lake, and it sits on the other side of the water. It's not a big lake, and you could easily swim from one side to the other, but it's perfect.

"This is beautiful," I say to Brooke, who had linked her arm with mine as we walked the short distance from the cabin. Sawyer and Liam, who are behind us, have carried armfuls of beach paraphernalia, including loungers and umbrellas.

"I love the lake. I don't come here nearly enough. I forget how stunning it is."

"I bet you had fun here as a kid."

"We did. We spent every summer here. The Coopers owned the cabin across the lake, and they had two kids similar in age to me and Sawyer. We spent hours at each other's places and down here on the lake."

"Do they still live there?" I ask, glancing across the water at the impressive-looking cabin. It looks even bigger than Sawyer's parents' cabin.

"No, they sold it a few years back. It's empty at the moment, and the new owners are overseas."

"I'd love to own a place like this to escape to," I say wistfully, knowing my teenage years would have been entirely different from Brooke's.

She bumps her shoulder with mine. "I'm sure Sawyer will bring you here again. He seems pretty smitten."

I smile at her before glancing over at Sawyer, who is setting up the loungers and umbrellas with Liam. He must feel my eyes on him as he looks across at me, a smile coming over his face.

"See? Smitten," Brooke whispers in my ear, and Sawyer winks at me, unaware of what his sister has said. I want to tell her I'm equally as smitten with him, but I don't. I don't want to jinx anything.

Brooke makes her way over to Liam, and I turn to look out over the lake. It really is stunning. Walking away from everyone, I slip off my shoes and make my way down the jetty. Wooden posts stick up out of the water every few feet, and I brush my hand against them as I walk past. When I reach the end, I sit with my feet dangling over the edge. The water is cold, but it's a welcome relief from the hot sun, and I gently run my feet back and forward in the water.

Despite the sun beating down on me, I shiver as my mind wanders to Matt and everything that's happened over the past forty-eight hours. Finding out yesterday my apartment had been trashed devastated me. It was the one place where I'd felt safe. Even when all this is over and that asshole is caught, I don't know if I could go back to living there knowing *he'd* been through all my stuff.

As much as I love being here at the cabin, I want my life back, and with each passing day, it seems to be getting further and further out of reach.

Chapter Twenty-Six

Sawyer

As I lie on the sun lounger, my eyes are fixed on Hallie as she sits on the edge of the jetty, her feet dangling in the water. It's taking everything in me to stay on the lounger and not go to her. I can only imagine how difficult the past couple of weeks—particularly the last forty-eight hours—have been, and I'm trying to give her some space. I've no idea if space is what she wants or needs, but she's struggling, and I don't want to overwhelm her.

I wait a little while before my desire to know she's okay wins out, and I make my way down the jetty toward her.

"You okay?" I ask as I sit next to her, my thigh pressing against hers. She nods before dropping her head on my shoulder. We sit in silence for a few minutes, and I worry I've let her overthink things for too long. Time to take her mind off everything.

"Do you want to go for a swim?" I ask, my hand stroking the skin of her bare thigh.

"I'd love to." She lifts her head from my shoulder and presses her lips to my cheek. Slipping my hand around her neck, I capture her lips with mine. My fingers tangle in her hair as I deepen the kiss, my tongue dueling with hers. Pulling away, I rest my forehead on hers, my breathing labored.

"I'd better stop before I get carried away," I tell her with a wink. She giggles as I stand, then I hold out my hand for her. Pulling her to her feet, I remove her cover-up and drop it on the jetty. My cock jumps as I take in her pale blue string bikini that leaves little to the imagination.

"I think I need to get in the water and cool down," I mutter, unable to take my eyes off her gorgeous body. Her eyes track over my chest, and from the look on her face, I can tell she's as affected by me as I am by her, and I love that she is.

Suddenly, she takes my hand and pulls me with her off the end of the jetty. A scream escapes from her as we hit the lake's cool water. I break the surface and laugh as Hallie gasps at how cool the water is—pretty sure she wasn't expecting the temperature to be this cold. She swims over to me, throwing her arms around my neck.

"It's freezing," she squeals as her legs come around my waist. My hands go under her, and I pull her into my chest. The cold water has pebbled her nipples, and I can feel them through the thin material of her bikini top. Despite the chilly water, holding her in my arms makes my cock hard. She must be able to feel it through my shorts.

"Do you want to get out?" I ask, hoping she says no.

She shakes her head and rolls her hips against mine.

"I've suddenly warmed up," she whispers, and I drop my forehead to hers.

"I wish we were alone."

She looks back to the beach. "It looks like Brooke and Liam are busy themselves," she says with a chuckle. I glance to the beach and wish I hadn't when I see my sister making out with Liam. Hallie rolls her hips against mine again, and all thoughts of Brooke disappear. All I can focus on is the beautiful woman in my arms. Her hands go into my hair before she drops her lips to mine. Her tongue slips into my mouth, and I kiss her like a man possessed. I don't want to kiss anyone other than Hallie for the rest of my life. Admitting that to myself should scare the shit out of me. Instead, it simply feels right.

Needing to stop before things go further than I know she's ready for, I pull back and let her catch her breath. "Maybe we should get out and dry off before we're missed."

She gives me a shy smile. "Can I sleep in your room again tonight?" she asks me, her voice full of uncertainty.

"Baby, you never have to ask me that. If I had my way, you'd spend every night for the rest of your life in my bed." Her eyes widen at my admission. "I'm falling in love with you, Hallie."

Her lips turn up in the most breathtaking smile before she buries her face into my neck. Tightening my hold, I pull her closer to me, giving her a moment to process what I've dropped on her. I didn't expect her to say the words back to me, but I couldn't hold in my feelings any longer. We haven't known each other long, and our relationship hasn't started in the most conventional of ways, but I've never felt like this before. I had to tell her how I feel.

"I'm falling in love with you too, Sawyer," she says as she slowly lifts her head and looks at me.

"What?" I ask in disbelief.

She smiles, and her mouth goes to my ear. "I love you too," she whispers.

Closing my eyes, I squeeze her tightly, my heart pounding in my chest. I can barely believe she feels the same way. Despite holding her close, she shivers when I swim to the jetty with her in my arms.

"Let's get out and warm up," I tell her as she pulls herself out of the water and onto the jetty. Following her, I grab the cover-up I tossed aside earlier and reach for her hand. I'm smiling like an idiot as we walk back toward where Brooke and Liam are each on a lounger, but I can't help myself after what Hallie and I just shared. Glancing across, Hallie's smiling as widely as I am. I snake my arm around her waist and pull her into my side, brushing my lips against her cheek.

"Where have you two been?" Brooke asks over her sunglasses, a smile playing on her lips.

Crossing the Line

"For a swim," I reply, my fingers squeezing Hallie's hip. Brooke smiles knowingly and pushes her glasses back up her nose. She looks between us before turning to Liam.

"Babe, will you run back to the house and grab the prosecco and some glasses? Looks like we're celebrating."

Liam's brows are furrowed in confusion, and I can't help but laugh. "What are we celebrating?" he asks, looking from Hallie to me then back to Brooke.

"Love, Liam. We're celebrating love," Brooke tells him.

He still looks confused, but he's been with my sister long enough not to question her crazy. Hallie wraps her arm around my waist, and I press her closer into my side.

"If you say so, sweetheart," Liam says, standing from his lounger.

"Don't forget the glasses," Brooke reminds him. "There are plastic ones in the pantry."

He begins to make his way toward the house when I shout to him, "Just three glasses, Liam. I'm working."

He raises his hand in acknowledgment, and I turn to Hallie, who frowns.

"I hate that we have all this shit hanging over us," she says sadly.

I turn and cup her face in my hands. "We're not thinking about any of that. Not today."

"I'm always thinking about it," she whispers, a single tear tracking down her cheek. I wipe her tear with my thumb. I wish I could tell her something good to make it go away, but I can't. All I can do is hold her and wipe her tears. She closes her eyes, and when she opens them, she gives me a small smile.

"You're right. I'm sorry. I'm not going to think about *him* today."

"Don't apologize. You never need to say sorry."

"Hey, Sawyer! Can I borrow Hallie?" Brooke calls from her lounger.

"I think I can share her for a few minutes," I reply with a smile.

My sister rolls her eyes at me before gesturing for Hallie to sit on the lounger next to her. Laughing, I take the one next to Liam and leave the girls to talk.

Reaching into the bag I brought with me from the cabin, I feel for my phone, my hand brushing past my gun as I search for it. Despite having a day by the lake, I can't let my guard down for a single second. I'm still Hallie's CPO. She has no idea I have my gun with me, and I've no intention of her finding out. I know how much she hates it. Finding my phone, I check for messages, relieved when I haven't got any. Whenever I speak to Logan lately, it seems to be bad news.

"Hey, man. I brought you a soda," Liam says as he passes me, his arms full of glasses, prosecco, and Bud.

"Thanks, Liam." I reach over to his lounger, where he's dropped all he was carrying, scooping up my soda. Brooke grabs the prosecco and quickly pours three glasses, passing one to Liam and one to Hallie.

"To being in love," Brooke exclaims as she holds her glass in the air. My eyes find Hallie, and I wink at her. She smiles back and holds up her glass.

"To being in love," Hallie repeats Brooke's words, and Liam raises his glass.

The girls continue with their conversation, and I'm guessing with how animated Brooke is, they are talking weddings. Brooke's been planning her wedding since she was about five, and from what Mom's told me, it's going to be an elaborate affair. She always wanted the big white wedding, and she's finally getting her dream. I'm happy for her. I'm happy for both of them.

"We're going for a swim," Brooke announces as she grabs Hallie's hand, pulling her toward the lake. Hallie looks over her shoulder at me, raising her hand in a wave as she's pulled along by Brooke. I grin and wave back, loving how happy and carefree she is. It won't last. Eventually, reality will catch up with her, but for now, she's happy, and I love seeing her this way.

I turn to Liam, and we chat about his bachelor party, which is happening next weekend. He's flying to Vegas for a few nights. I've been invited, but with work, I can't commit to going. I can't leave Hallie, and Liam gets that. Talking about Liam's bachelor party makes me realize I have no idea what Brooke has planned for her bachelorette party.

"So, you're off to Vegas," I say to Liam. "What's Brooke doing for her bachelorette party?"

"She's coming up here with the girls. There are about ten of them, I think. They've got some pampering shit organized or something," he replies, drinking down what's left of his prosecco. He reaches under his lounger and grabs a bottle of Bud. "You sure you don't want one?" he asks, gesturing to the bottle in his hand.

"I'm good," I tell him, glancing out to the water where Brooke and Hallie are deep in conversation. My stomach drops as I realize we can't stay at the cabin. If Brooke's having friends over, too many people will know where we are. Hallie's name and photograph have been splashed all over the news. There's no way people wouldn't recognize her, and I can't ask my sister to cancel her bachelorette party. I need to think of somewhere else we can go if this shit isn't over by then.

I drag my hand through my hair and sigh.

"You look worried. What's wrong?" Liam asks.

"We can't be here if Brooke is having her friends over. It's too dangerous," I explain.

"Fuck. Do you think you will still need to be here then?" Liam asks, suddenly grasping the implications of us being here with a load of Brooke's friends.

"I hope not, but it's a possibility, yeah. I'll find somewhere else to take her. I can't have that many people knowing where we are."

"What about your place?" I look over at him and shake my head.

"The guy after Hallie knows where I live. We can't go there. I'll think of something, even if it's a safe house."

"Will it be harder to protect her now that you're together? I couldn't imagine some psycho coming after Brooke. I'd want to kill the guy."

"Believe me, I want to kill the bastard for what he's done to her." I sit up and look out to the water, checking on Hallie. "I've never fallen for a client before. It's not something my boss will be too happy about. I'll do whatever it takes to protect her, though. There's no way that asshole is getting anywhere near her."

Liam slaps me on the back. "I couldn't do your job, man." I can't bring myself to respond to him as I'm not sure I *want* to do it anymore. The longer I spend with Hallie, the more I question my career. I would do anything to keep her safe, but when this is all over and Logan hands me my next assignment, the idea of leaving Hallie for God knows how long makes me feel ill.

After the girls finish their swim, we head back to the cabin for lunch. My parents join us back at the lake after we've all eaten, and the afternoon is spent sunbathing, swimming, and having fun. Seeing Hallie so relaxed with my family is gratifying. She was nervous about meeting them when they showed up unannounced, but she didn't need to be. My whole family loves her like I knew they would.

Seeing that neither my mom nor my sister is monopolizing Hallie, I jump up from my lounger and head over to her. She has her back to the beach and is looking out over the water. I slide my hands around her waist and pull her back into my chest. She stiffens in my arms for a few seconds before recognizing it's me. Her body sags against mine, and she drops her head back.

"Hey, beautiful. I missed you," I mutter against the soft skin of her neck.

She chuckles and turns around in my arms. "You missed me? I've been right here all afternoon." She loops her arms around my neck, a wide smile on her face.

"You haven't been right *here*," I tell her as I pull her even closer to me. "My mom and sister have monopolized you all afternoon."

She laughs and shakes her head. "Well, you get me all night," she whispers, and my mouth instantly goes dry.

"Do I now? Where has my innocent Hallie gone?" I ask, my voice barely above a whisper. She giggles and drops her head on my chest.

"It's you. You make me crazy." She lifts her head, and I capture her lips with mine. I'm about to deepen the kiss when she pulls away. "Sawyer, your parents," she mutters.

"What about them?"

"They're right there." She's avoiding looking at me, and I stay silent until she looks up.

"Hallie, I've told you before, I don't care who sees me kissing you. I'm not going to not kiss you because my parents are here, and when this is over and we're with your parents, I'll be kissing you then too." Her eyes widen, and I chuckle. "You better get used to it, baby."

I dip my head and take her lips again. This time she doesn't pull away. Her hands are in my hair, her tongue pushing into my mouth. As her moans vibrate my lips, I run my hands over the bare skin of her back.

I pull out of the kiss before I get carried away and watch as she catches her breath, her eyes sparkling.

"Did you know Brooke is having her bachelorette party here at the cabin next weekend?" she asks me.

"I didn't until Liam told me earlier today."

"She invited me. I've never been to a bachelorette party."

Excitement dazzles in her eyes, and it breaks my heart knowing I have to tell her she can't go. "Do you think we'll still be here next weekend?"

I sigh and take a step back from her before running my hand through my hair. "I don't know, sweetheart. If Bryant is caught, then we'll be able to go home." I pause and take her hands in mine. "Hallie, if he hasn't been caught, we can't stay at the cabin if Brooke is having her bachelorette party here. Too many people will know where you are. It wouldn't be safe." Her face falls, and I want to take it back and tell her she can go, but I can't.

"Where will we go?" she whispers, her eyes wide with fear.

"Somewhere safe. I will *always* keep you safe." She nods sadly, and I pull her against me, wishing not for the first time today that I could take all her hurt and fear away. "If he's caught, I'll drive you back up here myself, okay?" It's not ideal, but it's the best I can do at the moment.

"Okay, thank you," she mutters before going up on her tiptoes and kissing me. "You can't stay, though. It's no guys."

I laugh. "I know, Hal." I brush the back of my hand against her cheek, and she leans into me. "It's going to kill me to be away from you for that long, though."

"Me too. Maybe I can sneak you into my room." She wiggles her eyebrows up and down, and I laugh.

"I might hold you to that." Turning back to the beach, everyone is packing up. "Looks like we're heading back." I tug on her hand, and when she doesn't move, I look back at her, seeing she's looking out over the water.

"Everything okay?" I ask, my eyes following her gaze.

"Yeah. I thought—"

"Hey, Sawyer, if you can put Hallie down for five minutes, Liam could do with your help," Brooke shouts from behind us, interrupting Hallie.

I take no notice and concentrate on Hallie. "You thought what?" I ask with a frown.

"I thought..." She shakes her head and turns, smiling at me. "I think I'm seeing things. Come on." She walks past me, and I reach for her arm, stopping her.

"Hallie, what do you think you saw?"

She looks over her shoulder at me and out across the water again. "Brooke said earlier the cabin across the lake is empty. I thought I saw someone moving around inside. Maybe it's the new owners. Or maybe I've had too much sun, and I'm seeing things."

I'm suddenly on high alert and quickly turn her so she's behind me. My eyes frantically search the cabin's windows, looking for movement.

"Sawyer," Hallie whispers, her fingers digging into my waist.

Crossing the Line

Turning, I take her hand and walk her toward where Liam, Brooke, and my parents are waiting for us. Reaching for my bag that's still sitting on the sand, I pull out my T-shirt and turn, slipping it over Hallie's head. My hand goes back in the bag and straight to my gun, and Hallie gasps as I pull it out.

"Leave the loungers. We need to get inside. Now," I announce, already walking Hallie toward the track that leads back to the cabin. I can feel her shaking next to me, and I know she's figured out what I'm thinking. I also know she's panicking. I squeeze her hand to try and reassure her, my eyes darting around us as we make the short walk back to the cabin. I quickly glance over my shoulders to make sure everyone is following, breathing a sigh of relief when they are. As soon as we're in the cabin, I can take her in my arms and calm her down. But right now, my priority is to get her somewhere safe.

I have no idea if the cabin across the water is empty or not. The last time I came up here, the Coopers still owned it. It's been a while since Brooke was up here though, and things change.

My immediate thought—*Bryant has found us.*

But maybe the cabin's for sale and a realtor's showing someone around. Or maybe it was Hallie's mind playing tricks on her.

But if it *was* Bryant, I had to get Hallie away from him and fast.

Chapter Twenty-Seven

Hallie

"Leave the loungers. We need to get inside. Now," Sawyer says, his voice strained. His hand is still in mine, and before he's even finished what he's saying, he's pulling me along the path toward the cabin. His eyes dart left and right before he looks over his shoulder. The noises around me disappear, and all I can hear is the beating of my heart. My hands are tingling, alerting me I am minutes away from a panic attack. Sawyer knows it too, as he squeezes my hand. I need to get myself under control. Thinking back to the sessions with my therapist, I take deep breaths, counting them over and over in my head. By the time we reach the cabin, I'm calmer than I was, and the tingling in my hands has subsided.

Once we're inside, Sawyer drops my hand and guides me to Owen. "Watch her, Dad."

Owen's arm comes around my shoulder as Sawyer crosses the cabin and opens the door to the den, his gun raised. He comes out and jogs into the kitchen before heading upstairs, returning a few minutes later. "Everyone into the den and lock the door," he says, his voice tight. He stops to talk to his mom, but I can't hear what he's saying.

Crossing the Line

"Sawyer, what's going on?" Brooke asks.

"Please, Brooke, do as I say. Into the den and lock the door. *Now*."

She must sense the urgency in his voice, and she takes Liam's hand before doing as he asks.

"Come on, Hallie," Owen says, coaxing me to move. Letting Owen guide me into the den, my eyes fly to Sawyer as he follows us.

"Sawyer..." He looks at me and gives me a small smile before coming to stand in front of me.

"You think it was Matt I saw?" I ask him. He sighs, and I look up at him.

"I don't know, sweetheart, but I need to find out."

I frown. "What do you mean?" He can't mean what I think he means. He can't mean he has to go over to the other cabin.

"Hallie, I have to go and check if anyone's been in the house. I spoke to my mom. It's empty. There shouldn't be anyone there."

"Can't you call the police? You can't go in there alone. Please, Sawyer. Don't go in there alone." My voice is desperate, and I don't care that I'm begging him.

He closes his eyes and sighs. "It will take the police over an hour to get here, baby. We're too remote. I have to check. If it is, then all this will be over."

"No!" I shout. "What if he hurts you or... worse. Please," I beg. "Please don't leave me." My voice has dropped to a whisper, and I know I'm losing the battle. He's going to go, and there is nothing I can do to stop him.

"I'm coming back. I promise you."

"You can't promise that. He'll kill you, Sawyer. He won't think twice about it. The man is a psychopath!"

"I have my gun, Hallie. It's going to be fine."

In a last-ditch attempt to get him to stay, I say the only thing I can think of that might force him to change his mind.

"What if it's a trick? What if he's trying to lure you out of the cabin, and he comes for me while you're gone?" My hands grip his T-shirt, my eyes wide as saucers. I must look crazy, but I will do anything to keep him here and safe with me.

"Hallie..." Hope erupts in my chest that maybe, just maybe, I've convinced him not to go. "I know you're scared, but I *must* go over there. My dad has a shooting rifle, and all the doors will be locked. There is CCTV covering the front and back of the cabin. No one is getting in here, I swear to you."

My hope deflates at his words, and I know nothing I say will change his mind. Accepting defeat, I drop my head on his chest, silent tears pouring down my face. He wraps his arms around my body and holds me for a few minutes before pulling out of the embrace.

"I'll only be a minute."

I watch as he leaves the room, gesturing for his dad to follow him, and it feels like my heart is about to break. They must be right outside the door as I can hear them talking in hushed tones, but I can't make out any of what they're saying.

Brooke sits next to me and takes my hand. "My brother is the best at what he does. He'll be okay." I don't say anything, not trusting myself not to break down. She continues to hold my hand until they both come back into the den.

Sawyer kneels in front of me. "I'm going to be right back. You're all going to stay in here with the door locked. I've let Logan know what's going on, and he's letting Detective Wilmot know. I'm coming back, okay, Hallie?"

I throw my arms around his neck. "Please be careful." I whisper in his ear.

"I will." He pulls back and kisses me before standing, then walking out of the room. The lock clicks behind him as the room falls silent.

"I'm so sorry we came here and dragged you all into this," I say to Sophia, who has come to sit on the other side of me. My voice breaks, and tears begin to fall down my cheeks.

"You have no reason to apologize. This is *not* your fault, Hallie.

Sawyer knows what he's doing. He's going to be fine." I know she's trying to make me feel better, but I can see the fear in her eyes. I'm sure it mirrors my own. She wraps her arms around me, holding me while I sob against her shoulder.

After a few minutes, I pull myself together, noticing that Owen has pulled up the live feed for the CCTV covering the front of the cabin. My eyes fix on the television, watching to see if Sawyer's coming back yet. He's been gone about twenty minutes, and while I'm focused on the screen, Brooke and Sophia have been trying to make small talk with me about anything from the weather to how many siblings I have. I've tried to interact, but I'm mainly giving one-word answers, my mind swirling with what's happening outside. Although he hasn't been gone long, it feels like an eternity, and I wring my hands in my lap, my eyes darting from the television screen to the den door every few minutes.

After what feels like forever he appears on the screen, jogging up the driveway. Then a few seconds later, "It's me, open up," he calls through the door. I close my eyes in relief, my whole body relaxing when I hear his voice.

"Oh, thank God," Sophia mutters, jumping up off the sofa.

Opening my eyes, I look up as Sawyer enters the room. His eyes find mine as his mom pulls him into a hug. He embraces her, his gaze firmly fixed on me.

"I'm okay, Mom," he says reassuringly. Pulling out of her arms, he crosses the room and drops to his knees in front of me. "There's no one at the cabin. It's all locked up, and there's no sign of forced entry."

"We'll give you two some time," Sophia says as everyone leaves the room, and suddenly, we're alone.

He takes my shaking hands in his, his thumbs stroking my skin. "He's not there, baby," he whispers. "You're safe." The floodgates open, and I burst into tears. In an instant, I'm in his arms.

"God, I'm so sick of crying," I tell him after a few minutes of sobbing. "I've turned into this needy, pathetic mess. I hate it."

"Hey," he says sternly. "You are neither needy nor pathetic. There aren't many people I've worked with who could deal with this the way you have, and believe me, Hallie, I've protected a lot of people."

I give him a small smile and wipe my eyes, only imagining the mess I look with snot and tears everywhere.

"Have I told you how incredible you are and how much I love you?" I ask him, brushing my hand across the dark stubble on his face.

"Not for about an hour." He chuckles. "I'm happy for you to tell me you love me as often as you'd like, though. I love hearing you say the words."

"And I love telling you." He holds me for a few more minutes before I pull out of his embrace. "I wonder what it was I saw, then, if the house is locked up?"

"Probably your mind playing tricks on you. There's been a lot going on, and we're all a little stressed."

I sigh. "Yeah, probably. Maybe I'm losing it."

"No, baby, you're not. Come on. Let's get showered before dinner." I go to get up when Sawyer's phone rings.

"I bet that's Logan." He slides me off his lap and stands. "Hey, man... no, I'm good. It's all clear... I didn't have time to wait, Logan. You know that... she's okay. Shook up." He looks at me and smiles, and I give him a small smile back. It sounds like I wasn't the only one who didn't want him to go over to the cabin alone. "What... no!" He sounds annoyed, and I frown as he turns away from me. "I can't talk about this now. Is there anything I need to know?" He pauses while he waits for Logan to answer him. "Okay then. I gotta go... I will... bye." He ends the call and takes in a deep breath before he turns back around to face me.

"Is everything okay?" I ask nervously.

"Everything's fine." His voice is clipped, and it takes me aback.

"You sound angry."

He runs his hand through his hair and sits down next to me. "I'm sorry. I've just done something I've never done before, and it doesn't feel good."

"What do you mean?"

"I lied to Logan. He asked me if there was something going on between us, and I said

no."

"Why would you lie to him?"

He stands and paces the small space in front of the sofa. I frown, and nerves flutter in my stomach as I wait for him to explain.

"There's one rule Logan has, and I broke it the second I laid eyes on you." He runs

his hand through his hair again before coming to a stop in front of me. "I fell for my client."

"And no close protection officer has ever fallen for their client before? I find that hard to believe."

"Maybe, but it's pretty much his *only* rule. He'd remove me from your case and assign you someone else the minute he found out."

All his talk of *crossing a line* when he first kissed me all makes sense now. I don't want someone else. I want him, but clearly us being together will put his job, a job he loves, on the line. I would never ask him to choose between his career and me. He must see the look on my face, and he pulls me off the sofa and into his arms.

"I won't let that happen, Hallie. There is no way I'll leave you."

"God, this is all so messed up." I pull out of his embrace and take a step back. "I'm going to have a shower and lie down. I need some time alone to think." I go up on my tiptoes and kiss his cheek before turning and walking out of the room. I don't want to walk away from him, but I need some time to get my head around everything.

"Hallie, wait." I stop in the doorway but don't turn around. He sighs, and it takes everything in me not to go to him. "I love you," he says quietly.

"I love you too."

And I do.

I love him more than I ever thought possible.

And I know he feels the same.

But is that enough? It's a question I don't have the answer to, and my head hurts trying to process everything.

Despite shedding enough tears to sink a ship, I climb the stairs with tears running down my face. I suddenly feel exhausted and want nothing more than to close my eyes and forget what a clusterfuck my life has become.

Chapter Twenty-Eight

Sawyer

As Hallie walks out of the den, I drop my head. It feels like she's pulling away, and I hate it. I'll give her some time alone, but I refuse to let her distance herself from me. Not for Logan, not for Bryant, not for anyone.

I find my parents along with Liam and Brooke in the kitchen. They all stop talking when I walk in. "Where's Hallie? Is she okay?" Brooke asks as she rounds the breakfast bar and pulls me in for a hug. "That was some scary shit, Sawyer."

"She's gone upstairs to lie down. I've no idea if she's okay. I doubt it, but she wants to be on her own," I say as Brooke steps out of the hug. "Logan asked me if there was something going on between us, and I lied. He'd pull me off the case if he knew there was, and I can't let that happen."

"You love her, right? I wasn't wrong earlier at the lake?" Brooke asks, her hand on my arm.

"Yeah, I love her."

"Then give her a couple of hours and fight for her. There is no way she wants to push you away. She probably thinks she's ruining your career, and with everything else going on, it's no wonder she needs some time."

"I don't care about the job. I've already decided this is my last assignment."

"Then tell her that. She loves you, Sawyer. I can see it every time she looks at you."

My mom rounds the breakfast bar and kisses me on the cheek. "I agree with Brooke. Give her some time. I've got to admit, after this afternoon, hearing you say Hallie is your last assignment fills me with relief. I don't think I've ever let myself think about how dangerous your job is. Seeing you with that gun..." she trails off, her voice breaking. My dad comes to her side and pulls her against him.

"I'm sorry, Mom. I didn't mean to worry you."

"What are you going to do instead?" Liam asks.

"I think I might apply to the police again."

"Oh, great! Something else nice and safe," my mom exclaims.

"It's what I know, Mom, and I'm always careful. It's time I faced my demons and went back."

"Does Hallie know you used to be a cop?" Brooke asks.

"Yeah, she does. She doesn't know why I left, though. I guess we have a lot to talk about." She offers me a sad smile. "I'm going to take a shower."

Leaving everyone in the kitchen, I head upstairs, hoping Hallie will be asleep in my room. I silently open my bedroom door, my heart dropping at the sight of my empty bed. Crossing the hallway, I press my ear to Hallie's door, but I'm met with silence. She must be sleeping.

After a quick shower, I pull on some jeans and a T-shirt before padding across the hallway to Hallie's room. Opening the door, she's wearing my T-shirt and is fast asleep on top of the comforter. As I walk nearer to the bed, I can see from her red, puffy eyes she's been crying again. My heart breaks knowing I wasn't there to hold her. Sitting on the edge of her bed, my hands itch to touch her. I hold back though, not wanting to wake her.

Crossing the Line

Letting her sleep, I go back to my room and sit on the bed. My head is pounding after the afternoon events, and I rub my temples in an attempt to ward off the headache. A large part of me had wanted to find Bryant this afternoon so this nightmare could finally be over for Hallie. When I'd found no evidence of anyone at the cabin, I was frustrated and angry. It has been weeks since his escape, and we're no closer to catching him. Knowing we can't stay at the lake past the end of the week only frustrates me further. I don't want to take Hallie to a safe house, but I will if that becomes my only option.

Grabbing my phone, I pull up my emails, firing off a message to a contact at the Tybee Island Police Department. Now that I've made my decision to leave close protection, I want to get something sorted soon. I'd loved being a cop, and despite leaving on bad terms, something's telling me now is the right time to go back.

My phone rings in my hand, and I groan as Logan's name flashes across the screen. The last thing I want is to get into it with him about Hallie and me, but I have to speak to him. It could be important.

Sighing, I answer the call, "Hey, Logan. What's up?"

"Sawyer, we've found where Bryant's been hiding out." I jump up, pacing the room.

"So, you've got him?" I ask, almost holding my breath.

"No. Not yet. The cops stumbled across something when they were searching an abandoned warehouse in Savannah. He wasn't there, but he definitely has been."

"How do you know it was him? It could have been someone sleeping rough."

"There were pictures, Sawyer. Pictures of you and Hallie."

"What? Pictures from when?"

He sighs, and my stomach rolls. "Pictures of you both leaving your apartment on the bike, and pictures of you on the beach in Hilton Head Island..." he trails off.

"Fuck! Anything from here at the cabin?"

"No. Nothing."

"Did they find anything else? Anything that might tell us where he is now?"

"No. We still have no idea." I drag my hand through my hair and groan inwardly. We're still no closer to nailing this bastard. "We're watching the warehouse if he does come back. The cops are throwing every resource they have at this, Sawyer. They'll get him."

"I hope so, Logan."

"I'll let you know if anything else comes up."

I end the call, tossing my phone onto the bed. The bastard had been following us. I knew I'd missed something. Sighing, I lie on the bed and close my eyes, wondering how much longer this can go on. He has to mess up soon. This asshole's luck has to run out at some point.

I jolt awake when I hear a knock on the door, realizing I must have fallen asleep. Rubbing my hand down my face, I sit up. "Come in," I call out.

Watching the door open, I smile as Hallie stands in the doorway wearing my T-shirt. "Hey, baby. Did you sleep well?"

She nods, and I climb off the bed. Crossing the room, I take her hand, gently pulling her inside. "You okay?" She nods again, and I can see she's nervous. I lead her to the bed and sit, patting the space next to me. "Sit down, sweetheart. I think we need to talk."

"We do?"

"Yeah, baby. We do." I squeeze her hand, and she sits, a noticeable gap between us. "Nothing has changed for me, Hallie. I want to be with you."

"But, Logan, your job—"

"Hallie, I had already decided this was going to be my last assignment. I want a normal relationship, not one where I'm away from you for weeks at a time. Once this is over and Bryant is caught, I'm resigning."

She turns to me and frowns. "Resigning? But you love your job."

"I love you more."

She shakes her head. "I can't let you do this, Sawyer. You'll end up resenting me."

"Do you remember that first morning in your apartment when I cooked you breakfast?"

"Bacon and scrambled eggs. Yeah, I remember." She smiles, and her cheeks flush pink. I raise my eyebrows as she blushes.

"What else are you remembering?" I wrap my arm around her waist and pull her against me. She giggles. I love hearing her laugh.

"That was the morning I realized how hot you were. I'd known you less than twenty-four hours but found you practically naked in my kitchen."

"Practically naked? I had sleep shorts on," I exclaim with a chuckle.

"Yeah, and no shirt! Sawyer, I'd never even kissed a guy then, let alone had a half-naked one in my kitchen."

I laugh again and hold up my hands. "Okay, point taken. You thought I was hot, though?" I bump her shoulder with mine, and she rolls her eyes. "I'll take that as a yes. Anyway, that was the morning you asked me what I did before I was a CPO, and although I was a little vague, I told you I was a cop."

"I remember," she whispers.

"I loved being a cop. It's what I'd always wanted to do since I was a kid. I'd been with the Tybee Island Police Department for five years before, one night, it all went to shit."

Hallie reaches for my hand, and when my eyes meet hers, she gives me a sad smile. "You don't have to tell me, Sawyer. I can see how hard it is for you."

"No. I want to tell you. It's part of my past, and I want you to know everything about me." I take a deep breath. "I was on patrol with a guy I'd been through the academy with, Noah West. He was a great guy, and we were friends as well as work colleagues. Anyway, it had been a quiet shift, and we were parked when this car sped past us doing way over the limit. I was driving, so I hit the siren and started after him. It didn't take long to realize the driver wasn't going to stop.

It was raining heavily, and we were already doing over one hundred and twenty. Noah said a few times we should stop, but I wanted to get the guy, so I carried on."

I drop my head as that night comes flooding back to me. It's something I've conditioned myself not to think about, locking the memories away in a box in my mind. Hallie brings me back to the present as she squeezes my hand again.

"We hit some water, and I lost control skidding off the road, hitting an embankment, and the car rolled. Noah... didn't make it."

"Sawyer, I'm so sorry," she whispers.

"It was my fault he died. I should have listened to him and stopped the pursuit."

"No, Sawyer. It was an accident."

"An accident *I* caused. There was an investigation, and they deemed I was exonerated, but I couldn't forgive myself. So, I quit. That's when I met Logan."

"You know now it wasn't your fault, though?"

"I think I'll always blame myself, but now it feels like the right time to go back."

"You're going to give up close protection to become a cop again?" She sounds surprised. "Because of me?"

Lying down on the bed, I pull her down with me. "I want a normal life, Hallie. Meeting you made me realize that." Rolling her onto her back, I move over her, my arms on either side of her head. "I can probably count on my hands how many nights I've spent at my place in the last six months. I don't want that anymore. I want a life... a life with you. One where I get to go to bed with you in my arms and wake up the same way."

Her eyes widen at my admission. "You do?" she whispers.

"I do. What do you want, Hallie?"

She bites down on her lip. "I want that too. Are you sure?"

I lean down and brush my lips against hers. "I've never been surer of anything," I whisper against her lips. "Plus, I've lived with you for almost three weeks, I think I know all your bad habits by now." I smile and wink at her, and she smacks me gently on my chest.

"Hey! I don't have any bad habits."

"I'm joking, baby."

She holds my gaze, sadness crossing her face. "I was so scared when you went to check out the cabin. I don't know what I would have done if..." she trails off, unable to finish what she was saying. I roll off her and wrap her in my arms, her head resting on my chest.

"It's okay. I'm fine," I reassure her.

"If he finds us and hurts you because of me—"

"That won't happen."

She shakes her head. "You don't know that. You don't know what he's capable of."

I increase my hold on her, knowing exactly what Bryant is capable of. I hope to God she isn't aware of all he did to those poor girls he'd abducted and murdered. He's one sick bastard, and there's no way I'll ever let him anywhere near Hallie again. I know I can't convince her of that, though. She's scared, and after everything she's been through, I can't blame her.

"Let's not think about him, okay?" She nods. "Do you still want to talk to Jess? You can use my phone while I fix us something to eat."

"Yeah, if that's okay. I could do with my best friend."

I pass her my phone and unlock the screen for her. "Take as long as you need. I'll make us some dinner." I kiss her before heading downstairs.

I find my parents, Brooke, and Liam eating pizza in the den.

"Hi, sweetheart. How's Hallie? Where is she?" my mom asks, her voice full of concern.

"She's okay. She's upstairs on the phone with her friend."

"Did you guys talk?" Brooke asks.

"Yeah, we did. We're good. I told her about Noah and how I'm thinking of going back to the police department."

"I'm glad you sorted things out. I really like her," Brooke says.

"I really like her too," I reply, chuckling. "I'm going to make us some dinner. You need anything?" Everyone shakes their head, and I move toward the door.

"Hey, Sawyer." Turning around, I look over at Brooke. "Bring Hallie down later, and we'll play poker or something. Take her mind off everything."

"Will do. Catch you later." I leave them eating while I head to the kitchen. As we had pizza yesterday, I opt for a sandwich. I'm not starving, and I'm guessing with everything that's happened, Hallie won't be either. I hope she's managed to get a hold of Jess. As much as I want to be there for her, there's nothing better than a best friend.

Chapter Twenty-Nine

Hallie

"I'm okay, Jess," I say after pouring my heart out to her for the past ten minutes. I've told her everything that's happened since we left my apartment. It's hard to believe it was only two nights ago. It feels like weeks. She hasn't asked me where we are, so I haven't had to lie, but I have kept from her that Sawyer's family is with us. I don't want her to join the dots, even though I trust her with my life.

I want desperately to tell her about Sawyer, but it makes me nervous after what he said about Logan having him replaced. I don't think I could survive this without him.

"Enough about me. Tell me something good. What's happening with you and Grayson?"

"Oh, he's amazing, Hal. I can't wait for you to meet him," she gushes.

I smile, excited for my best friend. "So, you've been out with him more than once?"

She laughs, and God, I've missed her.

"You could say that! I've seen him pretty much every night since our first date. He's amazing, and fuck, can he kiss..." she trails off and goes quiet. "I'm falling for him, Hallie. It all feels a little too perfect, though. I'm waiting for the ball to drop." I can hear the uncertainty in her voice, and I wish I were there to hug her. She's dated some assholes over the years, so she'll be thinking Grayson is too good to be true.

"Don't overthink it, Jess. It sounds like everything is going great. Not every guy you meet is going to be an asshole. Give him a chance."

"You're right. I know you are. It's hard to put your heart on the line when it's been crushed before."

"I know," I tell her quietly.

"God, Hallie, listen to me going on and on. Ignore me. You've got enough to deal with without listening to my insecurities."

"Jess, you're my best friend. I'll always be here for you, no matter what's happening with me."

"I miss you, Hal."

"I miss you too."

"Where's Sawyer?"

"He's making dinner."

"He's well trained then," she says with a chuckle. "How is your hot close protection officer? I was pretty shaken up when we met him at the station, but even I remember how gorgeous he was."

My face flushes when she asks about Sawyer, and I'm glad she can't see me. She'd know straight away that something's happened between us.

"He's good," I tell her, not elaborating further.

"That's it? Just good? Girl, you'd have to be blind to not see how hot that man is."

"You sound like Kitty. Have you spoken to her lately?" I ask in an attempt to change the subject. Unfortunately, Jess can see straight through me, and she gasps down the phone.

"Did something happen between you two? Oh my God, it did, didn't it?" The excitement is evident in her voice. "Tell me everything!" she screams.

I close my eyes and groan inwardly. "Okay, okay. We may have kissed once or twice." It's not the whole truth, but equally, I'm not lying to her either. She screams down the phone again, and I can't help but giggle.

"I knew it! I'm so excited for you. Do you think anything else will happen?"

"I hope so," I say quietly.

"You like him, don't you?"

"I really like him, Jess."

She will know how much of a big deal this is for me. She knows how difficult I've found it to interact with guys, let alone try to date anyone.

"Hallie, he'd be crazy if he didn't see how amazing you are."

"I love you," I tell her, my voice breaking.

"I love you too. Will you call again?"

"Yeah, I'll call you again in a few days. I've missed talking to you so much."

"Knock, knock," Sawyer says as the door to the bedroom opens.

"Hey, I'd better go. Sawyer's here." I flash him a smile as he crosses the room, a tray full of food in his hands.

"I would say something inappropriate, but I don't want to make you blush in front of him," she teases. "Seriously though, Hal, stay safe."

"I will. Bye, Jess." I end the call and sit down on Sawyer's bed.

"Sorry, sweetheart. I didn't mean to interrupt your call with Jess," Sawyer says as he puts the tray on the dresser and sits next to me.

"That's okay. We were pretty much done anyway." I hand him his phone and take him by surprise when I climb onto his lap. His hands go under my T-shirt, his fingers landing on my waist.

"You okay?" he asks, his fingers stroking my skin. Goosebumps erupt on my stomach at his touch, and I love the feel of his hands on me. I lower my head to kiss him. He groans when my tongue pushes into his mouth. As I deepen the kiss, he pulls me against his hard erection. He peppers kisses along my jaw and down my neck.

"I'll take that as a yes," he mutters against my skin.

"I want everyone to know you're mine," I whisper.

"I want that too." His breath is hot against my skin, and I shiver.

"I wanted to tell Jess so badly I'd fallen in love with you."

He lifts his head, his eyes finding mine. "What did you tell her?"

"Only that we'd kissed. She was telling me how amazing Grayson is, and I wanted to tell her how incredible you are. I'm sorry. I shouldn't have said anything, but I trust her. She won't tell anyone." My words come out in a rush, and I drop my eyes from his.

"Hey, look at me." He waits until I lift my head. "Don't apologize. I love that you want to tell everyone about us, and we can when all this is over. I need to be here with you until Bryant is caught. I'd go crazy if I weren't here to protect you."

"I'd go crazy too," I whisper. He squeezes my waist, his fingers digging into my skin. "As much as I want to strip you naked and make love to you, you're not ready for that. So, let's eat, and then Brooke wants to play poker if you're up for it?"

Heat pools in my stomach at his admission, and his eyes drop to my mouth when my tongue darts out to lick my lips. As nervous as I am, I want to be with him. I've waited forever to meet the perfect guy, and now that I have, I don't want to wait any longer. I love him, and he loves me. I know he won't break my heart.

"I think I like the sound of your plan better," I say quietly.

His eyes widen as a slow smile appears on his face. "You do? Are you sure?"

"I've never been more sure of anything," I tell him, repeating his words from earlier back to him. He holds my gaze as if he's expecting me to change my mind. I take his face in my hands. "I want you, Sawyer."

He stands up with me in his arms, my legs automatically going around his waist as he climbs onto the bed, placing me gently on his pillow. His body hovers over mine, his hand pushing a piece of stray hair behind my ear before his lips brush kisses against the hollow of my neck. I drag my hands through his hair, pulling his mouth to mine. As I kiss him, my whole body ignites, a now-familiar ache beginning to build between my legs. Nervous excitement bubbles in my stomach, but I'm desperate to feel his hands on me.

Reaching underneath Sawyer's top, my hands find his hard chest, my fingers stroking over his skin. Suddenly, he pulls out of the kiss and sits up, pulling his T-shirt over his head. I sit up on my elbows as he tosses it onto the floor.

"You look so fucking beautiful in my bed. I've never wanted anyone like I want you, Hallie," he says, his voice husky. I bite my lip and rub my legs together, the ache becoming unbearable. His eyes drop to my legs, and a smile plays on his lips. "Tell me what you need, baby." I gasp as his fingers slowly stroke up my leg, my breathing accelerating as he reaches the inside of my thigh.

He stops when I don't answer him.

"What do you need, Hallie?" he asks again.

"You. I need you." I moan, my head falling back onto the pillow as his fingers reach the edge of my panties. My hips rise off the bed as he teases me, his fingers brushing lightly over my clit.

"Tease," I mumble, and he chuckles, his hands leaving my panties and coming under my T-shirt.

"I need this off," he whispers before pulling my T-shirt up and over my head, leaving me in only my panties. His head drops to my chest, his tongue circling my nipple. My whole body is shaking with desire, and I arch my back as his other hand pinches and flicks my other nipple. Leaving my nipple, he peppers hot kisses down my stomach, his tongue lapping at my skin. When his mouth reaches my panties, he kisses my clit through the material, and I raise my hips, silently begging for more.

"My greedy girl." He chuckles as his fingers slowly pull my panties down my legs. Panting, I watch him toss them on the floor next to his T-shirt. He holds my foot, licking the inside of my leg. By the time he's gotten to where I need him, I'm practically trembling with desire. If I weren't so delirious with need, I'd be embarrassed he has his head between my legs. Instead, I'm desperate for him to touch me. He blows on my clit, and my hands grip the comforter.

"Is this okay?" he asks.

"God, yes. Don't stop."

I've barely got my words out before his mouth is on me. I inhale sharply, never having felt anything like it. My hands go in his hair as his tongue continues its delicious assault. When he pushes a finger inside me, I nearly fall off the bed. His one hand holds me down as the other thrusts one, then two fingers inside me. He sucks my clit into his mouth, and I'm close to falling apart. Sawyer must sense it too, as his hand reaches up, his fingers swirling around my nipple.

That's enough to push me over the edge, and it feels like a tidal wave sweeping over me, drowning me in pleasure. Shuddering, I arch against his mouth, moaning out his name as my orgasm hits me. Wave after wave of pleasure rolls through my body, and it seems to last forever as his mouth draws out the last of my orgasm, my legs like a vise around his head.

When the last wave subsides, I drop my legs, my breath coming out in pants.

Sawyer crawls up my body, kissing me hungrily, and I'm surprised I don't mind tasting myself on his lips.

Pulling out of the kiss, he climbs off the bed and removes his jeans. He's not wearing any underwear, and my mouth waters as he stands at the side of the bed, naked. He's perfect. Sitting up, my eyes roam over his broad, tanned chest down to the perfect V that leads to his impressive cock, which is hard and jutting out in front of him. Before I can reach my hand out to touch him, he moves to the nightstand. His eyes are fixed on me as he opens the small drawer and feels around inside. He pulls out a box of condoms.

"Can I put it on?" I ask shyly as he takes a condom from the box and opens the wrapper. I've no idea where my confidence has come from, but I know I need to touch him. He nods and kneels on the bed in front of me. He passes me the condom, and I grip his shaft. He inhales sharply as I touch him. His eyes stay fixed on mine, and I pump his erection, his head dropping forward as his breathing accelerates.

"Hallie…" he whispers, his hand cupping my face. I continue stroking him until his hand rests over mine. "I'm going to come if you carry on, baby, and I want to be inside you for that."

Butterflies swarm in my stomach at his words, and although I have no idea what I'm doing, I take the condom, sliding it down over his erection. When I'm done, he gently pushes me back on the bed, bringing his body over mine.

"Are you sure, Hallie?" he asks, and I nod, knowing I want him more than anything. He kisses me as his hand reaches between my legs, his fingers circling my clit. I push my tongue into his mouth and deepen the kiss as his fingers work me up again.

Suddenly, his hand is gone, and his erection is pushing against my entrance.

"Breathe, sweetheart," he says against me lips, and I realize I've tensed up. He moves his mouth along my jawline, and as I relax, he gently pushes inside me. I gasp as pain hits me, and he stills. "Are you okay?" I can hear the concern in his voice, and I give him a small smile.

"Keep going," I tell him, and he brings his lips back to mine. He pushes again, and my hands go around him, my nails digging into the skin on his back.

"I'm all the way in, baby," he whispers, his voice strained. The initial pain I felt is ebbing away, and I've never felt so full. Wanting him to move, I roll my hips, and he groans as he drops his head into my neck.

"You're so tight, Hallie."

"Please move, Sawyer," I beg, rolling my hips again.

"God, I'm not going to last two minutes," he mumbles. "I promise next time will be better."

I giggle, only to be silenced when he pulls back and thrusts inside me again. There's some pain, but less than before, and soon the pain is chased away by pleasure. His thrusts increase, and I find myself moving right along with him. The now-familiar ache is beginning to build, but it somehow seems like more as he hits the spot inside me that takes my breath away.

"Oh, God. Oh, God," I chant as something builds, something incredible and overwhelming and like nothing I've ever felt before. I thought Sawyer touching me was amazing, but him making love to me is something else.

"Tell me you're close, baby. I'm not going to last much longer," he says, his breath coming out in pants.

"I'm close," I tell him.

He reaches down between us, his finger flicking against my clit, and that sends me soaring. I'm pulsing around his hard cock, and I cry out his name, pleasure engulfing me. My orgasm must trigger his own as he shudders against me, my name a whisper on his lips.

He collapses on top of me, his face buried in my neck.

We're both panting like we've run a marathon, and our bodies are slick with sweat. He's lying on me, and I love feeling his weight pressing me into the mattress. When he lifts his head, I grin.

"When can we go again?" I ask, and he laughs.

"Whenever you want, sweetheart." He kisses me as he slowly pulls out, and I wince at the sting left behind. "Are you okay?" he asks, concern etched on his face.

"Sawyer, I've never been better. Thank you for making it perfect." The back of his hand brushes across my cheek, and I lean my face into his touch. He moves his weight off me, and I miss him already.

"I'll go and clean up. I'll be right back."

He walks across the bedroom, my eyes fixed on his perfect ass. As he disappears into the bathroom, I stare up at the ceiling, hardly believing what's just happened.

I genuinely thought I'd never have a relationship after what I went through. The irony isn't lost on me that it's the reappearance of Matt that brought Sawyer and me together, and I can't ever regret that.

Chapter Thirty

Sawyer

Reluctantly leaving Hallie on the bed, I push open the door to the bathroom and get rid of the condom. Knowing she must be sore, I turn on the faucet, running her a bath. As the water fills the tub, I find myself standing in the bathroom, grinning like an idiot. I've been with my fair share of women, but it had never felt as good as it did with Hallie, and I couldn't wait to make love to her again. I know what a massive step it had been for her, and I hope I made her first time special.

Making my way back into the bedroom, my eyes find Hallie still lying where I left her, eyes closed. I sit on the bed, and she opens her eyes, turning her head to me.

"Hey, you," I say quietly, loving seeing the flush on her cheeks from her orgasm. I lean down and capture her lips with mine, unable not to be touching her in some way. "Are you sore, sweetheart?"

"A little. I like it, though. It reminds me of how good you felt." A blush spreads from her neck up to her cheeks, and I love how innocent she is. I hope I can always make her blush. Standing up, I scoop her into my arms and carry her into the bathroom.

"What are you doing?" she asks, squealing as I lean over the tub. Holding her with one arm, I turn off the faucet.

"I thought the bath might help with the soreness," I tell her as I lower her into the warm water, kneeling next to the tub.

"You're amazing, you know that?"

Grinning, I kiss her forehead. "I have an ulterior motive. I plan on making love to you again and again..." He grins. "I don't want you to be sore."

"Oh?" she mumbles, biting down on her lip. I wink at her before standing up. Her eyes drop to my cock, and it jumps under her gaze.

"I'll get your sandwich, baby," I tell her, leaving her to soak before I'm tempted to climb in there with her. Pulling on some shorts and a T-shirt, I pick up the tray from the dresser and take it into the bathroom.

"You're dressed," she says with a pout. "I was hoping you'd get in here with me."

"I'd love nothing more, but you need to eat. You need to keep up your strength for later." I raise my eyebrows at her, and she laughs, splashing the tub water over me.

After we've eaten and Hallie has soaked in the tub, we head downstairs, spending the evening in the den playing poker with Brooke and Liam. They're all leaving the cabin early in the morning, and I can't wait to have Hallie to myself. The evening is relaxed, and I'm grateful no one mentions what happened earlier.

As darkness falls, Brooke and Liam say goodnight, leaving us alone. There's a movie playing on the television, but neither of us is watching it.

"Do you want to head up to bed?" Hallie asks as she presses her body closer to mine. We're sitting on the loveseat, and I slip my arm around her shoulder.

"I was thinking maybe we could go in the hot tub if you're not too tired?"

She lifts her head and bites down on her lip. "What about your parents?"

"They're asleep. They won't come down again, and the patio is completely private." Her eyes light up before she stands.

"I'll run and get changed into my bikini."

I reach for her hand and tug her down onto my lap. "Don't bother. You won't need it," I whisper into her ear, feeling her shiver in my arms.

"Oh," she exclaims, and I chuckle as I stand, pulling her with me. "Wait here, and I'll grab two towels."

Leaving her in the den, I run upstairs and into my bathroom. Snatching up the towels, I stop at the nightstand and pick up a condom, just in case.

Ten minutes later, the hot tub is ready to go.

It's dark outside, but small fairy lights are strung around the patio, casting a subtle glow. As I drag my T-shirt over my head, I feel Hallie's eyes on me. I push my shorts down and step out of them, my eyes fixed on her.

"Do you ever wear underwear?" she asks, her eyes dropping to my cock.

"Sometimes," I tell her, laughing. "You're wearing far too many clothes, baby."

She pushes her yoga pants down her legs and quickly removes her top, leaving her in her bra and panties. "Better?" she asks, throwing her arms around my neck.

"Much better. Just let me..." I trail off and reach my arms around her back, undoing the clasp on her bra. Peeling the straps down her arms, I step back and watch as the black material falls from her body. Dropping to my knees, I slowly roll her panties down her legs, watching as she steps out of them. "There. Perfect." Her breathing is labored, and I love how receptive she is to me, especially as I've barely touched her.

Leading her to the hot tub, I hold her hand as she climbs in, and I follow. "Mmm..." She moans as her body sinks under the water. "The bubbles feel even better with no clothes on." She giggles and pushes through the water to me. Her arms slide around my neck as her legs straddle mine. My cock is already rock hard, and as she kisses me, she rolls her hips, grinding herself against me.

"Fuck, you feel good," I tell her, my hands holding onto her waist. Her breasts are above the water, and I drop my head, taking her nipple into my mouth. My tongue flicks backward and forward, and she drops her head back, pushing herself further into my mouth. Her pussy continues to grind over my cock, and it's not long before she's panting, her fingers pulling on the hair at the base of my neck.

"Shit, Sawyer, that feels so good."

"Are you still sore, baby?" I ask as I release her nipple from my mouth. She shakes her head and drops her hand under the water, her fingers finding my hard cock. She lifts herself and guides me to her entrance.

"Wait, Hallie." She stills as her eyes find mine. "I want you to come first, and we need a condom."

"Fuck. I can't believe I forgot the condom. You drive me crazy with need, Sawyer."

"I know the feeling, sweetheart." Her fingers are still wrapped around my length, and I inhale sharply as her hand slides up and down my shaft. Reaching my hand between her legs, my thumb circles her swollen clit. She drops her head again, her hand tightening around my cock. I push two fingers inside her, pumping them in and out.

"You're so hot and tight, Hallie. I can feel you gripping my fingers," I whisper against her neck, my teeth nipping her skin.

"Oh, God," she mutters. Her hand pumps my shaft harder, and I close my eyes, an ache building in my stomach. Needing her to come, I increase the pressure on her clit, my mouth dropping from her neck to her chest. As I suck her nipple into my mouth, her walls flutter around my fingers, and her breathing tells me she's close.

"I'm going to come, Sawyer," she pants, and as I bite down gently on her nipple, she comes, her whole body convulsing. Her eyes are closed, and her chest rises and falls rapidly with her release.

Watching her fall apart at my touch is quickly becoming one of my favorite things.

I reach over the side of the hot tub for the condom I picked up from the nightstand earlier. Moving Hallie off my lap, I step up out of the water, quickly rolling it down my hardness before pulling her back to me. Her hand dips under the water, taking my length between her fingers again, and I drop my head back on the edge of the hot tub. She positions herself above me, and I groan as she sinks down, her wet heat engulfing me. If possible, she feels even better than earlier, and I'm desperate to take charge and thrust up into her. I don't though, wanting her to be in control.

"Sawyer," she mumbles, lost in pleasure. "I can feel you so much deeper this way." She rolls her hips slowly, my fingers digging into her waist as I silently beg her to move. She makes more slow movements, and when I can't take anymore, I resort to begging.

"Please move, baby," I say through gritted teeth.

"I'm not sure what to do," she confesses, her voice small.

My hand cups her face and my thumb strokes her cheek. "Do what feels good, sweetheart. It all feels good to me." She places her hands on my chest. Lifting herself, she sinks back down and gasps.

"Sawyer!" She whimpers as she rocks harder against me, water sloshing over the side of the hot tub. I thrust into her, and her eyes roll in pleasure. I'm even more turned on watching her. Her perfect tits bounce as she rides me, and I move my hand from her waist, cupping one of them, my thumb circling her nipple. She leans down and kisses me, pushing her tongue into my mouth. My hand falls from her nipple and winds into her hair as I kiss her like I'm possessed. I can feel my orgasm building as she continues to move her hips, and I reach my hand between us, rubbing her clit. She gasps into my mouth as I feel her getting close.

"Fuck, Sawyer. I'm going to come," she mumbles, and I increase the pressure on her clit. Her hands are on my shoulders, and her head drops back. Her whole body shakes as she comes, deep moans escaping her lips. Her hips continue to rock against mine as she rides out the last of her orgasm.

Watching her come triggers my release, and I thrust twice, shuddering against her as I come hard. Her name is a whisper on my lips, and I wrap my arms around her as we both try to bring our breathing under control.

After a few minutes, Hallie pulls out of my embrace and smiles at me. "I can't believe we had sex in the hot tub." She giggles.

"A first for me," I tell her with a wink.

"Really?" she asks, a huge smile on her face.

"Really."

"I love that I get to share a first with you."

"There'll be plenty more firsts for both of us, sweetheart," I assure her.

"I hope so." She climbs off my lap, and I quickly sort out the condom.

"You feeling okay?" I ask as I slide up next to her. She nods before a yawn escapes. Laughing, I stand and climb out of the hot tub, wrapping one of the towels around my waist.

"Let's get some sleep." I hold open her towel for her, wrapping it around her body as she climbs out of the hot tub.

After checking everything is locked and secure, we walk hand in hand upstairs, drying off before sliding into bed. Pulling her into my arms, I hold her close.

Despite what brought us to the cabin, I can't help but be thankful for where we've ended up. Lying with Hallie pressed against me, I know I'm exactly where I should be.

Chapter Thirty-One

Matt

From the trees, I watch as Hallie fucks her close protection officer in the hot tub. Her tits bounce as she rides him, and my cock hardens. Pulling my gun from the waistband of my pants, I drop it on the ground next to me, reaching inside my jeans. Pushing them down my legs, my hand goes around my hard length. Pumping my hand up and down, Hallie's head drops back, giving me a better view. It's dark where the hot tub is located, but the string lights give off enough glow to see her outline.

Being locked up for the past ten years, I'd almost forgotten what a naked woman looks like. When I do get my hands on her, I'll be sampling the goods for myself. I hear her cry out, and as she does, ropes of hot cum shoot from my cock onto the ground in front of me. Dropping my head forward, I catch my breath before pulling up my jeans.

Hallie is the one who got away and the reason I was locked up. I won't be making the same mistake again. I need to bide my time and wait until the family reunion is over. I'll have enough trouble with her security guy, I don't need to take on the whole family. I'm willing to bet they're only here for the weekend and will be leaving tomorrow.

I can wait until then.

I will bide my time.

As they climb out of the hot tub, I slink farther back into the trees, not wanting to be seen. I need the element of surprise if I'm going to get Hallie away from her little fuck buddy, who, by the looks of it, has taken his role of close protection officer literally. Can't say I blame him. It seems Hallie has filled out in all the right places over the past ten years. I can't wait to get my hands on her.

As the lights go off in the cabin, I head back toward the lake and cabin across the water. I'd seen the commotion on the beach earlier, and I knew Hallie must have seen me through the window.

I'd gotten careless.

That won't happen again.

Despite the security guy coming over to check the place out, he hadn't found me hiding in the attic, and thanks to the key I'd found hidden under a plant pot, I hadn't had to break in. To the outside world, it looks like the cabin is locked up and empty. And it is. It's just locked from the inside and empty, unless you look in the attic.

It appears I'd got one over on them, and it's one I'm going to use to my advantage.

I have to wait.

Something I've gotten good at.

I've waited ten years.

I can wait a few more hours to exact my revenge.

The wait will be worth every single thing I have been through.

Chapter Thirty-Two

Hallie

After waking early and eating breakfast on the patio with Sawyer's family, we'd said goodbye to them, leaving Sawyer and me alone at the cabin. Brooke had made Sawyer promise to be at her wedding, and I'd assured her he'd be there. There was no way I'd let him miss her wedding, no matter what was happening with me.

The weather is beautiful again, and we spend the day sunbathing on the patio. After changing into swimwear with a pair of Brooke's denim cut-offs over the top, I follow Sawyer downstairs and through the cabin. There is a delicious sting between my legs as I walk, and I can't help but smile to myself as I think back to this morning. Despite being apprehensive about sleeping with Sawyer, now that I have, I can't seem to keep my hands off him. We'd made love again this morning after I woke to him with his head between my legs. Heat floods my face as I remember trying to be quiet, knowing Brooke and Liam were in the room next door to us.

"Why are you blushing, Hallie? What are you thinking about?" Sawyer asks as he slides beside me, his arm snaking around my waist.

My cheeks flush hotter knowing he's caught me, and I giggle, covering my face with my hands.

"You know exactly what I'm thinking about." I groan through my hands, and he chuckles as he pulls my hands away.

"Were you thinking of my hot tongue on your clit?" he asks, his voice low and husky.

My eyes widen at his dirty talk. "Are you trying to drive me crazy? Because if you are, it's working," I tell him, sounding breathless.

Before he can reply, his phone rings, and he groans.

"Hold that thought, baby. As much as I want to finish this conversation, it's Logan, and I need to take the call." He smiles apologetically, and I smile back, letting him know it's fine.

Reaching into the back pocket of my jean shorts, I pull out my phone. Although I can't use it for calls or texts, Sawyer told me if I put it in airplane mode, I could use the Kindle app and read. I haven't read anything in ages, and I'm looking forward to getting lost between the pages of a good book.

Flopping on one of the sun loungers, my eyes flick to Sawyer, who seems deep in conversation with Logan. The conversation is becoming heated, and he drags his hand through his hair before turning to me, gesturing with his head that he's going inside. I stand, knowing he won't want me outside alone.

Stopping on the patio, I put my phone into the front pocket of my shorts and reach for the can of soda I'd brought outside with me. Looking into the house, Sawyer's standing on the other side of the living room, his back to me. As I go to join him, an arm circles my waist, pulling me backward. Screaming, I drop the can in my hand, soda exploding all over the patio. Sawyer spins around as the barrel of a gun is pressed against my temple.

"Hello, Hallie," a voice growls in my ear.

My eyes widen, and fear erupts in my stomach as I recognize *that* voice. It's one I'll never forget and one I hoped I'd never have to hear again.

"Let her go, Bryant," Sawyer yells, his gun held out in front of him.

"Not a fucking chance." He starts to walk backward, taking me with him. He moves the gun from my head and points it at Sawyer. "Take one more step, and I'll shoot. She's coming with me."

"No!" I cry. "Please don't hurt him. I'll go with you."

"Hallie, no!" Sawyer shouts.

My eyes lock with Sawyer's, and I silently plead with him, even though he won't willingly let me go. I can't let anything happen to him. I couldn't live with myself if he got hurt because of me.

"I'm sorry, Sawyer. Were you hoping you'd get to fuck her in the hot tub again? I hate ruining your plans."

Nausea rolls through my stomach, and a cold sweat breaks out on the back of my neck.

"You were watching. You son of a bitch," Sawyer exclaims, taking a step toward us.

"Stop!" Matt shouts, bringing the cold metal of the gun back to my temple.

Sawyer stops dead in his tracks, his eyes flicking to me.

"And I did more than watch, Sawyer. It was hot."

"You fucking bastard."

"Don't worry. I'll make sure she's not lonely tonight."

I gasp at his words, knowing exactly what he's threatening, and he means every word. He moves the gun from my temple and strokes the barrel down my cheek. I move my face away from him before leaning over, my body retching.

A gunshot sounds out, and I scream, praying it's not Matt who fired the bullet. Matt's arm drops from around my waist, and I fall to the ground. A gun falls next to me, and I snatch it up, scurrying backward and away from him.

"Come to me, baby," Sawyer says urgently. Looking up, relief floods my body as he stands over Matt, who's on the floor clutching his shoulder. There's blood oozing from the wound as he writhes in pain. Sawyer still has his gun drawn and pointed at Matt as I crawl across the decking toward him. "Get behind me," he says, and I whimper, my whole body shaking.

"How long have you been watching us?" Sawyer asks through gritted teeth. When he doesn't answer, he presses his foot onto Matt's shoulder.

"Argh!" Matt screams.

"How. *Fucking.* Long?" Sawyer bites out, pushing down harder on Matt's shoulder.

"A couple of d-d-days," he stutters.

"It was you at the other cabin yesterday? Fuck!" Sawyer shouts, and I jump. "How did you get in?" Matt doesn't answer, and Sawyer fires another bullet, this time into his knee. Matt groans, and I scream, shuffling backward and away from them. "Answer me, unless you want a bullet in your head."

"Spare k-k-key."

"Where's the girl?" Matt shakes his head, and I close my eyes, waiting for Sawyer to shoot him again. "The girl!" he yells. "Where is she?" Matt still doesn't answer, and Sawyer reaches for him. "Get up, you piece of shit." With his gun still trained on him, Sawyer uses his other hand to drag Matt across the decking toward one of the patio chairs. Matt screams as Sawyer pushes him onto the chair, his hand pressing into the wound on his shoulder.

"Tell me where she is before I put a bullet in your other kneecap," Sawyer shouts.

"Attic," he groans out.

"Hallie, baby... I need you to fetch me the duct tape from the drawer in the kitchen. Can you do that?" His voice is soft and like the Sawyer I know, and I nod, even though he can't see me, his eyes still fixed on Matt. "Hallie?" he repeats my name when I don't answer him.

"Yes," I whisper. "I can get it." I stand on shaky legs, realizing I'm still holding Matt's gun. It feels like it's burning a hole into my skin, and I want to toss it away from me.

"I have his gun," I say to Sawyer, my voice breaking. "What shall I do with it?"

"Bring it to me, sweetheart." Without taking his eyes off Matt, he holds out his free hand, and I move slowly toward him, pressing the gun into his hand. He does something with the safety and slides it into the waistband at the back of his shorts.

Turning, I run into the cabin, not stopping until I reach the kitchen. Throwing open drawer after drawer, I pull things out, looking for the duct tape. Finally, after what feels like hours but is possibly only a minute, I find it. Snatching it up, I run back outside.

When I reach the patio, Sawyer and Matt are nowhere to be seen. Panic begins to form as I spin in a circle, my eyes wide with fear.

"I'm in the den, Hallie," Sawyer shouts, and I close my eyes, relief sweeping over me. When I get in there, Matt's sat slumped in the patio chair, but there's now blood coming from his head, and he's unconscious. His head hangs down, and I think Sawyer must have hit him with the butt of the gun.

"I've got it," I say, holding the duct tape in the air.

Sawyer finally puts his gun away and brings Matt's arms around the back of his chair. I pass him the tape, and he secures Matt's hands together behind him. He then duct-tapes each of his legs to the chair before taping his mouth. When he's sure Matt's secure, he walks toward me, his face soft.

"Come here." He opens his arms, and I throw myself at him, his arms wrapping around me. Tears streak down my face, and I can't stop them. My whole body is shaking. "It's okay, you're safe. It's all over," he soothes, stroking my hair. "It's all over."

My legs give way, and we both sink to the floor, holding onto each other. I've no idea how long we sit there, but eventually, my tears subside, and my breathing evens out. Glancing over Sawyer's shoulder, Matt is still unconscious, and I'm glad. I don't want him to wake up. Ever.

"Baby, I think the young girl Bryant took might be in the attic at the cabin. I need to go and see. The police are coming, but they'll be a while."

My fingers grasp onto the material of his T-shirt, and a fresh wave of panic threatens to overwhelm me. "Don't leave me here with him!"

"I would never leave you here." He strokes my hair until my breathing evens out and then pulls me up to stand. "Let's get you out of here." He guides me out of the den, not allowing me to look back. As he closes the door, the lock clicks behind us.

Taking my hand, he leads me outside and around the lake toward the neighboring cabin. "I'm going to need to check the house is secure, so I'll be going in with my gun, okay?" I nod, and he squeezes my hand. He knows I hate his gun, but I have to admit, I'm glad he had it with him today.

As we get closer, he reaches behind him, pulling his gun from the waistband of his shorts. Dropping my hand, he makes eye contact, putting his finger to his lips before pushing me behind him. Nerves swirl in my stomach as we stop outside the front door. Reaching into the pocket of his shorts, he pulls out a key. He must have taken it from Matt once he'd knocked him unconscious. Opening the door, I stay close to his back as he checks through all the rooms before heading upstairs. When he clears the upstairs too, he turns to me.

"You okay?"

I nod and point to the hatch that leads to the attic. "How are we going to get up there?" I whisper.

"I'm sure I saw some ladders in one of the rooms. Hang on." He disappears for a few seconds, returning with a large ladder. Putting his gun back into the waistband of his shorts, he leans the ladder against the wall and climbs up, slowly opening the hatch. I follow him and watch as he climbs into the attic. Reaching for his gun, he keeps it low by his leg as he turns and helps me up.

There is power up here, and the light is already on. Boxes litter the large space, and my eyes flit from one side to the other. "Poppy," I

Crossing the Line

shout. "Are you here?" We're met with silence, and my heart sinks. Matt could have been talking about any attic, or he could have been lying completely. "We're not here to hurt you. Matt's been caught. You're safe now," I call out, trying again. Suddenly, soft crying comes from the other side of the room. I grab Sawyer's hand. "She's here!"

Sawyer starts to walk toward where the crying is coming from, and I pull on his hand.

"Can I go? She's going to be scared." He squeezes my hand and nods.

Crossing the attic, I negotiate boxes and paintings, the soft crying getting louder the closer I get. A large pile of stacked boxes is right in front of me, and when I round them, a young girl is sitting on the floor, her knees pulled up to her chin. Her eyes are wide, and her face is pale as tears stream down her cheek.

"Hey, Poppy. My name's Hallie. We've come to take you home. It's over, sweetheart. You're safe, I promise."

Her eyes meet mine, and I can see the uncertainty in them, the indecision on whether she can trust me or not. I remember feeling exactly the same when Taylor found me on the side of the road ten years ago. I'd escaped one monster, and I didn't want to run straight into the arms of another one.

"Are you hurt anywhere?" She shakes her head. "Do you think you can stand?" I hold my hand out to her, and she slowly places her small hand in mine. I pull her up, and she throws herself into my arms. I hold her tightly, silent tears streaming down my face. Pulling myself together, I keep an arm around her and lead her from her hiding spot. I know the exact moment she spots Sawyer as her whole body tenses.

"Poppy, this is Sawyer. He's here to help you too. He won't hurt you." She takes a deep breath, her body still pressed tightly to my side.

"Hey, Poppy. Shall we get you out of here?" She looks up at me, and I smile encouragingly at her.

"Okay," she whispers, her voice shaky.

As we leave the cabin, sirens sound in the distance. Relief surges through me that this nightmare might actually be over.

Matt won't be able to ruin Poppy's life, and I'm sure as hell not going to let him ruin mine.

Chapter Thirty-Three

Hallie

Poppy doesn't utter a word as we walk back to Sawyer's parents' cabin, and I can't help but feel for her. She must have been terrified, locked in the attic, and I know from experience she won't feel like this is over until she's safely at home with her parents.

"Sawyer, do you think it would be okay if Poppy called her parents?" My gaze flicks from Sawyer to Poppy, whose eyes go wide at the mention of her parents, her whole face lighting up.

"Of course. Do you want my phone?" he asks.

"She can use mine. You might need yours." I dig my phone out of my pocket and take it out of airplane mode.

"Poppy, do you know their number?" She nods, and I pass her my phone. Her hands shake as she enters the number, tears tracking down her face as she waits for someone to answer.

"Mom," she whispers. "It's me." I can hear her mom cry out on the other end of the phone, and a tear slips down my cheek. I can only imagine what they've been going through this past week, and my heart breaks for them all. I try not to listen to their conversation, wanting to give Poppy some privacy. I hear snippets though, and Poppy assures her parents she's okay and not hurt.

"Hallie, where are we?" Poppy asks, her hand covering the phone. I turn to Sawyer, realizing I have no idea. I never asked, and Sawyer never told me.

"We're about twenty minutes outside of Summerville. I'll arrange for someone to take you back to Savannah once the police arrive," he says. She relays the information to her parents.

A few minutes later and we're almost back at the cabin. Poppy says a tearful goodbye and hands me back my phone. "Thank you," she says quietly. "It was so good to speak to them. I never thought I'd see them again." Her voice breaks, and I hug her, wishing she wasn't going through this.

"You'll be home soon, Poppy. Are you hungry?"

She shakes her head. "Can I have a shower?"

"I think the police will want your clothes for forensics," Sawyer says apologetically. "Maybe you should stay as you are until they arrive."

"Okay," she whispers, dejected. "Can I use the bathroom?"

"Of course," I tell her. "You can use the bathroom off my bedroom."

"Will you wait outside for me?" she asks, her voice shaky.

"I'll wait right inside the bedroom." She smiles gratefully at me as we arrive at the front door. Letting us in, Sawyer pulls me to one side.

"I'll just check on something, and I'll be right up."

I nod, not wanting Poppy to know Matt is tied up in the den.

I guide Poppy upstairs and show her where the bathroom is.

"I'll wait right in here, okay?"

She gives me a small smile. "Thank you, Hallie." She disappears into the bathroom, and I wait to hear the lock engage before I flop onto the bed. My mind swirls with everything that's happened in the past couple of hours, and suddenly, I feel exhausted, the adrenaline finally wearing off.

A minute later, a tap sounds on the door.

"It's me," Sawyer calls out.

"Come in." He pushes open the door and joins me on the bed. "Is everything okay?" I ask, raising my eyebrows in question.

"He's awake but drifting in and out of consciousness. He's not going anywhere. I've spoken to Logan. He's almost here. He also knows we've got Poppy."

"Logan is coming?" I ask in surprise.

"That's what the earlier phone call was about. He was calling to say he was on his way. He heard you scream, and I managed to tell him what was happening. He's the one who contacted the cops."

"Why was he coming here?" I frown, and Sawyer sighs, stroking my cheek.

"He was coming to see for himself what was going on between us. He wanted to make sure I could still protect you."

"I think you proved you can," I tell him with a sad smile. "Matt was going to take me. If you hadn't shot him..." I drop my head as the memory of what happened floods back. "If he'd hurt you, Sawyer, I never would have forgiven myself."

"Hallie, look at me..." I raise my eyes to his, and he cups my face with his hand. "I'm okay. We're both okay. It's over. He can't hurt you now." Sawyer tilts my head and brushes his lips against mine. He pulls me into his arms, and we hold each other until we hear the toilet flush in the bathroom. "I'll go and wait downstairs. Come down when you're ready," he says. I watch as he leaves the room. He looks as exhausted as I feel, and I can't wait for this day to be over so I can crawl into bed with him and fall asleep in his arms.

By the time Poppy is finished in the bathroom and we've come downstairs, the cabin is swarming with cops, some with guns and some without. Sawyer has positioned Poppy and me on the sofa in the living room while he talks to the guy I'm assuming is in charge. He's only a few feet away from us, but he's constantly looking over to check we're both okay.

Matt was removed under police guard by EMTs a few minutes ago, and I can finally breathe again knowing he's not here. Poppy had burst into tears when she'd seen him, her hand gripping mine tightly until he was taken out of sight.

Suddenly, the cabin door swings open, and Logan walks in. I've only met him once when I was introduced to Sawyer, but from memory, I'm sure it's him. He spots Sawyer talking to the detective and crosses the room toward him. He takes his outstretched hand and pulls him in for a hug. It's clear they're friends as well as work colleagues. Sawyer gestures in my direction, and Logan makes his way to me.

"Hallie, Poppy, are you okay?" he asks, his voice full of concern. "Have the EMTs checked you over?"

"Oh, no… I don't need an EMT. I'm okay," I assure him.

"Poppy, I think we should get you checked over." He gestures with his hand to an EMT waiting in the entryway, and Poppy's eyes go wide with fear. I take her hand and quickly explain that Logan works with Sawyer and is one of the good guys. A female police officer walks over with the EMT and escorts Poppy outside. She turns and gives me a small smile, and I raise my hand in a wave.

"I've arranged a car for you. It's waiting outside." He gestures with his head to the door.

"A car?" I ask, a little confused.

"To take you back to Savannah. This is all over. You can go home now."

"Oh, yes. Of course." I drop my eyes and fiddle with the hem of the T-shirt I put on before I came downstairs. "I thought I'd be going back with Sawyer."

"Sawyer needs to finish up here and then we will debrief. You probably shouldn't wait for him. It's for the best if you take the car." I slowly lift my head, and Logan smiles kindly. "Your parents are keen to see you." I nod weakly, feeling like my heart is being ripped from my chest. The last thing I want to do is leave Sawyer, but I also don't want to get him into trouble.

Crossing the Line

"I'll go and get my stuff," I tell him, standing from the sofa. I look across to Sawyer, who's deep in conversation with one of the officers. Not wanting to interrupt him, I quietly head upstairs.

Chapter Thirty-Four

Sawyer

After filling the detective in on what happened, I look around for Hallie and see the empty sofa in the living room. I saw Poppy go with the EMTs, but I was sure Hallie hadn't passed me. I head upstairs and knock on her bedroom door.

"Hey, I wondered where you'd gone," I say as she swings open the door. She frowns as she steps aside to let me enter.

"Did you speak to Logan?" she asks quietly, her hands wringing together nervously.

"No. He's talking to the police. Why?"

"He's arranged a car to take me back to Savannah. He said I shouldn't wait for you."

My jaw tics, and I want to punch Logan in the face. "The hell you shouldn't. You're going back to Savannah with me, Hallie."

She lets out a breath before giving me a small smile. "I wasn't sure what you wanted me to do. I don't want to get you in trouble."

She looks unsure, and I hate that Logan made her feel like that. I need to speak to him and soon.

"You won't get me in trouble, baby. Come here." I hold out my hand, and she comes to me. "Are you okay?" I lead her to the bed, pulling her down to sit next to me.

"I'm okay. Relieved it's all over." She pauses and looks across at me. "Where have they taken him?"

"To the hospital, but he's under heavy guard. Once he's been treated, he'll be back behind bars." She rests her head on my shoulder, her hand still enveloped in mine.

"Thank you," she whispers.

"What for?"

"For protecting me."

"There was no way I was letting him take you, Hallie. No way."

"How do you think he found me?"

"I don't know, baby. I didn't think anyone had followed us. He'll be questioned when he's been treated. Hopefully, they'll get something out of him."

"Where's Poppy? Is she okay?"

"She's still with the EMTs. They'll take care of her." She yawns. She must be exhausted after everything that's happened today. "Shall we go home?"

"Logan said you needed to be debriefed."

"Screw that. I want to take my girl home. Debriefing can wait." Standing up, I pull her into my arms. "Have you got everything?"

She laughs and looks down. "I'm wearing everything I came with."

"Good point. We did come a little light on stuff. Let's go home." I take her hand, but she doesn't move.

"Sawyer, can you take me to my parents' house? I don't think I can go back to my apartment. Not yet."

I nod but don't say anything. I knew she wouldn't want to go back to her apartment, but I hoped she'd want to stay at my place. I don't want to push her, though. She's going to want to spend some time with her parents after everything that's happened.

When we get downstairs, most of the cops have gone. The detective I spoke to earlier is talking to Logan, and I squeeze Hallie's hand as we walk into the living room. Logan turns as he hears us enter, his eyes dropping to our joined hands. He says something to the detective, who nods and walks out.

"Where's Poppy?" Hallie asks him as we get closer.

"The EMTs have taken her to be checked over at the hospital in Summerville. Her parents are on their way." His eyes flick between us before landing back on me. "Sawyer, can I have a word?"

Hallie drops my hand and takes a few steps back. "I could do with a soda. I'll be in the kitchen."

"Hallie—"

"It's okay, Sawyer," she says, cutting me off. "Talk to Logan."

I step toward her and brush her lips with mine. "I won't be long."

I watch her retreating as she walks toward the kitchen. Turning around, Logan's frowning.

"You lied to me." I can hear the hurt in his voice, and I sigh, dragging my hand through my hair.

"I'm sorry, man. I knew you'd pull me off the case."

"Damn right I'd have pulled you off the case. Fuck, Sawyer. You know the rules. Don't get involved with a client." He sounds disappointed, but I don't regret what happened. I don't regret Hallie.

"This isn't something that just happened, Logan. I fought my feelings for her. I didn't want to get involved."

"She's vulnerable," he yells before lowering his voice. "You made her feel secure when her world was falling apart. The lines have become blurred, and you're both reading more into it than is actually there." I bristle at his words and frown. "Don't get me wrong, I see the appeal. Hallie is beautiful, but this... this attraction... it's not real."

"You've no idea what you're talking about, Logan. This isn't just an attraction. I love her. I know how I feel." He rolls his eyes, and although he's only a couple of years older than me, it feels as though he's treating me like a child.

"You might know how *you* feel, but for Hallie, I guarantee this is an infatuation."

Anger courses through me, and I clench my fists at my side. How dare he say that about me? He's got no idea how either of us feels. "She's been through something traumatic, and you were there for her, that's all."

"I'm not listening to this," I tell him through gritted teeth. I need to walk away before I punch him. "You'll be getting my resignation in an email." I turn to leave, and he grabs my arm.

"You're resigning?"

I pull my arm away and turn back to face him. "I thought we were friends. I knew you'd be pissed I'd broken your stupid rule, but to say all that to me..." I shake my head. "Goddammit! What me and Hallie have *is real*. I want a life with her, and I can't have that as a CPO. Not that I owe *you* an explanation." I look behind me to the kitchen door, hoping Hallie hasn't heard any of our conversation.

"Sawyer—" Logan begins.

"Are we about done here?" I ask, cutting him off. "I need to lock up." I raise my eyebrows in question. "Oh, and Hallie won't be needing the car ride home. She's going back with me." He walks toward the front door, and I follow him. "I want to know when Bryant's back behind bars."

"Look, I'm sorry. Maybe I said too much—"

"Let's leave it there, Logan. I'm tired, and I want to go home."

He sighs. "Bye, Sawyer."

"Bye." I close the door and drop my head onto the wood. That's not at all how I thought this would go. I knew he'd be annoyed, but I never expected him to say what he did.

Not wanting to think about it anymore, I make my way to the kitchen, finding Hallie sitting on the countertop with a can of soda. "That went well," she says, giving me a small smile.

"Shit. You heard all that?"

"Most of it." I walk across the room and stand between her legs. Her arms wrap around me, and I sigh as I hold her close. "We didn't meet like most people do, Sawyer, but I know how I feel. It's not an infatuation. I genuinely love you."

I step back and cup her face in my hands. "I know, baby, and I love you too." I bring her mouth to mine and kiss her softly. My hands wind into her hair as she deepens the kiss. When I pull back, we're both panting. I rest my forehead on Hallie's, and she reaches her hand up and strokes my face.

"I'm sorry he said all those things to you. I hope this won't affect your friendship. I'd hate to be responsible for ruining that."

"You won't be responsible for ruining anything. He's managed that all by himself, sweetheart. I knew he'd be annoyed, but his reaction..." I trail off, not knowing what to say. If I'm honest, I'm furious. I thought after knowing Hallie and Poppy were safe, and my relationship with Hallie hadn't jeopardized me protecting her, he'd be happy for me. Clearly not.

"Shall we go home?" My hands go to her waist, and I lift her off the countertop.

She nods. "I can't wait to see my parents."

Taking her hand, I lead her through the cabin and outside, locking the door behind me. I've arranged for a cleaning company to come in tomorrow to deal with all the blood in the house from where Bryant had been shot. Brooke is coming to the cabin with her friends on Friday, so I don't want her walking into that.

Placing the key in the key safe, I turn to Hallie. "Ready, baby?"

"More than ready."

We walk around the back of the cabin, and I climb on my bike, holding a helmet out to Hallie. She slides on behind me, her arms winding around my waist. My hand goes to hers, and her fingers lace with mine. Starting up the bike, I ride slowly away from the cabin, leaving the nightmare of what happened firmly behind us.

Chapter Thirty-Five

Hallie

The reunion with my parents is an emotional one, and I'm crying before Sawyer even pulls up outside the house. They're waiting on the driveway for us, and I fly off the bike into my mom's arms. After multiple hugs from my parents, I turn to see Sawyer standing at the edge of the driveway. Walking toward him, I take his hand.

"Ready to meet the parents?" I ask with a chuckle.

"I've already met them," I remind her.

"Not as my boyfriend." I wriggle my eyebrows at him, and he laughs.

"I like hearing you call me that." He slips his arm around my waist and pulls me against him. "What do you think your parents would say if I kissed you right now?" His eyes drop to my lips, and my breathing hitches.

"I don't care," I mumble, and he chuckles.

"I think we'd better at least say hello before I start making out with you on their driveway, baby."

"Tease," I tell him, slapping his chest. "Come on, then. Time to face the music."

Turning around, my parents are grinning at us, and it seems they've already worked out something is going on. "Mom, Dad, you remember Sawyer? Sawyer, my parents, Brett and Aubrey."

After answering what seems like a million questions, I think my dad feels like he's grilled Sawyer enough, and we head inside to the living room.

"Saying thank you doesn't seem enough after what you've done for Hallie," my mom says to Sawyer, her voice breaking. My dad wraps his arm around her and pulls her into him.

"She's quickly become the most important person in my life, Mrs. Anderson. There's nothing I wouldn't do for her." He reaches for my hand, lacing his fingers with mine. My mom's eyes drop to our joined hands, and she smiles.

"I can see how happy you both are. It's all her dad and I have ever wanted for her." Tears track down her face, and I go to hug her.

"Happy tears, I hope, Mom," I say with a chuckle.

"You'll stay for dinner, won't you, Sawyer?" she asks, wiping her eyes.

"I'd love to."

After we've eaten dinner, I can't stop yawning. It's been a long day, and I'm more than ready to crawl into bed. I've no idea if I'm staying here tonight or at Sawyer's place. He hasn't mentioned it, and I don't want to ask. Wherever I stay tonight, I've no spare clothes, and I'm going to have to face my apartment tomorrow if only to get some necessities. I can't think about that now, though. I simply don't have the energy.

"Do you want me to make up the spare room, Hallie?" my mom asks. "Or are you staying with Sawyer?"

I bite my bottom lip as I look from my mom to Sawyer. "Umm..."

"I'll give you two a minute to figure it out. Brett, could you help me in the kitchen?" she says to my dad.

"I'd love nothing more, sweetheart," he says, sticking his tongue out at me as he puts his newspaper down and follows her into the kitchen.

Crossing the Line

Suddenly nervous, my fingers play with the edge of the cushion I've placed on my lap, my eyes fixed on my hands.

"Why are you nervous?" Sawyer asks, a trace of humor in his voice.

"What? I'm not nervous." My eyes stay on my hands, not daring to look at him.

"Really?" He takes the cushion off my lap and pulls me onto his knee, my legs straddling his. "You're not nervous?"

"Well, now I'm nervous. What if my parents walk in?" My arms reach around his neck, and I lean my head down, kissing him.

"I think we both know they aren't going to walk in." Pulling his head back, he waits until I finally make eye contact.

"Where do you want to sleep tonight, Hallie?" he asks, his fingers making circles on my back. "If you want to stay with your parents, I totally understand. But you should know, I want you with me."

"I want to stay with you," I tell him. "I wasn't sure if you wanted me to. You hadn't said anything, and I didn't want to assume..."

"Hallie, I'll always want you with me. I told you that at the cabin. Don't ever be afraid to tell me what you want. Okay?"

"Okay," I whisper.

Twenty minutes later, we've said goodbye to my parents and are on our way to Sawyer's place. As he pulls into the underground parking garage, I can barely keep my eyes open. Sawyer must see I'm about to fall asleep, and he scoops me up in his arms.

"I can walk," I tell him as I drop my head on his shoulder and close my eyes.

"Looks like it," he says with a chuckle, his lips pressing against my temple. "I like having you in my arms anyway."

"I like it too," I mutter, my eyes still closed. I must have fallen asleep as the next thing I know, Sawyer is laying me on his bed.

"Go to sleep, baby," he says as I open my eyes. I pull off my top and bra and wriggle out of my jean shorts, tossing everything on the floor. As tired as I am, there's no way I'll be able to sleep unless they're off. With only my panties on, I lie down and smile when

Sawyer groans. The bed dips, his arms go around me, and I press my body into his, knowing I'm exactly where I belong, safe and wrapped in his arms.

* * *

Sawyer makes love to me twice when we wake up, and I want nothing more than to stay in bed with him all day, but I know I'm putting off the inevitable. Sawyer knows it too.

"Do you want to pick up some clothes and things from your apartment today? I need to grab my things too. Maybe we could bring your car back?"

"Yeah. I guess I've got to face it sometime," I say sadly.

"I'll be right there with you, sweetheart."

"Thank you," I whisper, brushing my lips against his.

An hour later and we're pulling up outside my apartment building. It's only been a few days since we were last here, but so much has happened, that it feels much longer. Climbing off the bike, I stare at the building. Nerves swirl in my stomach, and I wring my hands. I don't want to go inside, but I have to. My parents had cleaned up as much as they could, but they weren't sure where all my things went, and I knew the apartment would be a mess. What I was struggling with was knowing Matt had been in there and through all of my things. It was hard to breathe thinking of him invading my private space, a space where I'd felt safe.

Sawyer slips his arms around my waist, and I lean against him, trying to bring my erratic breathing under control.

"I've got you, Hallie," he whispers. "Breathe, baby." I close my eyes and drop my head back on his chest. Taking in a deep breath, I turn in his arms.

"Let's get this over with." Leaning down, he brushes his lips with mine before taking my hand and leading me into the apartment building. "At least the press has given up camping outside," I say as we ride the elevator.

"I'm expecting the news of Bryant's capture to hit the stations by the end of the day. That, and Poppy being found. They might be back."

"Thank God I won't be here." The doors to the elevator open, and taking Sawyer's hand, we slowly make our way to my apartment. "Here goes," I say as I put the key in the lock and push the door open. I'm surprised to find the kitchen and living room are tidy.

"It looks like it always did," I say in relief. "It must have taken my parents hours to tidy up." My voice breaks, and my hand goes over my mouth.

"They love you, Hallie. They wouldn't want you coming back to how it was left."

I nod and pull myself together. "Let's get our stuff and get out of here."

I make my way down the hallway and gingerly push open the door to my bedroom. Other than a pile of clothes lying on my bed that wasn't there when I left, my room looks like it always has.

"Do you see anything missing?" Sawyer asks from behind me. Looking around, I shake my head. My iPod is on my dresser, along with my flat-screen television. I don't wear a lot of jewelry, and only have some cheap costume pieces. None of those seem to be missing, either.

"It looks like everything is here."

"That's great. I'll grab my stuff and be right back." He kisses my head before leaving me alone in my room. Sitting on the edge of the bed, I sort through all my outfits. It seems like all the items of clothing I own are on there. Matt must have emptied every drawer as well as my closet. I hope I can wash what I take to Sawyer's place. I don't want to wear anything that creep has touched.

Throwing what clothes I need to bring with me into a bag, I grab my hairdryer and makeup, looking around for what else I want to take.

"Are you looking for BOB to bring with you?" Sawyer asks from the doorway, his bag and pillow in his hand. He wriggles his eyebrows at me, and I roll my eyes. Picking up a cushion off my bed, I toss it at him, hitting him square in the face. He laughs. "I'll take that as a no!"

Crossing the room, I stand in front of him. "It's already packed," I lie, gesturing to my bag. His eyes light up, and now it's my turn to laugh. "I'm joking, Sawyer."

His face drops, and he pouts. "Tease! I'll wait for you in the living room." He's laughing when he leaves, so I know he's joking, but I reach under the bed anyway, pulling out the box with my vibrator and slip it into my bag. Nervous excitement swirls in my stomach at the thought of using it in front of him, but I push it down for now and continue packing.

Needing toiletries, I pad along the hallway to the bathroom. Flicking on the light, I gasp as I see a note on the mirror written in what looks like lipstick. Fear builds in my stomach, and my breathing accelerates as I read what's written.

I'm coming for you, Hallie, and no one will be able to stop me.
See you soon.

"Sawyer," I yell. "Sawyer, there's something in the bathroom."

Seconds later, he's behind me.

"Shit. Are you okay?" His eyes flick to the mirror before he pulls me to him. Being in his arms calms me, and I know this was written before Matt was caught, but it still unnerves me. "It's over, Hallie. He can't hurt you now."

"I know, it's just..." I trail off and shake my head.

"It's that he's been here. I get it, baby." He steps back, his hand going around my neck, his thumb stroking my cheek. "Move in with me, Hallie? You'll never have to come back here. I'll move all your things." My eyes widen, and I step back, his hand dropping from my neck.

"What?" I whisper. "We can't move in together. We've only known each other a couple of weeks."

"I know I love you, and I want this. It doesn't matter how long we've been together if it feels right." I bite my lip and stare at him. My heart is screaming yes, but my head is holding me back. How can I go from never being kissed to moving in with a guy in just over two weeks?

"Can I... can I think about it? Everything is moving so fast."

"Yeah. Of course, you can think about it." He drags his hand through his hair. "We're moving fast. I don't want to rush you into doing anything you're not ready for."

"I do love you," I tell him, hoping I haven't hurt his feelings.

"I know, baby. Shall we get out of here?"

I nod as he wets a towel in the sink and wipes the lipstick off the mirror.

"I wonder why my parents never saw the message."

"They probably never thought to check in here."

"Yeah, I guess."

"Come on. Let's go. Have you got everything you need?"

"Yep," I reply, snatching up my shampoo and conditioner before meeting him in the entryway. He's picked up my bag from my room and is waiting for me.

"Ready?" I nod, and he pulls the front door open.

"Oh, crap! My phone charger. I'll be right back." I race down the hallway and into my bedroom, unplugging the charger from the wall. "Got it!" I hold it in the air as I meet Sawyer back in the entryway. "You know what's weird?" I ask as we close the apartment door and turn around to lock up.

"What's that?"

"I don't have my boyfriend's phone number."

He smiles and holds out his hand. "Pass me your phone." I pull it from the pocket of my shorts, entering my passcode. Handing it to him, I watch as his fingers fly across the screen. His phone rings in his pocket, and he smiles.

"There you go. Now you have mine, and I have yours."

I grin like an idiot, reaching up on my tiptoes to kiss him. "Thank you."

He chuckles. "If I'd known my phone number would make you this happy, I'd have given it to you sooner."

"*You* make me happy—"

"Hallie?" I hear a voice call out from down the hallway. Turning, I see Kitty coming out of her apartment. "Oh my God, where have you been? Are you okay?" She looks between Sawyer and me and squeals. "You're dating the hot Marine!"

I laugh and roll my eyes. "I've missed you, Kitty." I walk toward her, and she pulls me in for a hug.

"God, I'd forgotten how hot he was," she whispers.

Reaching for Sawyer's hand, I pull him against my side. "Kitty, meet Sawyer, my close protection officer." Her mouth drops open, and I think for once she is speechless.

"Your close protection officer? I thought he was your brother's friend?" I can see the confusion on her face.

"I'm sorry I lied to you. Sawyer was assigned to protect me when Matt escaped. I said he was my brother's friend as it seemed... well, easier."

"You fell for your bodyguard! Hallie, that is so hot." She wriggles her eyebrows at me, and I can't help but laugh. I really have missed her.

"Yeah, I guess it is."

"Have they caught the guy yet?" I look across to Sawyer, who gives me a small nod.

"Umm, yeah. Yesterday."

"Good. I'm glad. I heard about your apartment. I'm sorry, Hallie."

"Thank you. I'm going to be staying with Sawyer for a while. Maybe we could meet up for a drink soon?"

"That sounds good. We could go out, the six of us."

"The six of us?" I ask.

"Yeah. You and Sawyer, me and Nick, and Jess and Grayson."

"That sounds great. Drop me a message, and we can arrange something."

She checks her watch. "Shit, I need to go. I'm late for my shift. It was so good to see you." She pulls me in for another hug, whispering in my ear, "I want to know everything. We need a girls' night! I'll text you." She pulls out of the hug and walks backward along the hallway. "Great to see you again, Sawyer." She waves before spinning on her heel and running for the elevator.

"She's still as crazy as she ever was," Sawyer says as he picks up the bags and slings his arm around my shoulder. "Shall we go home?"

"Yes, please."

My mind wanders back to Sawyer's question in the bathroom. *Could his place be my home?* I think, deep down, wherever he is will feel like home. I need my head to catch up with my heart. I hope it doesn't take too long.

Chapter Thirty-Six

Sawyer

Hallie's made herself at home in the few days since we got back from her apartment, and I love it. Her clothes are hanging in my closet, and her toothbrush and girly shit sit is on the glass shelf in the bathroom. I fall asleep with her in my arms and wake up wrapped around her. I finally feel like I'm exactly where I should be. I've had a couple of girlfriends in the past, but Hallie is *the one*, I'm sure of it.

The news of Bryant's capture and the rescue of Poppy hit *CNN* the afternoon after we arrived back from the cabin. As predicted, the press swarmed to Hallie's apartment, with Kitty messaging her to let us know. I was so glad she wasn't there. She's been through enough without having to face the paparazzi.

"So, Brooke's been messaging," Hallie says as we lie in bed, her head resting on my chest.

"Is she boring you to death with wedding talk?" I joke.

She hits me on the chest before sitting up. "No!" She bites her lip. "It is about the wedding though... kind of." I smile to myself, knowing precisely what Brooke's been messaging her about.

Crossing the Line

"She's asking you to her bachelorette party, isn't she?" She smiles. "You don't have to ask me if you can go, Hallie."

Logan messaged earlier to let me know Bryant had been released from the hospital and was back behind bars in Iowa. There is no reason for Hallie not to go, and I knew she'd wanted to when Brooke had asked her at the lake.

"You wouldn't mind if I went?"

"No, baby. I wouldn't. I'll miss you, but I want you to have fun." Her face lights up with a smile, and I grin back at her. "I can take you. The girls are meeting up tomorrow, aren't they?"

"Actually, Brooke has said I can bring a friend or two, so I've mentioned it to Jess. She's offered to drive."

"Okay, if she's sure. Is Kitty going too?"

She shakes her head. "She's working and can't find anyone to swap her shift with, so it's only me and Jess. I'll message Brooke and Jess now." Her eyes dance with excitement as she types out a message on her phone. I'm definitely going to miss her but I love how much she's looking forward to doing something on her own. After everything she's been through, she deserves to enjoy herself.

"I'll miss you," she whispers after she's finished on the phone.

"I'm going to miss you too." I push her gently onto the bed, bringing my body over hers. "I've gotten used to sleeping with you in my arms." I brush my lips with hers, and she raises her hands, wrapping them around my neck. Swiping my tongue against her bottom lip, she opens her mouth to me, and I deepen the kiss, hearing her moan against my lips.

Moving from her lips, I pepper kisses across her jaw, my tongue brushing over the pulse point on her neck. Making quick work of removing her top, I toss it on the floor, leaving her in her panties. My mouth finds her pebbled nipple, my tongue swirling around the bud. As I bite down gently, Hallie's back arches off the bed.

"Sawyer..." She whimpers, her hands going into my hair.

My mouth continues to move down her body, licking and kissing her skin. By the time I reach the edge of her panties, she's practically panting, and I love how responsive she is to my touch. Slipping my hand inside her panties, my fingers slide through her folds. She's so hot and wet, I can't wait to sink inside her, but first, I want a taste. My fingers circle her clit, and she moans, her hips lifting off the bed.

"What do you need, Hallie?" I ask, my fingers still working her over.

"Oh, God," she whimpers, her arm resting over her eyes.

"Tell me, baby."

"Your mouth on me," she says, her voice breathless. Smiling, I slowly pull her panties off, licking the inside of her thigh.

"Please, Sawyer," she begs, and I blow gently on her clit. My tongue licks through her folds, and I tease her, avoiding where she wants me most. Pushing two fingers inside, her walls grip me, and my tongue finally finds her swollen clit. She gasps and lifts her hips, pushing herself against my mouth. I lick and suck on her clit, my fingers pumping in and out. Her breaths are coming out in pants, and her head thrashes from side to side. As my mouth continues to work her over, her walls flutter around my fingers, and I know she's close.

Reaching a hand up, I pinch and roll her nipple between my fingers as she calls out my name, her body shuddering. Her orgasm seems to last forever as I continue with my mouth and fingers until she can't take it anymore and pushes my head away. Slowly I remove my fingers and put them in my mouth, licking them clean.

Hallie watches me, her eyes full of heat. "God, that's hot," she mutters, breathless from her orgasm. Sliding up her body, I kiss her, knowing she can taste herself on my lips. Her hands go to my chest, and she pushes me, so I roll onto my back.

"My turn," she whispers as she straddles me, her tongue licking and kissing down my chest. When she reaches my shorts, she pulls them down my legs, tossing them on the floor.

I'm rock hard.

My cock jumps as she licks her lips, her eyes on mine. Her soft hand grips my erection, and I drop my head back, groaning as she pumps my shaft, her thumb circling the head of my cock. Closing my eyes, my hips thrust into her hand, and I gasp when her hot mouth lands on me.

"Fuck, Hallie!" I groan, my hand going into her hair.

Her head bobs up and down, her mouth sucking and licking along my length. An intense pressure begins to build in the pit of my stomach, and my breathing accelerates. Knowing I'm going to come soon, I pull her up my body, and she squeals as I flip her onto her back.

"I want to come inside you, baby," I whisper in her ear before reaching across to the nightstand and grabbing a condom. Kneeling, I quickly roll it on before pulling Hallie onto my lap. Her legs go to either side of mine, and she lifts then slides down on me.

"You feel so good," I tell her as I thrust up into her. Her arms are looped around my neck as she moves against me, her head dropping back. She's fucking gorgeous with her tits pushed in my face. I lean down, drawing a nipple into my mouth. She breathes heavily as my tongue circles her bud. Needing more, I lift her off me and lay her down. Her dark hair fans out on my pillow, and my breath catches in my throat as I'm overwhelmed with love for her. Moving over her body, the back of my hand brushes her cheek.

"I love you so much, Hallie. I never thought I could feel like this."

Her hand cups my face, and she smiles. "I love you too, Sawyer."

I push inside her, and she moans, her eyes rolling. Kissing her, I show her exactly what she means to me, her breathing accelerating with each thrust. My lips never leave hers, and every time we make love, it's better than the last. Her kisses become more urgent as her hands tug on the hair at the base of my neck, and I know she's close. I increase my pace, and she bites down gently on my lip as she comes, my mouth swallowing her moans. Her body trembles as she chases the last of her orgasm.

Watching her pushes me over the edge and I groan as I come, dropping my weight on top of her. Her hands stroke my hair as we both catch our breath, our bodies spent.

Rolling off, I pull out, missing the heat of her body immediately. "I'll be right back," I whisper.

"Mmm..." she mumbles, her eyes closed.

I dispose of the condom as quickly as I can so I can get back to having her in my arms. As cliché as it sounds, I'm going to miss her so much this weekend it almost hurts. I want her to go and have fun, but I am a selfish bastard and don't want her away from me. I know she's looking forward to it, so I will need to overlook my possessive tendencies so she can have some fun without me.

She's fallen asleep by the time I climb back into bed, and I pull her body to mine, hearing her sigh contentedly. It's not long before her rhythmic breathing lulls me to sleep, my arms wrapped around her.

* * *

The following morning, Hallie packs for her weekend away, and before long, the intercom sounds. Checking the screen, Jess's face lights up on the door camera. I'd heard Hallie on the phone to her earlier in the week, telling her we were together. I swear I could hear Jess scream from across the room. I can only imagine their conversation on the way to the cabin.

Buzzing Jess in, I call Hallie to let her know she's arrived. A second later, she emerges from the bedroom with her small suitcase. She's wearing black skinny jeans and a green top that hugs her body in all the right places. Her hair is down, falling in waves over her shoulders, and she has something on her eyes that makes them pop. She looks incredible.

"You look beautiful, baby," I state, taking Hallie's suitcase from her and placing it in the entryway. Coming back, I pull her into my arms.

"I'll miss you," she says with a pout. "Maybe I should have let you drive and then snuck you into my room."

I chuckle. "As hot as that sounds, Brooke would kill me if I interrupted her bachelorette party. You're going to have a great time, and I'll be right here waiting when you get back."

"You could grab a last-minute flight and join Liam in Vegas?" she suggests, and I shake my head.

"Nah, it's not exactly my scene. I'm good. Besides, Logan messaged me earlier. He wants to come around and clear the air."

"Oh, that's great. I hope you can sort things out with him. I feel so guilty I've come between you two." She gives me a sad smile, and I trace my fingers across her back.

"You have nothing to feel guilty about. I'm sure things will be fine with us." I've no idea if they will be, but I don't want her going away for the weekend worrying about it.

There's a knock on the door, and Hallie bounces up and down in my arms. "That'll be Jess," she says excitedly. Pulling out of the embrace, she walks to the door, swinging it open.

"Jess!" she cries, hugging her best friend.

"God, it's good to see you." She looks over Hallie's shoulder at me and smiles. Pulling out of the embrace with Hallie, she comes over and I'm taken aback when she hugs me.

"Thank you for looking after her," she says quietly, her voice breaking. "And thank you for making her happy."

"She means everything to me, Jess. There's nothing I wouldn't do for Hallie."

Jess steps back from me and smiles, wiping a tear from her face. I can see Hallie feels a little embarrassed. Her eyes are trained on the floor, and her hands fiddle with the edge of her shirt, so I change the subject.

"Do you have everything you need, sweetheart?" I ask as I move toward Hallie and take her hand.

"I think so."

"Call me when you get there?" I ask, hoping she won't think I'm being too overprotective.

"Of course, and I'll call you before I go to sleep." Taking her in my arms, I kiss her, not caring that Jess is standing right behind us.

"Have a great time and drive safe."

Jess loops her arm with Hallie's, and I open the door, watching them walk with Hallie's suitcase to the elevator. Waiting at the elevator doorway, Hallie waves, and I manage a wave back before the door closes. I go back into the apartment, and I'm alone for the first time in over three weeks.

An hour or so later, the intercom sounds, and I flick off the movie I wasn't watching and buzz Logan in. I'm somewhat nervous about how this will go, especially after how things went down the last time we spoke. I want to straighten everything out between us. We were good friends, and I don't want to lose that if possible.

Awkward doesn't describe the mood when he arrives, and I offer him a beer to try and break the ice. He takes one, and I take a pull of mine, gesturing for him to take a seat in the living room.

"I need to apologize," he says as soon as we both sit. "I was an asshole at the cabin, and you deserve to know why."

"I'm listening," I tell him, not prepared to let him off the hook just yet.

He sighs and drags his hand down his face. "I fell for a client once, years ago. She was only my second assignment. Some guy was stalking her, and she came to us seeking protection while the police tried to nail the bastard. She was young and beautiful, and I knew I was in trouble the minute I saw her."

He closes his eyes and sighs before shaking his head and carrying on, "She was genuinely terrified of this guy. He was doing some freaky shit. He'd already broken into her place twice and shit in her bed. Then dead animals started arriving in the mail. Clearly a whack job, but a dangerous one. I moved her to a safe house, and we got close. You know how it is... hour after hour, day after day, just the two of you?" I nod, knowing exactly how it is.

I wait as he takes a pull of his beer before continuing, "We'd talk for hours, and she'd confide in me, things she said no one else knew about her. I fell hard, and she said she felt the same way. Things changed though, when the guy was caught and locked up. She went

Crossing the Line

back to her life and wanted nothing to do with me. I tried to talk to her, but she said her feelings for me hadn't been real. The situation we were forced into had blurred the lines, and she realized what she felt for me had been an infatuation rather than the *real thing*. I was devastated. I couldn't get my head out of my ass and walk away. It nearly cost me everything."

"That's why you have the rule," I say, his overreaction to my relationship with Hallie suddenly making even more sense.

He shrugs. "I knew from speaking to you on the phone something had happened. I could hear it in your voice when you spoke about her. Seeing you holding hands at the cabin, I saw myself all those years ago, and I didn't want that for you."

"I'm going to marry her, Logan, and she feels the same way."

"I know she does."

"You do?"

"She called me this morning." He must see the look of surprise on my face because I can't hide it no matter how much I try. "You were in the shower. She told me exactly how she feels about you, and after speaking to her, I've no doubt she loves you."

Stunned, I flop back on the sofa. She'd been worried about coming between Logan and me, but I had no idea she'd been worried enough to contact him.

"You're not pissed, are you?" he asks, and I shake my head. "She thought it was her fault we'd argued, and she hated knowing she'd come between us. I knew then I had to come here and explain why I'd been such an ass. She adores you, man. You're one lucky son of a bitch." He taps his beer bottle with mine before taking a pull. "We're good, right?" he asks.

"Yeah, we're good." I sit up and pull him into a one-armed back-slapping hug. "I'm sorry about the girl."

He waves his arm. "It was a lifetime ago."

I look at him, wondering if he means that. I've never known him to date or be in a relationship the entire time I've known him. This woman, whoever she was, clearly did a number on him, and

I'm betting deep down he's still hung up on her. I don't push it though, knowing he's probably opened up more today than he ever has.

"Well, if you ever need to talk, you know where I am," I tell him.

"Thanks, man. And I'm happy for you, even if I am losing my best CPO."

"I'm sure I'm easily replaced."

"Don't bet on it!"

We chat for a while longer, and I fill Logan in on my plans to go back to being a cop. He offers to put a good word in with someone in the Tybee Island Police Department and I'm grateful, happy to take any and all help offered. My phone vibrates in my pocket, and I pull it out, my face breaking out into a smile when it's a message from Hallie.

"I can guess who that is by the look on your face," he says with a chuckle. "Where is Hallie anyway?"

"She's gone back to the cabin with her friend for Brooke's bachelorette party."

"A bachelorette party! You're brave."

"Why brave?"

"Sawyer, surely you know what happens at a bachelorette party," he exclaims. "Strippers and shit."

"Brooke's not into all that. It'll be movies, alcohol, and girly pampering shit."

"You sure about that? Isn't it the maid of honor who arranges the bachelorette party?" I slide my eyes to him, and he laughs.

Dropping my eyes back to my phone, I open Hallie's message.

Hallie: *We're here. Your sister's friends are crazy! Brooke's already drunk! We're getting in the hot tub in a minute. I'll call you before bed.*

Me: *Have fun, baby.*

As I'm messaging Hallie, Logan's phone rings, and he walks out onto the balcony to take the call. His comment about strippers hasn't riled me. The cabin is so remote, I doubt they've managed to find a stripper who would travel that far. Pulling up Brooke's number, I shoot her a quick message to make sure.

Me: *There are no strippers this weekend, are there?*

Slipping my phone into my pocket, my eyes go to Logan on the balcony. He's pacing up and down the small space, his hand running through his hair. An uneasy feeling washes over me, so I stand, and I wait for him to come back into the room.

"We've got a problem. Do you remember we got a print from the black van used to bust Bryant?"

"Yeah, there was no match," I reply with a frown.

"They got a hit. A guy was taken in this morning for driving under the influence. They ran his prints and flagged him as a match to the Bryant case."

"And?" I ask, the uneasy feeling intensifying.

"Wilmot's questioned him, threatened to charge him with homicide. His prints in the van place him at the scene of the cemetery shooting. He's admitted to being the driver but denies killing anyone. He's given us the names of two of the shooters, and they've been picked up, but it turns out it wasn't Bryant who arranged his escape. They dealt with another guy, and it was all organized *before* Amanda died. The finer details like the date and time of the funeral were left until the day before."

"Fuck! He wasn't working alone. Did this guy give a name?"

Logan nods. "Blake Lambert."

"Never heard of him. Is he known to the cops?"

"A few minors as a kid. Nothing more. Wilmot's done some digging though, and it turns out he was in the foster care system at the same time Bryant was. Bryant's a few years older than him. They were in the same group home."

"That's the connection. Do they have him in custody?"

"No. They've checked his last known address, and he hasn't been seen for weeks. Wilmot's sending over his license photo now, and they're putting out an APB. The guy they brought in made a positive ID."

Just then, his phone beeps, and I watch as Logan opens the file. As he turns the phone around, the blood drains from my face when I see the screen. Anger and fear bubble up inside me, and I punch the wall, my hand going straight through the drywall. "I need to get to Hallie. *Now!*"

"I'll come with you."

I call Hallie and Brooke nonstop on the way to the cabin, but neither of them answers. I toss my phone at Logan and hit the steering wheel.

I promised her she was safe.

I promised all of this was over.

I promised I would never let anyone hurt her.

Fuck! I pray to God I can get to her in time to keep at least one of my promises.

Chapter Thirty-Seven

Brooke

"Someone get me some more alcohol," I shout from the hot tub. "My glass is empty!"

"Take it easy, Brooke. It's not even dark yet," my bridesmaid, Kristie, exclaims. "I don't want to be holding your hair back while you barf everywhere."

"I'm *never* sick," I assure her. "But if I were, the job of hair holding goes to the maid of honor, so you, Kristie, are safe!"

"Oh, great," Kendall cries. "Remind me why I agreed to be your maid of honor again?"

"'Cause you love me, bitch."

"It's a good thing I do."

"I'll get some more wine," Hallie offers, climbing out of the hot tub and grabbing a towel.

"See, at least my future sister-in-law is happy to keep my glass full."

Hallie's eyes widen, and her cheeks flush pink. She was quiet when she first arrived with Jess, even more so when I suggested going in the hot tub. I knew from Sawyer what had happened earlier in the week on the patio, but she seems to have loosened up a bit now. I hope she'll have a good time this weekend. After everything she's been through, she deserves it more than anyone.

"I'll be right back," she says, tossing her towel on one of the chairs.

"You might have to check the refrigerator in the garage. I think we might have already drunk what was in the kitchen."

She nods, and I relax back into the hot tub's bubbles. Closing my eyes, my head spins a little, and I know I'm well on the way to being drunk. It is my bachelorette party, though. I'm sure there is some unwritten rule somewhere that the bride is meant to spend the whole party drunk.

"Looks like your hot brother couldn't stay away from his girl," Kendall says with a laugh as my eyes fly open.

"What?"

"Your brother. You said he was her close protection officer, and that's how they met, but you'd think he'd let her have a girly weekend without crashing the party."

My head spins, and I've no idea what she's talking about. Kendall has never even met Sawyer. "My brother?"

"God, you're drunker than I thought." She groans, rolling her eyes. "Yes, your brother. Hot, tall, blond, currently pulling Hallie with him into the woods." My eyes widen in horror, and I jump out of the hot tub.

"Brooke!" Kendall cries as I grab her hand, pulling her with me toward the kitchen. "What's going on?"

"Sawyer isn't blond." I drag her through the kitchen and out the back door.

"Who the hell was that, then? I assumed it was Sawyer. He had his arms all around her."

"Did it look like she was being forced to go with him?" She shrugs, and I want to shake her. "Kendall!"

"I don't know, I didn't take much notice. I thought she was sneaking off for sex in the woods. I thought it was Sawyer."

My eyes flick around the back of the house, but Hallie is nowhere to be seen. Fear erupts in my stomach. Something is wrong. I don't know Hallie that well, but she wouldn't go off with someone she didn't know, especially with what she's been through lately.

"Brooke, what's going on?" a voice asks from behind me. "Where's Hallie?" Spinning around, Jess's face is etched with worry.

"I don't know. Kendall saw her out here with a blond guy. She thought it was Sawyer."

"Hallie!" Jess shouts. "Hallie."

We're met with silence.

My stomach churns.

"I need to call Sawyer." Pushing past Kendall and Jess, I head back to the den where I've left my phone. Snatching it up, I gasp when there are over fifty missed calls, all from Sawyer. Hitting his name, I hold the phone to my ear, praying he answers, "Brooke!" he shouts as he answers. "Where's Hallie?"

"Someone's got her, Sawyer." A sob escapes my lips, and the line goes silent. "Sawyer? Are you there?" I pull the phone from my ear to check the call hasn't dropped.

"Fuck! I'm fifteen minutes away. Get everyone inside and lock the doors. The cops are on their way."

"I'm going after her. I can hold my own. You taught me well."

"Brooke, no! I taught you a few self-defense moves. This guy likely has a gun and is dangerous. Do as I ask, *please*. I can't worry about both of you. Promise me you won't go out there, Brooke?"

"Okay," I say with a sigh. "I promise. But, Sawyer, hurry."

Chapter Thirty-Eight

Hallie

I'd felt more than a little apprehensive when I arrived back at the cabin. I hadn't thought about how I'd feel being back here, especially out on the patio. Brooke had seen I was struggling and quickly handed me a glass of wine. I decided then and there to push that asshole, Matt and what happened last weekend from my mind. It was over, and I was determined to enjoy the weekend.

As I pad barefoot through the living room to the kitchen, I chuckle when I see Brooke was right and there's no wine in the refrigerator. *God knows how many bottles they've already gone through.* Going out through the back door, I cross the small driveway, making my way to the double garage that sits directly opposite the kitchen. Woodlands surround pretty much the entire house, and hearing a noise in the trees, I glance across, seeing a familiar face.

"Hey, what are you doing here?" I ask, walking toward him. "Did Kitty change her shift?" I frown. "Hang on, I never told Kitty where the cabin is..." I trail off, an uneasy feeling washing over me. My instinct is screaming for me to run, but I'm not quick enough, and he grabs me, his arms trapping me against him.

"Let me go, Nick! What are you doing?" I struggle against him, but he's strong, and I'm not.

"Blake," he says with a smirk.

"What?"

"It's Blake, not Nick, and I'm finishing what Matt started," he bites out, and I still in his arms.

"What?" I whisper in disbelief.

Waves of panic wash over me.

I try to breathe but there is no air.

Knowing I stand no chance of getting away from him if I have a panic attack, I try desperately to keep it together. He's pulling me into the trees, and before I know it, I can't see the cabin.

"Matt wasn't working alone, Hallie. He might be behind bars, but I am finishing this." His words don't make sense, and my mind struggles to figure out what he is talking about. Suddenly, he lets me go, pushing me in front of him. I stumble on the rough forest ground, the stones and twigs cutting into my bare feet. When I turn around, he's holding a gun, and it's pointed straight at me.

"Walk."

I stare at him.

Nausea is becoming evident.

Terrified.

Panicked.

Despair.

Every emotion I could possibly feel rolls through me one after the other, pushing at the boundaries of my sanity.

"*Now!*" he yells.

I jump at his tone and spin, doing as he says. My eyes flick around, looking for some way of leaving a trail for whoever comes looking, but I'm only wearing my bikini. I'd taken my charm bracelet off when I got in the hot tub, or I could have discreetly dropped the charms, hoping they'd be spotted. Glancing down at my bikini, I look at the hot pink beads hanging from the edge of the bikini bottoms and wonder if I can pull any of them off.

Needing to keep him distracted while I try, I start talking, "Why did you go after Kitty in the bar?" I gasp as a thought occurs to me and ask, "Or is she part of it too?"

I hope to God she isn't. I'd never be able to trust anyone again. My fingers have stopped tugging on the cotton the beads are attached to as I wait for him to answer.

He laughs, but there's no humor. "She's got nothing to do with it." I let out a breath I didn't realize I was holding, relieved at his words. "I'd been following you for weeks. The plan was to hit on you. It didn't take me long to realize how uptight you were, though. So I knew I needed to find another way to get to you. Kitty was the answer."

I recoil at his words, feeling like I'm going to be physically ill. *How had I not known he'd been following me?*

Suddenly, the cotton I'm pulling on comes undone, and I can remove a handful of the beads. I drop one and hold my breath as I wait to see if he's noticed. I want to look back and see if it's visible, but I don't want to draw attention, so I keep walking.

A few seconds pass, and he hasn't noticed, so I keep him talking. "How do you know Matt?" I ask, praying someone will detect I'm missing soon. They have to, it's the only chance I've got.

"Let's just say we go way back. Matt watched out for me when no one else did. I owed him, and he called in the favor."

We walk in silence for a few minutes, and when he doesn't elaborate, I try again, dropping another bead as we walk.

"How did Matt know I was here?"

"I bugged your phone," he says flippantly. I frown, trying to think back to when he would have had access to my phone and I can't think of a single time.

"How?" My voice doesn't hide my surprise, and he laughs.

"Actually, Sawyer let me."

I gasp, and my stomach twists. "What?" I whisper, my hands wrapping around my body. I'm suddenly cold, and my whole body begins to tremble. There's no way Sawyer would let him bug my phone. No way.

"Well, 'let' is probably a bit of an exaggeration. I came over one day with some bullshit story that Kitty needed Tylenol. I planned to bug the apartment, then I saw your phone on the table in the entryway, and I changed my mind."

I drop another bead, relief washing over me knowing Sawyer wasn't involved. It's quickly followed by guilt at ever thinking he was. My mind flicks to the call I made to my mom after we arrived at the cabin, and that's when Nick or Blake or whatever his name is, found out where we were. *It's all my fault.* If I hadn't turned my phone on, Matt would never have found us.

"Where are we going?" He doesn't answer, and I shiver, the dense forest blocking out the sun's heat. We've been walking for about ten minutes, and it feels like he doesn't know where he's headed. The farther I get from the cabin, the less chance I have of anyone finding me, and I'm running out of beads. I've dropped all but two, and I've no idea if anyone will even notice them. Maybe if I can keep him talking, I can make a wide loop around and head back the way we came.

"Why was Amanda's funeral held in Savannah?" He doesn't answer, and I stop, turning around to face him. I glance behind him and hope erupts in my chest seeing one of the bright pink beads on the ground.

"Matt never said you were this chatty." He flicks the gun forward. "Keep moving." Turning back, I carry on moving a little slower.

"Amanda grew up in Savannah. Her aunt is her only living relative. Despite having nothing to do with her for years, her mental health isn't the best. Persuading her to have the funeral here was the easy part. We knew Amanda was dying. We just had to bide our time until we could put the plan into action."

"All this was planned?" I ask, my voice not hiding my surprise.

"All except Sawyer. We hadn't bet on him." I hope that's still true now. Sawyer has been coming here all his life. He knows these woods like the back of his hand. I have to hope Brooke or Jess have noticed I'm missing and have called him. I must keep him talking. It will take Sawyer a couple of hours at least to get here, and at this point I have no doubt this lunatic plans to kill me.

Why else would he be answering all my questions? There's no threat of me telling anyone anything if I'm dead. Shaking my head, I push down my thoughts. I can't fall apart now.

Dropping the last bead, I send up a silent prayer that it's enough.

"And the girl he abducted from the park?"

"That was all me. I wanted to know how it felt. We had plans for her, but that changed when we were able to track you here."

"What do you mean? What plans?"

"I'm done talking. Here is as good a place as any. Stop walking." His voice has changed, and it's suddenly emotionless.

I do as he says and stop. My body shakes again, and my breathing becomes erratic. Reaching my hands around my waist, I hug myself, imagining it's Sawyer's arms wrapped around me.

Silent tears fall from my eyes as I realize *this is it.*

This is where I'm going to die.

I'll never see Sawyer or my family again.

Chapter Thirty-Nine

Sawyer

The car comes to a sudden stop on the asphalt of the driveway as I throw it into park and jump out, then run to the cabin door.

"Brooke, it's me. Open up," I shout as I bang on the wooden door. What feels like hours pass as I wait for the door to open. When it does, I push past everyone and head for the den where I can pull up the CCTV. We have a camera covering the front door and the back of the cabin. I'm hoping one of them will show me which way Blake took Hallie.

"What are you doing?" Brooke asks as I pull up the vision on the television.

"Checking the cameras. I need to know which way they went." Rewinding the footage, I play it in fast forward until Hallie comes into view. I watch her walk toward the garage when she suddenly stops and turns. Anger courses through me as a figure walks out of the trees toward her. She even makes a move toward him, obviously thinking she can trust him.

"Oh my God!" a voice cries from behind me. "That's Nick." Looking over my shoulder, Jess has tears streaming down her face.

"You know him?" Brooke asks.

"I know him too. He's played us all." Turning back to the screen, my stomach rolls as he grabs Hallie. His hands seem to be all over her, and I want to kill him. She's struggling against him when she suddenly stills, and I can't help but wonder what he's said to her.

"Sawyer, look," Logan says from beside me, pointing to the screen.

I get close and drop my head.

"Fuck! He's armed." A gun is stashed in the waistband of his jeans, and I watch on helplessly as he drags Hallie into the trees and out of sight. My heart breaks knowing how terrified she must be. I have to find her.

I played in those woods hundreds of times as a kid. I have the upper hand on him, and I need to use that to my advantage. "I need to find her," I exclaim, standing up.

"Wait for backup, Sawyer," Logan says, his hand on my shoulder. "They'll be here soon."

"I can't wait," I tell him, shrugging off his hand. "She might not have that long. I can't lose her. I made her a promise, one I intend to keep."

He sighs and drags his hand through his hair. "Then I'm coming with you."

"Thanks, man. I appreciate it." Turning to Brooke, I pull her in for a quick hug. "Stay inside and lock the doors behind us. Don't unlock them unless it's me, Logan, or the cops."

"Okay," she whispers, her face full of fear. "Be careful." I squeeze her hand before heading to the kitchen. Once outside, I pull out my gun, keeping it by my side. Looking to Logan, I point to the section of the woods where Hallie was taken, and he nods, silently following me.

No one's been through here in a while, and the ground is overgrown. A small section has been flattened where someone has walked recently, so I follow it, not having much else to go on. My gun is out in front of me, and I jog along the recently made path. My eyes flick from left to right, but all I see are trees.

Coming to a stop, I drop to my knees. "Look at this," I say to Logan, picking up a small pink bead that's lying on the ground.

"Does it seem odd to you that this would be here? It's not weathered at all. I think it's been dropped recently."

"You think Hallie might be leaving us a clue?"

"Her bikini was the same color on the CCTV. I didn't see any beads, but her back was to the camera most of the time. It could have fallen off as she was walking, but keep a look out for any more. If I'm right, she might be dropping them for us to follow."

I hope my hunch is right. Time is running out, and I have to find her. Anything else isn't an option.

We find two more beads, and after finding the second one, I'm more convinced than ever that Hallie is dropping them on purpose. Suddenly, a gunshot sounds, quickly followed by a scream, and I stop, my heart thundering in my chest.

"That came from over there, right?" I say to Logan as I gesture in front of me and off to the right. Logan nods, and I take off through the trees, desperate to get to her. I run silently, coming to a stop when I hear muffled voices. Looking to Logan, he points to the left, and I edge to the right. I use the trees as cover to get closer, stopping when I can make out the voices.

"He was going to kill you, you know that, right? He said you were the one who got away. The one who brought everything crashing down," Blake says, his voice almost euphoric. "I never thought I'd be the one to kill you. I never thought I'd have that honor."

"Honor?" Hallie says. Her voice sounds strained, and I move, trying to get a glimpse of her. Blake is in the way, and I can't see her without giving away my position.

"You're fucking crazy. Why are you..." She pauses and groans. "Why are you doing this?"

"You have no idea what it's like to be in a foster home, do you?" Blake spits out. "Someone always wants something from you. Food, clothes, money, company…" I watch as he shakes his head. "Matt saved me more than once from some desperate sicko preying on young kids…" he trails off and is silent for a few seconds. "I wrote to him while he was locked up, and we became friends again. When he asked for my help, I couldn't say no. He saved me when I was a kid, and I owed him big-time."

"You don't have to do this, Blake. Please," Hallie begs. She sounds breathless, and I've heard enough. I look over to Logan, who's moved to the other side of where Blake and Hallie are located. His eyes meet mine, and I gesture with my gun, pointing at them. He nods, confirming he has my back.

Moving from my hiding place, I walk toward them. My eyes are fixed on Blake's back, but I still can't see exactly where Hallie is sitting. Thick bushes and undergrowth seem to be hiding her from me, and I'm frustrated I can't just kill this asshole. I can't shoot and risk hitting Hallie, not when I don't have a clear view. A twig snaps under my foot, and I silently curse as Blake spins around, his gun firing randomly in my direction.

Dropping behind a tree, I steal a look, only to see Blake dragging Hallie to stand, his gun pressing into her side. Blood is trickling from a wound on her thigh. Anger courses through me as I realize the bastard has shot her.

"Let her go, Blake!" I shout, moving out from behind the tree, my gun aimed at him. I finally have my eyes on Hallie, and my heart breaks. Tears are tracking down her cheeks, and her beautiful face is pale. Looking at the ground, I can see she's lost a lot of blood. I need to get her to the hospital and fast. Her empty eyes meet mine, and I know she's close to giving up.

I can't lose her.

I won't let that happen.

"It's over. Let her go," I repeat, discreetly trying to make eye contact with Logan but not being able to see him.

"No fucking way. I'm ending this," he yells back. "It's too late." A gunshot sounds out, and I watch helplessly as Blake and Hallie both drop to the ground.

"Hallie!" I scream, my heart pounding. Running over to where they both lie, I kick Blake's dropped gun away, falling to my knees next to the two tangled bodies. Neither of them is moving, and panic creeps up my spine.

"Sawyer," Hallie whispers, and relief floods me.

Pushing Blake's lifeless body off her, I see he has a bullet through the back of his head. Logan must have taken the shot. Still not seeing him, I reach for Hallie, and she winces as I pull her into my arms.

"I've got you," I soothe as she sobs in my arms.

"Is she okay?" Logan asks, finally appearing from the cover of the trees.

"I need to stop the bleeding." Not wanting to let her go but knowing I have to, I lay her gently on the ground, quickly removing my belt. Using it as a tourniquet, I loop it around her thigh, tying it tightly above the wound. She groans as the leather bites into her skin.

"I'm sorry, baby. It has to be tight." She nods, her eyes closing. Her face is deathly pale.

"Stay awake, Hallie. I need you to stay awake, sweetheart." Her eyes open briefly, and I pull off my T-shirt, wrapping the material around her leg in a makeshift bandage. Her eyes close, and despite begging, I can't make her open them again.

"I need to get her to the hospital," I tell Logan as I holster my gun and scoop Hallie up into my arms. Her head lulls onto my shoulder, and I carry her back along the path.

"He's dead. I'm coming with you," Logan says as he follows me back to the cabin. "I'll bring the cops back later. They should be here by now."

My eyes drop to Hallie, seeing she's still unconscious. "We found the beads, Hallie," I tell her, hoping she can hear me. "They led us to you." I watch her face for any sign of acknowledgment, but there's none. "I'm so sorry I wasn't here, baby. I'm so sorry..."

A feeling of dread settles in the pit of my stomach as I run with her, careful not to trip on any of the undergrowth.

After a few minutes, the path suddenly opens, and I can see the cabin. Relief surges through me as police cars and an ambulance come into view. EMTs run toward me with a gurney, and I gently place Hallie on it, following as they wheel her inside the ambulance.

"We'll get her stable, and then you can come inside," one of the EMTs says, and I watch as they close the ambulance doors. My whole world is behind those doors, and I've never felt more helpless. Falling to my knees, my head drops into my hands.

In an instant, Logan's next to me.

"She's in good hands, Sawyer," he says, his hand on my back.

"I owe you, Logan," I tell him, my voice breaking.

"You don't owe me anything. I'll always have your back."

"When I heard the gunshot..." I trail off and shake my head.

"You thought he'd shot her."

I nod. "I looked, but I couldn't see you."

"When he fired at you, I couldn't see Hallie," he says. "I couldn't risk hitting her if I took a shot, so I moved around, hoping he'd be concentrating on you. My hunch was right, and I managed to get behind him. I saw an opportunity, and I took it."

"You always were a better shot than me."

He squeezes my shoulder. "I was lucky, that's all."

"You saved her life."

"She'll be okay, Sawyer."

"God, I hope so." Hearing a commotion, I look up to see Brooke trying to force her way past a cop to get to me.

"He's my brother, let me go. He's right there," she yells, pointing across the driveway at me. The cop turns in my direction, and I stand up, gesturing for him to let her through.

"Sawyer," she cries as she throws herself into my arms. "Are you okay? Where's Hallie?" She steps back and looks me over, her face etched with worry.

"I'm fine. Hallie's... Hallie's been shot. She's with the EMTs now."

Her hand flies to her mouth, and she stifles a sob. "Is she going to be okay?"

I run my hand through my hair as I try not to break down. "I don't know, Brooke. I can't lose her. I promised I'd keep her safe. I promised."

"Hey! You did keep her safe. You got her away from him. She'll be okay, Sawyer. She has to be."

I stare, not knowing what to say. I know from experience willing someone to be okay isn't enough. It wasn't with Noah. I had to hope and pray I'd gotten to her in time. She's a fighter, and I knew she would fight to stay with me.

"We're ready to go to the hospital, are you coming?" the EMT calls from the back of the ambulance. Pulling myself together, I give Brooke a sad smile.

"We'll meet you there," Logan says, and I jog over to the ambulance.

"How's she doing?" I ask as I climb aboard, the EMT gesturing for me to sit next to Hallie.

"She's stable for now, but she's lost a lot of blood."

"Has she woken up?"

He shakes his head and positions an oxygen mask over her face. Scooping up her hand, I bring it to my lips, brushing a soft kiss on her cool skin. Watching her lying there hooked up to various machines, a cannula in her other hand, makes my stomach roll. Guilt overwhelms me. This was *never* how it was meant to be.

I should have been with her.

I should have stopped him.

"Did you do that?" the EMT asks, pulling me from my thoughts. Looking at him, he's pointing to the tourniquet, and I nod. They've left it in place but replaced my makeshift bandage with a proper one. Blood is still seeping to the surface though, and I can't help but wonder how much more blood she can stand to lose.

"I'm pretty sure you've saved her life. Any longer, and she probably would have bled out." He squeezes my shoulder before taking a seat behind Hallie's head.

Fifteen minutes later, we're pulling up outside the emergency room at Summerville Medical Center. I reluctantly drop Hallie's hand, stepping aside as they wheel her off the ambulance and into the building. Following the gurney, I'm stopped by a nurse as they take her through a set of double doors.

"I'm sorry, but you can't go through there." She takes my shoulder and gently guides me to the check-in desk. "Maybe you could give us her details?"

I answer all their questions before taking a seat in the waiting room, then drop my head in my hands and break down. I've held it together until now, but I've got no fight left.

If I lose her, I don't know what I'll do.

Chapter Forty

Sawyer

Unaware of how long I've sat with my head in my hands, I suddenly feel someone kneel on the floor in front of me. "Sawyer."

Looking up, I stare into Brooke's scared eyes. "Is she..." she trails off and clamps her hand over her mouth.

"No," I exclaim, standing up and pulling her into my arms. "At least, I don't think so. No one's been out to tell me anything yet."

She sags against me, and I hold her close. "I'm sorry I scared you."

Checking behind her, Logan has his arm around Jess, both of them looking as worried as Brooke.

Pulling out of the embrace, Brooke hands me something. "I brought you a shirt."

"Thanks," I tell her, pulling it over my head.

"Jess, do you have Hallie's parents' phone number?" I ask, knowing I need to let them know what's happening.

"I called them. They're on their way."

I nod, silently relieved I haven't had to make the call, as selfish as that sounds. I'd be pissed if someone was meant to be looking after my daughter, and she ended up getting shot.

I can only imagine how they're feeling.

The same nurse from earlier comes out from behind the double doors and makes her way to me. "We've stabilized Hallie enough to take her down to surgery. Are you her husband? I didn't see a ring."

I shake my head. "Surgery?" I ask, fear bubbling in my stomach. "No, we aren't married. I'm her boyfriend. Is she going to be okay?"

"She's stable at the moment. We need to operate to remove the bullet." She must see the look on my face and kneels in front of me. "She's in the best hands." The nurse gives me a small smile before standing back up. "Someone will be out with more information when we have it."

"Please take care of her," I whisper, and she nods before walking away.

We all sit in silence in the waiting room for what feels like forever, but it's more like a couple of hours when a doctor finally appears. "The family of Hallie Anderson," he calls out, looking around the room.

I jump up. "I'm her boyfriend."

"Is there a next of kin here?" My heart pounds, and a cold sweat breaks out on the back of my neck.

"They're on their way. Is she okay?" My voice must give away my desperation, and he seems to take pity on me.

"She's stable. She was lucky. The bullet missed her femoral artery. Half an inch to the left, and we'd be having a different conversation." I swallow the lump that's formed in my throat as I realize how close I came to losing her. "I've removed the bullet and repaired the damage. She should make a full recovery." Relief washes over me, and the need to see her is overwhelming.

"Can I see her?"

"She's still in recovery. As soon as we've moved her into a room, she can have visitors. If you'll excuse me, I need to get back. One of the nurses will let you know when she's settled."

"Thank you." I hold out my hand, and he shakes it.

Crossing the Line

"You're welcome, son." Falling back into my chair, I drag my hand through my hair.

"She's going to be okay," Jess says before she bursts into tears. Brooke goes to her and pulls her into a hug.

"Sawyer," a voice calls from behind me, and I see Hallie's mom. She looks across at Jess and bursts into tears. Brett pulls her against him, and his eyes find mine.

"She'll be okay. You've just missed the doctor. She's out of surgery and in recovery." I walk over to them, and Aubrey pulls me into her arms.

"Oh, thank God. Thank you, Sawyer. Thank you so much." She's sobbing, and I hold her to me, overwhelmed that she's thanking me.

"I should never have let him get near her."

She pulls back and wipes her eyes. "Sawyer, you had no idea this guy was even involved with Matthew Bryant." My eyes flick to Jess, who gives me a small smile. "Jess told us everything when she called. This isn't your fault. You found her and brought her here." I nod, despite not believing them.

"Have they said when we can see her?" Brett asks as he puts out his hand for me to shake.

"They're going to let us know when she's out of recovery," I reply, shaking his hand. His eyes drop to my jeans, and I glance down, realizing for the first time that I'm covered in Hallie's blood. Before I can say anything, a different nurse appears and calls out Hallie's name. Brett and Aubrey rush forward, and I hang back. As desperate as I am to see her, her parents will want to see her first.

"It's only two visitors," Aubrey says, looking back at me.

"You two go in first," I say. "Tell her I love her." She smiles, and I watch as they disappear behind the double doors.

"You okay?" Logan asks as he comes to stand next to me.

"I'll feel better when I can see her."

"I'm going to grab a drink. Do you want anything?" I shake my head and watch as he asks Brooke and Jess.

Ten minutes later and I'm pacing the waiting room. Hearing the doors open, Brett and Aubrey make their way toward me.

"She's asking for you," Aubrey says. "We'll give you some time alone. Through the doors, turn left. Third room on the right."

"Thank you," I say over my shoulder as I rush across the waiting room and toward Hallie. Coming to a stop outside her room, I take a deep breath before pushing the door. Her head turns as I walk in. When her eyes meet mine, she bursts into tears. I'm by her side in seconds. Sitting on her bed, I gently take her into my arms.

"Shh, it's okay. Please don't cry." Her hands clutch at my T-shirt, and it's as if she thinks I'm going to disappear. She mumbles something through her sobs, but I can't make out what. I hold her until she calms down, my hand stroking her hair. When she lifts her head, her eyes are bloodshot, and her face is red.

"I thought I'd never see you again." Her fingers continue to grasp my T-shirt, and I reach for them, gently taking her hands in mine.

"I'm so sorry I wasn't there, baby. I promised to keep you safe..." Closing my eyes, I bring one of her hands to my mouth, brushing my lips across her palm.

"You came for me," she whispers. I pull her against my chest. It feels so good to hold her in my arms again. There was a point earlier today when I thought I'd never see her again, let alone hold her.

"How are you feeling?" I ask as I lean back. She's wearing a hospital gown, her injured leg covered with a blanket.

"A little sore. Not too bad. I think they've pumped me full of pain meds..." she trails off. "How did you get to me so quickly?"

"We don't have to talk about this now, baby. You should rest."

"I want to. I need to get what happened straight in my head. It was Nick, Sawyer. How could we not have known?"

"He had us all fooled."

"He seemed so into Kitty. She's going to be devastated." Hallie shakes her head. "So how did you get to me so quickly?" she asks again.

"Logan found out some information while he was at my place... a name of someone involved. When the ID picture came through, I saw it was Nick and knew I had to get to you. I tried to call you and Brooke, but I couldn't get through."

"How did you know where he'd taken me?"

"The CCTV and I found the beads you dropped."

"You did? I didn't know if you would, but I didn't know what else to do."

"It was a great idea."

"I got him to talk. I thought if I could keep him talking, I could buy myself some time." I kiss her head, knowing how terrified she must have been. "He tracked my phone, Sawyer. That's how Matt knew we were at the cabin."

"What?" I ask, frowning. "When?"

"He said he came to ask for Tylenol for Kitty. He wanted to bug the apartment, but when he saw my phone, he changed his mind."

"Fuck! I remember him asking for Tylenol." Anger bubbles in my stomach, and I want to punch something. He was right under my nose, and I didn't have a clue. "I'm sorry, baby. Your phone was on the table in the entryway. He must have done something to it."

"Why are you apologizing? It isn't your fault, Sawyer. None of us knew Nick wasn't who he said he was..." she trails off. "You don't have to beat yourself up anymore. You didn't miss Matt following us. He was tracking my phone. When it died after we left Hilton Head Island, he must have lost us. I stupidly turned it on to call my mom when we got to the cabin. It was my fault he found me."

"None of this is your fault, Hallie. We were all fooled."

"He'd been watching me for weeks, long before Amanda died. I had no idea."

"That fucking bastard! They had everything planned."

She takes my hand and squeezes. "Everything except you. They couldn't plan for you."

I shake my head. "You got shot, Hallie."

"Sawyer, stop it," she says sternly. "I'm okay!"

"There were a few minutes in the woods when I thought I'd lost you. I don't know what I would have done if—" I choke on my words, unable to say them out loud.

"You saved me, Sawyer." She brushes her lips gently across mine. "The doctor told me if you hadn't put the tourniquet on my leg, I'd have bled out."

"I love you so much, Hallie."

"I love you too." She yawns. After what she's been through, she must be exhausted.

"You should get some sleep, sweetheart."

"Will you stay?" she asks.

"Try and make me leave." She smiles and moves over slightly in the bed, wincing as she moves her leg.

"Are you okay?" I ask, hating to see her hurting.

She nods. "Lie with me." She pats the space next to her, and I kick off my shoes before climbing on the bed. She drops her head on my chest, and I wrap my arm around her.

"Sleep, baby. I'll be here waiting when you wake."

And I will.

I'll wait forever for her.

Chapter Forty-One

Hallie

Opening my eyes, I move my leg, wincing as I forget in my haze of sleep there had been a bullet in it not too long ago. Looking up, Sawyer smiles at me.

"You stayed?" I ask, and he leans down, brushing his lips against mine.

"How are you feeling, sweetheart?" my mom says from next to me, and I jump, not realizing she was there. Turning my head, I smile as I see my parents sitting at the side of the bed.

"I'm okay," I lie. My leg is throbbing, and I know the pain meds are wearing off, but I don't want anyone to worry. "Have they said when I can go home?" I'm desperate to get out of here and back to Sawyer's. I'm more than ready for this whole nightmare to be over.

"No one's said, but you've been shot. I think they'll want you to stay overnight," my mom says. "They need to make sure there's no infection."

"I want to go home."

"I know, sweetheart." She reaches for my hand and gives it a gentle squeeze. "We'll go and see if we can find a doctor. See what their plans are for you. Jess and Brooke want to see you." My dad bends down and kisses my cheek, and I watch as they leave, closing the door behind them.

Turning to Sawyer, I frown. "Brooke is here?"

"Yeah, Logan brought her and Jess."

"No, no, no! It's her bachelorette party. She shouldn't be here."

"Hallie, she doesn't care about her bachelorette party. She cares you got hurt," Sawyer insists.

"But I ruined her bachelorette party."

"No, you did not," Brooke exclaims as she walks through the now-open door and crosses the room, pulling me in for a hug. "How can you think I care about a silly bachelorette party when some psycho kidnapped and shot you!" She releases me from her hug and sits in one of the chairs my parents vacated.

"But—"

"No buts. You're alive. That's all I care about."

"Told you." Sawyer smirks, and I smack his chest.

I smile at Brooke. "Well, for what it's worth, I'm sorry." She waves me off, and I turn back to Sawyer, seeing Jess in the doorway.

"Hallie," she whispers before bursting into tears.

Sawyer jumps up and takes her hand, bringing her to me.

"Hey, I'm okay," I assure. She sits on the edge of the bed, and I hug her.

"You're really okay? I couldn't believe it when I saw Nick on the CCTV. You must have been so scared."

"I'm really okay. I promise. You and Brooke should go back to the cabin and carry on with the party. I feel bad you're missing it."

She shakes her head. "I think I might go home. Sorry," Jess says sheepishly, her eyes flicking to Brooke.

"It's fine, Jess. I totally understand," Brooke tells her sympathetically.

"Are you okay to drive back?" Sawyer asks, knowing Jess and I drove up together.

"Grayson's brother is driving him up to the cabin. He's going to meet me there and drive my car back. Logan said he'd take me back to the cabin when I was ready. I had to check you were okay first." She takes my hand and squeezes it. "Will you call me when you get back home?" I nod, and she pulls me into a hug.

"I'll go and find Logan." She stands up to leave, and I grab her arm.

"Wait, Jess." I turn to Brooke. "Go back with them, Brooke, please. Go and enjoy your bachelorette party." I can see the indecision in her eyes, and I tell a little white lie to encourage her to leave. "I'm shattered and due more pain meds soon. I'll likely be asleep anyway, and Sawyer is here with me."

"Okay... but are you sure?"

"I'm sure."

"Sawyer, call me if you need anything, okay?" Brooke instructs, pulling me into a hug.

"I will. Go... enjoy yourself."

"I'll see you at the rehearsal dinner," I promise. She smiles, and I wave at them as they head out of the room.

"Finally, alone at last," Sawyer mutters, climbing back onto my bed and taking me in his arms. Just then, the door opens, and a nurse walks in. Sawyer groans, and I stifle a giggle.

"Mr. Mitchell, do you not remember our earlier conversation? The only reason you got away with being on the bed last time I checked on Hallie was because she was asleep. This is not a hotel. Please get out of the patient's bed," the nurse says, her voice stern. He raises his eyebrows at me before pulling a face, and I bite my lip in an attempt not to laugh. He climbs off and takes a seat in the large recliner in the room.

"Visiting time is nearly over. I'm going to have to ask you to leave soon," she tells him, putting a blood pressure cuff on my arm.

"I'm afraid I can't do that. I'm Hallie's close protection officer."

She raises her eyebrows at me and cocks her head. "Is that right, Hallie?" she asks.

Out of the corner of my eye, I see Sawyer nodding frantically behind her. "Yes. Yes, he is," I choke out, my mouth suddenly dry.

"Hmm..." she mutters, obviously not believing a word either of us is saying.

"I can get my boss on the phone," Sawyer offers. "Or perhaps you'd like to speak to Detective Wilmot of the Savannah Police Department?"

She looks between us before shaking her head. "That won't be necessary. You can stay." She finishes taking my vitals and leaves me some pain meds before heading for the door. "Mr. Mitchell?" She waits for Sawyer to look over. "Stay off the bed."

"Yes, ma'am," Sawyer says, saluting her. She rolls her eyes before closing the door behind her, and we both burst out laughing.

"You've made a fan there, Mr. Mitchell," I tease.

"She likes me, I can tell. Scoot over."

"You're going to get into trouble," I warn him as I shift over.

"I'll take my chances. You're worth getting into trouble for." I inhale sharply as pain shoots through my leg. Seeing me grimace, he picks up my meds.

"I know you're in pain, Hallie. Take them." He passes me the two white tablets and holds out a glass of water.

"They make me sleepy. I don't want to sleep." I pout.

"I'll be here when you wake. I'll always be wherever you are, Hallie. You're my home." His hand cups my cheek, and I lean my face into his touch.

My heart is so full of love for him.

When I was in the woods with Blake, I really believed I'd never see him again. I couldn't see a way out, and I knew if Sawyer hadn't shown up, Blake would have killed me. I'd wanted to scream and shout that life was cruel. I hadn't loved him long enough to lose him. Now I realize an eternity wouldn't be long enough. I want to make every second count, and I want it to start now.

"Do you remember what you asked me in my bathroom at the beginning of the week?" I look up at him uncertainly.

"Yeah, I remember."

"Ask me again," I whisper.

His face erupts into a smile, and butterflies flutter in my stomach. "Will you move in with me, Hallie?"

"Yes."

His smile grows even wider if that's possible, and his mouth drops to mine. "I'm going to marry you one day, Hallie Anderson," he says against my lips, and before I can respond, he's kissing me, pushing his tongue into my mouth.

I moan against his lips, my hands winding around his neck as the kiss intensifies.

Pulling back, he stares into my eyes. "I love you, baby."

"I love you too. I'm so glad you crossed the line," I whisper.

"Me too, Hallie. Me too."

Epilogue

Sawyer

Twelve Months Later

"You ready?" Logan asks from behind me.

"Never been more ready," I tell him as I turn around. "You've got the rings?"

He nods and pats his jacket pocket. "Let's get you married, then." He slaps me on the shoulder, and I follow him out of the hotel room toward the elevator.

As the elevator doors open into the lobby, Logan gasps next to me.

"What's wrong?" I ask, my eyes flicking to where he's staring.

"Dana," he chokes out. "What's... what's she doing here?"

"You know Dana?" I ask, frowning when I notice how pale he's gone.

"You know her?" he asks, his voice panicky. "Is she here for the wedding?"

"She works with Hallie."

"Fuck," he exclaims, his eyes never leaving her.

"Logan, what's going on?"

He runs his hands through his hair and sighs. "That's her, Sawyer. The girl I was telling you about." My eyes flick between them both, and I'm speechless.

"Dana? Dana's the girl you were in love with?" He nods, and I squeeze his shoulder. "Maybe this is your second chance."

He shakes his head. "There's no way she's single. Look at her. She's beautiful. Besides, she wasn't interested then, she won't be interested now."

"You still love her, though?"

He shrugs. "Does it matter?"

"She's single, man. Has been for a while. Apparently, her ex did a number on her." Just then, she looks over. Her eyes meet mine and then flick to Logan. I watch as her eyes widen, and her hand comes up to cover her mouth.

"Looks like she remembers you."

"Yeah, and I remember her breaking my heart. I'm not going there again. Come on. We've got a wedding to get you to."

I don't push it. There's something between them, no doubt about it, but they need to figure it out themselves.

Walking away from Dana, we head outside.

It's amazing to think how far Hallie and I have come in the last twelve months. My life's changed beyond recognition, but I've never been happier, and I know Hallie feels the same. She moved in with me as soon as she was discharged from the hospital, and we haven't spent a night apart since. She's back working in the library, which I know she loves, and I've been with the Tybee Island Police Department for about six months. Marrying her today is something I've wanted for months, and I can't wait to call her my wife.

As we walk to the beach where the ceremony is being held, I smile to myself as my mind wanders back to the evening when I'd proposed to Hallie three months ago.

. . .

"Where are we going?" Hallie asks excitedly as I lead her, blindfolded, from the car.

"I'm not going to blindfold you and then tell you where we're going. You'll have to wait," I tell her with a chuckle. "It'll be worth it, I promise."

I slip my arm around her waist, pulling her against me as I walk her along the pier at Myrtle Beach. It's just before sunset, and if I've timed things right, I'll be where I need to be as the sun is setting. Hallie is almost bouncing with excitement, and I can't wait to see her face when I remove the blindfold. I'm a little nervous as we near the end of the pier, and I pat the pocket of my jeans, double-checking the ring is still there.

"We're here. I'm going to take off your blindfold, but keep your eyes closed, okay?" She nods, a huge smile on her face. I gently untie the blindfold and can't resist brushing my lips against hers. "No peeking," I warn. She giggles, and I smile as I slip my phone from my pocket, pulling up "Perfect" by Ed Sheeran. Pressing play, I reach for the ring and drop to one knee.

"Open your eyes, Hallie." I watch her face as her eyes open and fix on me. Her hand covers her mouth when she sees me down on one knee.

"Sawyer," she whispers, her voice breaking.

"Hallie, I love you so much. You are the person I never knew I needed, and now I can't imagine my life without you. You inspire me every day to be a better man, and if you'll have me, I'll spend the rest of my life showing you exactly what you mean to me. Will you marry me, baby?"

Tears stream down her cheeks, and she drops to her knees in front of me.

"Yes, yes, yes," she exclaims through her tears as she throws her arms around me. "I love you," she whispers in my ear.

"I love you too." Pulling back, I reach for her left hand and slide the diamond solitaire ring onto her finger. Bringing her hand to my mouth, I brush my lips over the ring.

Crossing the Line

"Let's not wait too long to get married. I can't wait for you to be my wife," I tell her as I stand up and pull her with me.

"I'd marry you right now if I could, Sawyer. I can't believe how amazing this is. You're playing the first song we ever danced to, and you've brought me here as you know how special this place is to me. You're incredible."

"Not as incredible as you. Dance with me?" I wrap my arms around her, dancing to 'our' song as the sun sets over the ocean.

"You okay, man? You've gone quiet. Not getting cold feet, are you?" Logan asks, pulling me from my memories.

"What? No way! I was thinking back to the night I proposed," I tell him.

"I'm happy for you, Sawyer. I don't think I've ever seen two people so in love. You certainly proved me wrong." He pulls me into a one-armed hug as we reach the beach.

Pulling out of the embrace, I cast my eyes over to where I will marry the love of my life. It looks incredible. A raised floral archway sits a little away from the crashing waves, and rows of white chairs are laid out for the guests. Pink rose petals line the aisle, the flowers matching the archway. It's perfect, and Hallie is going to love it.

Ten minutes later, all the guests have taken their seats. Nervous excitement swirls in my stomach, and I can't wait to see Hallie. As the music starts, the guests stand, and I look over my shoulder, watching Jess walking up the aisle. She looks beautiful, and my eyes flick to Grayson, who can't take his eyes off her. Kitty and Brooke follow Jess, and my eyes drop to the small bump Brooke is sporting. She looks even more beautiful pregnant, and I couldn't be happier for her and Liam.

Tears well in my eyes as Hallie comes into view, her arm linked with Brett's. As she walks down the aisle, her eyes lock with mine, and she takes my breath away. She looks stunning in her strapless lace gown. Her hair is swept up off her neck, and she's carrying pink roses in her hand.

"You look beautiful, Hallie," I whisper as she comes to stand next to me. She smiles, and my heart races.

"You look pretty good yourself." Her hand finds mine, and we turn to face the officiant. Minutes later, we have exchanged vows, and I hear the words I've been waiting to hear since the day I met her.

"I now pronounce you husband and wife. You may kiss your bride," the officiant says, a smile on her face.

"Finally," I whisper as I slide my hand around Hallie's neck. My lips find hers, and I kiss her deeply. Applause erupts around us, and she smiles against my lips.

"I love you, Mrs. Mitchell."

"And I love you, Mr. Mitchell."

I fell in love with Hallie not long after we met, and I didn't think I could love her more, but with each passing day, my love for her grows. I know I'll love her more tomorrow than I do today.

They say *home is where the heart is*, and my heart beats for Hallie, and it always will.

THE END

Acknowledgments

Thank you to my beta readers, Anne Dawson, Bri Wignall, Jo Webb and Layla Rathbone. You are all stars.

Tracey Jukes you've been there when I've doubted myself and given me the kick up the bum I've needed. Thank you.

Finally to my family, James, Charlie and Isla who are my everything. I love you.

Printed in Great Britain
by Amazon